DOTWAV

Also by Mike A. Lancaster

Human.4
The Future We Left Behind

DOTWAV

MIKE A. LANCASTER

SKY PONY PRESS
NEW YORK

Sky Pony Press books may be purchased in bulk at special discounts for sales promotion, corporate gifts, fund-raising, or educational purposes. Special editions can also be created to specifications. For details, contact the Special Sales Department, Sky Pony Press, 307 West 36th Street, 11th Floor, New York, NY 10018 or info@skyhorsepublishing.com.

Sky Pony® is a registered trademark of Skyhorse Publishing, Inc.®, a Delaware corporation.

Visit our website at www.skyponypress.com.

Books, authors, and more at www.skyponypressblog.com

www.themindfeather.com

10 9 8 7 6 5 4 3 2

Library of Congress Cataloging-in-Publication Data is available on file.

Jacket image by © Shutterstock
Jacket design by Mumtaz Mustafa

Hardcover ISBN: 978-1-5107-0404-6
Ebook ISBN: 978-1-5107-0405-3

Printed in the United States of America

Interior design by Joshua Barnaby

This one's for Fran, Jon, Ian, and Alan.
If a person is defined by the company he keeps,
then having you guys as friends should make
me awesome—but actually, it just makes me
very, very lucky.

Contents

03: GOING VIRAL

If you think you are too small to make a difference, try sleeping in a closed room with a mosquito.

—African Proverb

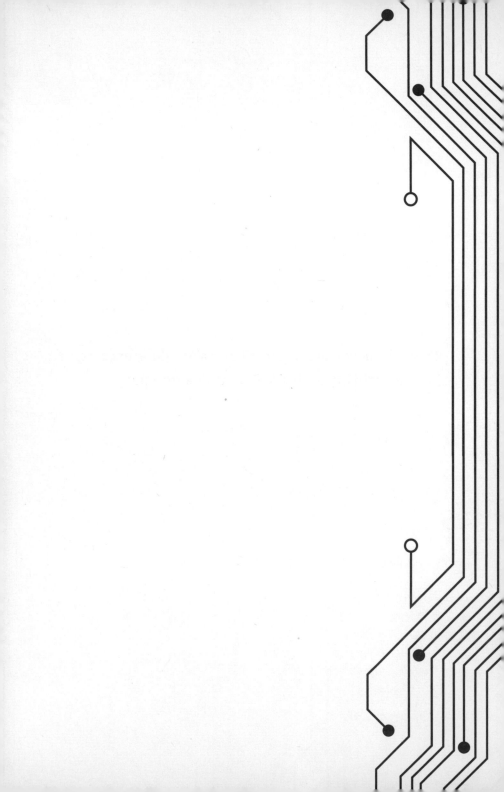

PART 01:
WHATEVER HAPPENED TO HARRY BREWSTER?

It took no comfort from our nurture
It never seemed to understand
We raised our game and fed it virtue
It raised its head and bit our hand.

"It Took No Comfort"
Precision Image

CHAPTER ONE: Ani

Ani pretended she was lost and went around the block again, just to make sure.

Second time around and the guy was still sitting there, behind the wheel of a car that really didn't belong on this street. You'd have thought that someone conducting "covert surveillance" would choose a car that blended in on a street in the Arbury Estate area of Cambridge.

A boy-racer GTI with under-lighting, perhaps.

Or a decade-old Subaru.

But not a brand-new, high-end beamer.

That meant a cop or a drug dealer, and the car wasn't pimped enough for it to be the latter.

Sore. Thumb. Anyone?

Suddenly the dull, pre-weekend day she had just spent at school—math, chemistry, English, and French—was forgotten.

She pulled her hoodie up around her ears, jerked the handlebars of her bike upward, hopped up onto the curb, and pedaled along the pavement away from the BMW. Then she turned out of sight on the other side of the building.

Ani rapped her knuckles on a curtained window around the corner, waited, got no reply.

The guy who lived in the flat was named Kinney, and she reckoned she knew him well enough for a favor or two, but she wasn't sure if Kinney was his first name or last.

She took out her phone and opened a web browser—a mobile version of the one she used on all of her computers. It was an updated version of the stripped-down browser she'd designed and programmed herself.

Even before the app was open it had already hooked itself up to someone else's wireless network and bypassed the user security key. She input the few details she knew about Kinney, pushed search, and it ran its trace using someone else's IP.

It took nine seconds to get the information she wanted and she copied over the number to the phone and pressed dial.

Two rings later Kinney's lazy voice squeezed "What do you want?" into two syllables: "Whadwant?"

"Hey, it's Ani. I live upstairs. Can you open your window for me?"

"Huh?"

"Open. Your. Window. Please."

Kinney made a noise that was probably how a question mark must sound when uttered alone.

A few seconds later the curtains twitched, then moved apart. Kinney's face appeared at the window, staring out at her with wide eyes. He did a half smile/half frown thing and raised the sash.

"Took your time," Ani said, handing the bicycle up to Kinney before he had time to refuse and pushing it through the open window. "Good job it wasn't urgent or anything." Kinney didn't have the time—or words—to object and he struggled with the bicycle, making a silent film comedy routine of the whole process as the front fork went left and right and Kinney kept guessing the wrong way and slamming it against the window frame.

"Do you think you could you make just a little more noise?" Ani whispered harshly. "There are people on the other side of town that haven't heard your inept bicycle wrangling . . ."

Kinney finally got the bike through the window and inside his flat. Then he moved aside and let Ani climb in.

"What is it this time?" Kinney asked, wheeling the cycle through his living room and toward the front door. "What have you got yourself into now?"

Ani shrugged.

"Probably nothing," she told him. "But the five-o out the

front has his eye out for someone from this block and the law of averages says it's either me or my dad, so . . ."

Kinney shook his head.

"Five-o?" he tutted. "Do people *really* call the police that?"

"Five-o. Feds. Cops. PoPo. Fuzz." Ani flashed him a smile. "You want more synonyms, or will those keep you going?"

Kinney shook his head again. Seemed like a habit he'd fallen into.

"How can you live like this?" he asked her as he opened his front door and wheeled her bike out into the corridor.

Ani gave him a wide grin that she tried to pour a whole cup of crazy into, just for the effect.

"How can you not?" she asked him, smacking her chest with her hand. "My heart is pounding. Adrenaline is coursing through my veins. In this moment, and others like it, I know with a hundred percent certainty that I'm alive."

Kinney let her take the bike.

"Try to keep it that way, huh?" he said, and closed the door before Ani could come back with a smart answer.

She shrugged and made her way to the elevator.

She traveled seven floors up in an elevator that smelled slightly worse than a public toilet, in the company of an old woman who kept looking at Ani's bike as if it were a personal insult to her delicate sensibilities.

Ani tried nodding a greeting, but that just made the old

woman's face curdle. Ani reckoned that the old dear must have seen a lot of things going on around the flats in her time, and her default setting was now one of suspicion and distaste.

Ani thought that it was probably a natural response to a world that had stopped making sense to the woman around the time that the Beatles had first played the Cavern.

There was a mirror on the wall of the elevator that was so stained and graffitied that it was unusable from just about every angle except the one Ani had chosen.

She saw a slim, dark-haired teenager reflected back at her with the slightly Asian eyes that she'd inherited from her rather more Asian mother. Her hair was shoulder length and straight, and her eyebrows were plucked into smooth arches.

Ani wondered what it was that the woman in the elevator saw when she looked at her. Probably another unfathomable teenager of mixed race and with unconventional dress—which made her just something else for the woman to be afraid of in a world that was rapidly losing all sense.

When the elevator reached seven, Ani wheeled the bike out and tried to think of something she could say that would make the woman less fearful.

Nothing came to mind.

The doors closed behind her.

And then Ani thought of the perfect remark.

She shook her head, saved the phrase for another day,

and approached her front door. Instinctually, she reached out for the door handle.

And stopped.

Man in the BMW downstairs, she thought. *What was wrong with that picture?*

She pulled away from the handle and propped the bike up against the wall as quietly as she could, moved to the side of the door, and put her back to the wall.

Her heart was still beating hard in her chest.

The man in the beamer had been staking out her building, of that she had been certain. But proper procedure for covert surveillance of that type, at least for law enforcement purposes, surely required *two* people. A second person would be on hand to witness—and indeed corroborate—the findings of the first. And to make sure that if the first guy missed something, the second wouldn't.

But the man on the street had been alone.

That could mean he was an amateur, but everything about him had said five-o: hair buzzed short; slightly arrogant set of the shoulders; reasonably tall.

Law.

Which meant he had a partner.

Alone in his car, meant his partner was . . . somewhere else.

She pressed her ear to the door.

Silence.

For most people, the absence of noise would have been reassuring, but for Ani it ratcheted up her alert level.

The flat where she lived was *never* silent.

She figured that her dad would be out, but Radio 5 live should have been blaring, because her dad was—it seemed to her—physically incapable of turning the radio off. It was on when he was at home and it was on when he wasn't, and only Ani seemed able to still its endless cycle of chatter and sports.

Her dad had lost his job at the electronics factory a few months ago after an annual review of inventory had uncovered some discrepancies, and he was always out in search of his next get-rich-quick scheme. Sometimes Ani didn't see him for days at a stretch, which might seem weird for most fifteen-year-old girls, but it was just the way things were to her and she accepted it without ever really *understanding* it.

But whether her dad was in or out: there should have been noise.

She took out her phone again and opened up the app that remotely controlled her computer inside the flat. She logged in, opened up iTunes, and selected a track by Skrillex. Then she upped the volume, put her ear to the door, and pressed play.

She heard the guitars at the front of "Bangarang" start up, loud, and then there were sounds of movement as someone slammed a door, opened another, and then scrabbled through the flat, heading for Ani's bedroom, where the music was coming from.

Clearly her dad, used to Ani's remote computer activities, wouldn't have been startled enough to chase down the sound.

Only one explanation made sense: someone else was in the flat.

By the time the bass synth and dubstep beats kicked in, Ani was heading for the stairwell, leaving her bike still standing up against the flat's wall.

She hit the stair door at a sprint and it flew open. When she heard it bang shut she was already down past the sixth floor landing, taking the stairs two and three at a time.

She didn't have time to think, just to react.

Hows, *whys*, and future plans to deal with them both were shelved, and she converted that anxiety into a little extra adrenaline to keep her moving.

She'd played this game when she was a little kid, running downstairs to see how fast she could make it to the ground floor, but the abrupt slam of a door up above her made that game suddenly seem so far away and long ago. Because that slam could only mean that the person who'd been waiting for her in the flat was now heading toward the stairs in pursuit.

Maybe he'd checked out front when the music went off, saw her bike propped against the wall, and had put two and two together.

She stopped for a second and could hear footsteps pounding down the stairs toward her, which meant that she had a floor-and-a-little head start on him. And, of course, he was some kind of law enforcement operative, while she was just a fifteen-year-old girl. His strides would be longer than hers and in a straight race there was no doubt who would be the winner.

Ani started running again, increasing her speed, and her mind was suddenly flipping through possible ways to make the race a little less straight, to make the odds a little less skewed in favor of her pursuer.

He would be able to hear her footsteps, just as she was able to hear his, so hiding on another floor was out of the question. He'd know precisely which one, and he'd find her. Eventually. And she didn't want to be found.

Jackie boy, what have you gotten me into? she thought as she passed another landing.

She'd been chatting with mates on IRC in the school IT suite at lunch when she'd gotten the message from Jack. A quick, urgent instant message: *ani i need your help.*

She hadn't heard from Jack "Black Hat" McVitie for weeks, not since he'd gone dark in the aftermath of their notorious Facebook hack. It had made the papers, even warranting a one-minute piece on the BBC news, and they'd agreed there'd be no contact until some of the dust had settled. Neither of them had boasted about the hack, and no one else knew they had been behind it. That had been the plan: the glory was in the act, not in taking credit for it.

She'd IMed with Jack, and he'd been even more paranoid than before, darkly alluding to "men in black" and covert surveillance.

It turned out that Jack—very much wearing his Black Hat—had been fishing around in some government server and had found a file locked behind multiple layers of encryption. Jack had had no idea what he'd found, but he'd taken the file as a personal challenge and had thrown an arsenal of hacking tools at it, cracking its encryption within a few hours. He said it had taken two, so Ani guessed it was more like six.

It was when he opened the file that the trouble began. Jack hadn't disconnected from the net, and the file called home. He saw what the file was doing and tried to block the transmission, but it was already too late. It went right through his firewall like it wasn't there, broke through the software he had running to stop pirated apps phoning home, opened up a socket, and told someone he'd opened the file. He'd never seen a safeguard like this, but he figured that whoever owned that file was probably already on their way. So Jack uploaded the file to SpeediShare, contacted Ani, gave her the link to the file, and told her that if anything happened to him he wanted the file out there.

He asked her to grab a copy and keep it safe.

She'd asked him the obvious question:

AniQui: What kind of file are we talking about here?

BlackHat: That's the thing. It's nothing. A .wav file.
A weird noise. That's all.

AniQui: A song? What?

BlackHat: No idea. A sound. A noise. But the file called home,
ani. They're after me.

It had sounded fanciful to her, at best. Jack had downloaded an audio file—an uncompressed .wav—and suddenly he was in danger?

Hackers were a paranoid bunch. They had to be to remain anonymous. But Jack had always taken his paranoia to new and extreme levels. Ani knew his hacker ID, that he lived *somewhere* in London, that he was a badass hacker and . . . and that was it. His name certainly wasn't Jack "Black Hat" McVitie: that was just a play on the name of the man whose death in the 1960s had been the beginning of the end for a pair of East End gangsters called the Krays.

Surely this had to be an example of his overcautious nature.

Who would come after him for downloading a sound?

But he had been persuasive and she'd snatched a copy of the file from SpeediShare and saved it to a flash drive, which was now sitting in her pocket.

 13

The thing about being paranoid, though, is that some-times you're right. It's the law of averages. You worry about enough things and one of them is bound to come true someday.

The internet was a digital shrine to paranoia and fear, with millions of people sharing their modern delusions on everything from a systematic cover-up about the existence of UFOs to the 9/11 tragedy being a false flag operation by the US government.

Ani had always taken such conspiracy theories with an ocean of salt, but when she'd tried to get in contact with Jack before going home he'd been offline.

Offline.

For most people that would be no big thing, but Jack was *never* offline. He lived on the net, and he had gadgets that allowed him access wherever he happened to be.

So was he just being cautious, spending time offline because he was scared the file had called home?

That had been her take on it, but then she'd arrived at the flat and found people waiting for her.

Coincidence?

She didn't think so.

Suddenly Jack's fears seemed very real indeed.

Ani hurtled down the stairwell as if the very hounds of hell were snapping at her heels. She felt trapped and afraid, but she had to put those feelings aside and come up with a way to get out of this. Her mind was buzzing with plans that all ended with a question mark. She needed to get out of the building, find a place to hide, and try to figure out what she'd just gotten herself into.

And, more importantly, how to pull herself out of it.

Ani heard a voice behind and above her and guessed that the man chasing her was alerting his buddy in the car below to her escape. He'd be moving to apprehend her at the entrance to the building, so suddenly "down" was no longer an option.

She hit the fourth floor and, through the steel-reinforced glass, she spotted the elevator, with its doors open.

She had no time to think.

She grabbed the handle of the stairwell door and was through it before she'd had time to contemplate what she'd do if the man cornered her in the elevator.

She sprinted for the opening, stabbing the top floor button just as the man appeared on the other side of the stairwell doors. He was young and dressed in a sharp suit, and he had a walkie-talkie in his hand. His dark eyes met hers just as the doors closed. The elevator started to climb.

Ani wondered if he could outrace it.

Doubtful.

Her lungs were burning with the exertion of the chase and she leaned her back up against the wall, hoping that no one pressed the call button before the elevator had completed its climb.

She checked her pocket for the flash drive and shook her head in disbelief. *How could something so small suddenly be the cause of so much trouble?*

The eighth floor light came on and the elevator shuddered to an unhealthy stop. She hit the doors open button five or six times, even though she'd heard that they had no effect and were only put there to give people the *illusion* that they had some control over the process.

Eventually, the doors did open.

She ran out onto the landing and headed for the access door to the roof at the end of the corridor.

A Yale lock sat square with the door frame.

She already had her library card in her hand when she reached it, and pushed the card into the crack next to the lock, shoving it left and right until the mechanism clicked open. It wasn't the first time she'd done the trick—a few of the local kids hung out on the roof at night, doing the kind of things their parents really wouldn't approve of—but this time was certainly the most urgent.

She went through the door, closing it quietly behind her, and then took the last few steps up to the roof.

Another door between her and outside, but this one was never locked and Ani guessed that someone had thought that the first door was enough to do the job.

She dashed onto the roof and then looked around her. The plan she'd formed in the split second between seeing the elevator and running for it had pretty much ended here: run the opposite direction to the one her pursuer expected.

Standing here on a windswept roof, she suddenly doubted the wisdom of her choice.

As it turned out, a roof was the ultimate dead end.

The only way off it was down.

And it would use gravity, acceleration, terminal velocity, and impact to turn her into a red stain on the pavement.

She had read somewhere that a four-story jump was survivable, but only in about fifty percent of cases. Each additional floor made survival even less likely. Sure, there was an outside chance that she'd get lucky (people *had* survived much greater falls), but you were getting into the realms of millions-to-one odds, and she liked her life far too much to risk it on a leap.

There were no external fire escapes—just as there were no ladders, ropes, or handily-parked helicopters with the keys in the ignition and a *Helicopter Flying for Dummies* book on the copilot's seat.

She looked around again, desperately, her mind whirring.

Above the door leading onto the roof was another flat roof. And a slope that led up to it, following the angle of the stairs beneath.

Suddenly Ani had herself a plan.

By the far edge of the roof was a cube of brick that acted

as some kind of vent. She took off her hoodie, emptied out the pockets, and then placed it on the ground, some of the dark blue material showing around the edge of the cube. She fluffed it up as best she could in an attempt to make it look more substantial.

Then she made her way back the way she had come in.

But much faster.

She ran past the door, to the edge of the building behind it, and clambered onto the sloping part of the roof. Then, as quietly as she could, she edged herself up the incline until she reached the flat part, and lay prone.

Squashed down, hidden, over the door.

And waited.

Of course if one of the men had been outside watching for her, this could all be in vain, but she kind of doubted it. When there was a chance that she was making for the exit, keeping a man outside would have been the sensible play; but when she'd started back *up* into the building, Ani was gambling that *both* men would be coming to search for her. It was a matter of strategy: two men could block off more escape attempts than one.

Lying there, though, she had a moment where she felt like giving in to panic. The molten fire of adrenaline was pumping through her veins; her throat was scorched dry with exertion; her heart was pounding in her chest. She had joked to Kinney about how it was better to feel alive, but right now those words sounded hollow and boasting.

She was fifteen years old, and already her life was traveling on a course that she no longer felt in control of. Indeed, it felt like it was spiraling into chaos and madness.

Here she was, perched on the highest point of her building while men in suits were hunting her down. Playing this scene in a video game would be a lot of fun. Experiencing it for real, she was suddenly asking herself a whole bunch of questions about the direction her life had taken.

Ever since she and Jack manufactured a virus to affect the cattle on the Facebook version of FarmVille—a piece of malicious code that spread through users' accounts and had quickly turned into a worldwide epidemic of digital foot-and-mouth disease—she had been living in fear of repercussions. They had concocted the plan out of utter desperation at the way people spent more time looking after digital animals rather than standing up for their real-life counterparts, but if you messed with a corporation like Facebook, it was certain that someone would be working on tracking you down.

But this incident seemed unconnected to Facebook. This was something else entirely, a .wav file that Jack had downloaded without knowing the kind of storm it would bring down upon his and Ani's heads. What could be so important about a sound file, for goodness' sake? Why was it so critical that these men retrieve it?

And who did she think she was kidding, hiding up here like a common criminal, when she should be in her flat doing her homework, listening to music, surfing the net, and waiting for her dad to get dinner ready?

It was too much.

Too . . . She broke off her train of thought and listened carefully.

There was a sound of footsteps beneath her, the scuffles and squeaks of someone trying to move quietly, but who ended up making more noise than they would have walking normally.

Her breath caught in her throat.

The door beneath her opened.

"Stay close," a voice ordered. "Don't let her reach this door."

"I'm not the one who let her get away in the first place," another voice replied. "So *you* keep your eyes open and fix your own mistake."

There was an odd metallic sound—a slide and click— that Ani knew she should recognize.

"A gun?" the second voice said. "Really? What, you're going to shoot a teenager now?"

"If I have to," the first voice answered.

"Are you listening to yourself? I mean, overreaction, or what?"

"Shut up and keep looking."

"*Jawohl, mein führer.*"

"Are you calling me a Nazi?"

"No . . ."

"Because it sounded like you just implied a similarity between me and Adolf Hitler. . . ."

"It's just something people say . . ."

"I'll have you know, my grandfather died fighting Hitler. . . ."

"What, in actual hand-to-hand combat?"

There was a full five seconds of silence where, it seemed, the exchange could go either way; it could escalate, or fizzle out.

It fizzled.

"You . . . you just look over there," the first man said harshly, but without real anger. "And keep an eye on this door."

As the second man obeyed, moving in the direction his partner had just indicated, Ani heard him say under his breath: "I wasn't calling you a Nazi. But if the jackboot fits . . ."

Ani risked a quick peek over the edge of the roof and saw that the two men were moving left and right and away from her. Still too close for her to make her move, but going in the right directions.

She saw the exact moment the man with the gun spotted her hoodie.

He was moving like the guys in TV cop shows, with the gun sweeping side to side in front of him like a divining rod, and then he did an almost comic double take as he saw the material poking around the corner.

He waved for this partner, motioning for him to approach from the left, while he went right.

Ani just waited until they were on the other side of the roof, dropped down from her vantage point, doubled back out the door they'd just come through, and bolted it behind her.

When she made it to the second door she could hear the two men banging in pursuit. She ignored the sound, slamming the door behind her, and promptly collided with someone standing in the corridor.

Ingy Havel was the kind of kid that the *Daily Mail* had fun writing about. A third generation immigrant from an Eastern European place Ani couldn't pronounce for its complete lack of vowels, Ingy was a petty crook, an all-round hard man, and wore his No Fear hoodie like it was a badge of belonging. Two of his lackeys—school bullies without a school—stood on either side of him, their eyes bulging in surprise.

"Whoa there," Ingy said, and Ani was relieved to see a smile on his face. "What's the rush?"

"Men. Chasing. Me," Ani said, trying to catch her breath.

"Police?" Ingy asked her.

Ani shrugged. "Something. Like. That," she managed to say.

"Hate to see a damsel in distress, don't we, boys?"

The two gorillas nodded and grunted agreement.

"We'll slow them down. You should go."

"Thank you," Ani said. "One of them has a gun."

Ingy smiled, wide and toothy, and his blue eyes sparkled.

"Now it gets fun." He shooed Ani away down the corridor.

She reached the elevator, stabbing at the button, and feeling a surge of relief when the doors opened instantly.

She heard Ingy shout: "We'll have to go out sometime." It sounded more like bravado in front of his friends than a genuine offer.

And then the doors closed and the elevator started moving down.

She rode it to the ground floor and ran out of the building, her mind racing. She needed to get away, but she had no idea where she could go. She kept thinking about the memory stick in her pocket and the value of the secret that it contained.

She needed to work out what it was she had, and find a way to get herself out of the mess she had suddenly found herself in.

She had to find someone who could help her.

Someone with mad skills.

Someone she could trust.

Someone who could tell her what the file *meant*.

It took her all of six seconds.

Uncle Alex, she thought. If anyone could help her, it was her uncle.

With her mind made up, she started into town.

CHAPTER TWO: JOE

Joe Dyson stood in front of the house and tried to remember why, exactly, he'd agreed to come here. Oh, he knew *why* he was here, and what he was supposed to *do* here; he just couldn't remember precisely how Abernathy had talked him into it.

The house itself was a beige-fronted terrace—what he'd have called a row house back in the States—with the front door and windows painted in some overpriced heritage shade from one of those "quaint" British companies who thought *Mouse Back* or *Baby's Breath* were reasonable names for types of paint. The bare branches of a twisting wisteria crept from right to left, so it looked like it was scratching at the wall with skeletal fingers.

It was a nice little piece of high five-figure/low six-figure real estate in an area that had seen a tremendous change in the last forty years.

Once the poorer, dirtier part of the borough of Kensington and Chelsea, Notting Hill had been far removed from the setting for Hugh Grant and Julia Roberts's romance in the nineties romcom. Big houses, with owners who could no longer afford to employ servants, were sold for dividing up into bedsits and cheap lodging houses, and the area began a downward slide into slumhood. It was only recently that the moneyed classes had moved back in and turned the place into one of the most desirable postal codes in London.

Joe doubted he could afford an hour on a parking meter around here.

He rapped at the door and waited.

And waited.

Rapped some more. Louder this time.

And waited some more.

Nobody in?

It seemed likely.

Residents of neighborhoods like this one weren't the kind of people who let someone knock loudly on their front doors without answering.

Certainly not twice.

After all, what would the neighbors think?

Joe took a look up and down the road. No twitching curtains. No nosy old ladies giving him death-ray glares. So he took a walk down the row of houses, counting them as he did, and found the alleyway that led to their backyards.

He weighed the risks against the gains and then ducked down the alley. The temperature seemed to drop by a few degrees the moment he left the sidewalk. Pavement.

Whatever. It got tiresome: thinking in two versions of the same language had become perfectly natural, but he was acutely aware that whenever he opened his mouth he needed to be sure the right one came out.

He reached the end of the houses and there was a foot-path leading left and right past garden fences. He took the right-hand path that led back parallel to the way he'd come and counted houses again, this time from the back.

He scanned the area, again keeping an eye out for nosy neighbors, then stopped in front of the house he was looking for.

What kind of trouble have you gotten yourself into, Lennie? he thought.

Only a couple of hours ago, Joe felt like his life was over.

He'd been standing by the Thames under one of the bridges that crisscrossed that mighty river, staring out across the water. Boats passed by, gulls wheeled across the sky, but he'd only been vaguely aware of any of it.

He was focused on his own thoughts, not the scenery.

The spring sunlight barely reached the shaded spot where he'd stood for twenty minutes, unmoving, and the single tear he'd cried had long since dried on his cheek.

A siren screamed through the morning air and snapped Joe back to the world with a sudden jolt. He shook his head to clear the dark thoughts that had been consuming him and, as if on a prearranged cue, a blue SUV came into view, slowed, and parked a few feet away.

A man got out and walked toward him, looking immaculate—as always—in his Savile Row suit and improbably expensive shiny shoes. Joe looked down at his own ratty jeans, rattier hoodie, and mud-splashed sneakers and shrugged.

"Thought I might find you here," the newcomer said.

"Don't you mean you checked the GPS in the chip inside my head and just followed me here?" Joe asked bitterly, making no attempt to hide the rough edges of his accent.

It was instinctive whenever he spoke to the man, a kind of unconscious *Reset to Default*.

Although he was seventeen years old, Joe always felt like he was about twelve whenever he was in the presence of Abernathy. Joe had worked for him for nearly four years and the closest he'd come to discovering a first name for him was "Mister."

"Half a million pounds of our government hardware in that head of yours entitles me, I'd think," Abernathy said.

"Come to reclaim it?" Joe asked. "I have a Swiss Army knife, and I'm sure it has a tool for removing experimental tech from inside kids' heads. It has a toothpick, too."

"I've come to reclaim you," Abernathy said.

"Not interested."

"You know, I wouldn't have to resort to digital *Where's Wally?* if you answered your phone every now and then."

"I'm guessing you mean *Where's Waldo?* Anyway, it's not going to happen."

"I need you. Someone's in trouble."

"Someone's always in trouble."

"That used to mean something to you."

"Used to," Joe said coldly. "Past tense."

"Two words will change your mind."

"No, they won't."

Abernathy looked Joe square in the eye. "Leonard Palgrave." He turned and walked away.

Joe waited a full five seconds before following.

The backyard of the last address for Lennie Palgrave had a high fence with a gate. Joe tried the handle.

Locked.

It figured.

The fence was old with cracks in some of the panels, so Joe put his eye to one and looked through. A large garden that was mostly given over to a lawn; a couple of silver birch trees; a bike propped up against the back wall.

He wondered what to do next. Climbing over the fence would probably lead to a neighbor calling the police and he hadn't brought the tools he'd need to open the gate quietly. He had no idea if Lennie even still lived here—the address Abernathy had given him was a month old at least, and there was no way to be certain that Lennie hadn't moved on.

Joe weighed the alternatives and decided that the vagueness of the information meant that breaking in would be a mistake.

He was about to give up on the house when he spotted movement in an upstairs window, as if a shadow had just passed behind the net curtains.

He made his way around to the front door and knocked again.

A lot harder this time.

Made it sound official.

There was a sound from within.

Someone was coming down the stairs.

Joe got himself ready for whatever it was that was about to greet him.

Abernathy took Joe to a riverside greasy spoon that was light-years away from the boutique cafés that Joe imagined he usually frequented. None of the chairs matched, the tablecloths were paper, and its smell of cooking bacon reminded Joe of a hole-in-the-wall diner near Coney Island that his mom had taken him to whenever she got back from a "business trip." That made it just about the finest smell in the world.

Abernathy bought Joe what was referred to as a full English breakfast—four strips of bacon, sausages, fried eggs, fried tomatoes, fried mushrooms, fried bread, toast— to which Joe added some hash browns, extra toast, and a stained mug of instant coffee with the curse taken off it with multiple sugars. Abernathy ordered mineral water. It was delivered in a slightly dirty glass, making his lip curl.

Joe ate like he hadn't had anything for a month and Abernathy just sat and watched him tear through his meal. Joe was pretty sure he didn't blink the whole time.

When he was finished Joe looked up, wiped his mouth with a napkin, and said, "No."

"I thought Leonard Palgrave was a friend of yours."

"Actually, you *know* he is. And his name's Lennie. And it's still *no*."

Abernathy studied the tabletop.

"What's he done, anyway?" Joe asked finally.

There was a slight twitch of Abernathy's top lip that could have been a smile or a sneer.

"That is the question I was hoping you would try to answer."

Joe shook his head. "Nice coincidence, isn't it?"

Abernathy raised an eyebrow. "I'm not sure I know what you mean," he said gruffly.

"Oh, come on. One of your operatives goes AWOL and suddenly you've got a case involving a friend of his?"

"Okay, I understand what you're saying. But I believe that the universe tends to put people in the places they're needed, at the times they're required. I understand your suspicions, but this isn't a trick to lure you back to duty. I would never be so"—he waved his hand in the air as if fishing for the right word—"transparent."

Joe tried to look unconvinced.

Failed.

Abernathy might be many things—among them haughty, overbearing, and arrogant—but he certainly wasn't a liar.

But the big thing was still unspoken between them, the elephant in the room, and Joe couldn't think about anything else until he'd drawn Abernathy's attention to it.

"I'll only let you down. You know I will."

"You've let no one down," Abernathy said.

"Tell that to Andy."

Abernathy paused. "It wasn't your fault."

"Says you. Not me."

"Just look into this one thing for me. Go save your friend. Maybe it will balance out . . ." He left the sentence unfinished.

Joe pushed his plate aside. "So I'll ask again: what did he do?"

Abernathy handed him a folded piece of paper. "That's his last known address." He stood up, pausing to brush a wrinkle from his suit trousers. "Find out how he's doing. What he's doing. Report back if you find out anything."

Abernathy paid the bill on the way out of the door.

He didn't look back.

While the person took their time answering the door, Joe got himself ready. First he chose the accent to match the situation, immediately disregarding the hybrid US/UK one he'd been gaining since moving here, and going for something a little more Notting Hill friendly. Then he loaded a few personality traits from the many he had stored away inside the chip in his brain.

Immediately, he felt his back straighten, giving himself an extra inch in height; felt his face set itself into just the right mixture of expressions: expressions that would make him seem friendly, concerned, and vaguely—indefinably—official. He reinforced the expressions by manufacturing the precise pheromones to accompany them.

The chip in his head was capable of a whole lot of really cool things, but pheromone control was one of the coolest. Sure, it had taken him months to learn to effectively use pheromones—chemicals produced naturally by the body that had subtle, subliminal effects on other people who encountered them—but they were now an indispensible weapon in his armory. Insects used them for marking territory, warning comrades of danger, attracting mates, calling other insects toward them, even calming distressed pals. Human pheromones were still a disputed topic among scientists, but Abernathy's Research and Development team were light-years ahead of the private sector, and Joe carried software that gave him complete control of their production.

It wasn't a miracle mind-control device or anything, but producing the right pheromones at the right time could subtly alter a person's perceptions. It gave Joe a small edge by chemically reinforcing his deception.

The door was opened by a pretty girl in her mid-to-late teens; she had expensive highlights in her hair and expensive clothes. Artist-precise makeup. Light blue eyes. The hand holding the door had perfectly manicured nails, not the hideous fake ones favored by so many of her peers.

"Hi," the girl said, sounding bored more than hostile.

Joe thought *what the heck?* and added *attract* pheromones into the mix.

"Hi there," he said. "My name's Joe. I'm looking for a friend . . ." He ended the sentence with the rising tone that made it sound like a question. *Antipodean rising inflection*: an Australian imported intonation that also managed to gently condition the listener to accept questions.

The girl's expression matched her bored tone.

"How very nice for you," she said. "I usually make friends the old-fashioned way, but if going door-to-door is working for you, then good luck with that." She looked ready to slam the door in his face.

Joe smiled, but it was a precise smile requested from, and executed by, the chip inside his head. Most people didn't even *consciously* notice the sort of expressions manufactured by his onboard hardware and software. That was because they were *micro-expressions*, the tiniest changes in the muscles of the human face that viewers analyze without even knowing they are doing so. Everyone's face makes them, but very few people have complete mental control over them. Reading micro-expressions makes it possible for some people to tell what others are thinking just by looking at their faces. It wasn't telepathy; just very small facial expressions of the type that Joe's chip was capable of faking.

This smile had a touch of vulnerability, which he—of course—underlined with the necessary pheromones.

The girl's face suddenly shifted. She sensed the change in Joe and looked concerned. Joe almost felt guilty manipulating her.

Almost.

"I'm sorry," he said, acting like he really *was* sorry. "I didn't mean to disturb you."

He emphasized the apology with a slight turn of his body as if he were about to leave.

Which he wasn't.

"That's all right," the girl said, her bored—then teasing—manner disappearing in an instant. "Look, don't go. How can I help?"

Joe made his face look grateful.

"I'm looking for a friend of mine. This is the address I was given by his parents . . ."

The girl now looked positively eager to help.

"What's his name?" she asked, and Joe was surprised to see her actually pout to stress her femininity, until he realized he hadn't turned off *attract*.

Still, the mix seemed to be working, and it would have been a shame to spoil a winning recipe.

"Lennie," Joe said. "That is, *Leonard* Palgrave. We went to school together. Kind of lost touch. . . ."

Something flickered in her eyes when he gave her Lennie's name, but he couldn't really get a feel for what it was; it was too quick, too vague, and she recovered very well and very quickly.

"I know Lennie. He lives here." A tiny frown crinkled her brow. "Or he did. I haven't seen him for a couple of weeks, maybe more."

"Oh." Joe tried *disappointed* as a facial and chemical combination, but retained the smallest trace of *attract*. "Do you know where he went?"

The girl shook her head.

"I don't know that he's moved out, exactly. It's just that I haven't seen him around. My folks rent out a couple of rooms," she explained, "so there's a fair amount of coming and going. It's just the last time Lennie went . . . well, he didn't come back."

"But he hasn't moved out?"

"No. I mean his stuff's still here. . . ."

Joe decided to shake her up a little and tried *worry* and *concern*. And *attract*. "I hope he's all right," he said, getting the pitch of his voice just right.

The statement seemed to shock the girl.

"Oh. I hadn't thought . . ." Joe saw an opportunity for a little *indignation*, contemplated how it would be mean of him, then used it anyway.

". . . that something might have happened to him?" He immediately scaled back on the *indignation* and went back to *concern*. "I just hope he's okay. His parents are worried. . . ." The shifts in chemicals kept the girl off balance, uncertain.

Once, long ago, Joe had found this sort of deliberate abuse of people's emotions distasteful, but once he'd started saving lives and putting bad guys away, he'd become more ambivalent toward it. Yes, it was manipulative and a little cruel, but it also got results where anything else would probably fail. But he had made a mental pact with himself that he would only use it for work, never for fun.

He mostly even kept to the pact.

The girl was riding his pheromone waves of *concern*, and he cut it off entirely in case she actually started crying.

"Should I have called the police?" she asked, her voice shaking.

"No, of course not," Joe said quickly. "He could be on . . ." He went to say "vacation" but realized it would ID himself as a nonlocal. ". . . holiday. Or maybe he's met up with friends. . . ."

This seemed to reassure her because her posture visibly relaxed.

"Look, do you want to come in? I mean, standing here on the doorstep . . ."

She left the end of her sentence suspended in the air for him to finish. It replicated the way he'd left the end of *his* last sentence hanging, and that was a pretty solid sign that she was starting to trust him. *Mirroring*, they called it in the courses that Joe had attended. He smiled, but not too much and with a little *relief,* and she ushered him into an immaculately neat hallway.

There were waxed oak floorboards underfoot, neutral magnolia on the walls, a few tasteful framed pictures and the sweet smell of jasmine in the air. Two of the pictures were of dogs, Joe noted; the other a country landscape.

She led him past the stairs and into a kitchen at the end of the hall. The kitchen revolved around an Aga stove, with a huge oak table and a breakfast bar close enough to take advantage of the heat the Aga was belting out.

"Can I get you anything?" the girl asked.

"I'm fine. And I'm Joe, by the way, Joe Dyson."

He'd already told her his name when she first answered the door, but she hadn't offered up hers yet and he liked to put a name to a face.

So did Abernathy.

It made filing reports a whole lot easier if you could list a name rather than refer to your subject as "attractive teenager."

"Ellie," the girl said. "Ellie Butcher."

Joe offered his hand and they shook. "Pleased to meet you, Ellie. You said your parents rent a couple of rooms . . . ?"

She looked a little embarrassed, but Joe eased it with pheromones.

"It's the economic downturn. It helps pay the bills."

"A great idea. Very sensible. And how long has Lennie been living here?"

"Not long," Ellie said, sitting at the table and gesturing toward a seat for Joe. "Two months, give or take. He answered a small ad, seemed nice . . ."

Joe sat down and nodded encouragingly. "He's a good guy . . . At school he . . . helped me out a few times. I feel like I owe him."

Sometimes getting information out of someone was as much about telling the truth as it was about lying.

Joe had met Lennie Palgrave during his first disorienting week at Horace Walpole Secondary School, near Windsor.

He'd been moved there midway through the winter term of what the Brits called Year 10. He'd been having trouble at his first English school because his ever-present anger issues had started rearing their ugly head again.

Of course, his feelings had been made stronger by being suddenly uprooted from the bustle of New York to the Hobbiton-like existence of rural England, and had culminated in his punching a bully who just wouldn't let up about Joe's accent. His mother had disagreed with the headmaster's solutions, so she'd called in a favor from a family friend—Abernathy—and Joe had transferred at the same time he became a youth operative for Abernathy's anticrime youth task force.

It had been a hectic transition from inner city public school to countryside private school—although for some mystifying reason the Brits used "public school" as a euphemism for what was really a *private* school—and it had carried a very steep learning curve.

So steep it was practically perpendicular.

Abernathy had supplied three private tutors to help speed up Joe's transition into the UK school system, but coupled with the increased complexity of the intelligence service training, Joe was still feeling out of his depth. At times he wondered if he hadn't made some hideous, embarrassing mistake.

Walking into his first English lesson Joe had done the *look around and watch people avoid eye contact* that had greeted him in every other class and was preparing to settle at an empty desk when suddenly one of the kids deliberately caught his eye. Joe had done a double take, and the kid had nodded at the empty seat next to him, smiling. Joe had felt spectacularly grateful for the gesture and ended up sitting down next to Leonard Palgrave.

Lennie was one of those pale kids with skin that seems just opaque enough to be solid, but transparent enough that you can see more than the usual amount of blood vessels through it. He was mousy-haired and quiet, but when he did speak he had a wicked sense of humor. He was a voracious reader and, although he could quote Plato, Feynman,

Proust, and Sophocles until the cows came home, he also had a deep and abiding love of science fiction.

Joe learned about all of that later, of course. On that first day Lennie was just a friendly face in the crowd.

"Hi, I'm Lennie," he'd introduced himself and offered a hand for Joe to shake.

Joe had immediately made the assumption that Lennie was unpopular, and that what Joe perceived as kindness in calling the new kid over had actually been a desperate act of loneliness, but that turned out to be far from the truth. Indeed, Joe would learn later, Lennie was very popular and had just made sure that he was sitting alone so he could invite the new kid over.

He'd done it so that Joe had a friend.

It was an act Joe had never forgotten.

Sitting there in Ellie Butcher's kitchen, Joe found himself wondering again what kind of trouble Lennie had managed to get himself into. The simple fact that Abernathy had asked Joe to check up on him set off all kinds of alarm bells, but Lennie didn't fit the profile of people that Joe was usually ordered to investigate.

He just wasn't the kind of kid who courted trouble. He was easygoing, bright, and—as far as Joe was aware—he'd never put a foot wrong.

"So what's Lennie been up to?" Joe asked casually, making it sound like gossip rather than an interrogation.

Ellie shrugged.

"To be honest, he keeps mostly to himself. I've had a few conversations with him but he always seems so distant. . . ."

Distant certainly wasn't a word that Joe would have used to describe Lennie, which was worrying. *Outgoing* was more like it. Maybe Abernathy *was* right and Lennie was mixed up in something.

"Has he ever brought home any friends? Anyone I can get in touch with?"

Ellie frowned. "He brings back some of those X-Core types occasionally," she said, pronouncing it *Cross Core*. "But I never got any of their names . . ."

"X-Core?" Joe asked, dredging through his memory for what that might mean and coming up blank. "What's that? A videogame? A new extreme sport?"

"It's a type of music," Ellie explained. "Apparently, it's going to be the next big thing." She paused. "I doubt it. It sounds like a bunch of tone-deaf people throwing fits in a scrap yard."

"That bad, huh?" Joe said, mildly disappointed. What kind of music Lennie listened to was hardly mission-critical information.

"Terrible. Thank heavens for headphones."

"Yours? Or his?"

"His." Ellie smiled. "He played it loud a couple of times, but I can be awfully persuasive."

"I bet you can." He stopped.

Lennie playing loud music? And, come to think of it, Lennie playing any music that wasn't classical?

Joe felt a tingle in his spine. Maybe this *was* mission critical. It sounded like there had been a distinct change in Lennie's behavior; there was a connection to some new musical subculture: it wasn't too much of a leap to imagine that music had led Lennie to more dangerous behavior. It certainly wouldn't be the first—or last—time that music had caused someone to drop out of society.

"What do you know about X-Core?" Joe asked. "I'm really out of touch with the music scene."

"It's like musical catnip for nerds. Techno/industrial noise, bands with names like Precision Image and Le Cadavre Exquis. I looked them up on a few sites, and it's geeky beyond belief."

"Geeky how?"

"You can't get their music on iTunes, Amazon, or any of the other commercial sites. You download X-Core songs for free from the bands' own websites. If you're good at maths."

Joe narrowed his eyes. Why Brits insisted on adding an *s* to *math* was a thing that still baffled him. Like their national obsession with tea.

"Maths?" he asked, sure that the sound as it came out of his mouth would betray him. But Ellie's last statement had come out of left field, and Joe wondered if he'd misheard.

"Wait here." Ellie got up and left the room. She was back

moments later with the brushed matte silver clamshell of a MacBook Pro.

She squeezed in next to Joe and popped the lid, searched for *X-Core*, and clicked on one of the results.

THE HOME OF PRECISION IMAGE, the website's banner informed them.

"Click DOWNLOADS," Ellie instructed, and Joe located the word on the menu bar and did as he was told. It brought up a page of a dozen or so songs with names like "It Took No Comfort," "Etude in Code," and "Democracy Theocracy." They all sounded deathly.

"Choose one," Ellie said.

Joe scanned the list, and chose a track called "TechnoLeeches" because it was the weirdest title there, and pressed the download button next it. Instead of a progress bar, a dialogue box appeared, similar to the CAPTCHAs that appeared on so many websites these days. The difference was this one was an equation—$x^2-3x-4=0$—with two boxes to be filled, and a SUBMIT button.

Joe said, "That's weird."

"Like I said: catnip for nerds. Solve a quadratic equation or you don't get to play." Ellie shrugged. "Seems like an odd way to grow a fan base."

"It's a gimmick," Joe said. "There must be a dozen sites and message boards where you can get the answer."

Ellie shook her head. "They change *every* time. Even for the same song. It means you basically have to solve a different maths problem—and give two values of x—to get access to any of the tracks."

Joe looked at the CAPTCHA on the site, worked it out in his head, and entered *4* in one box and *-1* in the other, then hit SUBMIT. The track started downloading.

"You're not just a pretty face," Ellie said.

Joe flashed her a grin.

"Maths club," he said, the sibilant an afterthought. "Just about the only thing I did learn there."

It was an easy lie that covered a top secret truth: optical character recognition software in his chip had translated the equation into something his chip could handle and it had done the rest. Sometimes dealers and terrorists used codes to mask illegal communications, so Abernathy had made sure that Joe was a walking, talking Enigma machine.

"It's like they only want a certain *type* of people to listen to their music," Ellie said, voicing a suspicion that was already building in Joe's own mind.

But what were they talking here? Bored nerds setting puzzles for people they thought could solve them? Or was there something more sinister at work here? A cult? Mathology? Joe didn't know.

"You ever listen to X-Core?" he asked.

Ellie shook her head. "Half a song maybe. Less, probably. Not my thing."

"I'm guessing you're into classical, right?"

"Death Cab for Cutie." She grinned. "You?"

"Anything that isn't R&B. Mind if I listen?" He pointed to the computer screen. It had finished downloading the song.

"Go for it." Ellie moved a couple of inches closer.

Joe double clicked the file and it opened in iTunes.

It took him about ten seconds to realize that the track had already started, and that he had been hearing it the whole time, but then he recognized a low bass note from a synthesizer that he almost felt as much as heard.

Felt it in his stomach, like a rumble, even through the MacBook's tiny speakers.

The synth panned from speaker to speaker, making it sound like it was in constant motion. Twenty seconds later there was a sudden, shrill screech of guitar tearing through the circling bass; highly distorted and processed that seemed to cycle through a disconnected four-note pattern, getting dirtier and more distorted with every pass.

A drum machine—again highly distorted—kicked in with a simple rhythm that drove on without changes or fills. More synths bled in and out, throwing odd, discordant moods and tones into the mix.

As the tune developed, Joe was struck by the lack of harmony between the different elements; they seemed oddly individual, as if the band had recorded each instrument separately from the others with little or no knowledge of what the other instrumental parts would sound like.

They fitted together—*sort of*—but it sounded more accidental than by design.

Delay and heavy reverb sent bass and guitar into rhythms that seemed at odds with each other, and odd samples of speech would drop in and out at points that sounded . . . *wrong* somehow, as if their cues were chosen for them to appear at precisely the worst possible moments for the listener to be able to work out just what had been sampled over sudden swells of noise and texture.

It made Joe feel on edge, uneasy, anxious.

He had a strange and totally inexplicable thought that the instruments weren't just circling around, but rather *getting closer*, like predators closing in on a kill.

Finally, a full two minutes into the song, the vocalist condescended to sing—although it could hardly be called "singing." It sounded more like a bored, monotonous recitation of a poem:

> *Their leeches bled us of our faith*
> *Drew our blood, let science in;*
> *Bloodless shells we cried for mercy*
> *Pagan shrines to insulin.*
>
> *With scalpels they rewrote the gospels*
> *Lumbar puncture stigmata;*
> *Broken altars, broken idols*
> *To autoclave automata.*

Trepan culture, Karma sutured
Our wounds are read and understood;
Their practice did not make us perfect,
It only taught us to be good.

From the local to the general
Did we build our promised land?
Anesthesia, cracked amnesia,
Hippocrates to guide our hand?

Did we slip the bonds of angels?
Learn to fall, forget to fly?
In Gray's anatomy found our scriptures,
Heart beats to set watches by.

Insanity did Kubla Khan
Find echoes of our distant past;
Vexed to nightmare by a CAT scan,
And an etherized Encephalograph.

There was no sign of a verse/bridge/chorus structure to the song, and its lyric seemed to be in constant conflict with the music, with no attempt made—it seemed—to match the rhythm of the song with the meter of the verse. Again, it was like the vocals had been recorded with no foreknowledge of the music it would be grafted onto. But somehow that very disconnect meant the words gained an almost unreal quality, and the monotone delivery started to become almost hypnotic.

When the track ended by winding down until just the bass rumbled on, Joe felt confused and uneasy.

"You certainly can't dance to it," he said in a small voice from a suddenly dry throat.

"It kind of gets to you, doesn't it?" Ellie rubbed her temples as though fighting a headache. "I feel like I need to shower after listening to it."

"I don't get it. I mean it has a certain power, I guess, but no one could honestly listen to that noise for pleasure."

"Lennie listens to nothing else."

"And does he often go missing?" Joe asked, changing the subject.

"Occasional nights away. Maybe a weekend. But nothing like this. Maybe I *should* call someone. . . ." The thought made her draw away from Joe.

"I'll talk to his parents. I'm sure they'll know what to do. It might help if I can tell them what he was like the last time you saw him. Was he worried? Depressed? In love?"

"Serious. But then, he's always so serious, isn't he? I mean, he can joke around but he's always very controlled. Very repressed. Forced, even."

"Tell me about it," Joe agreed, but he didn't recognize the portrait that Ellie was painting of Lennie. Sure, he was exceptionally smart and incredibly focused, but he had a really sweet, funny side that sounded miles away from the person Ellie was sharing her home with. "Are there any new friends that he might have taken off with?"

Again, something registered in Ellie's eyes and she thought about the question before nodding a little. "Not *new*, exactly. But like I said earlier, a few of those X-Core types started coming round . . ."

"Did they all have to wear headphones?"

Ellie bit her lip.

"They didn't play music," she said cautiously. "They just went up to his room and kind of sat there."

"Sat there?"

"I went up to offer them something to drink once, an excuse to check on them, really, because it was so quiet. The door was open and they were just kind of sitting there, silent. It was kind of strange, to be honest."

"Maybe they heard you coming and stopped whatever it was they were doing?"

"It's possible, but that's not the impression that I got. It just *felt* like they'd been sitting in silence the whole time. And it took them a while to realize I was there even when I asked them about the drinks. . . ."

"That is strange," Joe admitted.

"Even when they finally saw me there was a moment where they looked at me . . . like I was something they didn't recognize. And then the moment passed and they were all perfectly calm and lucid. Maybe it's some kind of meditation. . . ."

"Probably," Joe agreed. "Do you know who any of these other guys were, I mean, so I can tell Lennie's parents, maybe get them to call around . . . ?"

"I didn't know any of them. And Lennie didn't introduce them, which was kind of odd, too, now that I think about it. Usually his manners are perfect. But I know who one of them is."

Joe took a quick mental note of Ellie's demeanor. Her face showed that she was still a little cautious, but that was only to be expected. She had a kid she didn't know asking her questions in her parents' kitchen and no matter how practiced he was at this kind of thing—he'd been on dozens of training courses to learn his craft—it was still an odd situation for her.

He decided that pushing her could make her even more hesitant. If he made it seem as if he was too interested—too eager—to gather information, then caution might turn into suspicion.

He decided to play it neutral.

"I guess it could be helpful," he said quietly, making it sound like it didn't matter one way or the other.

Ellie stood up. She'd made her decision, and it was just the one Joe had been hoping for.

"Wait here," she said and left the room.

Joe sat there as she went upstairs and he knew that she

was going into Lennie's room. She came back a minute or two later clutching a piece of what looked like a card to her chest.

"I saw this the other day." There was a little hint of guilt in her voice. She was, after all, confessing that she'd been in his room. "I recognized one of the people from the night they were all just sitting there."

She handed Joe the card and he saw that it was a flyer for a Precision Image gig, illustrated with a photo showing the band performing live.

Ellie put a perfectly manicured nail on the lead singer and said, "That was him."

Joe nodded. So Lennie wasn't just a X-Core fan; he knew the singer of one of the bands. He didn't know whether that was a good or bad thing. Still, it *was* a lead. The flyer gave the date and location of the gig, and it was in Brixton, tomorrow night.

He tried to think of a way to get a quick look around Lennie's room, but any excuse would only make Ellie suspicious and probably wouldn't get him anywhere, so he wound up the interview, thanked Ellie, left her his number in case she thought of anything else that might help, told her everything was going to be all right, and left.

He was ten feet down the road when he pulled out his phone, dialed Abernathy's number and when Abernathy answered said: "Okay, you've got me interested. I think it's time you briefed me."

"All in good time. What do you know about Lennie's father?"

"Not much," Joe said.

"You must know that your friend's the son of Victor Palgrave?"

"I met Lennie's father a couple of times, a long time ago, on sports day at school, but I have no idea why you would have an interest in him."

Abernathy laughed.

"Read a newspaper sometime, Joe. They can really fill the gaps in your knowledge of current events."

"I only read the back pages."

"So if he was an overpaid Premier League player you'd know all about him?"

"Hey, look," Joe interjected. "It was *you* who taught me to cultivate an interest in soccer, because in this country—apparently—it's impossible to get anywhere with the male half of the species if you can't recite stats for a game that only lets the *goalkeepers* pick up the ball. . . ."

"Okay, it was a low blow. Anyway, listen up. And in case you're wondering, we're talking UK politics, Joe.

"The current government has, according to some Conservatives, become altogether too soft on immigration. The right wing of the party feels like the UK's borders are too porous, and a large section of the voters seems to agree. As a result there has been an alarming growth in right-wing parties and organizations. To placate these dissenting voices, a more traditional form of Conservative is secretly being tipped for a meteoric rise up the cabinet hierarchy. And that minister's name is Victor Palgrave—your friend's father. Some say he's going to be the next prime minister."

"Fascinating," Joe said. "Now, is there a point to this tale, or are you just going to fill me in on the progress of all my school friends—,'cause I'm pretty sure that's what Facebook's for?"

"I've just arranged a meeting for you," Abernathy said. "A personal audience with Victor Palgrave. Go have a chat with him. Then we'll talk."

"Okay. Send me the address."

"Already done," Abernathy said. "By the way, did you find anything out at Lennie's house?"

"X-Core."

"Welcome back, Joe," Abernathy said and hung up.

CHAPTER THREE:
UNCLE ALEX

Ani had never been "on the run" before, and it wasn't at all like the movies.

There was no romance, glamour, or sparkle to it; no big-budget special-effects sequences; no adrenaline-pumping, free-running set pieces; no excitement at all, really: just fear.

The town she had lived in all of her life had become sinister and threatening. Every unexpected car engine had her heart pretty much leaping out of her chest; every sudden appearance of a stranger had her swerving and changing direction; and every CCTV camera had her lowering her head in terror.

Even the streets looked different somehow, as if the scenery were changing to match her situation. Alleys looked longer and seemed to have more places for pursuers to ambush her; roads looked wider and more likely to contain hidden threats; and the buildings seemed to close in around her, making her feel trapped and isolated.

She thought about calling her dad, but hesitated when she took her phone out of her pocket.

She didn't dare.

Maybe *they* were tapping his phone.

Or hers.

Or both.

With the phone in her hand she started thinking about GPS and SIM cards and then she stopped to take the SIM and the battery out. She was sure there was no way they could track her if there was no power.

Or was she?

She was a tech-head, a hacker, a digital spitter-in-the-face of the great and self-proclaimed good, but suddenly all that she knew was up in the air. Uncertain. Unknown. Unknowable.

Who were those guys back there? They weren't cops— she was pretty sure of that, because of the guns, really—but that led to thoughts of darker, less defined law-enforcement agencies.

MI5?

FBI?

Interpol?

Intellectual property rights enforcement?

A Colombian death squad?

Thinking about it was getting her nowhere, but her mind kept picking over it anyway; teasing at the few details she knew, and trying to find a way to make some kind of sense of them.

Problem was, that way lay madness.

She knew this from school and from her online life, too. In the absence of information, of data, the human brain was remarkably adept at inventing stuff to fill in the gaps.

Soon she'd be as mad as Jack McVitie and his 9/11 *Truther* nonsense; or the old man she saw downtown sometimes, who shouted out random statements that were linked only by the power of his delusions.

I need data, she thought. *Solid, dependable data.*

Hence, Uncle Alex.

She just hoped he was home.

The Grafton Centre shopping center squatted on concrete haunches over the bones of an area of Cambridge that once made up part of a district called the Kite.

Urban decay had taken root in the area and, rather than taking steps to stop the rot through a program of gradual regeneration, the universities and city council had opted for a scorched-earth policy that saw a large area demolished and the four-hundred-thousand-square-foot Grafton Centre rise from its ashes.

As far as phoenixes went, this one had retail outlets for feathers.

Ani had heard stories from her dad about life before the

center was built, warm memories of a place where people used to shop in daylight before they were herded beneath the artificial lights of perpetual shopping time.

Of course Ani's dad wasn't an unbiased witness; she was sure his black and gray market goods—he was what was usually referred to as a "fence," the middleman that plied his trade buying what criminals had to sell and moving it on to other people at a reasonable though marked-up price—had found an easier outlet amid the run-down houses and pubs of the Kite.

Walking down Burleigh Street, past the Grafton, she was suddenly aware of the number of CCTV cameras that were needed to protect this brave new world. She had read somewhere that the United Kingdom was the most surveilled Western democracy, and today she saw that it could quite possibly be true.

She felt like the most surveilled person in a Western democracy today, and though it was just paranoia, she ducked her head and stared at the pavement. Tried to look like she was just a normal girl, walking normally. Even though she felt like she was going to suddenly explode from the panic that was filling her up.

The air was cool and she wished that she hadn't needed to sacrifice her hoodie to distract the guys who were following her. It made it harder to tell if she was shuddering from fear or because of the weather.

She passed Forbidden Planet—one of her favorite stores

in Cambridge—then a few thrift stores, took a right down Adam and Eve Street, hurried past the parking lot and out onto East Road. She hustled her way through the two lanes of stationary traffic, cut through the park on the corner, then headed up Mill Road just as it started to rain.

Uncle Alex lived on Devonshire Road—just off Mill Road, before the bridge and running nearly parallel to the railway line—in a bay-fronted Victorian house with windows that looked like they hadn't been cleaned since . . . well, the Victorian era.

A lot of the houses down here were broken up into student bedsits, and the one next door to Uncle Alex's house was a case in point, with a window open and the strains of Bob Marley's *Exodus* leaking out from within.

Ani hurried past Uncle Alex's and stopped ten yards down the road, as if she had just remembered something, even pretending to pat her pockets to make it look realistic. While patting, she checked she wasn't being followed, observed, or pursued by robot drones and then spun on her heels and made her way back to the house.

She walked down the tiny path that crossed the house's postage-stamp concrete yard, gave the door knocker a good hard rap, and stood and waited.

The door swung open and Uncle Alex stood there, eyes widening when he saw who was doing the knocking.

Her dad's brother was a tall, stick-thin man with a hairstyle that on anyone else she would find tragic. But somehow the black hair swept back into a ponytail had always seemed to fit Uncle Alex, even though the front was now starting to thin.

Somehow on him it seemed . . . well, rock 'n' roll.

Like the faded crew T-shirt from Nirvana's *Nevermind* tour he was wearing, a souvenir from when he'd had to stand in on a couple of nights as Kurt Cobain's guitar technician after the regular guy had fallen ill.

"Ani," he said brightly. "Claire's at her mother's and won't be here until next weekend. . . ."

He must have suddenly seen the tension in her face because he left the sentence unfinished, and his eyes narrowed.

"Can I come in?" she asked, and he nodded and stepped aside to let her pass.

"What's going on?" he asked when he'd closed the door behind her.

"I—I'm in trouble. Really big trouble." She was startled to discover that she was crying.

In a kitchen wallpapered with tour posters from bands of the seventies and eighties, over a cup of sweet, grape-tasting tea, Ani managed to get out the story.

Uncle Alex just sat and listened without interruption, occasionally nodding. He narrowed his eyes when Ani described the scene on the roof when the man drew a pistol but he let her tell it in her own way.

When she was finished he reached over and squeezed her arm. "That's a heck of a day you've had, kid. Are you okay?"

Ani gave him a fake smile and nodded.

It didn't fool Uncle Alex. "I'm glad you thought you could come to me," he said. "I don't know what this is all about, but I'll help you any way I can."

This time, Ani's smile was real, made up of equal parts gratitude and relief.

"I'm guessing you want me to take a look at—or listen to—that .wav file of yours," he said.

"Am I that transparent?"

He had no way of knowing, but Alex had just confirmed what she had always thought about him: that he was just about the coolest adult in the world. He had given her no grown-up lectures, had asked her no stupid questions. He had just homed straight in on the heart of the matter.

"Like a window. You want to come through to the Lab?"

Ani nodded. "Thank you."

"What for? We don't know that I'll be any help at all."

"You already have been. And that's what the *thank you* was for."

Alex opened a door in the kitchen, fumbled around for a light switch, found it, and then they were both descending the stairs that led to the cellar.

"The Lab" was an Aladdin's cave of recording and performance gear left over from the decades that Uncle Alex had been the go-to guy for obscure rock 'n' roll equipment.

Ani's dad had once told her that Uncle Alex could build a guitar out of scrap, and that it would be better than ninety percent of the guitars you could buy in a music shop. He also built synthesizers from scratch, and once mended one of David Bowie's performance amps with a chewing gum wrapper.

Ani looked around at the high-tech gear that filled every available piece of wall space in the vast cellar: stacks of amplifiers; keyboards of weird and wonderful designs; gadgets with wires spilling out that she had no idea what they could be.

In the center of the room, like an altar, was a mixing table with so many rows of lights, knobs, buttons, and sliders that she figured you'd need a degree to operate it. And coming off the side of it, so it made an *L* shape, was a Mac computer with a massive display.

"Take a seat," Alex said, pointing to a chair in front of the mixing table, taking the one in front of the computer himself. "Let's see what you've got on this thumb drive."

Ani took the memory stick from her pocket.

"It phones home," she warned. "Kicks holes in firewalls and tells its real owners where it is."

Alex smiled. "It might phone home on your hacker friend's system," he said, "but he sounds less careful than you and me."

Ani looked unconvinced, but handed the drive over anyway.

Alex plugged the stick into a USB hub and waited for it to appear on his desktop, then double clicked and pointed at the screen.

"This the file that's got you so scared?" he asked her.

There was a file called prime.wav in the finder window.

"That's the one. Careful. It bites."

Alex laughed.

And double clicked the file.

Ani held her breath.

"Hold on to your hat," he said.

The .wav file opened in a piece of editing software that made it appear as a series of jagged spikes on a timeline.

Alex studied them and wrinkled his nose.

"It's a .wav file all right. Kind of odd-looking, though. Wanna hear it . . . ?"

Suddenly a dialogue window appeared over the sound editing software: a familiar yellow warning triangle with a red skull-and-crossbones over it:

Ani watched as Alex clicked GENERATE and then he turned and saw the surprise on her face.

"Hey kid," he said, "I got moves, too. And you certainly didn't get your hacker skills from your dad, now did you?"

Ani smiled, suddenly thinking about how computer illiterate her father actually was, even needing her to set his DVR.

"I just keep forgetting there's a Vader edge to your Yoda," she said.

Alex rolled his eyes.

"I'm all about the edge. So, as I was saying before I was interrupted, wanna hear it?"

Ani nodded.

He reached across her and made some adjustments on the mixing table, flicking sliders and pressing buttons, then he grimaced theatrically, and pressed PLAY.

At first, there was nothing to hear.

Ani could see from the computer screen that it was because there was a flat line at the start of the file, which represented silence. Then the software's playhead marker started approaching the body of jagged lines and Ani felt a strange apprehension.

Whatever was in that file had gotten people excited enough to come to her house with guns. Suddenly, she was almost *afraid* to hear what it was.

When it hit, the result was nothing like she'd been expecting. And through Uncle Alex's setup, the sound was loud and incredibly clear.

First there was a low bass sound; a rumbling buzz that

she felt as much as heard. It worked its way through her until it felt like her whole body was vibrating right along with it. It wasn't an entirely unpleasant feeling; just a very, very strange one. She thought that maybe she felt the way a plucked string would on a guitar, if it were capable of feeling.

Then the bass notes plunged even lower—getting so deep they were almost all sensation and no noise—and this new frequency seemed to hit her in the stomach like a punch.

She felt a moment's panic—it was like a physical pain growing inside her. Then over the buzz, or, rather, *out of it*, came a weird rush of high-frequency sounds that seemed not to belong together, so ugly and discordant was their overall effect.

The feeling in her stomach now felt like a hand folding up into a tight fist, closing on her guts.

Hard and cruel.

She looked over at Uncle Alex, but he seemed utterly unaffected by the sound, almost bored by it.

By the time some mid-range sounds kicked in—again ugly and disorganized—the sensation was spreading out through the rest of her body. From her guts it reached outward, making her fingers and toes tingle from within, then she felt it squeezing itself upward, into her head.

Suddenly the sound was in her brain, right inside, and she saw the sounds starting to gain form in her mind's eye: a knot of strange, squirming patterns that edged out all other thoughts until there was nothing left, just . . . *sound-forms*—unsettling patterns—that were playing out in the cinema behind her eyes.

She didn't want to see them, but they wouldn't take *no* for an answer. So she watched as the patterns unfolded and evolved inside her head.

Now there was something distinctly *wormlike* about the images that had forced their way into her mind and she felt a sudden wave of revulsion but, again, she was powerless to resist them.

She was no longer aware of the sound that had made them appear: she was aware of very little except those squirming things in her head.

Her body was still vibrating, but it seemed distant and unconnected to her. The images were crowding out all other thoughts and sensations.

She felt sick as the wormy things grew clearer and more definite in form. They glistened wetly, and seemed to be growing, getting fat on her fear. Suddenly they split open, and hatched into her brain, pouring millions of tiny living threads into her mind and body.

She could see them clearly now: shiny and wet, boiling in a dense mass throughout her body. She realized that they weren't worms, or even particularly wormlike, it was just the closest her mind could come to describing them. Like the information she was receiving wasn't visual at all, but her consciousness was desperately trying to understand the input it was receiving, and images were just the *closest* or *most convenient* way to do that.

She didn't know.

But she did know one thing.

She knew one thing without a shadow of a doubt.

Whatever this data stream was that was flowing through her, it was *dangerous*.

She felt it probing, prodding at her mind, looking for a way in. It was filling her up, and its intentions were not good or honorable. It wanted her. It wanted to use her as a vessel. It wanted to keep splitting, keep hatching, keep writhing and poking until her defenses gave up. And then it would *be* her. It would flow into the spaces that made her Ani and push them aside, devour them, until it took her over.

That was what she sensed now, above all other things. The *hunger* of the sound, of the things that weren't worms. Its total and single-minded appetite for her body, for her mind.

There was nothing she could do.

There was no defense against it.

No happy thoughts that would defeat it.

Soon, it would eat her up and hollow out her body, and make her into *it*.

She felt the sound/worm/*soundforms* finding a crack in her mind. A backdoor into who she was.

She felt terror, loathing, sorrow, and loss and then . . .

. . . and then it was gone.

It didn't slow, then fade, then stop. It just disappeared. One instant she thought she was about to be consumed by the *soundforms,* and the next there was nothing.

The relief was like a physical force.

She opened eyes that she couldn't remember closing and was back in her uncle Alex's cellar.

The lights were suddenly very bright, but she didn't avoid them—indeed, she basked in their intensity.

Better to be dazzled than to have to look at those horrible *soundform* things for a moment longer.

Uncle Alex was standing over her, looking down at her, and his face was worried beyond belief.

"Ani?" he asked nervously.

"Only just," she managed to reply. "That was the most terrible thing that's ever happened to me."

Uncle Alex looked at her strangely.

"What just happened?" he asked. "I played the sound and suddenly your eyes rolled back in your head. . . ."

"How long was I out?" she asked. "I mean, that seemed to go on forever."

Again the strange look from Alex.

"The .wav file was about ten seconds long, but I cut it off after about five when you started looking demonically possessed. . . ."

"*Five seconds?*" Ani asked, thinking that Uncle Alex was playing some kind of joke on her. But his face didn't look like he was joking. It looked like he was terrified.

"It was six seconds, *max,*" he said. It sounded like he was apologizing to her.

Ani did the only thing she could to deal with what had just happened to her.

She fainted.

CHAPTER FOUR:
YETI

The Pyramus Club was on Dover Street, a mere stone's throw away from the pomp and luxury of the Ritz Hotel, but you really had to be looking for it to find it. It was hidden in plain sight, like the purloined letter in the Edgar Allan Poe story, and hundreds of people an hour hurried past without giving it a second glance.

Joe, on the other hand, had a cell phone and it led him straight to it.

It was an anonymous-looking building that hinted at a long and great history without giving many clues to the precise era it was erected. Only a tiny brass plate on the wall provided an identity, but it offered no clues to the type of club that lurked behind two stern oak doors.

Joe pressed the buzzer and posed for the camera in the intercom system.

A curt voice asked, "Yes?"

"I'm here to see Victor Palgrave," Joe said, upper class English accent very much in use. "I believe he's expecting me."

"One moment," the voice replied, then kept him waiting five minutes.

Standing there, Joe ran through the few facts he'd gleaned from Ellie Butcher, just to get them straight in his head before seeing Lennie's father.

Which, on the face of it, amounted to a whole lot of *not much*.

All he knew was that there was a new musical subgenre of dubious artistic merit that Lennie had gotten himself mixed up in. There had been a marked change in Lennie's behavior, maybe a change in his actual personality. And there was the odd thing about the math puzzles that allowed access to the bands' songs.

Joe would probably have thought X-Core was irrelevant if it weren't for two persuasive counterarguments: first was Abernathy's *Welcome back* when he'd mentioned X-Core. That meant he'd thought Joe had stumbled on to the right track; and second was the song he'd listened to on Ellie Butcher's MacBook. He couldn't put his finger on it, but it had sounded . . . *wrong* somehow, and he couldn't imagine that someone as sensitive as Lennie would find anything there to pull him away from his Chopin.

It was a puzzle, that much was certain.

And Joe suddenly realized that a puzzle was just what he needed right now.

Finally the door opened and a man dressed like a valet from

Downton Abbey appeared around it and gave Joe a rather withering look up and down. The man's center part would have looked appropriate for a stage play, perhaps, but not real life, his hair pasted down with Brylcreem, and his scalpel-slash-thin lips were pursed in what looked like perpetual disapproval.

"Ye-e-e-es?" The man stretched one tiny word into an entire sentence. It was both a question and a critique of Joe's outfit.

"Joe Dyson. To see Victor Palgrave?"

The man raised a beaklike nose into the air and spun on his heels, walking off inside without another word. Joe, guessing that he was meant to follow, stepped across the threshold, closed the door behind him, and followed the man across a luxurious foyer into the club. If Joe was to characterize the interior designer's choices, he would have to say that he had an almost single-minded fondness for dark wood panels and watercolors of hunting scenes.

The man led him through a reading room and toward some private rooms. Half a dozen pairs of eyes dragged themselves away from their newspapers to follow them past. Joe recognized one of them as a political talking head from the evening news.

The valet stopped suddenly and knocked on an ornate door with intertwined roses carved into the dark wood with quite some artistic skill, and a single bark from within must have served as an instruction to enter.

The cut-rate Carson held the door open for Joe, nose still up in the air. Joe was sure the man sniffed indignantly as he passed.

The door closed behind him.

Victor Palgrave was a long, lean man with intense dark eyes and a politician's smile—the kind that would make pain seem like pleasure and bad news sound good. He was sitting in one of a pair of enormous armchairs by a roaring fire, drinking coffee, flanked by two guys who made it look like the Secret Service was scraping the shallower end of the gene pool these days. When Palgrave saw Joe his face lit up, and it seemed genuine.

"It's good to see you, Joseph," he said, and gestured toward the empty chair. "It's been a long time."

Not good enough for you to remember my first name, Joe thought, although "Joseph" from "Joe" had been a pretty good guess.

The two gorillas in suits stood behind Palgrave, looking at the walls, and generally pretending not to hear a thing.

Strategy-wise, Joe decided that his real accent, Brooklyn diphthongs still not fully eroded by elocution lessons, would jangle more in Palgrave's cultured ear.

So it was the one he used.

"I hear you're doing pretty well for yourself these days, Mr. Palgrave," Joe said, sitting down. "It's good to see you, too."

Palgrave smiled, but the smile didn't quite reach his eyes. Could have been sadness. Could have been deceit. "Our mutual friend said you're helping out on this. I have to say I was delighted that Abernathy chose you. I appreciate it. I really do."

"I'm just trying to get up to speed, maybe get an angle on all this. I can't believe Lennie would get himself mixed up in anything . . ."

"Unsavory?" Palgrave finished, waving a hand absently in the air. "I find it hard to believe it myself. Leonard has always been such a sensible boy. This X-Core nonsense has kind of come out of the blue. What are your impressions?"

Joe shrugged. The truth was he had no impressions. X-Core seemed to be the key phrase, but since he'd only just heard of it, he had no idea why that should be. Still, it wouldn't look good to be hopelessly uninformed. "I was just briefed," he lied, "so it's probably better if I ask you a few questions. Try to put things in some kind of context?"

"Of course." Palgrave sat back in his chair and linked the fingers of both hands in front of his stomach.

Joe suddenly felt a little awkward, but such feelings would be counterproductive. He hid it immediately with a question. "Let's begin with an easy one: when did all this start?"

Palgrave shrugged. "I've been asking myself the same question," he said after a moment. "I keep going over and over it. Trying to find a precise moment where I could have stepped in and . . . helped . . . said something . . . I don't know."

He closed his eyes, unfolded his hands, and tried again.

"I meant it when I said that Leonard has always been a sensible child. Jenifer and I have always been so proud of him. It sounds a little trite, I'm sure, but I have always thought that he was destined for *exceptional* things. That the advantages he has had would make him—I don't know—somehow greater than the sum of his parents' backgrounds.

"I was a product of a state school. Jenny went to public school, but on a scholarship." (Joe wondered again at the euphemism "public school," and made a mental note to look up the etymology of the phrase sometime.) "We fought hard to climb upward through life. We thought that sending Leonard to the best schools in the country would give him a secure footing in the world. Allow him to scale even giddier heights than we ever managed . . ."

"There's a rumor that you're on a path that leads you straight to prime minister in a couple of years," Joe interrupted, mainly to get Palgrave back on track. "That's not so shabby for a kid from a state school."

Palgrave laughed, but with a hint of bitterness.

"I'm afraid that's just a case of right place, right time. I have the policies that seem to fit with the general mood of the country, and the educational background to make me more agreeable to voters. I'm under no illusion that the party truly stands behind me. It's just that they see me as a convenient lesser of assembled evils."

He sipped at his coffee, then thought better of it and knocked the last third of the cup back.

"Leonard has no political aspirations," he said. "Never had. I'm kind of glad. There's something essentially self-serving about Westminster, and he seemed to see it for the ship of fools that I fear it is in my darker moments. He was acing his way through school; I mean, when he hardly tried he was better than most, but when he gave something his full attention . . . he *excelled*. And that's not just a proud parent speaking. . . ."

Speaking? Joe thought. *Don't you mean "droning on"?*

He wondered if all politicians had a natural flair for saying little in a lot of words, or if it was something they learned once deciding upon their career path.

Or is he hiding something? Joe wondered, surprised at the thought.

None of these thoughts changed his pleasant, professional demeanor, however. Training. Never show what goes on under the surface.

"Oh, I remember," Joe said, smiling. "No one could touch him."

He saw Palgrave grow an inch as he took the compliment-by-association.

"And then something happened," Joe prompted.

Palgrave nodded.

"I keep looking back, trying to spot danger signs. But I can't find them. Every child rebels against his or her parents. It's something you wait for—the moment when the perfect storm of hormones and new ideas present you with this new person who suddenly seems so angry and resentful. Maybe they read Camus or Marx or Chomsky and start to question things. The thing is, I always thought that the process would be gradual. But it's like Leonard went through it all overnight.

"My mother used to tell me fairy tales, not out of books, just ones she remembered hearing when she was a girl, and she probably embellished them. But I keep thinking about one in which a woman started to be afraid of her own baby, only to discover that it had been switched out with a goblin baby—a *changeling*.

"Well, Leonard's shift from teacher's pet to obsessed X-Core fan was so swift, so total, that the story was the first thing I thought of."

Joe accessed his chipset and released a little *encourage*. "It's like it's no longer Lennie," he said gently, gauging the tone to match the pheromone.

Palgrave thought about the statement for a few seconds and Joe worried he'd gone too far, misreading the situation, but then Palgrave nodded gravely.

"If I didn't know better, I'd say that he was no longer my son." His face reflected the internal struggle it had taken to bring that thought to the surface. "I look into his eyes and

I don't see Leonard looking back at me. There's something harder . . . crueler, perhaps, that has taken up residence inside his head.

"I tried to get him some help . . ."

"What kind of help?" Joe asked.

"Counseling. Talks from people he used to respect. Tough love."

"And where did that get you?"

"Nowhere. Every attempt to help him just made him more and more distant. The last try was a full-scale intervention . . ."

Joe narrowed his eyes. "That thing where you get everyone in someone's life assembled in one room and confront him with his problem?" Something about that idea jarred with Joe, and he wasn't sure he fully believed it. It just didn't *feel* like Palgrave's style. Still, there was nothing to be gained in calling Palgrave out on it, and no reason he could find for him to be lying. Better to let him elaborate and see if there wasn't something to grab on to. "I'm guessing that's when he moved out?"

"Yes." There was a hint of something that could have been shame in Palgrave's voice. "I mean, the weird thing is that he's not some average teenager acting up and trying to assert himself in an adult world. He doesn't swear or steal or disrespect us. It's nothing solid. Nothing you can pin down. It's more like a total change in attitude. He no longer seems to be interested in anything but that music of his."

"X-Core. When did he become interested in it?"

Palgrave shook his head. "I stopped paying attention to the music he listened to a few years ago. It all sounds like noise to me. Back in the long-lost past, when he was buying CDs, he used to sometimes show them to me, but now he has his computer and iPod and whatnot—it's become a very different world. It's just data he downloads, and it's not as easy to check what he's listening to, what he's watching, even who he's talking to."

"And he took his computer with him, of course?"

Palgrave nodded.

"Shame. I would have liked to snoop through it."

"But our whole home network backs up onto a cloud server. . . ."

Joe raised an eyebrow. "So there's a chance that a lot of his data is still accessible?"

"I believe so. Do you think it will be any help?"

Joe was mystified why Palgrave *wouldn't* think it would be useful. But he shrugged to downplay it. "It could be. If you could give Abernathy the details, and any passwords, one of our techs might be able to mine it for relevant information."

Palgrave suddenly seemed cheered up by the idea.

"I'll do that as soon as I get home. Is there anything else . . . ?"

Joe thought about it. It seemed like getting their hands on Lennie's data might be a lead, though a weak one, but he wasn't really sure what more help Palgrave could be.

Sometimes gathering intelligence was just a matter of asking a whole bunch of questions and hoping that one of them opened up an avenue for further investigation. Usually it didn't amount to much, but sometimes a small detail became a clue.

It was obvious to Joe that Victor Palgrave had little insight into the circumstances that had led Lennie from "boy most likely to succeed" to "possible security risk."

Joe didn't know when Palgrave had stopped listening to his son, but figured it was probably a long time before X-Core got its hooks into him.

That's the curse of modern technology, Joe thought. It isolated people from their families, providing them with a whole slew of virtual "friends" to talk to, rather than the people who would traditionally have been there for them.

Sometimes it seemed like the price of progress was that people "talked" more to their online friends than they did to their own flesh and blood.

"I guess we'll see if we can find anything in Lennie's backed-up files, and see if that gets us anywhere."

Palgrave's face changed. It suddenly looked very earnest, grateful, and serious, and Joe realized that the man was pretty good at controlling his own micro-expressions. For the first time, Joe saw why people thought Palgrave was such a good politician: he could fake it along with the best of them.

Joe wondered again just how honest Palgrave was being with him. He had a sneaking suspicion that the man was holding *something* back, or covering something up, but he couldn't see a way through the politician's formidable defenses, so he just filed the impression away in his *things to think about* file.

"I appreciate everything you're doing," Palgrave said. "I really do."

Joe got up from the seat, smiled, and said, "I'll let you know when I have anything to report."

Then, before Palgrave could come back with any more carefully controlled words or expressions, Joe turned and walked out of the room.

Again, the first thing that Joe did once he was outside was call Abernathy.

"I hear nothing from you for weeks, and suddenly I'm back on speed dial. How did your meeting with Victor Palgrave go?"

"Tell me about X-Core."

"Ah, it's time for *that* chat, is it?" Abernathy said. "Why don't you drop by the office?"

It took a half hour to reach Whitehall, where Joe stood outside the building and psyched himself up to enter.

Just like he'd been psyching himself up the whole journey.

It had only been a few weeks since he'd last been inside, but it seemed like a whole lot longer. Time was like that, telescoping out to make the bad times last for ages, while good times flew by on fast-forward.

Since Andy died, time had done nothing but drag on. Bad days followed slowly on the heels of bad days—until today, when Joe'd set off for Lennie's house, and time had started moving at normal speed again. He was no longer being dragged back by feelings of guilt, sorrow, and regret.

Joe sighed, opened the double doors, and stepped inside.

Into a large lobby with another set of doors at the other end.

First up came the security desk, where Joe flashed his ID—a membership card for a snooker club on the Grays Inn Road, which was better than getting searched in the field and being found carrying an intelligence services ID—and waited while the rent-a-cop scrutinized the photo and Joe's face as if playing Spot the Difference. When the guy was satisfied they were one and the same person, he let Joe through.

On the other side of the doors, one could be forgiven for thinking that it was the office of a law firm or a corporate headquarters. People tapped away at keyboards and watched the fruits of their labors appear on widescreen LCD monitors. People shuffled papers and sat hunched over reports. People gossiped next to the watercooler. The air-conditioning was on and the air was cool and refreshing.

Joe felt a pang of shame at his ratty clothing and messy

hair, but walking through the open-plan area of the offices toward Abernathy's inner sanctum, he was greeted and nodded at by a half-dozen people.

They looked genuinely pleased to see him.

Soon there was even the hint of a swagger creeping into his step.

By the time Joe got to the door of Abernathy's unit, he felt genuinely glad to be back. He swiped his ID and then he was walking into the control center of YETI, the Youth Enforcement Task Initiative.

Okay, officially it was YETF, with the *F* standing for *Force*, but no one in the building called it by its unpronounceable acronym, referring to it instead by the humorous alternative. A much-derided memo had instructed operatives to think of the acronym as having a "silent vowel"— pronounce it "YET<u>U</u>F"—but it had achieved no noticeable effect. The name "YETI" even appeared on the few departmental signs around the place, but only because it was so easy to remove the horizontal stripes of a capital *F* with Wite-Out.

Abernathy had told them a few months ago that a leading cabinet member had taken to calling them YETI, too, which had had the entire control room in stitches when he'd done an impromptu impression using exactly the same delivery that the minister used when he was interviewed for commentary on the news.

The control room itself was a postmodern cube of vast displays and associated workstations. The people who operated it on a daily basis were all highly trained intelligence personnel, analysts with backgrounds in law enforcement, or the spying community.

What made YETI different, however, was the age of its covert operatives.

There wasn't one of them over the age of eighteen.

It was an utterly secret department, backed by the very highest authorities in the country, and answerable only to the home secretary and the prime minister. They remained out of public documents, and only once had a journalist gotten even a slight whiff of the organization, a "scoop" that had led—through the well-timed release of some incriminating evidence stored for just such an occasion—to the downfall of a leading Sunday tabloid.

As Joe made his way across the room he received respectful, solemn nods from the analysts at work there, and he felt for the first time in a while that he really did belong.

In the days following Andy's death Joe had believed that this life was behind him now, that he no longer belonged here, that his inability to help his friend had closed these doors behind him. He had been angry, riddled with guilt, and scared, and instead of throwing himself back into operations—to carry on the important work that Andy had died for—Joe had closed himself off and shut himself down.

Now he was beginning to see that reaction as a mistake, a knee jerk of shame and a snail-into-shell retreat from a lack of self-confidence.

Abernathy was waiting for him by the briefing room at the far corner of the control room and they both went inside.

The briefing room looked a lot like a classroom with desks lined up in front of a digital whiteboard. Joe sat down at a desk, and Abernathy moved to the front of the room and swiped the whiteboard with his arm to turn it on. Abernathy's ID was subcutaneous, implanted into his arm, and it also acted like a universal remote control for gadgets and doors.

"Glad you could make it, Joe," Abernathy said. The rare show of emotion made his voice sound less clipped and stern than it usually did.

"Glad to be back. Now tell me everything you know."

Abernathy nodded, and it was obvious that he was pleased with Joe's back-to-work attitude, because he gestured with his arm and the board suddenly displayed a high-resolution image of a group of teens, four boys and a girl.

"The picture you're looking at is a publicity photo of a band called Precision Image, the prime movers behind the whole X-Core scene." He double-tapped on the boy at the center of the picture and the photo zoomed in on a sullen white face with only the bright blue eyes showing any kind of life. A shock of bleached-blond hair, gelled into spikes, served only to make the boy look angry.

"I've seen him," Joe said, and Abernathy looked surprised. "Well, I saw a photo of him that came out of Lennie's room. Turns out he's a personal friend of Lennie's."

Abernathy lifted an eyebrow as he took that information onboard.

"Curiouser and curiouser. Anyway, he calls himself Null-A," Abernathy said, and Joe had a nagging impression that he had heard the name before. "Lead vocalist with Precision Image. Real name: Harry Brewster. Attended prep school in Dulwich; then a top school that boasts some of the best results—and wealthiest parents—in the United Kingdom. Straight As across the board. Son of James and Nora Brewster—he's a dotcom millionaire, developer of an online office manager for small businesses; she writes chick lit and is successful enough at it to have spawned two films and a TV series.

"Preliminary reports show that Harry's interest in music was limited to classical—he's a prodigiously skilled pianist—until about six months ago."

Abernathy fiddled with the board and brought up a picture of a boy with a haircut that looked like it had been done using a bowl and scissors. By his mom.

He was dressed in a dark blue blazer and tie. Thick-rimmed glasses magnified his eyes into saucers.

"This was Harry Brewster last year," Abernathy said, and Joe felt a jolt of shock that this could be the same kid from the previous photograph. "Traveling along a preordained course from expensive prep school to a Cambridge college like a Scalextric car locked into its metal groove."

Abernathy caught Joe's look of incomprehension.

He attempted another simile. "Or a train locked on its track."

Joe nodded.

Abernathy actually smiled. "Then . . . *something* happened." He swiped again and a school report appeared on the board. "Take a look at this."

The report showed the most glowing praise for Harry's efforts and achievements: "wonderful"; "a joy to teach"; "an original and lively contributor to class discussions"; "one of the best and brightest it has ever been my pleasure to teach."

Abernathy swiped again and brought up another report, dated three months later.

"Compare and contrast."

Joe could hardly believe that the report bore the same name on the cover page: "a disappointing term"; "taking big steps backward"; "uncommunicative and withdrawn"; "a spectacular disappointment."

"Was there anything going on at home to explain the sudden change?" Joe asked. "Divorce? Abuse? Bullying?"

Abernathy shook his head.

"If anything, his family life *should* have improved. Daddy sold his dotcom start-up to Google for close to a half a billion dollars. There's no evidence of any tragedies or hints of abuse. The academic downfall seems all Harry's own work."

"A hothouse student has a mental breakdown?" Joe asked, suddenly feeling like the last few weeks hadn't happened.

"Exactly what I thought." Abernathy nodded. "Anyway, I talked to his parents—they are devastated, by the way, and only too happy to help—and that was his parents' first thought, too. It turns out, though . . ."

Abernathy fiddled with the board again and the internet page Ellie had shown him earlier appeared on it.

"This is the home page of Precision Image. And this"— he tapped on the tab headed *Mission Statement* and a page of text appeared—"is a sort of online manifesto for X-Core. I draw your attention to this part." He double-tapped.

Joe read the text: *Mental weakness of any kind is anathema to the goals and culture of X-Core.*

"Anathema?" Joe asked.

"Something loathed and detested."

"Methinks they might protest too much," Joe said. "It wouldn't be the first time that someone said they were one thing and turned out to be another. . . ."

"Still as cynical as ever?"

"Realistic."

"Well, there really is no evidence to support the breakdown hypothesis one way or another. So I guess that will be high up on your list of things to find out."

Joe nodded. "It's weird," he said. "The kid in the first photograph had green eyes magnified by his unflattering eyewear, which suggests that now he's adopted contact lenses; his hair is styled as far away as it's possible to get from the kitchen-bowl hairdo from the earlier photo; it's like his whole purpose in the second image is to undo the image presented in the first. What has he told his parents?"

Abernathy shook his head.

"Zip. Nothing. Nada. He has cut off all contact with them. They've tried to see him, to talk sense into him, but he refuses to acknowledge their existence. His mother said it was like Harry was no longer there and this . . . character he's created . . . Null-A . . . has taken over completely."

"Null-A," Joe mused, the name still resonating in his memory somewhere. "Where have I heard that before?"

"The name comes from a trilogy of books by the science fiction writer A. E. van Vogt," Abernathy explained. "*The World of Null-A* was a 1948 novel, and it seems likely that Harry simply took his new name from there."

"A sci-fi nerd?"

"Oh yes," Abernathy said. "Nerd squared, by all accounts. Null-A is also notation for 'non-Aristotelian.'"

Joe's confused look was probably worth a thousand questions.

"Aristotle." Abernathy launched into the "schoolteacher" mode that he so loved to adopt. "Greek philosopher educated by Plato. Wrote on a wealth of subjects and is pretty much the first person to study logic. Van Vogt's books were based on the notion of overthrowing conventional logic."

Joe passed his right hand over his head, to demonstrate where Abernathy's words were going.

"It doesn't matter," Abernathy said. "Let's just say, for now, that the name Null-A works on a couple of levels: as a reference to some science fiction books, and as a rejection of formal logic."

"I'll take your word for it."

"You'll have to do better than that, Joe," Abernathy snapped. "We're already building the foundations of the character that you're going to need to play to get inside X-Core. The thing that Harry has in common with your friend Leonard—and indeed with all the music's followers and performers—is that they are all nerds. High-achieving, top five percent IQ, generally with a keen interest in scientific study, or, it seems, a taste for science fiction."

"It sounds like a strange pool for a music culture to be drawn from," Joe observed. "What is X-Core, anyway?"

Abernathy winced. "In terms of its sound, it seems to be nothing more than a throwback to the seventies and eighties darkwave bands—where gothic rock met synthesizers." Joe had to mentally stop himself smiling at Abernathy talking about "darkwave." "But it's the use of modern production, and a love of industrial sounds, that have given it a very modern edge."

"The one song I heard was pretentious and weird," Joe said. "I couldn't tell what it was actually about. Something medical, I guess. Is that typical of the stuff they sing about?"

"The word 'sing' is a little kind as a description of their vocal stylings," Abernathy said, "but lyrically, X-Core bands are almost exclusively obsessed with machines, metal, wires, circuitry, human-machine hybrids, more metal, more wires . . ."

"Has Gary Numan sued? It sounds like he ought to."

"Numan's not a bad choice for comparison, but where that particular pioneer of commercial electronic music had a cold, detached—but ultimately poetic—approach to his lyrics, X-Core is a little less elegant."

"The track I listened to was called 'TechnoLeeches,'" Joe said. "There was a lot of noise and . . . well, not much else. It's not exactly music . . ."

"You're starting to sound like a parent." Abernathy smiled. "But the scene is flourishing, with new X-Core bands popping up at an alarming rate."

"The math test worries me," Joe said, and saw Abernathy's eyebrow lift up again, this time in surprise.

"Good catch. It *is* odd, isn't it?"

"It's certainly not the best business model I've ever heard of. But it also seems . . . selective. It's almost as if the bands aren't interested in their fan base's money, but rather their intellect."

"That's the thing that scares me," Abernathy said. "The more I find out about X-Core, the more certain I become that this is unlike any other music culture we've seen before. It's not about fame—its major players eschew the media spotlight. It's not about fortune—they give their music away for free. It's not about politics—although it has a poorly conceived manifesto. It's not even about the rock 'n' roll lifestyle. It seems more like a cult than a pop trend."

Joe stared at him blankly. "Then what *is* it about?"

Abernathy looked at him gravely. "That, Joe, is what we need you to find out."

Joe leaned forward. "So how did it land on your desk? And how did Lennie get involved? He really isn't the type . . ."

"And therein lies the problem. Maybe he's *exactly* the type."

Abernathy pulled up a chair and sat down opposite Joe. "I told you that Leonard's dad, Victor, is tipped for big things in the world of politics. He's already in the cabinet—Secretary of State for Culture, Media, and Sports—but becoming PM would take him to a whole new level of scrutiny. The higher the post, the higher the levels of clearance need to be and Five performed a scan through Victor Palgrave's life—"

"You mean MI5," Joe interrupted. "Why do people think that it's okay just to say the number? Is it from watching too many spy dramas, or something?"

"And yet you knew *exactly* what I was referring to. Makes me wonder what your objection really is."

"The fact that I'm seventeen and know what 'Five' means. Like I know what 'collateral damage' is. And a 'sleeper cell.' And that I know these things from first-hand experience. . . ."

"Can you have a second-hand experience?"

"You know what I mean."

"Yes. I do. A fellow operative died, and you feel that it was somehow your fault. But it wasn't. It was the fault of a particularly nasty piece of work called Glenn Tavernier who is safely shut away behind bars, thanks to you. Now may I please continue?"

Joe nodded.

"Good. MI5 performed a routine vetting of the Palgrave family tree and your friend Leonard set off some alarm bells. . . ."

"That's ridiculous. Unless they are flagging people for having fancy accents or a strong desire to work in the city. . . ."

Abernathy shook his head. "It was his connection with X-Core that set off the alarms."

"So MI5 is already looking into X-Core?"

"No, they just saw it as a possible security risk."

"I don't get it. Why would an MI5 vetting flag the musical taste of an MP's kid?"

Abernathy sighed. "Music actually matters a great deal. Plato said that musical innovation was a danger to the state, that 'when the modes of music change, the fundamental laws of the state always change with them.' Translations of the quote differ, as do analyses of what Plato actually meant, but Five seem to have taken that one particular version of it rather literally.

"Ever since the 1950s, musicians have been routinely scrutinized, such as when the FBI asked Five to keep an eye on Larry Adler because of his communist leanings."

"Larry who now?"

"Adler. Played the harmonica."

"The mouth organ? And was famous for it? Talk about a different world."

Abernathy sighed. "During the 1960s, groups like the Beatles started spreading what were seen as counterculture ideas. Then the anarcho-punk movement of the late 1970s and early 1980s saw an upsurge in activism actually *encouraged* by musicians. Music is a powerful voice for change—look at Live Aid—and the intelligence services have thought it wise to watch musicians and their fans."

"So what is it about X-Core that has Five worried?"

"It's the demographic," Abernathy said. "Most musical subcultures are largely fueled by working class kids and are used as a kind of tribal rite of passage: a group of people to belong to who hold the same values as you, who dress the same, listen to the same music, talk in the same designer slang. It's a big scary world, and it's in small groups or subcultures that kids seem to feel most comfortable.

"Music trends are one of the easiest tribal groups to be accepted into. You just have to buy some records and don whatever uniform the tribe prefers."

"Records? What, to take home and play on their gramophones in the parlor?"

"I'll have you know that vinyl is making the most unlikely comeback since Johnny Cash," Abernathy said. "Anyway, it may sound incredible, Joe, but teenagers are a relatively modern invention. Pre-1950, there was very little difference between people in their teens and adults. Before that, there were, broadly speaking, only two ages of person: child and adult. Postwar affluence, and a desire for parents to give their kids the things that they never had in their own austere childhoods, served to create this new creature: the teenager. And the mechanisms of commerce and marketing seized onto it with barely concealed glee."

"Nice editorializing."

"My point is that these new creatures needed tribes of their own, to separate themselves from the children they once were and the adults they would ultimately become.

"And it came to pass, because—lo and behold—the music industry did verily provide them.

"Mods and rockers; skinheads and punks; new romantics and metalheads; house, garage, and probably shed and greenhouse, too; grunge and industrial; emo, screamo, pop punk, and grindcore; goth, death metal, darkwave; rap, R&B, drum and bass, and dubstep. A wealth of ready-made labels for young people to subscribe to.

"But these labels have, in the majority of cases, been a product of working class energy; the anger of those at the bottom, raging against the world's machine.

"X-Core skips the working classes almost entirely.

It seems to recruit its performers and listeners from the very best schools, and it wears its elitism very clearly on its sleeve."

"So where do I go next?" Joe asked.

"Home. I'll call you in the morning when we've both had a chance to think about where we are, in both the investigative and the personal contexts. This is your first day back, Joe, and I know it's going to dredge up ghosts, but I have to be honest with you: I need you on this. So have an evening of pizza, pinball, and PlayStation, and we'll resume tomorrow."

Joe wanted to protest, but he knew that Abernathy was right. He'd stepped back through the doors of YETI, and that was good, but he needed a little time to think about what that meant.

"Catch you tomorrow, boss," he said, and headed for home.

CHAPTER FIVE: A TRAIL OF BREADCRUMBS

When Ani came around, it was to the smell of rich roast coffee. A steaming mug sat on a small table nearby. She realized that she was horizontal, and that the surface beneath her was soft.

She sat up too quickly and felt woozy from the sudden rush of blood to her head. When that had passed, she looked around her and saw that she was in Uncle Alex's front room. He must have carried her up the cellar steps and put her on the sofa for comfort.

The room was a shrine to music, with one wall dominated by racks filled with records; another wall was filled with CDs. Hi-fi equipment sat on a designer rack; speakers circled the room.

Ani tried her feet and was almost surprised to discover that they still worked. She had a splitting headache and her balance was slightly off, but she was capable of functioning as a human being.

She'd just reached the living room door when Uncle Alex appeared, his face grave.

"Ani," he said, his compassion and worry evident in his voice. "Thank God you're up. I made coffee . . ."

Ani muttered a thank you, went over to the table, took the mug, and sipped its contents. It was warm and sweet and just what she needed.

"What happened to you?" Alex asked her, taking a seat on the sofa and looking at her solemnly.

She shook her head.

"There's something in that sound. Something bad. Something dangerous."

"It just sounded like a racket to me," Alex said. "What do you mean *something dangerous*?"

"Didn't you see anything?" Ani asked.

Alex looked puzzled.

"See anything? No. Except you turning into a space-case on me."

"It was the .wav file," Ani explained. "The sound, it . . . made me see things."

Alex looked concerned, but not like he thought she was crazy. Which was a relief.

He thought for a moment. "Can I ask *what* you saw?"

"Strange patterns. Sort of like worms. Millions of them. I think they were alive."

"Alive?"

"I know it sounds nuts."

"Not *nuts*, Ani," Alex said, "but extraordinary things sometimes have pretty simple explanations. It could be stress, hunger, dehydration . . ."

"I saw it," Ani said firmly. "And I really wish it was a dream, or a hallucination, but it wasn't. You really didn't see anything?"

Alex shook his head, and then his expression changed.

"But that doesn't mean you didn't." All doubt was now gone from his voice. "Look, maybe I'm too old to hear it."

Ani sat down next to him. "What do you mean, *too old?*"

"Well, you've heard about the Mosquito—a high frequency sound that most adults can't hear, but that's loud and clear to most kids?"

"The ringtone thing?" Ani asked. "So your phone can ring in class but the teacher won't hear it."

"That's the one. It was originally developed to put in urban spaces to stop teenagers loitering in or outside particular areas. It takes advantage of the fact that human hearing peaks in the early to mid-twenties and then starts dropping off. High frequencies are the first to disappear from an aging person's aural range."

Ani thought about it. "So this .wav file might have sounds that adults can't hear? Which is why I saw things and you didn't?"

"It's possible," Uncle Alex admitted. "It's also possible

that years of some of the loudest rock gigs in the history of humanity have impaired my hearing. But I've never heard of a sound that causes hallucinations. . . ."

"It wasn't a hallucination," Ani said. "It was real."

"Okay," Alex said, and Ani loved him for the way he didn't try to argue with her, believing her almost without hesitation. "But we need to work out what that means. *Real* is one of those words we throw around all the time, without ever truly understanding what it means."

"Doesn't it just mean that a thing exists?"

"But how do we know a thing exists?"

"We can see it. Or touch it. Or taste it. Or hear it. Or smell it."

"So is *time* real? Or *gravity*? Or *air*?"

"Okay, so we can measure it, too."

"So, we measure the things that we can't detect with our senses, and that makes them real," Alex agreed. "How about *love*?"

"That's one we feel."

"So, feelings are real? Jealousy? Rage? Embarrassment? They exist because we feel them?"

"Of course."

"Some people feel like they've lived before in previous lives. Others feel that they've been abducted—sometimes, that they've been experimented on—by aliens. Some people feel that there're ghosts in a room, or that their next-door neighbor's dog is telling them to kill people. Are these feelings real?"

"No. Of course not."

"But people swear that those experiences are true. They *feel* them as powerfully as you or I feel love or anger. You can see what I'm saying, right?" Alex asked.

"You're saying that I imagined it," Ani said, colder than she'd meant to. The truth was she didn't like the way this was going.

But Uncle Alex, as usual, surprised her. "Ani, Ani, Ani," he said gently. "That's not what I'm saying at all. I'm just trying to define our terms before we start. I'm saying that this label is not some hard and fast property of things that exist, but just one way we have of understanding the things around us.

"Ideas exist—I know that for a fact, I've had some—but what makes my idea for a design for a rotating speaker stack for Iron Maiden any different from the one I once had for making mouse-flavored cat food? The point is that thinking something doesn't make it real. It makes it a real thought, but not a real thing.

"Now, your criteria for something being *real* seem to be all about the ways that we can interact with them. They become real when we can prove they are by measuring them, whether it's with our senses, or with external apparatus. But how about things that our senses can't detect and that we haven't thought to measure yet? Aren't they real?"

"Such as . . . ?"

Alex smiled. "I don't know, but we can't be saying that

our twenty-one senses are enough to say we know every-thing about this universe of ours. . . ."

"Wait. Twenty-one senses?"

"The notion that we have only five is so last year. We have a lot more than that. For example, we can sense the passage of time; we can sense temperature, pressure, hunger, thirst, and itchiness. We have a mild, maybe vestigial, magnetic sense; we can tell which way up we are, and how balanced we are; we can tell without looking where our body parts are; we sense pain, tension, and chemical imbalances in our own bodies. And sight is really *two* senses—color and brightness; and taste, well that's five: salt, sweet, bitter, sour, and umami."

"I'm sorry?" Ani said. "I think I might have just stumbled into a parallel universe in which my uncle Alex is a science teacher."

Alex laughed. "Sound is physics and music is mathematics. So I read *New Scientist* and *Scientific American* rather than *Sound on Sound* and *Mix*. The point I'm trying to make is that we have this great selection of sensory equipment in our bodies, but they're things that have evolved along with us, that offered us an advantage at some point in our history, but that are, by no means, a *complete* set. Yet we use them to construct our model of reality—let them determine what we decide is *true* or not.

"But there are things we can't sense. Does that make them any less real, just because our tool kit tells us so? What

I'm saying, Ani, is that something happened to you just now. Something that I didn't experience, but don't think for a second that means it wasn't real. I believe you. There is something . . . different about that sound file. Something dangerous. Something secret."

"Secret?"

"The fact that armed men turned up at your home seems to support that."

Ani nodded. "So where did it come from?" she asked. "I mean, how can we find out?"

"Way ahead of you there, kid." There was a hint of a smile on his lips. "Care to come back to the lab?"

Back in the cellar, Uncle Alex sat her down in front of the computer screen.

"Have you heard of Shazam?" he asked.

Ani nodded. "I have it on my phone. If there's a song playing and you want to know what it is then you open it up and it tells you what it's called and who it's by."

Alex pointed at the screen.

"Well, this is Shazam evolved. The next generation of sound identification. If I hum a few bars of a song, then this software will be able to tell you what song it is."

"And this helps us how?"

"I just fed it your .wav file. And I got a lot of hits. Seems it appears in quite a few songs, although it's buried beneath a lot of other noises, so you can't actually hear it.

"Have you ever heard of X-Core?"

"Some kind of new music. I read a post about it. Uses encryption on its files, or something. Someone had cracked the code on a few tracks and was sharing them. I didn't download them, sounded like some dumb gimmick."

Uncle Alex raised an eyebrow.

"And here I was thinking that if something said *encrypted file* that was exactly the sort of thing you'd be downloading."

"So many encrypted files, so little time."

"Well, the songs my software found the sound in all belong to X-Core bands. The sound in X-Core songs matches the .wav file by eighty-five percent, but it's too close to be a coincidence, don't you think?"

"They're putting *that* sound in their tunes?" Ani said, horrified. "But that doesn't make sense. Why would two people with guns be so keen on keeping it a secret if it's available through tracks that people can download?"

"I don't know," Alex admitted. "Maybe you can ask them. The main offenders, Precision Image, are playing a club in Brixton tomorrow night." He showed her an ad for the gig.

Ani studied the digital flyer and nodded. "I can't go home until I find a way to clear myself of this mess and get some answers. Maybe Brixton is just the place to start looking for them."

Uncle Alex shrugged. "It's not something that I would ordinarily advise," he said. "I mean, we have absolutely no idea what we're dealing with here. But I think it's safe to say that going home is out of the question."

"The men waiting for me . . ."

"Exactly."

Uncle Alex sighed. "Look," he said after a few seconds. "I'll square things with your father, explain as much as I can. And I'll start on analyzing your .wav file, reach out to a few sound-tech friends, see if we can't get some kind of a handle on just what this is.

"Your friend, the one who downloaded this file . . ."

"Jack."

"Where is he from?"

"London."

"Handy. Might be worth seeing if you can track him down. But if something looks hinky, then get yourself away as fast as you can."

"Did you say *hinky*? Did you just use a *Scooby-Doo* word?"

"That's *jinkies*. I must be crazy. Aiding and abetting a fugitive. Encouraging you to play private investigator. Even financing the trip . . ."

"Financing?"

Uncle Alex reached into his jeans pocket and drew out a wallet, flipped it open, and pulled out a debit card. "For my favorite niece, I figure what the hey?"

"Your only niece."

"Lucky I got a good one, no? Anyway, you can take three

hundred pounds a day out of an ATM with this. You'll definitely need some travel money. And you'll also need to buy yourself a few new pay-as-you-go SIM cards, use them, swap them, and discard. I have a friend who lives in Islington and I'm sure she'll put you up. I'll scribble down her address. She's good people. Just don't get her involved. Keep quiet about the .wav, space worms, and men with sidearms."

He held out the card to Ani.

"I can't," she said.

"That's just an account that I sling a bit of spare money into. There's a couple of grand in it, that's all. You're worth a whole lot more, kid. And this isn't up for discussion."

Ani took the card. "Thank you doesn't *begin* to cover it," she said. "But it's all I have at the moment. So thank you."

Uncle Alex blushed.

"I have no idea if the people after you will be watching the train station. It seems unlikely, but I'm not sure I'm willing to take the risk. I'll take you to the station, but that school uniform is kind of a giveaway. Claire leaves some clothes here for when her mother lets her visit, and they might fit. You know where her room is. Help yourself."

Ani felt overwhelmed with his generosity, could even feel tears of gratitude forming in her eyes.

Uncle Alex just smiled.

"It really is the least I can do. There's hair stuff and makeup up there, too. I usually roll my eyes at Claire using them, so I can't believe I'm *telling* you to. Try to make yourself look as different as you can. Don't think of it as makeup, think of it as a disguise."

Ani took the stairs to Claire's room two at a time.

CHAPTER SIX:
DOWNTIME

Joe felt wired and tired in equal measures when he got back home, and he spent the first part of the evening trying to get the place back in some kind of order.

Mission: impossible.

Home was an open-plan loft on Mortimer Street, huge now that Andy was no longer around to share it.

Actually, to be honest, it had been huge when he *was* around.

Abernathy had paired them up a year ago and brought them to the apartment that was to be theirs. Both Joe and Andy had been stunned by the size of it.

And by the size of the account that Abernathy had opened for them simply to deck the place out.

It was furnished in teen chic, but the kind of teen chic probably reserved for kids whose parents were multi-millionaires.

The first thing they'd bought had been two pinball machines—*Game of Thrones* and *South Park*—that stood in the darkest corner of the loft and had been the focus of a lot of their downtime. Then had come a home cinema projection kit, the latest game consoles, and computers. Finally, they'd bought the things ordinary people would have bought first: beds and kitchen stuff, sofas, chairs, and tables.

Looking at it all now, Joe just felt sad.

Everything here had history, and Andy was inextricably linked to every bit of that history. They had been two kids with a blank check, egging each other on to more and more extravagant purchases. Now it all seemed tawdry and useless.

After clearing away most of the mess that had accumulated during his downward spiral following Andy's death, Joe sat down on his bed and looked around.

Everywhere reminded him of Andy.

He thought about calling someone to try to pull himself out of his mood, but he couldn't think of anyone *to* call, so he hit the punching bags and ran through fighting programs from his chipset until he settled upon Wing Chun and pounded the bags until he was exhausted.

A vast library of fighting skills were kept on files within Joe's chipset, and activating them served to encode moves, punches, kicks, and stances into muscle memories: the mental process that allowed people to become proficient at any physical activity, whether it was riding a bike, playing "All Along the Watchtower" on a guitar, or blazing through the levels of a video game. The eidetic reflexes software tricked the body into thinking it knew—and had practiced—physical actions, so that with minimal practice (and often,

112

none) the physical action could be called out of the chip and used in the real world. They had been arranged in what Abernathy's tech-heads, the Shuttleworth brothers, called context-specific action groups, which meant that it was the situation that dictated the most effective strategies and sent them to Joe's muscles.

It meant that Joe could fight like an Ultimate Fighter contestant with only the barest amount of training.

But, although preprogrammed moves that faked muscle memory could get a man out of a close scrape, they also played havoc on a body that hadn't earned the skills through practice, so Joe showered, toweled dry, rolled himself up in his duvet, and fell asleep almost instantly.

Glenn Tavernier is grinning as he turns around with the gun in his hand; the endgame of four months of operational planning and establishing cover IDs coming down to that single moment of shock and horror.

Joe tries to move, but his legs feel as though they're stuck in concrete. He tries to shout out a warning to Andy, but his voice does not work. He's helpless.

Andy sees the gun and his eyes widen. Suddenly, the gun seems bigger. Huge. The hole in its barrel is dark and massive. There is a roar and it's the loudest sound that Joe's ever heard.

Andy falls.

Joe woke around dawn and knew that more sleep was out of

the question. Dim light was angling in through the blinds and kept hitting his eyes and the dream—a simplified and, therefore, factually inaccurate restaging of Andy's death—was so vivid that he got up, sat at a computer, and started a search for X-Core to take his mind off it.

After an hour Joe had learned little that he hadn't already known. For a new musical genre, X-Core left as small a digital footprint as it was possible to make on the multifarious paths of the internet.

Which left two possibilities: either 1) it wasn't a huge deal, or 2) someone was going to extraordinary lengths to keep mentions to a minimum.

Joe scoured music blogs and message boards, following every tiny reference to X-Core, and got the sense that most people treated it as some kind of novelty, or worse, a joke. No X-Core followers ever waded in in defense of the music; no flame wars broke out; the threads never lasted long enough for anyone to bring up Hitler.

It left him feeling a little baffled.

Either no one was passionate enough to weigh in for X-Core, or idle internet chat was beneath its devotees.

He gave up and opened another browser, the secured YETI network, and searched through his in-box. It was full of the mail he'd been avoiding for the last few weeks, and he scanned through it, allowing himself to grin at the number—and growing insistence—of Abernathy's emails.

Abernathy might have left him to grieve in the real world,

but he had sent dozens of emails trying to tell Joe that nothing had been his fault, and that YETI wanted him back as soon as he could face it. He had been thoughtful enough to stop short of visiting the apartment, perhaps realizing that coming here would've been an intrusion on Joe's *grief*.

Other emails of condolence from support staff and Human Resources stayed unopened.

His eye stopped at one that gave him a moment of shock:

Hope You're Okay 🖨

LESLEYDYSON@SECUREMAIL.GOV.UK
to me ▾

Dearest Jonah,

I am so sorry to have heard about Andrew, and hope that you are doing okay. I know it's been a long time since we last spoke, but you know how totally I lose myself in my work, and, if anything, that drive seems to be increasing the older I get. Still, recent events have galvanized me into action, so I am sending you this email to offer my thoughts in the hope that they can be of help to you in this difficult time.

I know you take things to heart dreadfully, my dear boy, and that you must be doubting yourself and your role in life at the moment, but I want you to know that the pain you are feeling is not a purely negative thing. It may feel like the end of the world, but I want to tell you that this tragedy, when the sadness has passed, will only serve to make you stronger.

I know this: the things you do are important. More important than even you know. Losing a friend and fellow operative demonstrates how high the stakes are, but it also shows you how much the organization needs you. You have rare and precious gifts that save lives every day. There are few people about whom I can say that.

Email me back if you need to talk.

Mother

Joe read the email through, then closed the window and sat back in his chair. He hadn't heard from his mother in months, and the fact that she had heard about Andy and felt the need to reach out to him made Joe feel a little better. His relationship with her was . . . complicated, to say the least. And her self-imposed exile from his life—and the outside world—was a mystery that he wished he could ask Abernathy to sign off on investigating.

Except, of course, Abernathy knew exactly where she was and what she was doing there. It had been Abernathy who'd brought her to the UK in the first place, head-hunting one of the brightest operatives from the US intelligence community to front some top secret project in London. He'd made Joe aware that the information was so classified that all he could tell him was that she was safe and well.

Joe hit the treadmill and set it for 6K, all the time thinking of a way to get through the gloom that threatened to envelop his mind every time he thought about Andy. Even a much-loved playlist of fast rock songs at high volume couldn't wipe the memories away.

Abernathy was right that it hadn't been his fault. Andy had been killed by a bad guy, and not by a mistake that Joe himself had made. Unfortunately, that didn't make it any easier. Because if it had been an error, then maybe Joe could correct it, ensure against it, make sure it never happened again. Knowing that there was no fault was like knowing that death was a natural part of the work they did, a risk they took that no amount of training, guile, or cleverness could ever truly prevent.

On a basic level, Joe had joined YETI to make a difference. To stop bad things from happening. To make the world a safer place for kids his age and for the rest of the ordinary people who just wanted to go about their lives without the threat of gangs, violence, and terrorism hanging over them like a cloud of doom.

But there were a couple of other layers of motivation that sat beneath the desire to protect and serve.

First up, his mother had raised him that way. From an early age, Lesley Dyson had taught her son to care about the world and the people around him. She had schooled him in military history and tactics, and in the workings of law enforcement and espionage organizations, portraying the self-sacrifice and determination they took as the purest of human achievements. It was almost as if YETI was a career path she had always envisioned for him. Which was crazy— the organization hadn't even existed then.

The second layer was by no means as credit-worthy.

Joe had had problems with anger for as long as he could remember. There was a physiological reason for it—it was called Intermittent Explosive Disorder by a couple of specialists his mother had consulted before Abernathy had offered his hardware/software control system as a treatment. The anger had gotten Joe into a lot more trouble than he should ever have found himself in. He'd usually managed to direct it at bullies and thugs, but it had made his teachers think that he was out of control.

YETI had offered him control.

With a 6K run and hardly an exertion spike on the graph, he hit the showers. High pressure: very hot. Fluorescent shower gel with bits in it that the label said was meant to take off dead skin. Joe wondered how good it was at taking a friend's blood off your hands, then squashed the thought before it could grow. He toweled himself dry instead, then dragged a razor across his chin to tidy away the few hairs that clung there.

He took his time over his wardrobe selection, knowing that the day could go down a lot of different ways, so he tried to gauge an average outfit that would cover many possibilities.

In the end, he went with something that was practical, reasonably put together, but would also fit in with the vaguely preppy look that X-Core seemed to favor in the few photographs he could find, just in case the day ended with him taking a trip to Brixton for the X-Core gig from Lennie's flyer. Joe went for an Original Penguin button-down shirt in powder gray and royal blue, a pair of khaki trousers, a gray/ blue striped seersucker jacket, and a pair of black loafers.

He looked at himself in the mirror and shook his head. All the items he was wearing were new, hung in the wardrobe for the time that they might be the order of the day, and he could see why he hadn't worn them before. It was the kind of look that Andy had been more likely to pull off; it all fit Joe's body a little too tightly.

Still, it would do.

Joe changed outfits so often to fit in with his work that he no longer knew what his style was. Jeans, a T-shirt, and sneakers made up an anonymous look that he wore most often, but he had no idea how he would dress if the pressure wasn't always on to blend in.

The truth was he had no idea *who* he would be if it weren't for YETI.

He spent a little time working gel into his hair to achieve a look that accompanied his outfit, consulting Google for pictures of the shaggy cut that fit.

Then he looked at himself in a full-length mirror, called the person reflected there a rude name, and set out through the front door and into the world.

He saw Mrs. Meakin on the stairs and she gave him a look that was equal parts concern and pity. A downstairs neighbor, Mrs. Meakin was in her fifties and the kind of busybody who managed to *always* be on the stairs when someone was passing.

She either had a motor function problem or a wonky mirror, because her lipstick skills had all the subtlety of the Joker's.

She'd heard about Andy—the official story, anyway: that he had been in the wrong place at the wrong time and had been killed in the cross fire of a gang war—and she really didn't know how to bring up the topic, so she just stood there and gave him what she probably thought was her compassionate look.

"Hi," Joe said as he passed.

"I was just checking for the mail," Mrs. Meakin said. "It seems to get here later and later every day."

Joe nodded, not sure if that was true or not, or if he cared or not, and made his way to the front door before she plucked up the courage to ask him anything personal.

CHAPTER SEVEN:
CHASING SHADOWS

Uncle Alex walked her into the station and watched as she went through the ticket barrier to the platform. She waved to him as she headed for the platform for the London train.

It was already there, waiting.

She found a seat by the window, pretty much fell into it, and sat there trying to stop her head from spinning.

The day had been too dramatic, too surreal, and for a second it felt like she was having a panic attack—breathing too fast and jagged, heart pumping hard but *wrong* somehow, sweat on her brow, and a sick taste in her mouth—but she concentrated on slowing her breathing, calming herself down, and by the time the train got started she was feeling *almost* in control.

Her life had never been boring or average, but today's developments had her wishing—only for a couple of seconds, but that was more time than she had ever spent on such thoughts before—that her life was normal.

More normal, at the very least.

In just a few short hours, everything about her life had suddenly been thrown up in the air. She still had no idea how the pieces would look when they had finished falling.

So she tried not to think about it all and watched as the flat, green landscape spilled past the windows. Horses and sheep chewed at grass turned lush by recent rains; farmhouses stood like silent sentinels; tiny villages flashed past and were gone.

Within twenty minutes she realized that she was bored.

But with the day she'd just had she would've said boredom was impossible. Even getting the train had been a nervy process: the hypervigilance approaching the station; the cautious entry into the foyer; the relief that men in dark suits didn't have the place on lockdown.

Ani turned away from the window and looked around.

The car was three-quarters full, and about a half of that number was studying their smartphones or working on iPads and laptops.

It suddenly made her feel like she was missing a limb.

Her computers, an Apple laptop and a Windows desktop—she was an equal opportunity geek—were both at home, and her phone was safely disabled until she bought it some new SIM cards.

Before cell phones and laptops, Ani had no idea what people used to do to fill the time on long journeys. Watching the countryside pass by had limited appeal.

Maybe you were supposed to use journeys to get some

thinking done, but, to be honest, thinking was about the last thing in the world Ani wanted to be doing.

She didn't want to think about the men looking for her and secret files, and she *certainly* didn't want to think about what had happened to her when she was listening to that stupid file at Uncle Alex's.

Of course as soon as she decided not to think about it, her mind would think about nothing else.

There had been something utterly terrifying about the experience, something that was still raw, still ugly, still . . . *there* . . . in her head. She caught flashes of it when she closed her eyes—of the way those *things* squirmed their way into the parts of her that made her who she was. She thought she could still sense their hunger for her mind, and their disappointment that Uncle Alex had shut off the sound before they could devour it completely.

She felt trapped in something that she could not see the shape of, and that scared her.

Ani suddenly, and not for the first time in her short life, feared for her very sanity.

And that fear opened a door to an event in her past.

Her mind slipped back to one of the worst memories she carried with her.

It's summer break and she's been out all day, practicing falling over on her backside in front of friends at the skate park at Jesus Green.

She's been working on landing an ollie for weeks now but those attempts have all been on her own, on the flat, and most of them have been performed while stationary.

This is the first time she's taken it out to the park.

To do it on a slope.

While moving.

In front of people.

An hour—and many bruises and a multitude of aches—later and she's landed maybe three ollies, earning her enough high fives and slaps on the back that it's actually been worth the pain and embarrassment.

She's feeling pretty good about herself when she reaches the front door, although the aches are tightening up and the bruises already coming into full color. Mastering the ollie opens up a whole new level of skateboard tricks, and she feels—finally—that she's well on her way to becoming a proficient rider.

She knows that something's wrong the moment she opens the door. Even before she sees what is waiting in the hall.

Not a sixth sense, exactly, but more like a fifth-and-a-half sense that is really all the other senses screaming out in unison that there is something off about the atmosphere of home today; about the way the air feels charged with something; about the way her mom isn't calling out her name like she always does when she hears Ani come into the apartment.

Ani steps through the door with a weird feeling; a nervousness that is based on nothing but the opening of a door, the sensing of an atmosphere, and her mom's failure to call out a greeting.

Then she steps into the hall.

The leaden feeling that is developing in her stomach tightens by three or four notches.

The full-length mirror that hangs in the hall has been smashed to pieces, leaving only the dark wooden frame on the wall, which has become an art display for some bad eighties wallpaper.

There is no mirrored glass at all in the frame, not even small pieces trapped in the frame edges.

Ani narrows her eyes, thinking that some of the glass should remain, and then she sees what's on the floor farther up the hall and confusion takes hold.

Twenty or more stacks of mirror pieces have been carefully arranged on the hall carpet, and as she gets closer she can see that each pile is made up of mirror fragments of roughly the same size, as if someone has smashed the mirror and then spent time—quite a lot of time, actually—gauging the size of the shards and arranging them, carefully, into ordered stacks.

Ani parks her board on its tail against the wall, wheels pointing outward, and calls, "Mom?"

There's no reply.

The silence becomes almost deafening.

A red, raw fear settles inside Ani then in that single moment. The first cut of a mental scar that she still carries around with her today.

She knows that something is wrong; something deeper and more destructive than just a shattered mirror. She doesn't know how she knows, but she does. Even before she ventures farther inside, something is telling her that each step is taking her toward something that will change her life forever. That she is crossing a line that can never be uncrossed.

She takes the steps slowly but surely, ignoring the doors to the left and right, heading straight for the one at the end.

Again, she doesn't know how she knows that that door is the one she needs, any more than she can explain why a few piles of broken mirror glass should fill her so full of fear.

Her mom is in the kitchen standing at the sink with her back to Ani and seems completely unaware of her presence.

"Mom?" Ani asks, her dry throat making it into more of a croak than a question.

Her mom just carries on doing whatever it is she is doing at the sink.

Ani takes a step closer, and suddenly she can hear the sounds that her mom is making, so quiet that they were barely discernible when she was farther away.

"Stupidstupidstupid," Ani's mom is whispering to herself, over and over again as she scrubs at something in the sink with a wire pan-cleaning brush. "Why are you always so stupid? Stupidclumsystupid."

"MOM?" The urgency of Ani's own voice surprises her; it sounds like it belongs to someone she will grow up to be, rather than the twelve-year-old kid she is.

"Stupidstupidwhyareyousostupid?" her mom mutters, her words pushed together in a harsh tone full of self-loathing and anger.

She scrubs harder with the brush. Muttering.

"Mom, you're scaring me," Ani says, and then she is directly behind her mother and she can see into the sink and there are no pans or plates there, just her mother's hands, and she's scrubbing at them with the brush, swapping the brush over when she has drawn more blood from the hand she is working on.

Her mom's hands are raw and bloody and don't have much skin left on them, like it's just meat that sits at the end of her wrists.

Ani screams but her mom continues to scrub away at the mess in the sink, and Ani tries to stop her, grabs hold of her arm, and tries to wrench it out the way of the wire brush, but her mother is strong and resists, and suddenly they are struggling against each other and it's then that her mother finally turns to face her.

The fight goes out of Ani immediately and she lets go and just stares, uncomprehendingly, at her mom's face.

If Ani didn't know better, she'd think that someone else was standing before her—an evil twin maybe, or someone wearing a mask—but that was just the stupid stuff that came from stories.

It was *her* mom.

That was what made it so much more terrifying.

Because it would be better if the woman in front of her was an imposter, someone who was pretending to be her mother; because that would mean the insane look in the woman's eyes belonged to an imposter, too.

Lé Sang—her name later anglicized to Sandy Lee, the surname Ani had retained at the request of her father, partly as a reminder of her mother's heritage, and partly because Ani Lee sounded a whole lot better than Ani Murch—had escaped the war-torn country of Vietnam as one of the "boat people" in the 1980s when she was still a child, and Ani knows that her mom had lived through a lifetime's worth of bad stuff before arriving in the UK.

What she knows of her mother's journey from a village just outside Hanoi all the way to Cambridge has been pieced together from overheard snippets of conversation, and from a few details that her dad has kind of let slip to explain some of her mom's darker moods.

Her mom, of course, never speaks of her journey, but she always carries it with her. You can see it in the set of her face, a kind of wary watchfulness that never relaxes. In the way she carries herself, making herself as small as possible, as if to avoid unnecessary attention. But, most of all, you can see it in her eyes.

They are haunted eyes that have seen too much, as if the world—with all its pleasures and treasures—is nothing more than a distraction from an interior landscape that sees very little daylight.

Ani has heard the story of young Lé Sang's escape from communist forces intent on placing her and her family into one of the forced "re-education" camps—camps where people went, but rarely came out unchanged.

If they came out at all.

Ani'd heard about the desperate escape, the two-hundred-plus-mile walk the family had endured to reach the coast, and the discovery that not only was the boat they were gambling their lives on barely seaworthy, but that the escape plan consisted of nothing more than aiming the boat toward a major shipping lane and hoping that they were 1) spotted, and 2) rescued.

And she knew that her own grandfather did not survive the voyage, dying of hunger and exhaustion just days before a French freighter spotted the boat and effected a rescue.

So Ani is used to seeing the silent, guarded, perpetual pain in her mother's eyes; but today that pain is gone. It has been replaced with anger and shame and all the colors of madness.

Ani realizes that now, when her mom looks at her, she is seeing a stranger. Maybe it's a ghost from the past, replayed by memory, amplified by time and her inability to talk about the things she's seen; but Ani feels a slice of herself wither and die to be on the receiving end of such a look.

Her mom starts making a strange sound: somewhere between a whimper and a scream—a combination Ani would have believed impossible if she wasn't hearing it now.

Pain and fear and rage intertwine in that terrible sound, and it goes on and on. It doesn't even look like her mom is breathing. Ani steps toward her and that's when her mom raises her hands to defend herself from an attack.

Ani suddenly feels very sick.

Her mother has taken most of the skin from her hands with the wire brush and they are tattered and red and dripping with blood.

And that's not even the most awful part. It takes a couple of seconds for Ani to process exactly what that is.

But when she does, it is the worst thing that she has ever seen.

Dozens of the thinnest, cruelest slivers of mirror glass have been systematically driven into the flesh of her mother's arms, arranged in perfectly spaced rows from her wrists to her biceps. A grid of horror that would almost look like acupuncture if it weren't for the raw redness of the wounds.

Ani has heard about self-harming—there'd even been discussions at school and the concept had been so alien to her that she'd been sure she misheard the teacher, naïvely thinking she'd said "cell farming," much to the amusement of the class—but seeing what her mother has done to herself brings it all home to her with crushing force.

That her mom has been in such pain and no one has noticed, that she'd suffered in silence for so long that she and her dad had just stopped noticing, it's all too much for Ani. She wants to reach out, to take her mom in her arms and try to take away even a fraction of the hurt, but she sees the "you're a stranger" look in her mom's eyes.

"Mom. It's Ani. Your daughter." She says these things calmly, matter-of-factly, but no recognition creeps into her mother's eyes. "It's okay, Mom. Everything is going to be all right."

It sounds hollow even as she's saying it. How, exactly, was this going to be okay? Ever?

Her mom's brow furrows and it looks like she's reaching out

for Ani, spreading her arms upturned toward her. Ani feels a sense of relief. Maybe recognition didn't show in her eyes, but this is an open, welcoming gesture, and Ani goes to take a step toward her mother again.

And that's when her mom suddenly smacks her hands into her own shoulders, closing up her arms at the elbow, and drives those glass spikes even deeper into her arms.

At the hospital the doctors had called it a "psychotic break," and though other names had come along to better describe her mother's condition, that was the one Ani always remembered.

Clung to, even.

Because if it had been a *break*, then that meant that it had been a sudden thing without any warning, like a lightning strike or a tsunami. That meant that it couldn't have been predicted, prevented, or even noticed.

She clung to it because it was so much better than thinking that there had been signs, like those "danger of death" plates on electricity substations, or the biohazard logos you saw on TV shows, and the people closest had just ignored them. Or that they had let her mom's mind fall apart, piece by painful piece, without taking the time to notice.

Her mom had been admitted, and now resided long-term in the local psychiatric hospital, Fulbourn, ruled to be a danger to herself, and maybe to others. Ani's dad had told her that the chances of her mother ever being allowed out were very slim. She no longer recognized Ani or her husband. She was hard-pressed to recognize her own reflection in the mirror.

Mental illness, Ani had since learned, was often hereditary, and she lived with a nagging fear that whatever had happened to her mother could just as easily happen to her.

Sitting on the train, thinking about the sound that had tried to invade her mind from a .wav file suddenly made her realize how close the boundary between sanity and madness actually was, and how easily it could be crossed.

For the first time in her life, Ani suddenly thought that insanity might not be such a bad thing. Because if what had happened to her was real, it made madness seem inconsequential by comparison.

CHAPTER EIGHT:
FIREWALL

Outside the clouds were low in the sky, but they were already starting to break apart. It looked like it was going to be a lovely day. Joe adjusted the collar on his shirt and then pulled out his phone.

Not many numbers were stored in its memory, and the first one that came up in his address book was Abernathy. He pressed CALL and the man picked up on the first ring.

"Joe." Abernathy's voice was warm and friendly. As if he was actually pleased to hear from him. "What plans do you have for today?"

"I was thinking I'd scope out the venue for the Precision Image gig in advance."

"Any particular reason?"

"Tired of sitting on my hands."

"Want to make a stop on the way?"

"Where?"

"Here."

"Twice in a week? People will talk."

"Twice in twenty-four hours, and they're already talking. They're saying you're back and it's about time. See you soon?"

"Of course."

Oxford Street was already wide awake, and Joe dodged through the crowds and signs for golf sales and made his way toward the tube station. En route, he grabbed a cup of coffee from a stand and sipped it outside the station. Hot, strong, and only vaguely offensive. Then he went inside and headed to the Victoria line, walked straight onto a train, changed at Green Park, and made Westminster within twenty-five minutes.

He took the front door into YETI and found Abernathy in the control room, talking to a couple of analysts. Joe stood off to the side waiting for him to finish. He seemed animated, and maybe just a little bit annoyed, and Joe wondered—not for the first time—what it would be like to be shut in a confined space with him all day, every day.

Abernathy was difficult to read (and Joe prided himself on his cold reading skills) because it was nearly impossible to get through the exoskeleton of the man's surface personality to the obvious depths that lurked beneath. Yesterday had been the closest that Joe had come to seeing the "real" Abernathy, when the man had finally managed to speak about Andy, but he still remained an enigma to Joe.

Watching him interacting with the adult members of

the team was always a revelation. Abernathy was a completely different person when he was addressing his YETI operatives.

Kinder.

Less . . . cranky.

Abernathy spotted Joe and waved him over.

"Firewall," Abernathy said by way of a greeting.

Joe shrugged, confused. "Firewall to you, too," he said.

Abernathy grinned. "It seems that all it takes to get Research and Development working again is to get *you* working again. We have a chip upgrade scheduled. One that R&D has been working on for a couple of weeks. Although clearly not all that efficiently, because as soon as you walk back through these doors, suddenly it's completed."

"A firewall?" Joe asked, puzzled.

"Well, that's what they're calling it. It's more like a neurological bulletproof vest." Abernathy started walking, a sure sign that Joe was meant to follow. "I've been worrying for a while about putting some kind of protection around that chip of yours, something to stop someone else gaining control of it, and then your mind."

"Gaining control of my mind?" Joe said, horrified at the thought. "People can do that?"

"No." Abernathy steered him toward R&D. "Yes. Maybe. Look, there's not a computer system on this planet that can't be hacked, but most of them aren't wired up to a person's brain. I'm just being careful."

Joe gave Abernathy a look that said he believed that *at least part* of his explanation was the truth, and then they walked into the R&D lab.

It was one of Joe's favorite parts of the building, probably because it was as close as he'd ever come to walking into Q branch, the fictional home of the people who gave James Bond all his neat little gadgets. Okay, it was nothing like that really. There were no people testing booby-trapped phone booths, or rocket-launching briefcases. But this was where a lot of the tech that made it out into missions was designed and tested.

The Shuttleworth brothers, Geoff and Greg, stood at lab benches on opposite sides of the room, busily soldering components onto tiny circuit boards. It was like a mirror line had been drawn down the center of the room: each brother's desk was laid out as a reflection of the other. Of course the word *fairground* had to be added in front of the word *mirror* if the simile was to hold true, because Geoff was tall and spindly, while Greg was short and kind of rounded.

The heads atop the bodies were very similar: identical Coke-bottle glasses perched atop two aquiline noses; near-lipless slashes for mouths; all underneath red sprawls of hair.

They stopped what they were doing when Abernathy and Joe came in. Geoff had his soldering iron in his right hand; Greg's was in his left.

"Sir!" they said in unison, Geoff's voice a low baritone, Greg's an octave higher.

Joe half expected a salute.

Abernathy nodded toward Joe. "Firewall," he said curtly.

Both brothers took a step forward.

"Joe. Lovely to see you again," Geoff said, smiling widely.

"'Again' meaning 'You're back!' rather than 'since yesterday.' Which makes it sound like 'you're back' is a criticism, rather than . . ." Greg tried to clarify, frowning.

". . . the delight it really is. And twice in twenty-four hours says 'back for good,'" Geoff said brightly.

"We hope," Greg said gloomily.

"Definitely," Geoff said. "We hope."

This back and forth between happy and gloomy voices, between short, fat brother and tall, thin brother, had taken Joe a little time to get used to. At first he'd thought it was a joke, a little bit of nerd playacting the pair put on.

But it wasn't. It was exactly how they were.

All the time.

"We've finally got a handle on a thorny problem," Greg said.

"Sounds painful," Joe deadpanned.

A two-second delay as the joke sank in was rewarded with some staccato laughter that sounded like a cross between a motorbike backfiring and a release of high-pressure gas.

"That's funny," Geoff said. "*Thorny* as in *thorns* . . ."

"Yeah," Greg said. With the small talk over he was able to go full-on nerd. "Anyway, we've been working on the problem of finding a viable protective infrastructure for your chipset to limit the possibility of a hostile agent or agency gaining remote access."

"An organization's technology can be both its strongest asset and its Achilles' heel," Geoff said, also in fluent nerd. "Think Facebook FarmVille and the foot-and-mouth outbreak that they still haven't completely dealt with; or the Vatican and its embarrassing JPEG switcheroo, where all official images on their site were replaced with creatures from the stories of H.P. Lovecraft."

"Reference also: PayPal, YouTube, Sony, the Church of Scientology," Greg continued without missing a beat. "All compromised by determined hackers with mischief in mind. Now, your chips have in/out sockets, and that means—in theory at least—that you are 1) discoverable, and 2) hack-able."

"That's why we have produced the first security update for your hardware," Geoff said. "It uses four bit hexadecimal encryption, with heuristic packet filtering at the moment. It's crude, sure, but it should keep you from being compromised until we get something sturdier together."

"We've even included a quarantine vault for malicious code," Greg said brightly. "Like the one you get in any good antivirus software—for Trojans, worms, and anything that will try to gain control of your root directory."

"Which, in this case, is your brain," Geoff offered.

As usual, the brothers' tech-speak meant next to nothing to Joe.

"The throne awaits," Greg said, pointing to an office chair at the back of the room.

Joe sat down and grasped the arms.

While Greg gently peeled back the inch-square area on Joe's scalp that concealed his access port, Geoff readied the input data on his laptop and then plugged the cord into the port. It felt like . . . well, like someone sticking a small plug into his head.

"As usual . . ." Geoff said.

". . . this might feel weird," Greg finished.

"Because you have to reboot the chip," Joe said. "I know."

"I'd love to know how it feels," the brothers said dreamily, in unison.

Geoff pressed RETURN on the laptop.

There was an odd feeling of loss as the chip in his brain switched off. It was like a part of his brain had just stopped working, and there was a moment when his whole mind seemed on the verge of going dark. It was only when the chip was switched off that Joe realized how much he had come to depend upon it.

He'd thought the chip he'd been implanted with was standard field equipment when he'd joined YETI, only discovering slowly, over time, that he was the only operative who carried one.

Initially he'd been given many reasons for this by Abernathy, and indeed from other members of the team, ranging from budgetary restrictions to the complicated nature of the implant procedure. It was only recently that the Shuttleworths had confessed to Joe that he was a one-off in the enhancement department; that previous recipients of the chip—lab animals, and one human subject—had been unable to integrate with it. In the human subject, any benefits had been outweighed by the fact that it caused nausea and migraines, neither of which were particularly useful in the field.

The medical examination Joe had undergone before joining YETI had revealed a genetic flaw that had indicated he might be a candidate for the enhancement hardware. The same genetic brain abnormality that had made Joe literally unable to control his temper, and that had led to him being labeled a "troublemaker" throughout his academic career, allowed him to be the first computer-enhanced YETI agent.

Finally getting a rein on his terrible rage problems had been a bonus.

He was not only YETI's first nonnative-born operative, but also the only one able to interface with its hottest tech.

Sitting in the chair, Joe felt a sudden flash of the old anger—red, raw, and frighteningly intense—and his hands grasped the chair arms until his knuckles were white, but then the chip rebooted and its calming influence reasserted itself.

He felt the anger drain away.

His hands relaxed.

Upgrade: complete.

"So why the security upgrade?" Joe asked Abernathy as they crossed the control room toward Abernathy's office.

"You don't think preventing your brain from being hacked is a good enough reason?" Abernathy said scornfully.

"It's a great reason. I was just hoping for the *real* reason."

Abernathy laughed. "I *have* missed you, Joe. I've missed your default setting of distrust, and your inability to take the first answer you're given. It's annoying, frustrating, and borders on the insubordinate, but it's what makes you a good operative."

They reached Abernathy's office and went inside.

Abernathy sat down on the big chair behind his black slate desk. Joe had to settle for the kind of seat they had in doctors' waiting rooms: tubular steel and really uncomfortable. Abernathy liked people to be uncomfortable. It wasn't a power thing, or sadistic. Just a practical measure. People tended to get their business wrapped up faster when they were denied comfort. Meetings were shorter and more focused.

On the wall behind Abernathy was an LED panel, and there was another panel set into the desk itself.

"So where are we with X-Core?" Joe asked.

"I'm becoming more and more convinced that we're dealing with some form of cult." Abernathy had his hands behind his head and was leaning back in his chair. "But most of the home-grown cults we keep an eye on target the vulnerable, and they sweep up their followers from supply lines that are the result of societal failures. Psychiatric hospitals, drug dependency clinics, and places the homeless frequent are rich hunting grounds. Cults provide, with offers of friendship, accommodation, and acceptance, an alternative to lives that are in the process of unraveling. You can see how someone perched on the edge of an abyss might join a group that seems to have all the answers.

"But X-Core targets the privileged, and it's hard to see that the same indoctrination procedures that work on the people who've fallen through society's cracks would work on people who aren't even aware that those cracks exist."

Abernathy touched the desk in front of him and a keyboard lit up within the surface of slate. He turned on the two screens and, after a little bit of searching, called up a file marked MKULTRA.

"I don't know if you've ever heard of the MKULTRA project," Abernathy said. "It's part of conspiracy theory folklore."

"Wasn't it a CIA investigation into the potential for mind control?" Joe asked.

Abernathy raised a surprised eyebrow.

"You know my mom," Joe said. "She told me bedtime stories about brainwashing."

"I think the CIA preferred the term *behavior modification*. But yes, it was an attempt to find ways to manipulate people's thoughts and actions. At its height MKULTRA consumed over five percent of the CIA budget, and some put that figure at closer to ten percent."

"Why would the US spend a tenth of their intelligence budget on science fiction? I thought the government released all the MK files and they showed that all their projects failed."

Abernathy gave him a wan smile. "There's a big difference between releasing *some* of the files and *all* of the files. Over twenty thousand documents were released in the 1970s, but they amounted to little more than a smoke screen. Later, all MK files were declassified, but by then all the important documents had been destroyed. If they were to release the true findings . . . well, let's just say the results would be incendiary."

"Are you telling me that the CIA succeeded in manufacturing mind-controlled assassins?" Joe said skeptically. "That the US *actually did* perfect push-button killers?"

"Ask JFK," Abernathy said. "Your beloved ex-president. Oh, wait, you can't. A preprogrammed patsy cut him down with an assassin's rifle.

"There are hundreds of examples of the human will being defeated, and people acting in ways that they normally wouldn't have. The point is that mind control is *not* science fiction. It's proven fact. And none of us truly knows the mechanisms by which it works.

"Adding a layer of protection to your chip seemed . . . *overdue*."

Joe's eyes widened.

"Do you think X-Core is manipulating its audience?" he asked breathlessly. "You think that we're talking about actual mind control?"

"Yes. No. Maybe. Definitely not. Delete as non-applicable. I don't know what I think. It's frustrating, like we're playing catch-up. I hadn't even *heard* of X-Core forty-eight hours ago, and now it's at the very top of my to-do list, so excuse me if I'm getting fanciful in my old age.

"I do have a question for you though, Joe. Not only is it science fiction hypothetical, but it's the kind of question that would get me fired if I put it in an official report: if a musical subculture wanted to start controlling its listeners, what would be the most efficient way of doing it?"

Joe was angry he hadn't already asked himself the same thing.

"They'd use the music."

Abernathy nodded, and tapped the keyboard in his desk.

A video file started.

A title card that looks to have been stenciled appears on the computer screen:

EXPERIMENT #73/1843/MAJESTIC - TOP SECRET

Then there is a quick cut to black-and-white footage of a man in a room. He's in his twenties, with a buzz cut that suggests he's US military. His outfit matches the haircut: a mid-dark shirt with a stenciled number on it, combat trousers, webbing belt, a sidearm holstered at his hip.

The camera is fixed, giving a wide view of the room: two white walls are visible, no windows, a door to the left. The back wall behind the man with the short hair is made up of speakers: big woofers and tweeters, like the stacks you see at live gigs for stadium rockers.

The man keeps looking over at the speakers warily. His eyes keep darting back to them, even when he's trying to look at the camera. It's like he's terrified of them, but can't stop himself from looking.

Suddenly a low sound can be heard: a dull rumble like distant thunder. The man reacts to the sound with wary concern, and his glances over his shoulder become more and more frequent. Even with the relatively low-def quality of the vintage camera, sweat can easily be discerned on the man's brow.

The sound deepens, and the volume of the recording drops significantly. Joe thinks that maybe the people who recorded this footage got a little worried that their experiment would have an effect on viewers of the film. Or maybe the film was once shown to military top brass who felt its effects firsthand.

The man on-screen puts his hands to his ears and starts pressing tightly. Another stenciled card informs the viewer that this is:

73% INTENSITY

The man sinks to his knees. His hands come away from his ears and fall loosely to his sides. His face, just seconds ago tense and fearful, becomes slack.

95% INTENSITY

The man's eyes change. They get wide, and then they start to bulge as if there's pressure building inside his head.

100% INTENSITY

The man's eyes are bulging out too much. Joe can see the flesh from the insides of his eyelids and he's suddenly glad the film is in black-and-white. There is still a slackness to the man's face, as if he is unaware of the pressure building within.

Then, suddenly, the pressure is gone. His eyes return to their sockets.

The man smiles.

He reaches down and unsnaps his holster, takes out a pistol with a long barrel, and brings it up to the side of his head.

He holds it there for a couple of seconds.

His smile deepens.

Then he pulls the trigger.

Joe winces, is about to turn away, but the hammer falls on an empty chamber. So the soldier pulls the trigger again: empty.

And again: empty. And again: empty. And again: empty. And again: empty.

The sound cuts off completely.

For a few seconds the soldier remains still, gun to head, but then he seems to come out of the state he was in. He looks puzzled and lost. He examines the gun that he's been holding to his head.

He stares at the camera.

The look in his eyes is pure terror.

The screen goes black.

"What do you make of that?" Abernathy asked.

Joe looked at the screen with horror.

"If that gun had been loaded . . ."

"He would be dead. I'm sure an official report would have said it was suicide."

Joe shook his head. "The sound," he said. "The sound made him do it."

Abernathy nodded. "A US science research program in the mid-1970s discovered a sound that could compel certain people toward self-destructive acts. And by certain people, I mean certain *already mentally unstable* people. The guy in the film was suffering from what they called combat shock back then, and what we call PTSD these days. He already *had* self-destructive tendencies. The sound did nothing but amplify those tendencies. Untold millions of dollars sunk into a project that worked on a tiny percentage of people, getting them to do something that—deep down—they already wanted to do.

"Not exactly a great return on investment, now is it? Needless to say, the project was discontinued. The equipment that produced it was mothballed. Presumably it's in the same warehouse as the Ark of the Covenant."

"And you think that the people behind X-Core could be using sound as a way to control their audience?" Joe said, horror-struck.

Abernathy looked grave. "Of course I don't. I've just been spending two days trying to find a way to put X-Core into some kind of context, and I dragged this old film out as an illustration of just how desperate I am.

"But if we were to believe it *was* mind control, for even a second, it would lead us to a rather overwhelming question, don't you think?"

"And what might that be?" Joe asked.

Abernathy looked grave. "Controlling them to do what?"

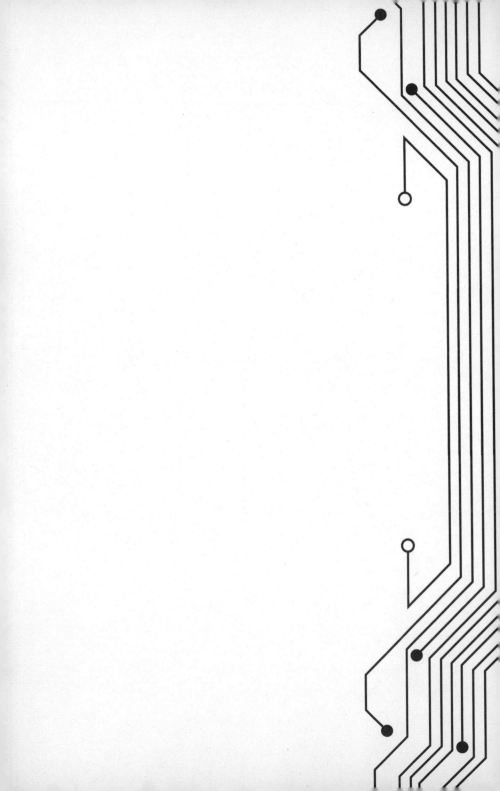

Part 02:
The Ceremony of Innocence is Drowned

Dreams of metal
Dreams of freedom
Locked up inside the cage
We call the human heart
I feel the wires
I hack your system
I scream and scream and scream
But no one seems to hear.

"Systems of Error"
Le Cadavre Exquis

CHAPTER NINE:
GRETCHEN

Ani looked at the piece of paper in her hand and checked it against the number on the door of the house in front of her.

They matched: she knocked. She was feeling so awkward about imposing herself on people she didn't know that the knock was so faint it hardly made a sound.

Someone inside, however, heard it and the door opened.

Ani was looking up at the tallest woman she had ever seen. Over six feet in height and stick-insect thin, the woman greeted her with a wide smile and said, "Ani, right?"

Ani nodded, rendered speechless by the woman's sheer daunting physical presence.

"Hi, I'm Gretchen," the woman said brightly. "Come on in."

She ushered Ani inside, into a long hall surfaced with immaculate oak floorboards. Five doors led off the hall, three to the left, two to the right.

"Alex called and said you were in a tight spot. I told him to send you on over." She smiled warmly.

"Thank you. This really is kind of you."

"Nonsense. Any friend of Alex's is automatically on my list of favorite people in the world."

She led Ani to the second door on the right and into a living room that was shelved out, wall-to-wall, and had more books on display than she had ever seen in someone's home before. Ani noted that there was very little fiction. It was mostly books on every conceivable subject from contract law to particle physics.

"Wow," she said, and Gretchen smiled.

"*Wow*'s good. You must be exhausted. A cup of tea?"

The tea was dark and rich and tasted of rose petals. It was like no tea that Ani had ever tasted before: exotic and strange and delicious. Ani sipped at it as Gretchen sat next to her, cross-legged and wide-eyed.

"I'm not going to pry," Gretchen said. "I want to help. Alex told me you needed somewhere to hide out. I figure you probably just need a bit of space."

Ani smiled, relieved. It felt like a heavy weight that she hadn't even known she was carrying had been lifted from her shoulders. She wouldn't have known where to start, anyway. All of it sounded crazy, even to her, and she'd lived through it.

She looked around the room, her gaze sweeping the bookshelves again. "You have a lot of books," she said, immediately regretting stating something so obvious.

Gretchen seemed not to notice her awkwardness and nodded. "This is just a few of them. I guess you'd call it overflow."

"Overflow?"

"The books that didn't fit into the main collection." There was a sparkle in Gretchen's eyes. "You want to see the actual library?"

"Library?" Ani said. "Sure."

So Gretchen led her farther down the hall and stopped in front of the last door on the left. She put her hand into the neck of her blouse, pulled out a key on a chain, and used it to unlock the door. She gestured for Ani to enter, and Ani shrugged and did as she was asked.

The library was huge.

Absolutely huge.

Ani was sure that the room must have been really spacious even before its conversion; but then its generous Georgian proportions had first been doubled by having it incorporate the neighboring room, then redoubled when the ceilings of both rooms had been removed. Four rooms had effectively been knocked into one, making a grand, light, and beautiful library: one vast room with every available piece of wall that wasn't a window or a door shelved up to the upper floor's ceiling twenty feet above. Although there were mezzanine galleries halfway up the structure, the upper shelves were still only accessible by the use of the kind of sliding ladders Ani had only ever seen on TV and in films.

The shelves were packed with books.

Many, many thousands of books.

More books than in her local municipal library and her school library combined.

Then tripled.

But there weren't any of the lurid paperbacks, celebrity biographies, or motivational books of the *How to Be a Winner* variety that seemed to fill the bookshops and libraries these days. Just thousands of leather-bound volumes that were arranged in what, to Ani, seemed like totally random order.

Looking at a nearby shelf, Ani saw a book on microbiology sitting sandwiched between a book on comparative religion and one on Chinese grammar. Next came a book on knots and splices, which was followed by a biography of Charles II, and then a copy of an *Advanced Listener's Guide to Wagner's Ring Cycle*.

Gretchen must have seen a look of puzzlement on Ani's face because she laughed.

"I know, it must look like a pretty chaotic shelving system."

"It's certainly not alphabetical by author. Or organized by subject . . ."

"Believe it or not, there *is* a method to my madness," Gretchen told her. "Ask me a question. Anything. Popular culture. Political history. Geography. Geometry. Philosophy. Physics. Biology. Botany. Literature. Languages. Anything."

"We were talking about US presidents in class yesterday. . . . Err . . . okay, who was the eleventh president of the United States of America?"

"Easy," Gretchen said, grinning. "The closest book containing that information is . . . by your left hand. Not that one, two along. That's it."

Ani took out the book that Gretchen had guided her to. It was thick, bound in green leather, and had *The World in Numbers* stamped on the spine in gold letters.

"Page seventy-eight," Gretchen said, then she squinted a little and added, "line twenty-four."

Ani raised an eyebrow and then located page seventy-eight. It was immediately obvious that she was in the right place because there was some run-on text at the top of the page, then a little way past that was a title: *US Presidents Chronologically.*

Ani counted twenty-four lines down the page and came to a name. To double-check the answer, she counted to eleven down the list of presidents.

"James K. Polk," Gretchen told her. "As I said, an easy one. There are one hundred and seventy-nine other books in this room that could have given that answer, but you would have had to move farther to find them. One is even a biography of Mr. Polk—a fascinating man, and well worth looking into."

"Okay," Ani said. "That's mentalist creepy."

Gretchen shook her head. "It's just the way I organize information. And to be honest it's the only way I *do* remember things. For some people feats of memory are accomplished by leaving pieces of information along a familiar route, by inventing mnemonics, by associating ideas with things, or by building elaborate memory palaces. Me, I remember everything I have ever read, and where every book I have is located."

"You remember *everything* that you read?" Ani's voice was halfway between amazed and incredulous.

Gretchen nodded. "Well. Yeah. Sort of. My brain files information away in a really weird way. Always has. A strange cross-referencing thing. Don't fully understand it myself. But then I don't need to. Long, tall, and short of it is if I've read the answer somewhere, then my brain will tell me the book/page/line that I need to answer the question. If it's an easy one like James K. Polk, I'll know the answer, too. In fact, most of the time I'll know the answer. Just thinking book/page/line will get me to recall it—the hard storage of the library is analogous to my brain's filing system. If what I'm trying to remember is *really* obscure then I sometimes have to follow book/page/line and then look at the answer in the hard copy."

"That's amazing."

"It's just the way my brain works."

"It's still amazing."

"You really think so?" Gretchen actually looked grateful for the compliment, and Ani found herself wondering how other people reacted to her hostess's remarkable gift. She knew from bitter experience that being perceived as even a little different could lead to some pretty cruel treatment from one's peers. Gretchen wasn't just different. She was, Ani was sure, unique.

Ani smiled and nodded.

"If I get on *Who Wants to Be a Millionaire* then you are definitely going to be my 'phone-a-friend.'"

It was when she was sitting at Gretchen's dining table over a vast assortment of tasty carry-out treats from a nearby Gujarati restaurant that Ani realized just how hungry she was.

She was wolfing down something made of beans that tasted of coconut and sweet chili when she noticed that Gretchen was studying her. Gretchen's face was friendly and warm, but there was something else in her eyes and Ani thought it was concern.

Ani finished her mouthful and then said, "Uncle Alex told me not to involve you in my problems."

"He's overprotective. To a fault. Let me tell you something about your uncle Alex. He saved my life. Long story, not particularly relevant, but basically I met him when I was at a crossroads in my life. Could have gone either way. He showed me kindness and understanding. Put me onto a positive path. Showed me that the thing that made me weird in most people's eyes was actually the thing that made me strong.

"Now my gift means that I earn a healthy living. I compile information for companies and provide research services for authors, scientists, and historians. I'm the go-to girl for quiz show questions. I even provide statistics for government bodies, selected multinational companies, opinion pollsters, and economists. I've turned a neurological quirk into a career.

"I owe it all to Alex. And if I can repay a tiny part of the kindness that he showed me by helping out his niece in an hour of need, then I'd like to do that. I really would."

"Overprotective or not, Uncle Alex is right about this. I can't drag you into it. I've been chased by men with guns."

"You're kidding, right?" Gretchen looked horrified. "Guns?"

Ani nodded.

"Then I'm afraid I'm going to have to insist that you tell me the whole story," Gretchen said sternly.

Ani put her fork down on her plate. "But Uncle Alex . . ."

"Alex sent you here. To me. It wasn't an accident. He *chose* me. No matter what he might have said, he thinks that I can help you. So let me help."

Ani narrowed her eyes, saw the earnest expression on Gretchen's face, and her resolve weakened. "Well, okay . . ."

Gretchen sat, openmouthed, throughout Ani's story. She

was mostly silent, too, only occasionally asking a question to better understand a detail.

When she was done, Ani felt exhausted at the effort of mentally reliving it all.

"Then I came here. And met you."

"That is the single most extraordinary thing I've heard in a long, long time. And I can't imagine what you're going through. But it does present us with two areas for immediate inquiry." Gretchen held up a finger. "First: these men with guns. There aren't *that* many people in this country allowed to carry a sidearm; fewer still without some kind of uniform. It's possible that it was one of the intelligence services, but the behavior you described of the men waiting at your place sounds undisciplined. Sloppy, even. It ignored the operating procedures for all the major law enforcement agencies, and that leads us to considering less official bodies.

"I'd guess that we're talking about freelance operators, out of their depth in UK urban environments. So that would seem to suggest that the men were mercenaries, guns for hire, ex-military men who have seen a lot of overseas action and are picking up work back home doing this kind of odd job.

"That's good, but it's also bad. It means that orthodox law enforcement and intelligence services aren't in play here, which means this won't end up on your permanent record. You're not being chased by the government. Or the police. Or Jack Bauer and CTU. Or the Peacekeepers from *The Hunger Games*.

"The bad news is exactly the same. It means orthodox law enforcement and intelligence services aren't in play here, which means we have no way of knowing the rules of engagement. Whoever is giving the orders is free of all moral and legal obligations and government oversight. If they decide that *shoot-to-kill* is a viable strategy, then shoot to kill is what they'll do."

Gretchen caught Ani's shocked expression and winced. "Which is *very* unlikely," she said hurriedly. "They seem to want something from you. Unfortunately, it all means that our first area for inquiry ends here. Without more information we cannot know our enemy."

She held up two fingers.

"Area two, however, may be a little more fruitful. X-Core. Something definite and tangible. We can find out more about it."

"How?" Ani asked. "You're not telling me that you have total recall of all musical subcultures?"

Gretchen shook her head.

"I was thinking Google."

In an office upstairs that housed a computer system that had Ani as close to drooling as she got, they made a breakthrough.

Gretchen had seen Ani's look of amazement and had misread it.

"You thought that just because I had a lot of books that I wouldn't be interested in tech?"

"Not at all. It's just that looks a lot like a liquid-cooled Digitechnic with, what, i7 processors . . . ?"

"Actually they're an i9 prototype that will never see commercial release, with eight core multi-threading processors. Top level Intel employees issue. Way more than I'll ever need, but it was a gift from a grateful client."

"Some gift."

"He was some client. I can't tell you his name, but if you know computers, you'll have heard of him."

"You're full of surprises."

"We all are. It's just so few people actually choose to do anything constructive with them."

Twenty minutes online and another surprise surfaced: a publicity photograph of the band Precision Image that had four guys and an older-looking woman looking at the camera with moody impatience.

"Huh," Gretchen said.

"Huh?"

Gretchen was looking at the photo with narrowed eyes. "I know her." She tapped the area screen the woman occupied with her fingernail. "At least I recognize her from somewhere."

She studied the woman's face, then closed her eyes.

"*The Times*. Three years ago. Beginning of September . . . no, that's not right . . . it was a Saturday . . . August—August the twenty-first. There was a photograph. Definitely her. Page two. Second column."

"Okay, that's pretty creepy and amazing," Ani said. "What was she in the news for?"

Gretchen typed quickly into Google's search bar, clicked on the first link, and showed Ani a news story. Sure enough, there was a picture of a woman who bore an uncanny resemblance to the woman in the Precision Image photograph.

August 21st

SCIENTIST LEFT RED-FACED OVER "ALIENS ARE COMING" MESSAGE

"Alien" Signal Merely a "Telescope Glitch"

For two frantic hours last night, scientists across the globe were furiously preparing for a "first contact" situation, convinced that they had just picked up a message from alien beings in an area of deep space.

Though it may sound like a scenario lifted straight out of a science fiction movie, there are advanced protocols in place for just such an occurrence, and within minutes of the signal being detected, observatories around the world were training their telescopes on a distant part of our galaxy in the belief that something out there had just announced its presence.

It all began simply enough: with a series of lights sparkling on the instrument panel at the Pabody/Reich Observatory in Shropshire. Dr. Imogen Bell—the researcher in charge of Pabody/Reich's new SETI (Search for Extraterrestrial Intelligence) program—was routinely monitoring a remote part of the galaxy, following the path of a signal that was broadcast into space in 1974 from the Arecibo Observatory in Puerto Rico. The Arecibo signal contained a basic set of details about the human race—the formula and structure of DNA, a diagram of our solar system, a picture of a human being and a representation of the telescope itself—and was transmitted at a frequency of 2,380 MHz.

"It was strictly a symbolic event, to show that we could do it," explained Donald Campbell, Cornell University professor of astronomy, who was a research associate at the Arecibo Observatory at the time the message was sent. The signal was nothing more than a demonstration that such messages were possible, and it was aimed at a group of stars named the Great Cluster in Hercules, Messier 13, a destination that it will not reach for 25,000 years.

The Pabody/Reich radio telescope has been a part of the SETI program since the start of the year, when Dr. Bell—daughter of Nobel Prize-winning physicist Professor Maurice Bell—secured independent funding for a fresh attempt at scouring the heavens for signs of alien life; an ambition that seemed to have been fulfilled last night when Bell, herself, picked up a weak transmission from space that triggered a global attempt to understand the message, and to confirm her findings.

Within two hours, however, it became quite obvious that this was not a case of ET trying to phone home. Detailed analysis showed that the signal had been a radio telescopic artifact: a kind of digital hallucination caused by the feedback, and misinterpretation, of data.

By then, Dr. Bell had already contacted observatories across the world, and cabinet sources say that the prime minister was notified, and may even have been preparing a speech to announce the news that we are not alone in the universe. Dr. Bell should be relieved that the embarrassment of such an announcement was avoided.

Story continues page 4

Ani looked at Gretchen, who stared back with a baffled expression on her face.

"Messages from space? I think we can safely say that both our days got just a little bit weirder."

Ani couldn't think of a thing to say in reply and just stared at the screen, feeling like things got a tiny bit clearer, but a whole lot more terrifying.

CHAPTER TEN: X-Core

Joe had thought that when the flyer had said "Brixton Warhouse" that it was a misprint; that someone had simply forgotten an "e" from the word *warehouse*, but it turned out it was actually the name of the venue.

He found it easily enough; it was set back from the Brixton Road between a Caribbean grocery store and a dry cleaner's, but there were still a few hours to go before the show and the place was locked tight and deserted.

Joe circled the building to make sure, found a homeless guy and his dog but no way in, then walked a couple of hundred yards down Brixton Road and found somewhere to drink coffee and think things through.

A kid on the other side of the street gave him a weird look, but Joe didn't rise to the bait and refused to meet his eye.

The Costa/Starbucks coin flip came up "Costa" and Joe stood in line, paid twice what a coffee should cost, then waited while a barista fussed over his cup.

Overfussed with it, Joe thought, wondering when it was that coffee turned into such a fetishized ritual. Why did a simple drink require so much gleaming chrome, so many manly handles and valves? When had coffee become machismo in a cup?

Finally the man brought over his vanilla latte, and Joe took it with a muttered "thanks" and sat down at a table.

He'd been in a few too many coffee shops recently where the drink had been spelled *latté*, and it made Joe as mad as he got over those shop signs that put an idiot apostrophe into plurals—carrot's; DVD's; biscuit's. Joe thought that people with a poor grasp of grammar should never be put in charge of writing signs. Ditto people who put pretentious diacritic accents onto words like *latte*.

It was at that precise moment, when he found himself railing against coffee and grammatical errors that hadn't even occurred, that Joe realized he'd been spending far too long on his own.

It wasn't healthy.

If Andy had been around when he'd seen the *latté* signs, they'd have made a joke about it; they'd have rolled their eyes and felt superior about it for a while, and then it would have been forgotten.

Joe realized that he had started to dwell on things: tedious, tiny, petty things that he should just be letting go. Without the pressure valve of a friend, Joe could feel his control slipping.

He couldn't afford to slip.

Joe decided that the very next time he saw Abernathy he was going to ask for a new partner. It wouldn't be an insult to Andy's memory. It was just something that he needed to do for his own sanity. Being alone didn't suit him.

He drank half the latte, then left the coffee shop.

His step felt light and free as he made his way down the street with purpose and determination.

Joe sensed trouble two seconds before it arrived: his chip-enhanced senses ringing with an alarm bell that gave him enough warning that he wasn't caught totally off guard. He turned and ducked, knowing how stupid it would look if it was a false alarm, but prepared to take the chance.

The baseball bat swished by his head only inches away and Joe spun around and came up under its arc. It had been a poor swing, more Pee Wee league than World Series, but pretty much what you'd expect in a country that didn't actually play baseball. He slammed his shoulder into his attacker's midriff and the guy took a couple of steps back. It gave Joe time to clock the face behind the attack: the kid he'd seen over the road just before going into Costa, with a couple of friends in tow.

As he swept toward the baseball bat kid's ankles with his right foot, Joe realized that he could easily have prevented this if he'd been less wrapped up in his own thoughts.

The kid's name was Lou Brakespeare, and he was a petty criminal that Joe had run up against over a year ago during an operation to infiltrate a gang that had been steal-ing high-performance cars to order. Lou had been low down on the food chain—just a grease monkey in one of the chop shops the gang used—but Joe and Andy had targeted him and a couple of his mechanic friends, charmed their way into their circle, and had started to work on Lou, whom they'd identified as the weakest link in the operation's chain.

Poor, hapless Lou had ended up vouching for Joe and Andy, getting them inside the gang and leading to the downfall of the whole crew.

Joe hadn't thought he'd ever see him again.

That was the thing about going undercover.

You made friends with people, socialized with them, spent time with them, and then—after the bust, after that peculiar endgame of the investigation, arrest—you dropped them in it and left. You changed your identity and moved on to the next case. Within a week they were forgotten. By the end of a year, you needed a pretty good reason to remember them.

Like someone suddenly swinging a baseball bat at your head.

Joe could have switched to his chip to help manage the fight—his *eidetic reflexes* settings would certainly guarantee a swift resolution to this confrontation—but he felt that he needed a little field exercise, and to let off a little steam, so he went in without augmentation. His foot smashed into both ankles and Lou's weight shifted very unevenly. *Feet together* was never a good attack position, and Lou had just found out why. Spread your feet and you're balanced. Bend your knees and you've got yourself a pair of shock absorbers. Stand up straight with your feet together, and you've just made yourself a whole lot less stable.

Ask any lumberjack: hit a tree near its base with an axe and eventually: *TIMBER*!

Lou was unstable.

He wheeled off to the left and Joe followed closely, looking only at Lou's right hand because it was the hand that was holding the bat. His friends were still a couple of seconds away from reacting in any kind of meaningful way, so Joe quickly grabbed Lou's right wrist in his left hand—vise-tight—then yanked it forward, abruptly, to unbalance him even more. Joe held onto the wrist, making sure Lou's arm was straight and under tension, then delivered a single, hard blow with the heel of his right palm into the middle of Lou's forearm.

He dropped the bat and made a thin reedy sound so Joe went behind him, still holding the wrist, and brought Lou's arm up behind his back. Any move that Lou made was liable to break his own arm, so he lapsed into swearing and cursing, but stopped fighting.

Joe put his foot on the baseball bat and looked around.

The other two guys seemed undecided. This wasn't their fight, but Lou was a friend, so Joe could see the conflict in their faces. What they wanted to do was run away, Joe was pretty sure. They'd gone along with Lou when he had a bat, a plan, some adrenaline, and something that passed as dignity to uphold. But they'd watched as he shed all those things in a little over five seconds and now they needed a reason to retreat without losing face.

They'd be gone already if there were a way to do it without Lou thinking less of them.

"Tell them it's not worth it," Joe growled low in Lou's ear. "Tell them to stand down."

"No way . . ." Lou began, but Joe steered him away from any negativity by twisting his wrist and pushing it up toward his shoulder blades.

Lou's defiance turned into a sustained *uhhhhhhh* and Joe maintained the tension on the arm, but pressed it no further.

"One more chance," Joe said. "Forget pride. Forget revenge. Tell your friends to walk away or I will break your arm, and I will make sure that it will never work again. Not properly. Not without pain. You'll curse me every time you try to tie your shoelaces or pick up a PlayStation controller. You'll remember this moment when you could have ended it before I was forced to use extreme measures, and every time you'll curse yourself for letting pride overtake reason. Your choice, though."

Predictably, Lou Brakespeare chose his arm over his pride.

"He's not worth it," Lou said, his voice bent out of shape by pain and shame. As far as back-downs came, it was hardly original, but it gave his friends an out.

"Scram," Joe told them. "When you're out of sight I'll let him go."

The pair looked at Lou for advice and he nodded.

They turned and hurried away.

Joe released Lou's arm and pointed after them.

"Don't look back," Joe told him.

Lou scuttled off.

A few people on the street had stopped to watch the whole encounter and looked like they didn't know whether to laugh, cheer, or phone the police.

Joe just shrugged, picked up the bat, and dumped it in the nearest trash can.

"Sounded interesting," someone said, and it sounded just like Abernathy.

Joe spun round expecting to see the man standing behind him, but there was no one there. He looked around. Still no one. He was beginning to think he'd imagined it, but then a thought struck him.

It hadn't actually sounded like Abernathy was behind him.

It had sounded like Abernathy was much, much closer than that.

"Surprise!" Abernathy said, and this time Joe knew that the man was in his office in Whitehall, probably laughing like a school kid at a teacher saying a bad word.

"The firewall upgrade," Joe said wearily. "Couldn't you have told me that I was now a walking bug?"

"What? And spoil the fun?" Abernathy chuckled. "How am I coming through?"

"Loud and bloody clear. You spies and your toys. So, what, I'm wired for sound now?"

"Indeed. We finally ironed out the wrinkles in the software. Now if you hear it, we hear it. Plus we get to chat like this. Pretty good, no?"

"Great. Now I have you in my head 24/7? Or are there privacy settings?"

"It's only for when you're out in the field on a specified mission. I wouldn't dream of listening in on anything else."

"Yeah, well, just make sure that it doesn't *mission creep* into my personal life."

"Believe me, we have no interest in what you get up to in your downtime," Abernathy said, feigning hurt. "We only activate the audio when you reach the GPS location of somewhere there might be something worth listening to."

"Okay. I'm not going to go into how it would have been nice to have been asked, or, I don't know, *warned*."

"Whose arm were you threatening with eternal pain, anyway?" Abernathy asked.

Joe was making his way down Brixton Road and was aware that, to an outside observer, it would appear that he was talking to himself. So he took his phone out and held it to his ear, just to make sure he didn't look like a crazy person.

"You remember that stolen car ring in Soho?"

"I remember the expense account claim," Abernathy said. "I also remember you and Andy enjoying putting a *lot* of miles on a Ferrari."

"You're not *still* whining about the Ferrari, are you? You gave a couple of kids a *supercar* to buy their way into a criminal organization and you're complaining about the mileage? Anyway, I just ran into one of the mechanics from that job. And he brought a couple of playmates along. Oh, and a baseball bat."

"You okay?" Abernathy's voice softened.

"What do *you* think?"

"I think that even with that chip in your head, you need to keep a tight rein on your anger."

"C'mon. I just stopped three thugs with barely any violence and some threatening language," Joe said.

"Then forget I said anything." Abernathy sounded contrite. "So where are we?"

"Brixton."

"I mean, in the investigation."

"The place's deserted. I'm in a holding pattern. That's why I took a walk and ended up bumping into an old friend."

"Unlucky, but not totally unexpected, I suppose. Oh, did I tell you that Victor Palgrave granted us access to his cloud storage? He said it was your idea."

"To be honest, I wasn't holding my breath waiting for it. Mr. Palgrave keeps his cards exceedingly close to his chest."

"Practically inside his rib cage. Anyway, there was nothing of any value or importance. If I was a slightly more cynical man, I might suggest that the data he gave us was incomplete."

Joe's mind went back to his meeting with Palgrave and his thought that the man knew more than he was letting on. Now, that suspicion was only deepening.

"Are you saying he cleaned the data?"

"*You're* saying that. I am simply nodding to a tune in my head. Which you can't see, obviously. By which I mean the head, not the tune . . ."

"Earth to Abernathy. Anything else?"

"Yes. How would you like to be a blogger for an hour?"

"Yeah, sharing my meaningless thoughts with the jaded masses sounds just the thing to make my day."

"Because if you want to interview some X-Core fans, get yourself down to a place called the Beehive."

"Oh, that kind of blogging I can handle. You know, the kind where I don't actually have to blog. Are you tracking X-Core fans using satellite technology, or by hacking their smartphones?"

"I've been reading Twitter, actually," Abernathy said, his distaste for the social site obvious in the venom with which he said the word. "When are people going to realize that using social media to tell everyone where you are is *never* going to be a good idea? 'Hi, I'm out. Come rob my house!' Anyway, Puppet609 just tweeted that he was meeting friends before the gig."

"Puppet609? Does that mean six hundred and eight other people beat him to the name 'Puppet'?"

"Hmmm. According to his online profile: Science Artist, Vegan, X-Core, and Bleach. I suppose he dyes his hair."

"*Bleach* is a Japanese manga and anime—sorry—comic and cartoon series. Very popular."

"I'll take your word for it, my little cultural encyclopedia. Anyway: Beehive, blogger, Puppet609. Skedaddle."

"I'm on my way."

The guy serving had a goatee that covered up a very weak chin, and he didn't meet Joe's eye as he ordered a latte. As weak chin fussed with the drink, Joe looked around and found his targets with ease.

It wasn't as if the place was busy.

He thanked the server, paid, and took his coffee toward the three guys gathered around a table about halfway across the room.

The place itself was pretty big—according to the quick search he'd done, it had been a shoe store once upon a time—and its decor had been copied from similar joints up and down the nation. It, too, had embraced the modern habit of having screens up displaying the news, with the volume down and subtitles on.

Joe made his way to the table with the three guys and offered his most apologetic smile, backed up with chemical reinforcements.

Contrition, Joe thought, *the new fragrance from Calvin Klein.*

"Excuse me . . ." he said, "are you waiting for the gig later, too?"

Three pairs of eyes looked at him with a mixture of contempt and hostility. Not the showy, cultivated hostility of close-knit groups that wanted to deter outsiders, but rather almost a reflex of distrust. Their body language was oddly hostile, too, as if they were, by nature, all tensed up and edgy.

Joe did a quick visual scan.

There was very little discernible difference among the members of the trio. All males in their late teens/early twenties, and if black was the in color this season, then these three were going for straight As. Black hair, T-shirts, sweaters, and jackets, and black jeans and boots. Joe couldn't see the socks and boxers but he would have bet on them being black, too.

"Move along," one of the three said. "Nothing to see here."

The other two laughed—a single, violent bark—as if there was anything remotely humorous in the comment, and that instantly established the group dynamic for Joe.

Move Along was the leader.

The alpha.

The one to work on.

The other two would pretty much go with the leader's flow.

"Look, I'm sorry to interrupt. My name's Elliot Carpenter

and I'm killing time. I just thought that we might have common ground . . ."

Move Along gave Joe the quickest of once-overs and then shook his head. "We have absolutely nothing in common," he said matter-of-factly, and there was a superior tone swimming through the upper-crust accent.

"We're going to the same event."

"Yet you understand nothing of what you will be hearing." Move Along looked away, dismissing Joe.

"So why not explain it?"

There was a full ten seconds of silence and Joe was about to leave when Move Along spoke.

"Do you teach calculus, Mr. . . . what was it? Carpenter?" he asked, without turning around. His friends didn't look Joe's way, either. It had to be the first time in his life that Joe felt snubbed while the person doing the snubbing was actually talking to him.

"No," Joe said hesitantly, sensing a trap but unable to see its trigger mechanism. "I have to confess that I have never done that."

"But if you did, would you teach it in a lecture theater, to students of mathematics, or in a field, to livestock?" Still Move Along faced away as if Joe were somehow below him.

Joe could see that this was the trigger for the trap.

All he had to do was say that he would teach it to students and Move Along would slam down the lid with a simple, "And that's why I won't explain anything to you."

A mildly clever way of comparing Joe to a beast of the field. If he played along.

But Joe knew that if someone was winning in a game that they, themselves, had set the rules for, then the only way to beat them was to shift to a set of rules that you could win by.

Or, if the opponent was proud, arrogant, or both, it might be better to force a draw.

Joe put a micro-smile on his lips, just in case one of the three turned to look at him.

"Your analogy is entertaining to a point," he said, "but it breaks down as soon as you actually start to *think* about it."

Joe was reinforcing his words with equal doses of *sincerity* and *pity*.

He saw Move Along's back stiffen.

"Because if the livestock in the field suddenly *asked me* to teach them calculus, then I think the opportunity would be too singular, too remarkable, and too tempting to miss."

He turned his back on the trio and started back toward the counter.

Five steps, he thought.

It actually took three.

"Hey! Wait!" The voice was still haughty and arrogant, but it had another quality to it now. The slightest of hints, sure, but that was a start.

The quality is, Joe thought, *curiosity*.

Joe spun on his heel and the trio was looking at him,

three sets of eyes in a row. They were giving him their attention now. Like they were seeing him for the first time: a new species of life that they were suddenly interested in.

He tilted his head a fraction, aware that any larger movement or grand pronouncement could undo the work that he had just done. He needed to be enigmatic. He needed to be a puzzle that the trio felt compelled to solve. So an almost infinitesimal tilt of the head and a steely, neutral stare back gave more layers to that puzzle.

"Would you like to join us?" Move Along asked, and there was that same thread of uncertainty running through the question.

Joe waited three seconds, gave a curt nod, and then said, "Sure."

Everything was controlled, planned, and carefully executed.

And it bought him a seat at their table.

They introduced themselves and the hostility evaporated instantly. It was replaced by an almost predatory curiosity.

It turned out that Move Along was actually named Curtis Madsen, and he introduced his friends as Thomas Grant and Mickey Warren. Joe didn't know which one was actually Puppet609, but thought it could be any of them. Joe's feeling that Curtis was the alpha of this particular group was borne out by the fact that he did almost all of the talking.

He revealed that they were college friends, second year physics majors at UCL. Then he asked what Joe was studying.

Which made a fork in the path forward.

Joe could carry on letting them think he was "livestock," which might limit the amount of information they were willing to share, or he could surprise them, trump their academic endeavors, and maybe throw them off enough to get more information out of them.

"Natural Sciences," he said without missing a beat and amping up on the chemical *confidence*. It was a rollback to a cover ID recent enough that his subject knowledge could stand up to pretty close scrutiny if required. "Caius College, Cambridge."

"Huh," Curtis said. He tried to cover the fact that he was impressed by immediately changing the subject. "So what brings you to Brixton? You don't listen to X-Core, obviously."

Joe had no idea why that was "obvious," but Curtis had phrased it as a statement, not a question. He decided to ignore the statement and answer the question before it.

"To be honest I'm late on a blog entry," Joe said, going with Abernathy's suggested "in." "I write music reviews for the online edition of *Varsity*—the university newspaper. An unforgiving editor is breathing down my neck, and all that was playing in Cambridge was a Pink Floyd tribute act, and I thought I'd rather cut off my ears than suffer that indignity. A friend told me if I wanted to see the next big thing in music, then to get myself over to the Warhouse tonight."

Curtis made a low sound in his throat that might have been a chuckle.

It might have been a growl, too.

"The next big thing," he said in a monotone. His two companions looked at him. Something passed between them, but Joe couldn't tell what. Some subtle expression maybe? An inside joke? Joe decided the best way to deal with it was to ignore it.

"So what have I got to look forward to?" Joe asked.

Curtis closed his eyes.

"When the global economic crisis hit, people were surprised," he said, a slow drawl that seemed entirely unconnected to Joe's question. "Even though economists had been sounding alarm bells for years about the unsustainability of financial structures built on foundations of credit and bad debt.

"The war on terror was nothing more than a war on the Middle East and a power play for oil, an excuse to settle ideological and religious differences. It ended up creating the very radicals it was supposed to destroy.

"People cling to material goods, utterly oblivious to the fact that it is those very things that are dragging them down.

"Religion. War. Violence. Intolerance. Untrammeled greed. Climate change denial. Fear. Distrust.

"Tonight . . . tonight you get to see the alternative."

Curtis opened his eyes and looked at Joe earnestly. His

friends started nodding their heads in eager agreement, as if he had come up with something more than a group of poorly thought-out and barely connected statements. It had sounded like headline extracts from a second-rate manifesto with important linking passages omitted.

Joe wondered how the intellectual elite that X-Core self-selected could settle for such gnomic garbage. It was the kind of stuff that trolls posted on just about every message board on the net.

It wasn't that Joe didn't sympathize with the problems Curtis had outlined—mostly he did—it was just that it was more like a collage of teen angst protest subjects than an actual belief system.

A set of bullet points rather than actual, cogent thoughts.

If X-Core was a cult that demanded its fans belonged to an intelligent elite, then Joe was bitterly disappointed at the caliber of those followers. He wondered if Lennie Palgrave was subscribing to such a threadbare ideology.

And Harry Brewster.

Something didn't scan.

Joe couldn't quite put his finger on it, but something felt *off* about this whole "alternative to the world's problems" shtick passed off as gospel truth.

The more he thought about it, the less comprehensible X-Core became to him. The examples of X-Core music he'd heard were hardly inspiring. Muddled musical ideas, ineptly played, terribly produced, and lyrically naïve—it was hardly a bold step forward. In lieu of songs, Joe had been expecting something sensational *behind* the music; something that explained its cultish status among bright, influential kids. An ideology. A purpose.

The core of X-Core though, if these three fans were anything to go by, was empty—and that seemed incredible to Joe. Maybe these three were not representative of the movement as a whole, but he feared that they were.

He decided that there was nothing to be gained by tiptoeing around, and he altered his strategy. To be honest, Curtis irritated him. The kid was quite obviously privileged, but all the good breaks and private tutors in the world had not resulted in the creation of a likeable person.

Or an interesting one.

Just a shallow and arrogant one.

"There's nothing that chills the blood of a music writer more than hearing something described as *alternative*," Joe said, making sure to meet Curtis's eye and feigning boredom. Boredom, Joe had found, was unlike most of the other emotions he could have used to slam home his message. Boredom was subtle because, if it was real, it was absolutely honest and inarguable. It was critical without the need for confrontation. As a result, it was much harder to dismiss.

Curtis blinked, surprised, and then spent a couple of silent seconds formulating a reply.

"That's because most times you hear something described as an alternative, it's usually just a lesser evil, rather than a true alternative. Like Diet Coke as an alternative to Coke: the choice is loaded. Labor or Conservative? Whoever you vote for . . ."

". . . the government gets in," Joe finished, pretending to stifle a yawn. "So is X-Core political?"

Curtis shook his head.

"Anti-political?"

Curtis shook his head again.

"Apolitical?" Joe tried.

Once more with the head shake.

Joe felt frustrated, like he was getting nowhere. Slowly. Either Curtis was toying with him or he really wasn't as smart as he wanted Joe to think he was.

Again, Joe felt disappointed by the level of Curtis's thinking—or at least his ability to *discuss* his thinking—but covered it up with a liberal dash of *encourage,* changed tack, and asked, "What makes X-Core different from any other musical genre?"

The trio exchanged an odd look among them, and it was almost as if Curtis was asking the others' permission to reveal more. Joe manufactured more *encourage,* sipped his drink, and waited.

And waited.

The trio had stopped talking.

Joe was about to say something else when, suddenly, Abernathy was speaking inside his head.

"I've just checked out our three friends," he said, as if it was perfectly normal to be communicating in this manner. "And they are pretty typical X-Core targets. All but Mickey Warren come from wealthy families. Curtis's father is a top London barrister, Tommy Grant is the son of Ellie Grant, a fashion photographer who regularly features in *Vogue*. They all attended elite schools—Mickey on a scholarship, he's a truly gifted physics student—and they're all engaged in research on theoretical particles. Or they were.

"Their research had even earned a rare undergraduate visit to the Large Hadron Collider at CERN when . . . well, something happened. It seems that about a month ago they dropped out of school. Diligent, conscientious, and gifted students, they suddenly stopped attending college. Their advisor is baffled. I've got someone speaking to her at the moment. If I find out anything else, I'll let you know."

Joe had been studying his companions while Abernathy was talking, and it was as if they had suddenly just been switched off. They sat there, unmoving.

And Joe suddenly realized something else.

Not only were they not moving, but for the duration of Abernathy's message they had been *unblinking*, too.

Their eyes had a far-away look, not quite glazed over, but definitely as if they were looking elsewhere, somewhere in the distance, somewhere farther away than the walls.

The word *cult* just kept rolling around in Joe's head. Was

this how people behaved when they were under the influence of an ideology or a belief system? Was this brainwashing in action?

He'd had enough of thousand-yard-staring X-Core fans.

Joe slammed his coffee cup on the bare table, deliberately avoiding a nearby coaster, and there was a sound loud enough that it attracted the attention of the server, who looked over disapprovingly.

The three X-Core fans appeared not to hear it.

It baffled Joe.

If one of them had just faded out, then it wouldn't have been so weird. People phase out. They get lost in a thought, and screen out the world around them. They're in the room, but they're not.

It happened all the time.

Make it three people, though, and it started looking sinister.

Very good acting, or a sudden epidemic.

It was time to test which.

Joe reached over and drove his knuckles into the meat of Curtis's right bicep, rotating at the wrist and drilling into the upper arm. Curtis blinked at an incredibly rapid rate, his body went into spasm, and then he slumped, as if asleep.

Joe might have thought he *was* asleep, if he hadn't suddenly begun speaking.

"A storm is coming," Curtis said in a low monotone, eyes closed, body loose and relaxed. "And the world is running out of places to shelter from it. What are you going to do, Elliot Carpenter? Are you going to run around with the rest of the cattle, sensing death flashing toward you, but too scared, too bound by tradition and manners to do anything about it? Or are you going to hide? Cower and quake as the sky falls in above you?"

Joe felt a frisson of fear that painted his arms with a cold coat of goose bumps.

It wasn't *what* Curtis was saying, although that was part of it. Joe wasn't big on apocalyptic ravings, but the certainty with which they had been delivered would have given him pause, regardless of the context.

It was the *way* Curtis had said it that disturbed Joe most.

Almost as if he was reciting it with little or no knowledge of what he was actually saying.

As if they were ideas that had been hammered into his brain so deep that they came out as a kind of reflex.

Brainwashed?

Or something worse?

Curtis and his friends remained there, slumped and unresponsive. Like marionettes with their strings cut.

Then he noticed something.

At first Joe thought he was imagining it, and he had to double check to be certain.

Curtis's foot was moving.

It was gently tapping.

Tapping out a rhythm.

He checked the other two and their feet were tapping, too.

To the same rhythm, Joe was sure.

Then, completely in synch, they started nodding. Nodding their heads to what looked like an insistent, driving rhythm. The only problem was—there was no music playing.

Joe thought about the military film and the soldier who would've blown his own brains out in response to a sound. Was X-Core *music* a mind-control technology? Did Curtis and his friends hear it in their heads even when there was no music playing?

Were they listening to it now?

That last thought jarred him. *How could they be listening without MP3 players or smartphones?*

He stood up and hurried toward the door, pulling out his phone as cover and holding it to his face.

"Abernathy?" he said. "You listening?"

"Of course," Abernathy only took a few seconds to answer.

Joe was already on the street, moving back toward the Warhouse.

"I suddenly thought you might have something better to do than monitor me."

"Don't be crazy. What have you got?"

"Just a thought. You know we had that science fiction chat earlier, about mind control, about sounds making people do things . . . ?"

"What of it?"

"I was just wondering, how carefully have we analyzed X-Core songs?"

"All the lyrics have been carefully examined by literary scholars and cryptographers looking for patterns, recurring images, motifs, words that might have extra meanings . . ."

"Have you analyzed the music itself?"

There was a pause, then Abernathy said, "I wasn't seriously suggesting that we had an MKULTRA situation here. So, no, we haven't analyzed the music. We've been concentrating on the people, rather than the music."

"A music-based threat. That video you showed me, and you haven't thought to analyze the music?"

"We've listened to it . . ." Abernathy said defensively. "A couple of musicologists wrote a report on its crude, brutalist soundscapes . . ."

"That's not the same thing. I just sat down with three of our X-Core fans and they fell into . . . I don't know, some kind of trance. Anyway, they were oblivious to the world around them. And they were listening to something. Without music playing. Without headphones."

"I'm not sure what you mean, Joe . . ."

"I mean that we might be looking at this whole thing the wrong way. What if the X-Core subculture isn't following the usual cult model—charismatic leader forms cult through force of personality and will—what if it's because there *is* something actually *in* the music?"

"But that was just me speaking hypothetically . . ."

Abernathy was silent, and Joe knew that he was ordering tests on X-Core tracks in his most unhappy voice.

Ten seconds later he was back.

"So how were Curtis and friends listening to X-Core without, you know, listening to X-Core?"

"You don't mind me thinking aloud?"

"I'd welcome it at this point."

"Earlier, I got fitted with a firewall for my chipset and its software,'" Joe said. "And I guess that's got me thinking about the way the human brain reacts to information. We're talking about music, so I started thinking about the way that we can get hung up on a song, find it hard to get it out of our heads . . ."

"Ohrwurms," Abernathy said.

"Gesundheit."

Abernathy forced out a laugh. "Ohrwurms, or earworms, are musical phrases that the brain latches on to and keeps playing back," Abernathy explained. "It's also called *sticky song syndrome.* . . . I seem to recall it has even been used as a defense in at least one murder case. In extreme cases, medication is prescribed to people who can't shut out a particular song. . . ."

"That's scary," Joe said. "But if we put a piece of code onto a computer that did the same thing that you're describing, wouldn't that be called malicious code? Wouldn't we call it a computer virus or a worm? Wouldn't people start worrying about it? My question to you is this: can a song *infect* a human mind? Not just get caught in it, but actually infect it."

"Oh my," Abernathy said. "It's not possible."

"*Possible* is a relative term. And calling something *impossible* is a luxury we can't afford. Run every sound analysis program you can think of on X-Core tracks. Then find someone else and get them to think of some more. Look for things that might not register to your dulled adult senses. High frequencies, low frequencies, sounds hidden behind walls of noise."

"And you? What are you going to do?"

"I've got a X-Core gig to attend."

"If there's something in the music, what makes you think you'll be immune?"

"I've listened to X-Core, remember? Apart from it making me want to listen to some decent choons, it didn't have any lasting effect on me."

"Be careful." Abernathy's voice was grave.

"Oh, I will be," Joe said. "It's been a long time since I've been to a killer gig. This one might be. Literally."

CHAPTER ELEVEN: LAST RITES FOR A DYING RACE

Ani exchanged a five-pound note for an ink stamp on her hand and joined the gathering crowd inside the Brixton Warhouse.

She'd spent the whole morning with Gretchen—who Ani now had on speed dial in case she needed her—trying to track down the elusive figure of Jack "Black Hat" McVitie. A three-month-old cell phone number had come back disconnected. Emails and IMs brought them no more luck. Gretchen had tried tracking IP addresses and examining metadata—the kind of methods that Ani herself would have employed—but Jack was paranoid enough to hide behind a number of proxies, to scrub metadata, and her efforts turned up nothing.

Gretchen had apologized for her failure by making an awesome lunch and then, after Ani had eaten half her body weight, they'd both tried chasing down Imogen Bell, the woman behind the alien first contact false alarm, and now—it seemed—involved in the X-Core movement.

They already knew that Imogen had deserted her post at the Pabody/Reich telescope, and she had dropped off the radar straight after as if she had fallen off the world, like Jack. Ani wasn't surprised that she'd disappeared. People—especially the press—had been less than kind. In the world of media, the failings of a scientist seemed to be given extraordinary coverage, as if it highlighted an inherent distrust of science. There was even a satirical cartoon about her in the *Guardian*, showing her—unkindly—as a fat, deranged Chicken Little figure, running around in a flurry of feathers, trying to convince world leaders that the sky was falling, when in reality it was merely an acorn—adorned with a picture of ET—that was hitting the roof of the observatory.

Ani thought that she'd probably want to disappear, too, if people were *that* horrible to her.

She'd been worried that the people on the Warhouse's door wouldn't let her in, but twenty minutes of Gretchen working magic with makeup meant that no one called her on her age, if indeed an age limit even existed. In fact, the kids on the door hadn't given her so much as a second glance.

Or, for that matter, a first glance.

Once inside, Ani saw plenty of people as young as her and realized she and Gretchen had been overcautious. Still, the makeup made a pretty good disguise if anyone was looking for her.

The Warhouse was an old building. Taking an "e" out of

the name hadn't changed its industrial beginnings. It was purely functional. Exposed ducts and pipes were the closest the place came to a theme.

The relief at gaining entry was in direct conflict with the fear she felt about *what* she was entering.

She had been hiding from the reality of being here. In truth, she'd had to. It was what kept her traveling the straight line between point A and point B. But now she was in the venue of a X-Core gig, surrounded by people she didn't know, miles away from home. The fear was taking over.

She had heard the sound that these groups encoded into their songs and it had almost cost her her mind. Her plan, such as it was, had just delayed things. If that sound played again, would it finish its work, whatever that work was?

Had these people gathered here also felt its power? Were they under its spell? Would she soon become . . . *one of them*?

One of them . . .

What did that even mean?

Again, she was aware of the speed with which her life had flipped from *fairly normal* to *snafu*. It was as if she had suddenly discovered the velocity of monumental events, the power that drove strange mechanisms hidden from human consciousness.

There was certainly something strange about the audience here tonight. She had been to gigs before, but this one seemed different. There was no chatter. No excited buzz.

No thrum of anticipation. The people gathering here were silent. They seemed detached from the proceedings. They weren't even talking to each other. There was none of the usual expectation, no sense of excitement at the event that was about to occur.

It was like the crowd was *here,* but their minds were *somewhere else.* She thought about the *soundforms* that had tried to worm their way into her brain, and developed a leaden feeling in her stomach. Was this what people were like if the process wasn't interrupted? Were these people who had listened to the .wav file and been *changed* by the process?

Suddenly it was all too much for her. What did she think she was doing here? Putting her mind at risk just so she felt like she was doing *something,* anything, to explain the chain of events that had brought her here.

Who did she think she was kidding?

There was no shame in running away. In returning home and trying to figure things out from home, in Cambridge, with people she knew, in an environment she understood.

She had just made up her mind to leave when a voice announced the arrival onstage of Le Cadavre Exquis and things went quickly downhill from there.

"Good evening," the singer announced as he snatched the mike from its stand. "Listen to this."

He was tall and painfully skinny with a shock of bleached-blond hair. Baggy black combat pants only served to accentuate how thin he was, as did the plain black T-shirt with cap sleeves. Behind him the drummer did a quick tour of his kit, heavy on the toms. A couple of notes from the bass guitar were followed by a distorted scrape of an electric guitar. A few notes from a keyboard and then . . . silence.

The stage in darkness.

An expectant hush.

Pin-drop quiet.

Suddenly a tape-looped voice started up, a strange American-accented voice that sounded both eloquent and insane, backed up by a low throb of bass guitar and a cycling, stereo-panning effect from the keyboards.

Slow, deep drums started pounding out a heartbeat. Spotlights danced over the stage. The guitarist fired off a set of random notes: their only unifying theme seeming to be that they were all spiky and unpleasant. The bass picked up the heartbeat. The singer closed his eyes. A wall of noise was building behind him. When it reached its peak, he raised his fist and the band fell into the first song. Red light blasted behind the band, rendering them into silhouettes.

"They lie, you die, never tell you why," the singer growled as much as sang. "You stick out your neck as they cash the check. You try, they lie, you die, we cry. At the edge of chaos, they never tell you why. At the edge of chaos. Living at the edge of chaos. The edge of chaos. Chaos. CHAOS! CHAOS! CHAOS!"

Ani wrinkled her nose. The music was okay—a little

loose, a little sloppy, a little all over the place—but the lyrics were awful. If she'd handed them in on an English exam, she'd barely have passed. She looked around her and saw that everyone else in the place seemed to be singing along.

The vocalist churned out another few verses, each as lousy as the first, and then just screamed out the word "CHAOS!" over and over again. The crowd started punching their fists into the air every time he did, and it looked to Ani much like the Nuremberg rallies must have looked to an outsider.

An instrumental break—which, to be honest, seemed to be taking the word "chaos" a little too literally—started a slow, low, churning in the pit of her stomach, bass vibration that made her feel sick . . . and . . . and . . .

Ani suddenly put her hand to her head because of a sudden pulse of discomfort from her stomach to her head, as if it had physically shifted locations.

She felt her body resonating, as if the music had suddenly become a physical thing within her, and she realized with horror that she recognized the feeling. She couldn't hear it, but she knew that the .wav file was buried beneath the music. The same .wav she was carrying in her pocket on the flashdrive. Knew it because of the way she suddenly felt like she was the instrument playing the music—that she was a plucked string from which the sound was issuing. She felt the physical blow that she'd felt in Uncle Alex's lab, the clenched fist in her guts, the tingling sensation that started at her extremities and then forced itself into her head.

The *soundforms* followed swiftly and unstoppably: the wormlike shapes that danced across her mind's eye, squirming as they took root in her brain. She felt divorced from her own body as the wet, shining worms of sound writhed and wriggled through her mind, breaking open and disgorging more of the *soundforms*. They were probing at her, trying to find the quickest and most effective way into her core, trying to find a way in so they could fill her, overwrite her, *become* her.

Even her terror seemed distant and dislocated, as if it was happening to someone else.

But, somehow, it felt *different* this time, and she couldn't figure out why.

It was as if the *soundforms* themselves had changed. They seemed harsher, more electric, and there was something buried inside them that seemed to be saying *"OBEY! OBEY! OBEY!"* over and over in her head.

She thought of the last time this had happened, and how it had been Uncle Alex who had saved her by switching off the sound. She knew that no one was going to turn the sound off this time. She was defenseless. Thinking happy thoughts wasn't going to get her out of this one. This time—with their constant refrain of *"OBEY!"*—this time they would *own* her. She felt her will ebbing.

The *soundforms*.

They were unstoppable.

She let out a moan and felt her legs giving out beneath her weight.

There was nothing she could do.

Nothing she . . .

In desperation she tried to think of things to throw in the way of the *soundforms*, to visualize objects that would slow down—or even stop—their terrifying onslaught. She pictured a brick wall around her brain. It was shattered in seconds. She tried an old-fashioned metal safe. It corroded and cracked, and she was vulnerable immediately.

There was no defense, or her concentration was just too weak to stand up to the *soundforms*.

She tried picturing her father's face, then Uncle Alex's, but they offered no resistance to the hungry entities that were threatening to devour her mind.

And then, unbidden, a mental picture of another member of her family rose to take their place.

Not a nice image—her mother, hands and arms red with blood, mirror shards lining her arms like the spines of some strange dinosaur—but a powerful one, encoded with so much fear and regret and revulsion that Ani felt the wormlike forms pause before it.

She concentrated on the image with a supreme act of will, bringing it into sharper and clearer focus. All the emotions that she had the memory tagged with came through with bitter clarity. She let it grow and grow, and she let the cruel despair she'd felt in the moment she'd seen what her mom had done to herself loosen, and she was shocked and elated to feel the *soundforms* wither in proximity to her memories.

Some tried to ride the flash of elation back down into her head, but she suppressed the feeling and replaced it with sorrow and loss and horror and pain and drove them back.

Negative emotions, she thought, *bad memories are a barrier against the invaders.*

She had no idea why this should be so, but now that she had a weapon against them she did something that she had never allowed herself to do before.

Something she had never wanted to do before.

She allowed herself to *wallow* in the terrible memory of her mother's self-mutilation.

She let it overwhelm and overtake her.

She let it *be* her.

Let it control her.

Let her weakness finally become a strength.

She saw, truly for the first time since it had happened, the bloodied wounds and the intersections of skin and glass. Where she always blocked out the details to lessen the pain, to diminish the horror, now she allowed those details to come to the forefront of her consciousness.

Firewall, suckers! she thought. *Now get out of my head.*

Ani visualized her mom's eyes, and the depths of the madness that they transmitted.

She opened eyes she hadn't even realized she'd closed and stepped out of the nightmare.

Into.

Another.

Nightmare.

The rest of the crowd had succumbed to the sound.

They were standing there, eyes closed, facing the stage but no longer seeing it or the band upon it. The band had stopped playing. They were listening to the *soundforms*, too, it seemed. No one was moving. It was eerie and silent, and in such contrast to what she'd experienced while the sound played that it felt unreal.

Then, as one, the crowd began nodding their heads, exactly in time, and there was an odd sound that Ani identified as every member of the audience tapping their feet.

It was as if they were listening to music, but there was none to be heard.

Ani felt a primal impulse to flee, to get as far away from this place as possible, and it was only when she saw the people flashing past her that she realized that it wasn't just an impulse; it was an action her body was actually putting into practice. She was already heading toward the wanly lit EXIT sign. Her body was in full flight mode, controlled by an instinct that had her self-preservation as its priority.

The people in the crowd around her stood, fixed to their respective spots, and she threaded herself between them, horrified at the thought of what was happening *inside* each and every one of them. Whatever those wormlike *soundforms* were, it was hard to believe that they meant anything but harm.

She was overwhelmed by fears, the worst of which was what the crowd would do to her if they came out of their stillness before she'd made it to the exit. Would they hunt her down? Pin her down? Force her to listen to the sound until it stuck? Until the *soundforms* could complete their dark and sinister purpose?

She was fifteen feet from the exit when a hand fell on her shoulder and she thought her heart would burst.

Joe arrived at the Warhouse in plenty of time and, after paying money at the door, tried to blend in with the crowd. Alarm bells were already ringing in his mind at the group's behavior, which seemed too quiet, too ordered to be normal. The word *cult* didn't seem powerful enough to explain the lack of talking—and the absence of any signs of excitement—that the people here exhibited. To Joe, the word *cult* suggested a brainwashed religious *happy-clappy* state of mind, where overall responsibility for one's actions had been handed over to a charismatic leader with his own agenda, which was usually as simple as fleecing the members of his flock and building up a personal fortune.

There was nothing happy here.

In fact, there was no emotional engagement at all.

People seemed almost blank, as if the act of being here was not in the pursuit of pleasure, or happiness, but for some other reason altogether.

He'd tried talking to some of the X-Core fans, but had received pretty much what he'd gotten with the three physicists earlier: a big fat zero. He even saw Curtis Madsen and his two friends, but they looked at him blankly, as if they didn't even recognize him.

Way to make a guy feel unwelcome.

Joe kept his eyes and ears open, but there was pretty much nothing to overhear and nothing sinister to observe. Apart from the fact that the whole thing felt sinister to him. On every level the people in the Warhouse felt *wrong*, but the feeling was far too nebulous to put into words.

It was almost a relief when the announcement for the first band came over the PA, but then the band started playing and things turned very weird, very quickly.

At first, he thought it was just his heightened senses playing tricks on him; that, on the lookout for something strange, he'd actually invented something to fill the gaps.

The lead "singer" of Le Cadavre Exquis—a young biochemistry prodigy by the name of Fulton Barnabas Peck, according to Abernathy's files, who had dropped out of academia to pursue his "music"—was droning on about chaos to a musical backdrop that sounded more accidental than planned, when Joe suddenly had the strangest sensation, as if something buried within the music was trying to worm its way inside his mind.

A horrible sensation that felt like physical pain and mental torment. His mind's eye was suddenly full of disturbing shapes. Something that looked like maggots, or threads, or magnified bacteria, that were assailing his consciousness, as if they possessed life and were hungry for his mind. Squirming threads that made his body tingle and his guts feel like lead.

Immediately recognizing the threat, the firewall programming kicked in and banished the invaders, pushing them away with brutal efficiency, but Joe was left feeling violated and nauseated. For a moment, he felt as if he could no longer tell what was real and what wasn't, so violent and unwelcome had been the intrusion.

He looked around at the other people in the crowd and was shocked to see that they were all locked in the same disturbing battle with the music. Their eyes were closed and their bodies immobile, and Joe was sure that the wormlike intruders hidden within Le Cadavre Exquis's music were threading their way into each and every one of the audience members.

Then Joe saw them doing exactly the same thing that the three X-Core fans in the pub had been doing: tapping their feet and nodding their heads to a nowexistent beat.

Joe found himself absurdly grateful for whatever it was

that Geoff and Greg Shuttleworth had installed in his chip's architecture. They had pretty much saved his mind for him, preserved his sanity.

He realized that things were darker and more danger-ous than any situation he had ever found himself in. There *was* something . . . *bad* . . . hidden behind the industrial noise of X-Core. Something that seemed to have a life of its own. And an agenda of its own, too.

"You listening, Abernathy?" Joe asked.

"Of course," Abernathy replied instantly. "We're picking up some really strange readings from your chipset. Is every-thing okay?"

"No. No, it's not. This is worse than we thought."

"Define *worse.*"

"Precise definition pending. But it's bad. Really, really bad. There *is* something terrifying hidden within X-Core. It tried to . . . take control of me, I think. It's got the whole audience."

"Get out of there, Joe!"

"How soon can you get a team here?"

"Three minutes," Abernathy said. "Why?"

"I think we need to grab a X-Core fan and run some tests on him."

"Kidnapping? Experimentation?" Abernathy sounded shocked.

"They . . . they're all immobile, except for heads and feet. They're listening to music even though there's none playing." Joe caught movement out of the corner of his eye. A girl was heading toward the exit. "Send people," he said. "Take a guinea pig. I'm off in pursuit of someone who seems unaffected."

"Be careful, Joe."

"Of course."

Joe hurried after the girl, catching up with her just before she made it to the exit of the Warhouse. She was small, dark, part Asian. And in a complete panic. Joe reached out his hand and touched her on the shoulder.

Ani turned and looked at the stranger with equal measures suspicion and fear. He was a couple of years older than her, about a foot taller, and had one of those intense faces that looked like its wearer was carrying the whole weight of the world on his shoulders. She looked into his eyes and thought she might have made a mistake about his age: they looked *older* somehow. Wiser and more cynical than the eyes of a typical teenage kid.

He's seen things that he shouldn't have, not at his age.

She thought about photos she'd seen in history class of the war in Bosnia, and remembered being shocked by the eyes of some of the kids who had lived through the atrocities. They'd seen too much. And that was how this kid's eyes looked to her.

He was staring at her with concern, but it quickly turned into something else.

Something that looked a lot like relief.

"It's okay," the stranger said with a warm hint of an American accent. "I'm not going to hurt you."

"You'd better not even try," Ani said, bravado masking her fear. "I'm a black belt in . . . in some made-up martial art that isn't fooling anyone."

The stranger smiled, and he looked young again.

"Let's hope you don't have to demonstrate it," he said. "I haven't trained in any imaginary defense strategies. They're my Kryptonite. We should get out of here. Before those . . . weirdos wake up."

Ani felt oddly comforted by the stranger's presence and nodded.

They left the Warhouse and stood on the pavement outside. The street was busy enough that it created an odd juxtaposition with the scene they had just left. People were walking around, oblivious and carefree. Ani and the boy both stood there for a couple of seconds, marveling at the normality and ordinariness just feet away from the extraordinary events they had just witnessed.

Finally the stranger spoke. "Hi," he said. "My name's Joe."

"Ani."

"Pleased to meet you, Ani," Joe said, shaking his head. "Do you have any idea what on earth happened back there?"

Ani hesitated. The events of the last twenty-four hours made her feel cautious and vulnerable, and she didn't know this kid from Adam. How could she be sure that he wasn't . . .

one of them, whoever *they* were? Adrenaline was pumping through her body, and she no longer knew who to trust.

Joe seemed to concentrate, his brow creasing for a second, and she felt herself relax, suddenly sure that Joe was actually an okay guy.

Of course she could trust him.

How could she not?

Joe reached out a hand and squeezed her arm very gently.

"Everything's going to be all right," he told her, and she knew that he was telling her the truth. She just didn't know quite how she knew that.

"I've got to get you somewhere safe," Joe said. "Somewhere where we can figure all this out. I need your help, Ani; maybe the whole world needs your help, if this is as bad as I think it might be. You just proved yourself to be unique in that crowd. You're still you, while everyone else in there just went blank. Can you trust me, come with me, tell me your side of what just happened?"

Ani nodded.

"Not quite unique, though," she said.

"Huh?"

"You were in there, too," she said, and Joe smiled again.

He pulled out his phone, dialed, and then said to the person on the other end, "Get me a car. I'm coming back to HQ. Oh, and I'm bringing a friend."

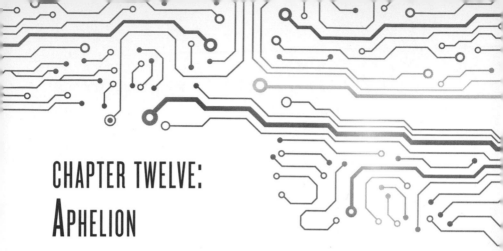

CHAPTER TWELVE:
APHELION

Whoever this Joe kid was, Ani had to admit that he traveled in style.

Within minutes of his call a chauffeur-driven, coal-black Mercedes was pulling up to the curb: latest model, latest reg, shiny and impressive. Ani narrowed her eyes and Joe shrugged before opening one of the back doors and waving her in. Then went around to the other side and got in next to her.

"Who are you again?" Ani asked, surrounded by a new car smell that didn't come out of a can.

"Joe Dyson."

"Heir to the vacuum cleaner empire?" Ani asked, only half jokingly.

She saw there was a moment when Joe's face seemed guarded, as if he were making a decision, then he smiled and said: "Special agent of a secret youth task force. Investigating X-Core with an eye to, you know, saving the world."

Ani laughed, then saw that Joe was being totally serious. "Really?" she asked.

"Really."

The Mercedes glided away from the curb.

"Don't spare the horses," he told the driver. "I think we just reached DEFCON Doomed."

The driver spun a neat turn and accelerated back the way he'd arrived.

Ani sat back in the plush upholstery and thought, *I could get used to this.* If life had been getting stranger and scarier with every passing hour, it had finally taken a turn that she actually approved of.

But she had a lot of questions buzzing around in her head—as well as the aftereffects of the second *soundform* experience—and the journey seemed like a good opportunity to get answers to at least some of them.

"So tell me, Special Agent Joe Dyson, how does an American kid become a British secret agent?"

"Just lucky," Joe said. "I guess it helped that my mom was CIA."

"And where are we going?" Ani asked.

"We are en route to the clandestine headquarters of the Youth Enforcement Task Initiative," Joe said, and he seemed relaxed and controlled, as if the craziness they had just been through hadn't even happened. "Which just so happens to be my place of work."

"YETI?" Ani snorted as she worked out the acronym. "How old are you, anyway?"

"Seventeen. I've been a YETI operative for over three years now."

"And what does being an operative involve?"

"Kids do bad things. Or are *made to do* bad things. If you want to infiltrate an organization, gang, or terror cell that is using kids to do their dirty work, then you need kids to do the infiltrating. And take down the baddies when the case is made against them."

"You're serious?"

"Always. I have to be."

"Isn't it dangerous?"

"Usually."

"Is that even ethical?"

Joe turned to look at her and his eyes looked old again. She realized that her first impression had been correct: he *had* seen a lot of things that a seventeen-year-old probably shouldn't have.

"I volunteered," Joe said gravely. "Anyway, is it ethical to use kids as suicide bombers? Or smuggling mules? Or to use them for mind-control experiments masquerading as musical fads?"

"Is that what you think X-Core is?" Ani asked.

"I can't think of another explanation."

"Then get me to your headquarters. I think I may

have another theory that I'd love to get a second opinion on."

Joe raised an eyebrow, but Ani just sat back in her seat.

Joe allowed himself to relax completely when the car got moving. It felt good.

He was hyped up by the events of the day, and he knew that things were probably going to get pretty hectic when he got back to HQ. In his experience, it was small moments like car journeys that provided the space to slow himself down, to recuperate mentally, and to prepare for the next storm to come.

Ani was an enigma to him: a young kid, smart and witty, but with reinforced steel somewhere in the construction of her personality. She had remained pretty much unfazed by the weirdness at the Warhouse, had accepted his revelation about YETI without so much as blinking, and then revealed that she had a theory as to what was really going on.

Who are you, Ani? he thought. *Who are you, really?*

He'd gone through the usual list of possibilities— bystander, perp, ally, or victim—and thought that she probably fit in category three: *ally*. There was just something about her that reassured him, that made him want to trust her— he'd had to use a blast of pheromones to convince her *he* was trustworthy—while Ani just needed her natural character to do the same thing to a cynical law enforcement agent.

He smiled.

Abernathy's going to love her.

Okay, so "theory" might have been overstating it, Ani thought, but her mind had been churning over and over on the information that she, Uncle Alex, and Gretchen had uncovered, and she was starting to draw together the disparate strands into something that made some kind of sense.

If it could be called *sense.*

It sounded crazy and creepy and it was probably totally wrong, too, but something about Joe made her want to impress him. When he'd admitted that he was a teen secret agent she'd at first been skeptical, but now she accepted it without question. It just *seemed* true, and a pretty cool idea. The kind of opportunity she would have liked herself if she'd gone to as good a school as Joe obviously had.

A fee-paying school, obviously.

The proof of that wasn't just in the accent he was concealing, but in his manner.

Or *manners*, actually.

He conducted himself entirely differently from any other kids his age that she could name. Better. More considerate. Really, he conducted himself better than most adults she could name, too. Maybe that could be a cultural thing— perhaps explained by that hint of an American accent she'd detected the first time he opened his mouth—or just something unique to himself.

He behaved as if he were an old soul in a young body:

an old soul from another time, when knights roamed the kingdom righting wrongs and protecting the innocent.

Not that she was sure that such a time ever existed beyond TV and books. But Joe struck her as a sort of modern-day knight errant. She realized again that she kind of envied him. Sure, she was a hacker and a technology freak, but she always saw what she did as a kind of inherently *decent* act.

Even the Facebook hack had been born out of a frustration—an anger—at people who spent *real* money on digital livestock and crops for farms that didn't even exist in the real world. Jack and Ani had bonded over a shared hatred of people deciding that their meaningless entertainment was somehow more important than making the world a better place. With all the world's problems—with all the poverty, social inequality, starvation, and needless deaths in the world—people still chose to squander their time, money, and energy on digital geegaws that served no purpose but to feed some insane need to develop nonexistent farms. Paying money for imaginary food while the rest of the world starved.

A world like that needed heroes.

If she could help him, then maybe she'd feel less ineffectual in this crazy world they existed in.

She guessed that that was one of the things that she'd always felt: ineffectual. It was probably the result of being born into a poor family, of being raised in public housing, and—of course—of being half Vietnamese. It was a perfect storm of social factors, and society's reduced expectations were leading Ani on a narrow path toward social immobility—a societal version of the Red Queen's race from Lewis Carroll's *Through the Looking-Glass*, where it took all the running a person could do just to keep in the same stupid place.

She was starting to feel a little angry, but knew that she was traveling down that particular thread of thought so she could crowd out the other thread that wanted examining. The one that was practically demanding her attention. The one that made her feel sick with fear.

The one that was built out of scraps—the things she had learned and experienced—and conjecture: the only frame that she could put everything into that explained it all.

When she got to wherever it was they were going she would have quite the tale to tell.

They pulled up to the barrier and the guy on the gate raised it and waved them through without asking for ID. His hand didn't stray anywhere near his weapon. Joe thought about every time he'd come through the entrance with Abernathy, when you'd have been forgiven for thinking the whole place was on security alert, and wondered if the guards only put Abernathy through more thorough scrutiny because they were afraid not to, or whether they just liked making Abernathy wait.

They pulled into the parking lot and Joe led Ani inside. When the guard refused to let Ani through the inner doors, Joe got him to call Abernathy who, judging by the distance the guard held the phone away from his ear, wasn't happy to be kept waiting.

The place had an atmosphere of suppressed hysteria, with people working off multiple screens and multiple phones as the urgency of the investigation was suddenly becoming apparent. He received fewer nods, but didn't take it personally.

Ani followed at his heel.

For a random kid walking in after the weird events at the Warhouse, she seemed to be taking things pretty well. As they made their way toward Abernathy's *sanctum sanctorum*, her eyes darted about, curious, and Joe wondered if the expression on her face was a mirror of the expression he'd worn when he'd made the walk through the offices for the first time.

"You *work* here?" she asked him, in genuine wonderment.

He nodded.

"Well, mostly I work undercover. But this is my base of operations."

"That's *so* cool. Have you got a number?"

"A number?"

"You know, like James Bond."

"No number. That would be like admitting we existed."

"Top top secret." Ani smiled. "More like Ethan Hunt."

"I don't know who that is. But yeah, we're pretty hush-hush. You'll have to sign the Official Secrets Act."

"No way!"

Joe nodded.

He realized that he liked having Ani around.

He approached the door to the control center, flashed his card at it, and the door opened.

"You think you've seen cool? Ani, you really ain't seen nothing yet."

They stepped over the threshold.

If the building had impressed her, the inner area took her breath away.

Literally.

She stood on the edge of a room that was like a hacker's dream. The computer setup was beyond amazing, like an exhibit from a tech expo five years in the future, and it made even Gretchen's computer look a little out of date. Three huge 4K displays collated text data, photos, video, and sound from the multiple individual workstations, giv-ing—she thought—a clear overall picture of a few different situations.

Or cases, she supposed.

In one window there was camera footage of people entering the Warhouse that must have been mounted upon the photographer's head from the angle it was taken.

She was following the action when her attention was

suddenly drawn to the main screen and she was alarmed to see a photo of herself, taken from a hidden surveillance camera, on her and Joe's way in to the building. She could see databases being accessed next to the picture, and facial recognition software results that gave her name, address, and other pieces of information that someone must have pressed *hide* on, because they disappeared from the screen just as she was about to read them.

A door at the side of the room opened and a tall, gray-haired man who looked about fifty stepped out and gestured for them to join him.

"The boss," Joe whispered, and they made their way over to him. "His name's Abernathy, and he can be a cold fish but he'll warm to you, I'm sure."

"Good to see you, Joe," Abernathy said. "And Ms. Lee, it is a rare and wonderful pleasure to meet you."

He offered her his hand and she realized that he wanted to shake. She offered hers up, awkwardly, and he gave it a soft squeeze.

"It really *is* a great pleasure," he said. "I'm a big fan of your work."

Joe looked at her oddly and she gave him a look that hopefully said she had no idea what he was talking about.

They went into the room, and Abernathy waved at a couple of chairs and then sat down behind his desk.

"Well, this is all very exciting," Abernathy said. "I want

to hear about it all, of course, but Joe—you should have told me who you were bringing in with you."

"I think I might be missing something." Joe looked a little embarrassed. "Why doesn't someone fill me in?"

Abernathy smiled, looking at Ani the whole time. "Ms. Lee here is kind of a legend," he said, and Ani felt half filled with pride, half sick with fear. "Under the hacker name 'AniQui' she has been behind some of the most audacious pieces of computer activism that this country has seen in the last few years. Facebook, McDonald's, the British Nationalist Party, Abercrombie & Fitch . . . it's quite a portfolio, young lady. While the Facebook Farms thing is the most elegant implementation of your skills, I have a real fondness for the Abercrombie & Fitch assault."

Ani felt like she had stepped through the looking glass into the weird world on the other side. She'd thought that all her exploits had been secret. That no one could possibly know.

"You're a computer hacker?" Joe asked in a small voice. "Like a famous one?"

"Apparently," Ani said. "I thought I was anonymous rather than famous, but there you go."

"Well that's . . . weird—" Joe began, only to be cut off by Abernathy.

"So, Ms. Lee, why are you caught up in this X-Core madness?" he asked. "Are you a fan?"

"Definitely not. You got time for a little story?"

"Always."

Ani thought about it, decided it couldn't get her in any more trouble than she was already in, and told Joe and Abernathy her tale.

When Ani was done Joe puffed up his cheeks, exhaled a gust of air, and then turned to Abernathy. "She's good."

Abernathy shook his head. "No, Joe, she is *exceptional*. Absolutely exceptional. She has managed to learn more about this whole business than we have, and on her own. And with resources she pretty much put together on the fly." He turned to Ani. "These . . . *soundforms*, did you call them? You think that they're what led to the scene at the Warhouse?"

"I'm certain of it."

"And you perceived these *soundforms* as threatening? You felt that they meant you harm?"

"Absolutely. It was as if they were trying to overwrite me, to replace who I am with something new."

"And it is precisely the same sensation you had when you played this .wav file?"

"Similar, but not identical. I was thinking maybe the .wav is more concentrated."

Abernathy nodded. "Well, then," he said. "I'm very interested in hearing your theory. . . ."

Ani looked shocked. Joe knew what she was thinking:

she had only mentioned the existence of a theory to Joe, and she knew that he hadn't told anyone about it.

Abernathy pointed to Joe. "He's wired for sound. So how do *you* put these pieces of information together to form a pattern?"

Ani hesitated. "You'll think that I'm insane. . . ."

"I doubt that."

Joe was stunned by the difference he was seeing in Abernathy's whole demeanor. All his rough, irritating, pompous edges had been rubbed off and he almost seemed human.

"I authorize Joe's expense claims, so I'll believe anything."

Joe grinned but felt a little peeved that Abernathy was making a joke at his expense in front of this total stranger. The feeling lasted only a couple of seconds though, because suddenly he understood what was happening here.

Even if Ani didn't know it, she was being interviewed.

Abernathy was being sweet and flattering and tolerant because he was *recruiting*.

Ani fixed Abernathy with a level glare. "I think the .wav file that's threaded through X-Core music is more than just a threat to teens," she said confidently. "And its relationship to the false *first contact* story seems clear to me. They both have a person in common: Imogen Bell. An astronomer who heard a message from space and decided to become a musician."

Ani paused and waited for that to sink in. Joe saw that she was studying Abernathy's face, waiting to see some kind of response in his features. Abernathy must have obliged because she continued on.

"It's too coincidental. I know that humanity has a problem with seeing causal links where there are none: if a man does a dance and then it rains, it's possible for him to say that it rained *because* he did the dance, but that doesn't mean that there's cause and effect—just that event followed event. But here, the two strands I've been following seem connected.

"Imogen Bell leads to the .wav file that leads to X-Core, and X-Core leads back to Imogen Bell. She's where you should go next." Ani shrugged. "What do *you* think?" she asked.

"I think I'd like to offer you a job," Abernathy said.

Ani handed over the flash drive containing the .wav file, and Abernathy hurried it through to his tech guys, and then he sent Joe off for a debrief, before asking her more questions.

"These people with guns that came looking for you," he said in a concerned voice. "Who do you think they are?"

"I was thinking government. Or some branch of the police." She remembered what Gretchen had said about the behavior of the men. "Now I think it's more likely that they were freelancers, maybe mercenaries, but how they link up with the scenario I outlined, I don't know."

"We're running an inquiry of our own on that as I speak," Abernathy said. "Now I have a huge favor to ask you. Feel free to say no, but please say yes."

Ani raised an eyebrow.

"I want you to accompany Joe on a trip to the Pabody/ Reich radio telescope in Shropshire. And I want you to have a look at the setup there. If I give you something that is guaranteed to hack into their computers, do you think you can have a little poke around and see if they're hiding anything?"

"Of course. You were serious about the job offer?"

"I would have tracked you down eventually. I'm always on the lookout for fresh talent to increase our skill set here at YETI, and at first glance I'd say you definitely qualify. But I have to ask, would you be interested in joining us?"

Ani took a couple of seconds to think about it, knowing that she was on one side of a line that, once crossed, would change her life forever. She had always looked for something to turn her talents to, and now she was being offered an opportunity to make that dream a reality.

"How did you know who I was? I mean, how could you possibly know that I'm AniQui just from a surveillance photo?"

Abernathy smiled. "I'm in the intelligence business. Have you heard of PRISM?"

"The electronic communications monitoring system," Ani said. "It's been in the news."

"It's the very small tip of a gigantic iceberg. PRISM is nothing more than a piece of technology that it was decided the public was ready to find out about. It was outdated years ago. SPECTRUM, on the other hand, is PRISM evolved: a heuristic network that runs by itself, monitoring communications in a proactive fashion. Your communications were tagged over a year ago, and whenever you type your hacker name into IM, email, or IRC, SPECTRUM logs every detail, and takes a snapshot from your webcam. You have never been flagged as a high priority target—just a person it might be worth keeping an eye on."

"You're not going to prosecute me for hacking?"

"Certainly not. A talent like yours is too useful, too rare."

"I'm in. For the record, you had me at 'big fan of your work.'"

"Then how about we make this trip your job interview? A field exercise. Pass it and you're a YETI operative. Wheels go up in ten minutes. I'll make sure that there's someone from the observatory on-site by the time you arrive. Find out everything you can. Your mission, should you choose to accept it, is to help save the world."

"So where's this hardware that's guaranteed to hack into their system? I really want to get a look at it."

Abernathy smiled, stood up, and gestured toward the door. "Follow me."

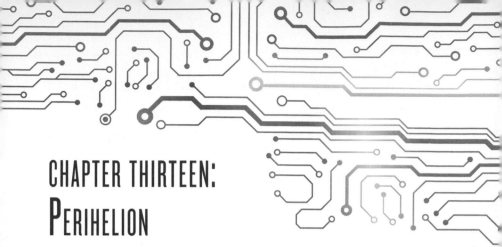

CHAPTER THIRTEEN:
PERIHELION

Joe requisitioned a vehicle—a midnight blue SUV—and proceeded to sling it through the city traffic with the comfortable familiarity of a London taxi driver. There was very little *mirror, signal, maneuver* to his driving, but there were occasions when he'd use two of the three. Most of the time he just seemed to trust his skill and the two-ton bulk of the vehicle.

Ani sat in the passenger seat, one eye on Joe's driving, the other on investigating the tablet that Abernathy had just given her. She'd genuinely never seen anything like it.

"This is one sweet piece of tech," Ani said, her voice betraying her wonder. "It's like an iPad from the future. On steroids. It's lightning fast. There are three operating systems accessible with the press of a button. Dual desktops in Windows and Mac OSX flavors; and then there's a Linux command line OS . . ."

"Yeah, but can you play Angry Birds on it?" Joe asked.

"Play it? With this, you can hack the app and make them

a whole lot less angry. I can't believe that I just got handed a tablet computer that's better than any laptop I've ever used."

"Abernathy loves his toys." Joe braked abruptly and gave an apologetic smile.

Ani waited until they were moving again and then asked, "So what's the deal, anyway?"

Joe needed to slow down again, but this time he feathered the brakes, swung the steering wheel, accelerated, and then threaded the SUV through a clump of traffic.

"The deal?"

"Yeah." Ani put the tablet down on her lap and turned to look at Joe. "I can understand law enforcement using kids to infiltrate groups of other kids. It makes a lot of sense. I can even see YETI using someone from across the pond as an asset. But sending *us* to interview adults—what's that about? Is this really just an interview for a job?"

Joe laughed.

"Abernathy is patched into levels of government the rest of us don't know exist, and has resources beyond measure. The fact that he's not using them tells me he has something else in mind. Three things, probably, because that's the kind of game Abernathy is always playing. Every move he makes tends to accomplish more than one goal. And he thinks many, many moves ahead.

"First thing: I've been off active duty for a while, and this is my first operation back. I think that he needs to see that I can still handle things—any things—that get thrown at me. Second: the interview. You are an unknown quantity. Computer savvy, obviously, but how will that translate into street smarts? Investigative fieldwork is a good way to test your temperament and abilities in relative safety.

"Finally, by sending *us* instead of some seasoned investigators, I suspect he's seeing how we work together. Seeing if we *can* work together."

"So you really think that if I do okay here, I get the job?"

"Yep."

"He does know that I'm still in school?" Ani said, her brow wrinkling. "I mean, hello!"

"If you make it onto the YETI payroll, they'll educate you as well. It's just that surveillance techniques, interrogation tips and tricks, and hand-to-hand combat will also be on your syllabus."

"And you're basically a spy . . . ?"

"You, too, now. But 'spy' is just one part of the job. It's much more useful to think of YETI as a network of undercover teen operatives. Kids. People forget to take us seriously. They have no idea how serious we are."

Ani shook her head.

"It's all too much, you know? I don't know what's real and what isn't. Two days ago I was just a normal kid. . . ."

"A normal kid who brought those stupid farms on Facebook to their knees," Joe reminded her.

"And now it seems I'm running from one insane scenario to the next. In Brixton, back there, you saw those kids, what they were becoming. There's something in that .wav file, Joe. Something dark and dangerous and very, very scary."

"That's why we have to stop it from happening."

"But how do we stop a sound? A file can travel in cyberspace, can be in a million in-boxes with the click of a mouse button. . . ."

"One click?"

"Sequence shortened." Ani laughed. "For demonstration purposes."

"An i-Gag?" Joe said. "Are you a real, actual computer nerd?"

"Virtually. And here I had almost given up hope."

"About what?"

"About finding kids who actually stood for something. About young people who care enough to want to make a difference. Whole blocks of our generation are getting a little forgetful about their responsibilities, and a little too dependent upon what they think of as their rights."

"Is that what the whole hacker thing is about?" Joe asked. "That's not sarcasm or rudeness or irony. I am genuinely interested." He did a comic double take out the car's windshield.

"Did that sign just say A406?" he asked.

"I think so. Why?"

"Hang on." Joe grinned, then floored the accelerator and swung the wheel so far over to the left that they leapt across two lanes of traffic, only just making it through two of the tiniest gaps in traffic before hurtling down the exit ramp they needed.

Ani had just managed to grab hold of the tablet and was trying not to look too traumatized.

Which was quite the job.

"I should have said *don't worry*," Joe said apologetically. "That maneuver was calculated and executed by computer."

Ani tilted her head.

Joe waited until they were off the ramp before explaining.

They'd been in the car for about an hour when Joe realized again just how much he had missed this: the simple act of discussing the job, YETI, his hardware, a case.

Ever since Andy died, Joe had had no one to just chat and banter with.

To talk about the job with.

Or to impress with his secret hardware.

Explaining his onboard computer to Ani was better than explaining it to anyone else because she not only got it, but she *really* got it. Joe could tell by the way her eyes widened and her voice became sort of breathy.

"Wow. A computer integrated into your brain? That is just . . ."

"Awesome?" Joe tried to finish the thought.

"Uh-unh," Ani said, shaking her head. "Ben & Jerry's is awesome. Skrillex. Vans. *The Nightmare Before Christmas*. The Large Hadron Collider. Dropbox, and this tablet computer, and *Wil Wheaton's TableTop*. They're all awesome. A brain computer? That is so far beyond awesome that it deserves a new superlative."

Joe actually felt his cheeks redden a little.

"It's a prototype. A tool that offers me a little edge in the field."

"It's a science fiction movie idea," Ani said. "I'd love to get a look at the specs."

Joe nodded. "Me, too," he confessed. "You know when you download the latest iTunes and get a bunch of those terms and conditions to agree to?"

"Sure."

"I never read them. And I have no idea what I've actually got implanted in my head. I just click 'agree' every time."

Ani smiled, and Joe went quiet and watched the road.

Ani grew tired of watching the night scenery rushing past the windows, so she took out her phone—which Joe had been impressed that Abernathy had let her keep—changed the SIM, and dialed Gretchen.

"Hey Ani," Gretchen answered after the first ring. "You had me worried. Is everything okay?"

"My day is getting weirder by the minute. So same old, same old, I guess."

"But you're all right?" Gretchen sounded worried and Ani felt guilty for not contacting her sooner. Of course she was worried. When they'd parted, Ani had been on her way to a gig where it was likely she'd run into the sound from the .wav file again. That hadn't gone well the first time.

"I'm absolutely fine. I'll explain everything that's been happening as soon as I can. Have you heard from my uncle?"

"Alex has called several times. I've reassured him that he has nothing to worry about, and he'd said he'd pass that on to your dad."

"Thank you. Do you think it's true?"

"Do I think what's true?"

"That he has nothing to worry about?"

Gretchen laughed. "One hundred percent true. You've got my number if you need any help, so use it, okay?"

"I will." Ani was about to hang up when a thought struck her. "Actually, I could use help with something."

"Shoot."

"Imogen Bell. Anything else you can tell me. She feels like the key to this whole thing."

"There's not much to find. Every reference to her is about her academic career, and then her fall from grace. Past that . . ."

". . . past that is the challenge. Ideally, I'd like an address."

"I'll see what I can do. I'll get back to you if I find anything. You could call your dad, you know? Put his mind at ease."

"I know. I just don't want him getting into trouble because of me. He gets himself in enough of it without my help."

"Still . . ."

"Message received," Ani said and hung up.

She dialed her father's cell number and let it ring twice. Then she called back and let it ring three rings. Once more: five rings. Dad's code when he was out doing some shady deal; it meant *I'm okay.*

Joe turned to her. "It's good that you've got people you can trust. But you have resources beyond imagination at your fingertips now."

"I have a feeling that we're going to need them."

Sometimes driving through the dark was an act of faith: at seventy miles an hour, you needed to just believe that the road continued ahead. Driving up a slight incline, Joe had a sudden thought: *what if I reach the top and there's no road behind the brow of the slope? Just a drop?*

Stupid, sure.

But he was kind of glad when a car overtook him and he could follow behind it.

He studied the road in front of him, keeping just below the speed limit and making sure he had plenty of time to react if the car ahead decided to do something stupid. It was a good policy. People *always* did something stupid on the roads if you gave them long enough.

He had no idea who Ani had just called, but figured that she had some pretty good resources of her own. Maybe it would be an ideal test to see if her friend could deliver for her. . . .

Abernathy's voice came through loud and clear.

"Joe. We're already running traces on Ms. Bell. I'll let you know when we've got something."

"I think we have it under control," Joe said, ignoring Ani's puzzled look. From her perspective he was suddenly talking to himself. "Ani here has lines of inquiry open, maybe we should see how they pan out . . . ?"

"I think that I should be the judge of that. And, while I see little harm in another brain working on gathering intelligence, I'd still like the opportunity to continue through *official* channels, if it's all right with you."

It took a second or so for Joe to figure out that letting Ani's friend do his research for him was actually a little bit of a blow to Abernathy's pride. Maybe that explained his immediate reaction to Ani herself—putting her straight out in the field with no training. This was Abernathy's version of *if you can't beat 'em, join 'em.*

"Look," Joe said. "The way I see it, it's a race. Your government resources against Ani's phone-a-friend."

"I'm running the search myself," Abernathy said and his voice betrayed how much he would take it as a personal affront if he was beaten to the information by an amateur. "I'll get right back to you."

"You're not talking to yourself, are you?" Ani asked. "*Wired for sound*, that's what Abernathy said earlier. You're talking to him now, aren't you?

Joe nodded.

"So does your boss listen in on *everything* you say and do?"

"It's still new to me. A very recent upgrade."

"How do you switch it on and off?"

"I don't. Abernathy does."

Ani shook her head. "It shouldn't be too hard to work out a way of shutting it off and on from your end."

"We're looking into that," Abernathy said.

"Apparently that's coming in the next version," Joe told Ani.

She smiled.

So did Joe.

The Pabody/Reich telescope array was hidden away in countryside outside Shrewsbury; three radio telescopes that looked alien and strange as they rose above the land, curved science fiction dishes with scaffolds focused into a pyramid shape, mounted upon metal towers.

An iron fence with a matching gate blocked their way to the site, but there was a buzzer and speaker by the gate and Joe got out of the car, pressed the buzzer, introduced himself to the person on the other end, and the gates swung open.

"Looks like Abernathy called ahead," Joe said when he was back behind the wheel. "Wanna go do some investigating?"

"Am I Daphne or Velma?" Ani asked.

"Huh?"

"From *Scooby-Doo*. Do I stand around looking gorgeous, like Daphne, or do I ask pertinent questions like Velma?"

"Play it by ear," Joe said, then pretended to be offended. "Does that make me Fred or Shaggy?"

Ani looked him up and down.

"Scooby," she said, and they both laughed.

Joe followed a single-lane road to a high-tech building at the end. It seemed to have been spun by a silkworm that was now working in steel and glass. Or maybe Joe's imagination was running wild.

They got out of the car and made their way to the entrance. Another buzzer, but this time the door was opened by a human. Joe noticed a black half globe above the door, which he recognized as a high-end CCTV camera.

A small, middle-aged man stood there with a puzzled expression on his face. He had an overabundance of hair in his eyebrows that seemed to be sympathizing with the lack of hair on the top of his head and standing in solidarity with the bubbly froth of gray hair that started about level with his ears.

"I've been expecting you," the man said, offering his hand. "I'm Donald Klein. Professor Donald Klein."

"Joe Dyson. And this is Ani Lee."

"I was told to offer you full assistance, although I was expecting someone . . ."

"Older?" Joe asked.

Klein nodded. "I was told to expect government agents. . . ."

"That's us. They start training us young these days." Pheromones underscored his statement, and it seemed to appease Klein.

"I'm sure I have no idea what this is all about." Klein gestured for Joe and Ani to follow him into the building. "We're just an observatory, you know. Now twice in a week we get visitors . . ."

"Twice?" Joe felt a prickling sensation down his spine. "Who else has been here?"

"Men in black," Klein said, scratching his bald head. "Well, men in suits, anyway. Two of them. Odd fellows. Had some very official-looking IDs. Asked strange questions."

"About?"

"That was the thing. Awfully vague questions, actually. Didn't seem to know much about radio astronomy at all.

Didn't seem to have a clear reason for being here. I just figured it was a security check, or some such nonsense."

They'd walked down a corridor as they spoke and Joe had spotted another three cameras on the ceiling. Klein stopped and they stood outside a door. He opened it and ushered them inside. A simple office, star charts and hi-res photos of nebulae and galaxies and planets. A grown-up version of a child's room, with computers and charts instead of toys and posters. Joe took a seat in front of the desk and Ani took another. Klein settled down behind it and leaned forward, steepling his index fingers and then resting his chin on the apex.

Joe looked around the office and spotted the camera in here, too. "I see that you have a great security system," he said. "CCTV cameras, motion sensors."

"Part of the burden of getting insurance for a building stocked with state-of-the-art equipment," Klein replied.

Joe waited a moment then asked, "Do you have footage of your two previous visitors?"

"We must. It'll be in the security office, stored on hard drives. May I ask why you're interested in seeing them?"

"Just wondering why they came, is all. I hate coincidences."

Klein made a sound that implied he hated coincidences, too.

"Did you leave these men alone at any point?" Joe asked.
"No. Of course not."

"Did either of them ask to use the toilet?"

Klein narrowed his eyes, which had the unfortunate effect of lowering his eyebrows over them, making them looked thatched. "One of the men *did* visit the facilities. But he was only gone for a moment."

Joe nodded. "You'd be surprised what a well-trained operative can do in a moment. We'll need to see the recordings in a while. First we have a few questions."

Klein looked at him impassively.

Joe turned to Ani. "This is Ms. Lee. She wants to know about a former colleague of yours."

Klein lifted one of those eyebrows and it looked like a caterpillar jumping. It was as if he were seeing her for the very first time.

"I'd like to hear about Imogen Bell," Ani said. Joe didn't hear even the slightest fluctuation of nervousness in her tone. Indeed, she sounded supremely confident.

She's good, he thought.

"Ah, of course." Klein sighed. "Why doesn't anyone ever want to hear about the rich wonder of the heavens? The composition of the colossal expanse that surrounds us? The life cycles of stars and the sublime power of the event horizon of a black hole? But, no. Let's just keep bringing up *that.*"

"I'm sorry," Ani said lightly. "I don't mean to come in here from London, barking annoying questions at you that you've answered a thousand times before. It would just be really helpful to us."

The sudden look of vulnerability she affected had Joe mentally applauding her technique. Equally good was the subtle reminder of how far they'd traveled to talk to Klein.

As a package, it certainly flustered the professor.

"No . . . look, I'm sorry," Klein backtracked. "Look, of course I'll answer your questions. It's just that the topic of Imogen Bell is still a bit of a . . . sore point here."

Ani nodded her encouragement and left a silence for Klein to fill. She was raw and untrained, Joe thought, but she had a natural, easy way of guiding people. With a pheromone factory and some detection software, Joe guessed she'd be a force to be reckoned with.

"A promising astronomer, Imogen was a keen and, I thought, gifted addition to our team here. Her postdoctorate research subjects were SETI-related. When she wasn't searching through space looking for alien life, she was at the whiteboard trying to find a new equation to replace Drake's."

Joe had no idea what the professor was talking about, and was surprised when Ani started nodding agreement.

"It certainly needs replacing," she said, "though, of course, Drake's equation was never intended to be a method for estimating the number of alien civilizations in our galaxy. It was just supposed to provoke debate about the kinds of questions we need to be asking if we want to find those civilizations. That UFOlogists have used it as a *proof* of the existence of extraterrestrial life seems a little dishonest."

Joe watched the shock settle across Klein's face. He wondered if his own was betraying surprise, too.

Ani turned to Joe and winked.

She wasn't just good.

She was *ace*.

Ani was relieved that her short-term memory storage hadn't let her down.

She'd read about the Drake Equation on Wikipedia the night before because of a paper that Imogen Bell had put up on the net a few years ago. The essay had been dry and dull and Ani had only skimmed it, but it had a link to the Wiki entry on the equation, and she'd read that. The information had stuck with her.

Lucky, really.

Or maybe Gretchen's mental magic was rubbing off on her.

Whatever the explanation, it was worth it for the look on the professor's face.

Shocked disbelief. And a little bit of respect. More than he'd given her before, anyway.

"Yes," he said after a long pause. "Imogen thought it was time that humanity stopped looking at the question of *What will we do if we meet intelligent extraterrestrials?* and started focusing on *What will we do* when *we meet them?* For her there was no doubt. Intelligent life was out there, we just needed to find it. Her attitude started to strike me as increasingly unscientific, her ideas based entirely on faith. But a project like SETI needs single-minded individuals to put in the hours, so I kind of let it go. Especially when you see some of the types a project with ET at its center brings out of the woodwork. I'm sure you can guess.

"Anyway, Imogen certainly worked hard, that much can't be denied. I'd started to value her as a part of the team, but then the whole signal fiasco happened and it all went downhill really very fast."

"Ah, the signal from space." Ani made direct eye contact with the professor, which seemed to unnerve him a little, so she held it. "How do you explain—or account for—Dr. Bell's overreaction regarding the *message* she claimed to have received?"

Klein threw up his hands in something that looked close to surrender.

"Strain of work. The pressure to justify project budgets. Or a genuine mistake. I only have a *take-your-pick* kind of answer."

Ani noticed Joe narrowing his eyes in response to something Klein had said or done that she'd missed.

Which, to be honest, made her feel a little bit annoyed.

She thought she'd been doing so well.

She reviewed Klein's list of reasons again and, in the few

seconds it took, she noticed that he was starting to sweat. It looked like dew on an egg.

What are you suddenly nervous about, Professor Klein? she thought, then glanced over at Joe. The look they exchanged told her he wanted her to press Klein further.

With pleasure. Either he's hiding something, or he's scared. I want to know which.

"This 'message' that Dr. Bell supposedly intercepted, what form did it take?"

"Form?" Klein's eyes slipped left and right and Ani was sure that it was because he didn't want to meet her gaze any more. "What do you mean, 'form'?"

"I assume it was recorded? And it exists as some kind of digital file?" she pressed.

"There was a file . . ."

"Was?" Ani arched an eyebrow.

"It was a radio-telescope artifact, nothing more. A binary glitch . . ."

"But Imogen Bell thought it was something more?"

"She *wanted* to see more," Klein snapped. "It's called *confirmation bias*: people choose to pay attention to the information that supports their beliefs, and to discard that which contradicts them."

"So she detected a radio-telescopic glitch, but heard an alien message?" Ani asked.

"Exactly." Klein seemed pleased with himself. He even met her eye again.

Ani's memory flashed to another detail from Wikipedia and she thought it was worth a try. "Didn't the Arecibo telescope in Puerto Rico have a similar incident a few years back?"

Caterpillars knitted themselves together on a crinkled brow. "It's exceedingly likely—" Klein began, but Ani stopped him before he could complete the lie that she now *knew for certain* he was trying to pass off as truth.

"*Likely?*" Ani said, making her voice sound one respectful notch below actual mocking. "I find it hard to believe that you are unaware of a near-identical situation occurring at SETI's headquarters. One that, unless I am very much mistaken, was every bit as dramatic."

"Well, of course there have been other mistakes. . . ."

"Genuine mistakes that didn't end with the person reporting their observation having their reputation dragged through the media mud." She was surprised with the level of outrage she was actually feeling. But something here wasn't right. And Professor Klein knew more than he was telling them, she was sure. "So why the level of hysterical overreaction?"

Klein puffed himself up and his features settled into a look of cunning that was both unexpected and odd. "I'm not sure I appreciate the way this conversation is going," he said slyly, watchfully. "I cannot be held responsible for the way the media treated Imogen which, while shameful, was hardly within my power to control. . . ."

"If you're uncomfortable with the line of questioning

then I apologize," Ani said, "but the media would surely only respond to the information they were given. It seems to me that you hung her out to dry, let her take full responsibility for this supposed glitch. . . ."

"It's a fact," Klein retorted. "Unless you're implying that there actually *was* an alien transmission and that I'm covering it up while using Imogen Bell as a smoke screen."

He tutted and settled back in his chair, as if he thought that he had demonstrated the ridiculousness of the idea.

Ani simply changed her tactics.

"I honestly hadn't thought of that," she lied. "What an odd conclusion to draw from a few random questions."

This seemed to wrong-foot Klein and he stared down at the surface of his desk as if seeking answers amid the papers and computer equipment in front of him.

Joe stood up and pointed to the door. "Perhaps you could show me the security tapes of your other visitors now."

"Of course." Klein seemed pleased to escape Ani's questioning. "Follow me."

He stood up and Ani did, too, but Joe shook his head.

"Could you stay here and try to contact HQ?" he asked her in a voice that suggested he was telling her off, excluding her for making the professor uncomfortable. "See if they have any messages for us. You could ask if they want copies of the footage, for identification purposes."

Ani understood the instruction and the tone instantly. She nodded humble agreement and Joe turned to the professor and offered him an apologetic look. The relief on Klein's face was plain for them both to see.

She took out her phone and looked ready to make a call.

Klein led Joe out into the corridor and closed the door behind them.

Ani put the phone away and got to work.

Klein led the way to a small room that seemed pretty much an afterthought at the end of a long corridor. A person would have been excused for thinking it was a janitor's closet. The professor opened it with a keycard and ushered Joe inside. It was a tiny security station, three monitors showing eight camera viewpoints each—*twenty-four cameras? Seems excessive*—a couple of computers, and a bank of hard drives that would make up the digital vaults where the footage would be stored. What it was missing, Joe thought, was a security guard, or anyone to watch the monitors. There wasn't even a chair in the room.

"You sure *do* have a lot of cameras here," Joe said, trying to make it sound like he was impressed when really he was more than a little suspicious.

"We have a lot of very expensive equipment here," Klein said proudly. Joe was surprised that he felt the need to revisit his earlier comment. He wondered whether it was just absentmindedness on Klein's part, or an imagined need to bolster up the existing statement. "Now let me see . . ."

He pulled an iPad mini out of his jacket pocket and

tapped and swiped his way to an app and page that he needed.

"11:55 a.m," he muttered. "Three days ago . . ."

Klein leaned over one of the computers, pointed and clicked his way to a file, adjusted some parameters in a pop-up box, clicked again, and then stood back and pointed to the monitors.

All the screens were now showing recorded CCTV footage of the site from three days before. Each screen was time-stamped 11:54. Most of the screens were just showing scenery; only three had people on them: Professor Klein himself, sitting in his office, staring blankly at the wall; a young technician in a white coat monitoring a vast bank of computers in a sort of central hub; and another older man leafing through a bunch of printouts. It seemed a small number of personnel for such a large building, but Joe had to admit he really didn't know anything about radio astronomy. Maybe that was normal. He didn't have enough data to formulate an opinion either way.

Or did he?

"Three people to man this whole place?" he asked, pointing to the monitors. "Seems like a skeleton crew."

"Budget cuts mean we can only afford to have three permanent staff members."

"Dumb bean counters. Do you get any visiting astronomers?"

"Occasionally." Klein pointed to a screen that showed the gates of the Pabody/Reich complex. "Here they come."

A man got out of a BMW in front of the gates. The car matched what Ani had told them about the people who'd been chasing her. Joe noted the registration number, clocked that there was another man inside the car, and then received a welcome interruption.

"There are supposed to be between eight and twelve people working out of Pabody/Reich," Abernathy said. "And Klein's funding is on the rise, not falling. Plus, looking at the figures I have in front of me, the professor is burning a lot of energy. Electricity usage has gone up tenfold, and he has no problems paying for the extra. I wonder why he's lying to you, Joe."

"I wonder . . ." Joe said aloud and Klein gave him a strange look.

"I was wondering if it would be possible to zoom in on his face," Joe said, covering.

"No need. There'll be plenty of opportunities to get a better look at both of their faces."

They watched the gates open and the man get back in the BMW, then Joe shifted screens to watch them arrive at the front of the main building. They got out of the car and approached the door: two stocky men in their late twenties or early thirties, dressed in matching gray suits.

Joe moved on to the screen showing the feed from the

dome camera he'd spotted over the front door, where the vantage point was ideal. He watched the two men approach until they were close enough for him to get a really good look at them.

Ani had said that she thought they were freelancer operatives, and the way the men held themselves screamed army or ex-army—a near-identical straightness and stiffness in the way they carried their obviously well-developed upper bodies that he'd noticed in a lot of the soldiers he'd encountered, on both sides of the Atlantic. The suits looked pretty expensive, cleverly tailored to downplay each man's considerable physique, and looked way too high-end for a government budget.

He squinted at the screen at a bulge that showed under the left arm of one of the men as he lifted his right to rest it against one of the steel porch supports in front of the door. It stretched the material of his suit enough for Joe to make a couple of observations. First, the guy was wearing an underarm holster, and second, by the shape of the bulge it made, Joe thought it housed either a Glock 29 or a SIG Sauer P239. He looked a little closer and the guy moved again and Joe decided it was more likely the SIG, because the material had stretched tighter and outlined the pistol a little better. It had a longer grip than would appear on a Glock without some sort of customization.

If it had been the Glock, then maybe—and it was very much a long shot kind of *maybe*—it could have been a law enforcement agency issue weapon. Certain specialist firearms units in the metropolitan police carried Glocks. Joe knew that only too well because a plainclothes cop had pulled one on him during an undercover investigation: a gross misunderstanding that had almost gotten Joe killed and eventually led to the officer involved being disciplined.

The SIG, on the other hand, wasn't carried by any UK force or department that Joe was aware of, suggesting that it was the guy's weapon of choice, rather than one he'd been assigned.

Freelancers?

Joe found himself nodding in agreement with Ani's conclusion.

Clever girl, he thought. *I hope you're taking advantage of your time alone in Klein's office.*

There were a ton of hacking tools on the tablet that Abernathy had given her, but Ani didn't like the look of them and downloaded a set of her own from her Dropbox. While the tools were downloading, she checked to see how much space she'd have to copy Klein's files, and was shocked to find a terabyte's worth of solid-state hard drive. A lot of space for a tiny computer, but she was still going to have to be picky about what she saved to it.

With the tools downloaded and installed, it took about thirty seconds to crack the wireless protection key and three minutes to bypass the pretty meager security on the Pabody/Reich network.

But then the tablet was blazingly fast and her tools brutally efficient.

The network administrator, or more likely Klein, had committed the cardinal but very common mistake of making his password memorable by changing the complicated but reasonably secure alphanumeric one into something short, and by making it a single word. Ani's software—which she called Cid after a character in one of her favorite video game series—basically threw a dictionary at the network router, and kept at it until it found the right password or phrase. It always astonished her that people were still so sloppy protecting their computer networks. When you considered all the sensitive data that sat on people's computers, one would think that people would make an effort to protect it. Ani had found networks and systems that were still protected by the password "password," or "PASS01."

Klein's entire network security rested upon his belief that no one would try the word "perihelion."

Unfortunately for him, Ani had a feeling about Klein, and had specified that Cid throw words relating to astronomy at the network first.

Half a minute later, she was discovering that the computers on Klein's network were—theoretically—almost as easy to crack. Klein had granted himself access to all computers on-site, and he'd used the same password on all of them. But then Cid had floundered trying to find it and Ani, aware that time was very much of the essence, had called Gretchen.

"I'm trying to crack a network," Ani told her. "I need a password."

"Who and where?" Gretchen asked.

Ani told her.

"Hunting down Imogen Bell, huh? Why don't you try *jansky*."

"Jansky?"

"Karl Jansky, the father of radio astronomy."

Ani tried it. "Nope."

"Of course not. We're talking a place that searches for alien messages. Try *tesla*."

Ani typed the word in.

Access granted.

"You got it in two," Ani said admiringly. "Tesla?"

"Nikola Tesla," Gretchen explained. "A pioneer in electrical engineering, genius with OCD, and the first person to detect signals from space as a response to his own electrical stimuli. In 1899, actually."

"You are *so* amazing," Ani said. "Catch you soon! I've got secrets to rifle through."

"Seek and ye shall find," Gretchen said cheerily, and hung up.

Ani was just wondering where to start looking when suddenly a window opened up on the screen of the tablet computer: a stylized photo of Abernathy that made him look like he'd been painted by Van Gogh, along with a rudimentary chat box.

>You're in, Abernathy typed.

>Yep, Ani replied, once more impressed by the tech that Abernathy had at his disposal.

>Wondering what to steal?

>Any pointers?

>Let's grab it all. Icon on your home
 screen—the Starship *Enterprise* from
 Star Trek. Open it.

Ani did as she was instructed, even though having the *Enterprise* for a hacking tool was so nerdy that even *she* inwardly groaned. The groan became audible when tapping on the icon made the noise of a *Star Trek* communicator. A window opened up showing what looked like a rotating wormhole in space. It was followed by a dialogue box that featured Leonard Nimoy as Spock in 8-bit graphic form. A couple of seconds of waiting brought up the query:

Wireless network detected: PabReich17c5
Computer detected: Kleino1
Mount drive? YES   NO

Ani smiled and tapped YES. Klein's computer appeared as an icon next to the wormhole.

"That's pretty cool," she said to herself.

>Drag drive into the warp, the program instructed, so she did as she was told, picking up the drive icon with her finger and sending it into the center of the wormhole. There was a whoosh and then the drive icon shattered into thousands of pieces that were sucked into the wormhole.

She went back to the chat box.

>Is that doing what I think it's
doing? she typed.

>It's sending us everything on the
entire network at pretty much the
speed of light. Was that what you
were thinking?

Ani shook her head in admiration.

>Looks like hackers like me are
redundant.

There was a pause, and then Abernathy typed back.

>There are few hackers like you. With
our help you will be legendary.

Ani waited as every piece of information on Klein's entire network was copied to the servers at YETI HQ.

If I get out of this alive and with my mind intact, she thought, *then I am* definitely *taking Abernathy up on the job offer.*

The two men in suits, once inside the observatory's main building, systematically ran rings around Klein. For Joe it was almost embarrassing to watch. Klein, viewing the footage for the first time, must have felt like a prizewinning fool. Swapping his attention from screen to screen, Joe watched as the men took turns distracting Klein while the other got up to various flavors of no good.

He saw the first guy—the one with the SIG—point to a security camera as the other picked Klein's pocket for his keycard. Then the first guy kept Klein talking while the second cloned the card with a pocket-sized skimmer before slipping the original back in the pocket it had come from. In the office, the second guy buddied up to Klein while guy number one put some kind of device underneath the desk. Then guy number two got directions to the bathroom and, instead of heading for them, used the keycard on a succession of doors and took photographs of documents, copied files onto a credit-card-sized hard drive, and generally snooped around while Klein and guy number one traded jokes.

Watching it all played back in front of him, Klein went through the ascending order of behaviors that led, pretty inevitably, to anger. First he wrinkled his nose in incomprehension, and then, as it became apparent what the men were up to, his brow creased and his cheeks started burning red. Observing guy number one planting something under the desk reversed the last phase, and Klein's face drained of color. Seeing guy number two with free run of the facility, using a cloned version of his own keycard, made Klein's hands tighten into rigid claws at his side. As Klein watched the guy stealing information, Joe thought he could actually hear the professor grinding his teeth together.

"What do you think they were looking for?" Joe asked, careful not to mention how easily Klein had been duped. Joe needed the professor to feel like Joe was on his side.

Klein shook his head. Suddenly, he didn't look like the confident, almost arrogant man that had let them into the observatory. Now he seemed like a spoiled kid having a temper tantrum over not being allowed an ice cream.

"We're an observatory," he said sharply. "We're hardly MI5."

"They certainly seemed like they were interested in something," Joe prompted, adding some *encourage* into the mix. "And they had the technology and skills to hunt it down."

Klein looked genuinely baffled. "We search through space looking for things that will help humankind understand its place in the universe," he said. It sounded like a prepared speech. "And we use what we find to help generate theories to explain how everything in the universe got where it is. We don't actually have any secrets. We're scientists. Everything we discover is available on the internet."

"Do you think it could be connected with Imogen Bell?"

"How could it be? *Why* would it be?"

"It's why *we're* here."

Klein looked at Joe with suspicion. "Yes, why is that again?"

Joe watched the men leave on-screen, shaking hands with Klein before getting back into their car and driving off.

"Imogen Bell believed that she had intercepted a message from outer space. I think that perhaps other people believe that, too."

Anger and suspicion turned to scorn, and Klein even let out a single note of derisive laughter. "Well, they're as crazy as she is. Is that why *you're* here? Chasing little green men? My goodness, I hope my taxes are being spent better than financing science fiction nonsense."

Joe gave him a puzzled look. "Isn't a large part of what you do here tied to SETI?" he asked.

"Not a large part, no," Klein said. "We *do* get some serious science done here as well, you know."

"But nothing worth dispatching two mercenaries to rifle through your files and hard drives?"

"Mercenaries?"

"That's what those guys looked like to me."

"Okay, maybe they weren't government agents, but isn't it more likely they were tabloid journalists trying to plaster some more embarrassing stories across the hysterical front pages of their gossip rags?"

"Unless journalists have started packing heat, I think that's pretty unlikely."

"Weapons?" Klein roared. "What are you talking about?"

"Automatic pistols in shoulder holsters. Why don't you copy over the footage of those two men onto my colleague's computer and start telling me everything you can about Imogen Bell?"

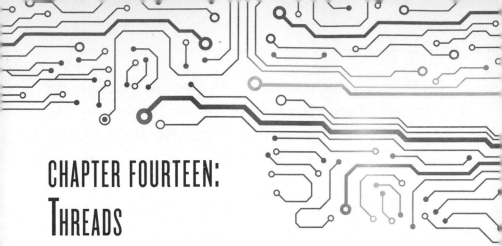

CHAPTER FOURTEEN:
THREADS

By the time Joe and Klein returned, Ani was already done uploading terabytes of information to Abernathy's data-hungry computers.

The speed with which it had happened was staggering.

Frightening, even.

Sending data from one computer to another over a hundred and fifty miles away at a rate that was simply breathtaking. There was no commercial tech available that could transfer data that fast. Nothing she'd even *heard of* like that in development. Whoever was making the tech for Abernathy and YETI was someone that Ani really wanted to meet.

She'd even had time to mess around on the tablet—more wonders to discover!—and then sign in and check her email.

Her heart started pounding when she saw one from JMcV—Jack "Black Hat" McVitie, the missing hacker who had started her on this crazy trail—with the subject line **HELP!**

She was about to tap on it to read the message when the door opened and Klein followed Joe into the room. Joe was calm and poised, but Klein was in a terrible mood. His face was all blotchy and his eyes were practically bugging out of his head.

"This is insane," Klein insisted forcefully, as if simply saying a thing loudly and firmly enough made it true. "Absolute insanity. Imogen Bell was mistaken. The harm she did to this institution is incalculable! She made Pabody/ Reich a laughingstock by jumping the gun . . ."

Joe gave Ani a despairing look, then surveyed Klein with an icy glare.

"So what *was* this message from space, exactly?" Joe asked, then seemed to remember something, and moved toward Klein's desk. He felt around underneath it, bringing out a black device and putting his finger to his lips. He showed it to Ani, then Klein, then crossed the room, exited, and returned a few seconds later, empty-handed.

"Can't be too careful," he said, closing the door. "Someone might have been listening in."

"Do you know how insane that sounds?" Klein protested. "This is a radio telescope setup!"

"So you keep telling me," Joe said. "The message?"

Klein made a *hmmmph* sound before going over to his computer, tapping the keyboard, and clicking his mouse. There was a crackle from his computer speakers.

Ani went cold. Fear hammered at her. He was about to

play the .wav file, the terrible sound that had almost invaded her mind twice already!

Her hands were halfway up to her ears to try to block the sound when suddenly she stopped.

Puzzled, she sat there, staring at Klein and trying to figure out what was going on.

The noise coming from Klein's computer was the sound of static, with occasional *bleeps* and *bloops* and then a strange high-pitched *eeeeeeeeeeeeeeeee*. The whole thing lasted about twenty seconds, and she knew that she had never heard the sounds before.

It certainly wasn't the .wav file.

"That's the message that Imogen Bell thought proved intelligent life was trying to contact us?" Ani asked, trying to keep the disbelief—and, something that surprised her, *disappointment*—out of her voice.

"You were expecting a greeting in the Queen's English?" he said sarcastically.

Klein was lying. She didn't know exactly how she knew it, or what it was about the man's demeanor that made her so certain, but he knew more than he was saying.

That wasn't the message that Imogen Bell recorded, but that was *the message that got sent out to all the other observatories across the world. That was the message that made her a laughingstock.*

"Were you here the night that Dr. Bell thought she'd found proof of extraterrestrial life?" Ani asked.

Klein looked at her oddly. "Of course. I practically *live* here. This is my life—"

"Did you *hear* what she thought was a message *before* she sent it to everyone and started the process that ruined her reputation?" Ani asked, cutting him off.

"Of course . . . that is, no . . . I mean . . ." Klein was too flustered to put together a coherent sentence. Ani was shocked that he honestly, bafflingly, hadn't figured on anyone asking that simple question. Which meant, of course, that he was completely unprepared for it, and his burbling contradictions said a lot more than his words ever could.

Gotcha.

Within a couple of seconds he had recovered his composure, but by then, Ani didn't believe anything that came out of his mouth.

"She sent it worldwide without me hearing it," Klein said with all the certainty Ani expected from a reasonably good liar. "Left me out of the loop. She must have wanted the glory, but was unprepared for the resulting humiliation."

Ani realized that Joe was studying her intently. She thought that the expression she detected on his face was approval. It gave her the courage to try something extreme.

She connected the tablet to SpeediShare, downloaded the .wav file to the home screen, gestured for Joe to cover his ears, turned up the volume as high as it would go, opened the file, and stuck her fingers in her ears.

ooo

Joe watched Ani deal with Klein and knew that she was going to make a great addition to the YETI ranks. Hacker skills notwithstanding, there was a calm, focused quality to her that reminded him a lot of Andy. That reminded him of himself. It was a quality that he and Andy had been taught, that had come only after months and months of training and simulations. Ani, with only natural talent and raw instincts, had cut through to the heart of things with a couple of questions and, Joe was sure, had managed to show Klein up as the liar he was. He was hiding something, that much was obvious. And it was all tied up with the .wav file that Jack had found.

Joe was pretty certain that the sound that Klein had played them was *not* the sound Ani had been expecting, which meant it wasn't the sound that lay at the dark heart of X-Core. Which also meant that either they were wrong about the .wav file being the same as the one that Imogen Bell had recorded from space, or that Klein had somehow switched out the file transmitted to other observatories around the world for analysis.

But why?

Why would Klein send out the *wrong* file?

Unless . . .

Unless . . .

Ani gestured for Joe to cover his ears and he realized that she was about to play the *real* sound file. He nodded his approval—Klein's reaction might tell them all they needed to know—but he didn't think Ani saw. She was too busy.

Joe covered his ears, Ani covered hers, and the .wav file played.

Ani had thought that Klein's face would tell her the truth— that his expression would show that he recognized the sound. In that instant, she reasoned, he would give himself away.

And yes, Klein gave himself away all right.

It just wasn't in the way she'd thought.

But then it was like nothing she could have imagined.

When the .wav started, Klein's body seemed to seize up. He was turning his head toward the source of the sound and then suddenly stopped dead, jerked back to how he had been positioned a couple of seconds before, moved again, stopped dead, and jerked back again. He was stuck in a kind of physical loop, repeating and re-repeating the same tiny action. The sight was so strange, so unexpected, that Ani could do little more than stare at him. It was as if Klein were an automaton and the clockwork mechanism that powered him had slipped a cog and become stuck.

He didn't so much as blink, nor did he seem to real-ize that he *was* stuck. The expression on his face did not change.

The .wav played on and Ani realized that she could hear it, although this time it sounded like the first time at

Uncle Alex's; there was less electricity threading through the experience, and the *"OBEY!"* command was missing. She jammed her fingers into her ears and opened her jaw to increase her ear canal pressure, like she'd done on the only plane trip she'd ever taken—to Spain a couple of years ago—and it shut out most of the sound. She was relieved to find that she couldn't hear enough of it for the *soundforms* to try, once again, to invade her mind.

She continued, fascinated and chilled, to watch Klein, all the time wondering what was actually happening to him. She leaned in a little for a closer look and that was the precise moment that Klein broke out of the loop and suddenly lifted his head, causing her to recoil. His eyes rolled back, showing all whites. His hands twitched into rigid claws at his sides.

And.

Then.

Suddenly.

It.

Happened.

At first she thought that it was because she was tired, and maybe her brain was trying to tell her so. Then she thought maybe it was a trick of the light, or a trick that her eyes were playing on her brain. Because, right in front of her, Klein suddenly went fuzzy, like he'd been encircled in the kind of heat haze you saw on roads on really hot days. His edges seemed to blur, to lose definition, and Ani made herself blink to try to clear the effect. It didn't work. It only seemed to make the man's edges blurrier.

She dragged her eyes away and looked at Joe, who was staring at Klein with what looked like disbelief. It made her feel a tiny bit better that he could see it, too, but then she thought, *He's a trained government spy and even* he *doesn't know what's happening*, and she felt even more scared. When she turned her eyes back to Klein, she thought that she'd lost her mind.

Professor Klein was no longer human.

Or, at least, he was no longer *just* human.

Over the entire length of his body, Ani could see an unearthly, hazy disturbance; a pattern of interference that made him look like he was covered with a dark, grainy texture—almost as if another layer had been superimposed over him in an image-editing program. The "layer" looked like it was made up of a grayish sandlike substance, and it was in constant, flowing motion, as if the particles were shifting across Klein's body. He was completely enveloped in the stuff—*or made of it?* Ani thought grimly—and it made her think of the sculptures she'd seen on beaches, where people built incredibly detailed models out of sand.

As she watched, another layer was added to Klein and it nearly made her throw up. Neon splashes wormed their way across the gray sand, looking too much like those awful *soundforms* for Ani to bear. Her instinctual horror of the wormlike shapes was calmed only slightly by the wonder of seeing them in the real world instead of inside her own head. They writhed and swirled across Klein, sinking through the sand texture, only to emerge again fatter and more defined.

Neon worms, she thought. *He's covered in neon worms.*

That was *almost exactly* what they looked like, but she didn't know if that was just her mind's desperate need to make sense of the shapes.

She felt the air in the room changing, becoming charged. There was a harsh electrical smell and she could taste it in her mouth, like she was licking a battery. Her scalp prickled and the hair on her arms started to stand up. Her mouth felt dry. Her eyes started to hurt.

The *soundforms* continued to crawl across Klein's body, more and more of them every passing second. She saw a fat worm of light enter Klein's mouth and exit through one of his eyes and it was so horrible and unexpected that she forced her right hand to move, slowly, away from her ear and toward the tablet in her lap. The sound of the .wav file was louder, not just because she had taken a finger out of her ear, but as if the tones had been picked up by Klein's body and were resonating through it, amplified and purified into a wall of noise—high-pitched, low-pitched, and every pitch in between—and when she saw the *soundforms* in her mind's eye, she knew that she was running out of time.

She willed her hand to travel faster, but it was like moving through molasses. *Soundforms* danced inside her, hungry for her sanity.

With a supreme effort she reached the tablet screen and closed the file, just as the *soundforms* began to change the structure of Klein's body entirely. As the sound died, Ani had a momentary glimpse of what the .wav file had been trying to do to Klein's physical form.

She saw his arms start to elongate, stretching and curling until they were like the whip tentacles of a giant squid, but made of a gaseous, foggy substance that was partially transparent. Through the clear surface she could see the *soundforms* passing back and forth like a new circulatory system that was pumping sound around his body instead of blood. His head seemed to bloat, also transparent, and the *soundforms* were gathering in the area of his skull that should surely contain his brain, wrapping themselves around each other, dissolving into a throbbing mass.

Klein's eyes stretched, grew longer, then divided like cells reproducing, then divided again and again and again until the front of his now-ovoid head was covered in them. But they were not like eyes she was used to seeing. These were perfect spheres barely connected to the face itself, and they pushed against each other like soap bubbles, so many . . . so many . . .

She got the feeling again that her mind was just trying so hard to understand the visual information it was receiving, it was simply picking things that were *close enough* for her to interpret what they were, rather than showing them exactly as they were. Klein's body seemed to suddenly flip inward, feeding back into itself like water flowing through a plug hole, or a black hole dragging matter inside it, and then . . .

. . . and then it was over.

Klein was just Klein.

No sand, no worms, no soap bubble eyes. Just a man.

The worms inside her own head disappeared.

The static charge in the air was dispelled.

Klein snapped back to his previous position and his head turned to face the source that the .wav had come from.

"She didn't follow protocol," he said, continuing on from his last statement, as if nothing out of the ordinary had just happened.

Ani looked down at the .wav file on the tablet screen and felt a tremendous sense of unreality wash over her.

What she had just seen had no place on this planet, she was sure of that.

Whatever was contained within that sound file was not from Earth.

It was something that Imogen Bell had found in outer space and—completely unknowingly—had dragged down to this planet by recording it as a sound file. Ani didn't know what it was, or where it was from. She didn't know what it wanted, or how many other people—like Klein—were carrying it around inside of them.

But she did know something.

It was alien—utterly, unbelievably alien—and Ani was certain that it was no longer content to remain trapped as a sound file on a computer hard drive.

Joe and Ani managed to hold things together just long enough to say their good-byes, thank Klein for his time, and get out of the observatory and into the night air. All the way to the door Joe was expecting Klein to change form again and prevent them from leaving, but the professor had just led them to the exit and shut the door behind them.

They tried to make it to the SUV before what had just happened hit them full force.

They failed.

They took about three strides and then looked at each other in a mixture of terror and awe.

Joe tried to speak, but it all came out in a torrent, muddled up and disjointed. "Did you see . . . ? I never . . . it was horrib . . . his head . . . I mean, what was that? . . . You did see it, right?"

He watched Ani as she tried to speak, but words failed her.

For a few moments back there, Joe had thought that he had been hallucinating, that his chip was malfunctioning, and that what he had thought he had seen Klein suddenly turn into was not really what had happened. Then he'd seen Ani's terrified face.

They had just witnessed the effects that the sound file from space could have on the human body; they had seen Klein *change*, before their very eyes, into something that had no place outside of a nightmare. Klein not realizing they'd seen the change, Joe was certain, was all that had saved them. If he *had* known, then maybe he would have had no choice but to prevent them from leaving so they couldn't tell anyone else.

A lucky break.

And thank heavens for it.

Finally Ani managed to get out the rush of words that had been twisted inside her mouth. "His . . . he was . . . he's not . . . what just happened? Did we just see an alien? I mean, Joe, seriously, tell me that we did not just see an alien back there!"

Joe shook his head.

"I don't know what we just saw. Abernathy?"

There was a moment when Joe was sure that his handler wasn't there, that he and Ani were on their own, but then the voice appeared in his head.

"What just happened, Joe?" Abernathy asked.

"You need to get a team down here stat, and you need to secure this facility. We need an armed team, we need scientists. . . . Abernathy, the guy in charge of Pabody/Reich is a bloody alien!"

"An alien, Joe?" Abernathy couldn't keep the disbelief out of his voice.

Joe understood Abernathy's doubts, but really didn't have time for them. Joe could hardly believe it himself, but the evidence of his senses was going to have to be enough if they were going to prevent what suddenly looked like it could be an alien invasion.

"Look, I know how it sounds," he barked. "Ani and I just saw Professor Klein turn into something that cannot, by any stretch of the imagination, be classified as human. He responded to the .wav file. It changed him. You need to get down here and find out what he is, because from where we're standing 'alien' is the only word that fits."

"Team's on its way. Are you both all right?"

"We're fine," Joe said. "I think we should stay in case that . . . thing decides to leave."

"Negative on that," Abernathy responded. "We need you back at HQ. Both of you. I thought I heard Klein saying he practically lives at the telescope. If that's true, he'll be there when we get a squad to your location."

"Any other news?" Joe asked.

"You told us to pick up some test subjects from the Warhouse, so we did. It was nothing like you reported in, just some kids at a concert, but we invented probable cause and scooped some off the street outside, brought 'em back here, and are currently experimenting. Should have preliminary reports waiting for you when you get back. I've also got the Shuttleworths throwing every test they can think of at Ani's .wav file. Again, I should have more for you when you return."

"Okay, boss," Joe said. "Might be worth blasting the .wav file at the kids you scooped up, just so you can see what we're dealing with here. Anyway, we're heading home."

There was a pause and then Abernathy came back, concern and resignation in his voice. "I don't know, Joe. This might have just gotten to be a little too big for us now. There's no shame in admitting that things have grown out of our remit. It might be time to hand the investigation over . . ."

"Call in whoever you need to, but we're not backing away from this. No way."

"As soon as I call the people I have to call, this will probably get taken out of my hands, anyway. They'll tell me that this was not why YETI was formed, and remind me that my operatives are all children who are hardly prepared to start defending the Earth from extraterrestrial threats."

"And you will inform them, politely but firmly, that an organization of kids is *exactly* what is needed. We fight aliens every day on our laptops and PS4s, and if anyone is more knowledgeable about extraterrestrial threats than a bunch of kids raised on a diet of science fiction movies, comic books, and cartoons, then I'd like to meet them. You've got government favors owed to you. It might be time to cash 'em in."

Abernathy laughed, a dry chuckle, but a laugh all the same.

"I'll see what I can do. I suspect it might be wise to wait a little while before I make any calls, and give us a chance to have something more substantial to tell them than 'the aliens are here!'"

They got in the SUV, and Joe spent a couple of minutes organizing his thoughts before he started it up, gunned the engine, and headed back toward London.

They shared almost hysterical re-creations of what they had seen at the observatory. The conversation had flowed along through disbelief, terror, awe, more terror, and then right on back to disbelief again. The human mind hadn't evolved to deal with stuff like that. It had evolved to process a hairless ape's progress through a complex, textured world, at medium speed, and to instill hunter/gatherer skills.

When faced with the truly terrifying, it tended to shrivel and hide.

Eventually, they fell silent while Joe concentrated on getting them back to London in the right number of pieces. He used the time to try to put what they had experienced into some logical, comprehensible order. It was like doing a jigsaw puzzle with an unknown number of missing pieces, no picture on the box, some of the pieces three-dimensional, and others that kept hiding.

In the end, he gave up and just tried to make his mind

stop racing. Ani played with the tablet computer, occasionally getting excited over some new feature—the battery life of the device initiated a ten minute mini-lecture on comparative battery studies—and Joe felt glad just to have her beside him.

Suddenly, Ani slapped her forehead with the palm of her hand.

"Are you okay there?" Joe asked.

"Apart from being an idiot, fine I guess. Back before Klein turned into whatever that was, I'd just gotten an email from a hacker friend. The one who went missing after sending me the .wav file."

"It's not really surprising it slipped your mind. What's it say?"

Ani stabbed and prodded at the tablet's screen and then said. "The subject line is *Help*; I can't imagine it's going to be good news."

"Read it out loud."

"'Ani. Gone dark because they're after me. Keep that file safe. Meet me tomorrow, outside Benedict's Place. Two p.m. Urgent. JM.'"

"Sounds like we caught a break. We'll have to make that meet tomorrow."

"I don't know London. And I definitely don't know where Benedict's Place is."

"Search it."

Ani did.

"Nothing comes up. And Jack McVitie is as paranoid as they come. He believes that there's an internationally-run project, ECHELON, that monitors all emails, phone calls, and other forms of communication, scanning for keywords. When Edward Snowden blew the whistle on PRISM, Jack's fears that the NSA and GCHQ listened in on just about everything only grew. Jack wouldn't put an address in an email."

"You do know that PRISM and ECHELON are just the distracting tips of the real iceberg? Information leaked out to cover the real systems that *are* analyzing *every* piece of information transferred across the globe, with thinking software that makes commercial AI seem like 10 print 'I'm thinking'; 20 goto 10."

"Abernathy *did* inform me, yes."

"So, where are you supposed to meet him?" Joe asked, baffled.

"It must be a code. Maybe if I wasn't so tired, I'd even see it. Hang on, that's weird . . ."

"What?"

"He signed the email 'JM.' He always just signs 'J.'"

"Is it significant?"

"It's the key to the code." Ani was silent for a couple of minutes. Then she looked up and smiled. "Nerd."

"Excuse me?"

Ani chuckled.

"Jack's a nerd. And I know that he's obsessed with Sherlock Holmes. It's something we have in common. Benedict is Benedict Cumberbatch. JM is Jim—James—Moriarty."

"So we just need to find out where Benedict Cumberbatch lives?"

Ani shook her head.

"Nothing that complicated. Benedict plays Sherlock. Sherlock lives at . . . ?"

Joe nodded. One of the most famous—if not *the* most famous—fictional addresses in the world. "Smart," he said. "But I didn't think 221B Baker Street was a real address."

"Well, when Conan Doyle wrote the original stories, Baker Street didn't go up to 221, but the city expanded, and now it does. The Abbey National Building Society took up 219 to 229 for a long time, but the Sherlock Holmes Museum—even though it actually sits between 237 and 241—is now, officially, 221B."

"And you called Jack a nerd?"

"I even know how many steps there are on the staircase to Sherlock's rooms."

"You're joking."

"Seventeen."

Joe shook his head. "I don't know how many steps there are on the staircase to *my* room." A thought occurred to him. "Hacker Jack, he listened to the .wav file, didn't he?"

"Yeah. That's how he knew it phoned home."

"That's what I thought." Joe sniffed. "So why didn't the .wav file affect him?"

Ani was silent for a while as she thought it through. He could almost hear the whirr.

"You said that you listened to it at Lennie Palgrave's place. Why didn't it affect *you*? Maybe we're talking about a sound quality, or volume thing. I've only listened to that sound through excellent equipment, and its effects were immediate. But why would there need to be more than one X-Core song? Maybe most people listen to it in MP3 form— compressed, less dangerous. Then it becomes a cumulative effect, getting people more and more into the sound until they go see a X-Core band live . . ."

Joe nodded. "Makes sense. But Jack listened to the uncompressed .wav version. So I ask again, why wasn't he affected?"

Ani had no answer.

They were coming to the end of the long journey back when Joe's phone started trilling. He answered it through the SUV's Bluetooth and was surprised to hear the clipped and careful voice of Victor Palgrave.

"Joe," Palgrave said with a practiced PR warmth that faded right after the first word. "I was just wondering how things were going. Are you making any progress in the hunt for my son?"

"We haven't found him yet, but we're busy chasing down leads. You know how it is. You gotta put in the shoe leather. Have you heard from him?"

There was a short silence.

"No," Palgrave replied. "And we are . . . that is Jenifer and I . . . are worried sick. Could I ask what kind of leads you have?"

Joe knew the guy, liked his son a lot, and didn't get calls from government ministers all that often, but he wasn't about to give away operational details, even if it was to a rising political star. He tried to deflect the question by asking some of his own. It was like a reflex action.

"I know this is probably going over old ground, but do you happen to know any of Lennie's X-Core friends? A name, maybe? A place that he used to meet them? Any detail that can help us pin him down . . ."

"I'm afraid not," Palgrave said. "I haven't paid as close attention to my boy as I should have. If I had listened . . ."

He left a space for Joe to add some phony-baloney reassurance that it wasn't Palgrave's fault, but Joe was too wired and exhausted to play that kind of game. If Palgrave needed absolution, maybe he should try a priest.

"Like I said, we're doing the best we can. We're just short on leads. . . ."

"So he wasn't involved with the whole Brixton debacle?" Palgrave shot back. The comment caught Joe off guard, but then he realized that a power player like Palgrave would have his fingertips on the pulse of every piece of news flowing through Whitehall's circulatory system. Still, for some reason it got Joe's back up.

"I haven't heard yet," he said, his tone clipped. "Has Abernathy been keeping you briefed?"

"I get reports." Palgrave sounded like he didn't think he received *enough* reports. "This is my son we're talking about here. I need to know that he's okay."

"I haven't heard anything to make me think he's not okay. Look, I'll be back at HQ soon. How about I find out where we're at as a team and then I'll call you?"

"Where are you now?" Palgrave asked, a little too eagerly.

"Coming back from something that turned out to be a dead end," Joe lied.

There was another moment of silence.

"Is that the dead end that has armed units converging on Shrewsbury as we speak?" There was a steely reproach in Palgrave's voice that made Joe feel like a naughty schoolboy who'd just been caught vandalizing a desk.

"I can't discuss mission critical information without Abernathy's say-so, Mr. Palgrave. We have a chain of command, just as I'm sure you do. If you want to find out what the weather's like up top, ask the head, not the feet."

"I was hoping that 'the feet' would be more willing to give me a straight answer."

Ani was looking at Joe with an odd expression on her face. He raised an eyebrow and she mouthed "Victor

Palgrave?" at him, silently stressing the first name. Joe nodded and Ani looked stunned. Joe just grinned back.

"Just so there are no misunderstandings, I feel I should point out that Lennie is only part of the problem we're looking into. He's my friend, and that gives me an added incentive, but I can't discuss an ongoing case with you, no matter how well we know each other or how high up in the government hierarchy you might be."

There was a long silence on the other end of the phone, and then Victor Palgrave let out a sigh. "I'm sorry, Joe. I didn't mean to come across all heavy-handed, putting you in a difficult position. I'm just very, very worried."

"I understand. Give Abernathy a call. He's got the big picture, while I can only see small details."

"Thank you, Joe."

"My pleasure."

"Bye."

Joe switched off the speakerphone and looked at the road ahead. Something about that call just didn't feel right to him. Sure, he was probably being paranoid, but he didn't like the way that Palgrave had deliberately set him up to catch him in a lie. Nor did he like the way he'd seemed to know so much about the case.

"You know Victor Palgrave?" Ani asked. "The MP? Personally?"

"I went to school with his son," Joe said. "Now he's caught up in the X-Core scene. He's probably hiding one of those . . . *things* inside him like Professor Klein was. How do I tell his father that?"

"If you want my opinion, Palgrave didn't call you for an update on the case. It sounded to me that he already knows everything that's going on. Which makes me wonder what that call was *really* all about." Ani got out the tablet and started tapping the screen.

Joe thought it over. They were both probably right. Palgrave *had* come in to the conversation pretending to know nothing, but he'd known just about everything, which was an odd way to conduct a call.

Which meant . . . ?

Which meant . . . what, exactly?

Ani continued to play with the tablet and Joe wondered what she was up to. Probably checking her emails or hacking into the Pentagon's mainframe. The hacker bit of her *sort of* made sense, but Joe wondered if it was truly about digital freedom, or if she just liked causing mischief. He thought it was probably the former, but to see someone so absorbed in technology made him feel a little uneasy.

He could use computers but preferred not to let them take over his life. To step into a world of trivial, unimportant, time-devouring nonsense, where people chatted to "friends" who weren't really friends, and logged the minutiae of their lives on social networking sites as if the world really cared about where they were eating out, or how many kittens their cat had just had. Joe was deeply suspicious of people who spent too much time on the web, mainly because it took away time they could be spending doing *real world* things. An interaction over the net was dubious. It required you to believe that the identities of the people you were chatting with were, indeed, the identities outlined in their profiles. Joe liked face-to-face conversations where you could see that the girl you were talking to really wasn't a fifty-year-old construction worker from Bolton. Or Baton Rouge.

"Give me your number," Ani said.

"Huh?"

"Your cell phone number."

Joe did and Ani input it into the tablet. Then she spent a few minutes in silence, scrolling through pages of something that looked highly technical. Finally she cursed.

Joe turned to see her face was sculpted out of anger and indignation.

"What?" Joe asked her.

She shook her head. "So, I was thinking, what was the *real* purpose of that telephone call from Victor Palgrave? He got no new information, except perhaps that it was you who called for the team to secure the Pabody/Reich facility. But apart from that? Zilch. And he must have known that you wouldn't give out information on the operation. So the question was nagging at me: *Why did he make that call?*"

"And?"

"And I hacked into the local cell towers, the ones that

would have dealt with the call. Abernathy provided us with the software to hack pretty much anywhere, so we could steal Klein's entire computer network, and I just needed to tweak a couple of parameters and add a few lines of my own code, and suddenly I'm seeing the cell traffic data for a few miles around. Bang in your number and I can suddenly see your phone. It's still connected to Palgrave."

"It isn't. I hung up."

But he checked the phone anyway to make sure.

Nope.

"I know," Ani said. "But looking at the data log from the 4G connection I can see that you downloaded about 300K of data while talking to Palgrave."

"I don't understand . . ."

"I know, but don't sweat it." She swiped through another couple of pages of data. "Check your GPS."

Joe went to his home screen and checked for the compass icon that told him the global positioning satellite software was running.

It was.

"And that, Joe Dyson, is how Victor Palgrave is now tracking us. He sent you a piece of code that has forced your GPS to squeal on us, turned it into a digital informer. Right now, it's shouting out our location, and I figure we have company mobilizing to head us off before we get back to YETI HQ."

Joe felt sick. It was just so unreal. What possible reason could Victor Palgrave have for doing such a thing? For betraying his trust so blatantly?

"You hearing this, Abernathy?" Joe suddenly needed to hear his handler's voice to reassure him, to tell him what they should do.

But he just heard silence.

Joe felt cold and alone and more terrified than he'd felt for a long, long time.

Abernathy picked up the phone and barked, "Where are we with the kids from the Warhouse?"

Dr. Emari Ghoti, the sharpest medical mind in the building, told him how little they'd figured out so far, and how they hadn't had time to even *begin* investigating what was going on with them, and Abernathy was ruder and harsher than he meant to be before slamming the phone back into its cradle.

He felt guilty immediately, but the frustration was becoming unbearable. He liked to be in control, to know exactly what was going on all the time. Having stray variables floating around just made him angry.

The truth was, he didn't like it.

Any of it.

Not one bit.

He'd sent Joe and Ani out into who knows what at the radio telescope and he knew it was pretty much dumb luck that had gotten them out of there in one piece. Then they'd reported their findings and his whole worldview threatened to shatter like toffee under a hammer.

Aliens?

Really?

Standard procedure for the outlandish claims they'd made meant he should be calling the pair of them in for psych evaluations. It sounded like a *folie à deux*—a shared madness transmitted from one person to another—but Abernathy knew Joe better than that. He was levelheaded and utterly dependable. Whatever Joe said, no matter how unlikely it might sound, had to be the truth.

Except . . .

Abernathy sighed.

Except, Joe had been off active duty since Andy was shot, and he was now taking this whole case personally because Lennie Palgrave was involved. Had he misjudged Joe's readiness for duty? Had he missed obvious warning signs in his desire to get Joe back into the field?

Without corroboration, Joe's claims certainly sounded like madness. Klein, an alien? Sound files from outer space?

But what if he's right? What if it's all true?

Abernathy struck his desk with his fist and then stood up, crossed the room, threw open his door, and yelled out into the control center, "Can anybody tell me *anything*?"

The analysts jerked around like they'd had an electric current passed through their seats and they made assurances that as soon as they had more information he would be the first to know.

He nodded curtly, and turned to go back to his desk.

And stopped.

The chip in his arm—the one that opened doors and monitored a few critical systems around YETI HQ—was vibrating.

And Abernathy knew, all too well, what that meant.

The piercing sound of the alarm that tore through the air confirmed it.

YETI had been breached.

Proximity sensors had detected the presence of unauthorized people entering the building. There was very little time.

"Evacuation protocols!" Abernathy shouted above the squeal of the alarm. *"Get out!"*

The procedure had been timed to perfection in drills that the YETI personnel had grudgingly performed, but this was the first time that it had been needed as a matter of urgency. Still, Abernathy was glad to see the speed and efficiency with which his staff grabbed laptops and hard drives and made for his office. Abernathy went to his desk, pushed the button he'd thought he'd never have to use outside of the emergency drills, and opened up the escape route in his back wall.

As he ushered people into the stairwell that led down

from the secret exit, which appeared on no plans or schematics of the building, he reflected that paranoia and being overcautious were really valid forms of self-preservation. He waited until the Shuttleworth brothers, carrying flight cases, made their way across the control center and into his office before activating the lockout protocol on his office door. As he input the last digit of the code into the console on his wall, he saw the first wave of intruders making it through into the control center.

Four figures clad head to toe in assault outfits with gas masks and goggles and very big guns gazed around the empty room in bewilderment, their weapons following their lines of sight. Abernathy kept the door open a crack and saw another five men, all dressed the same, enter the room.

He shut the door, heard the deadbolt fall into place, and made his way toward the exit.

Taking the stairs three at a time, he quickly reached the bottom.

Standing in a tunnel beneath Whitehall that had once been a part of the original Underground system, he took a quick head count, gestured for everyone to follow him, and led his staff into the darkness.

Joe put his foot down on the accelerator and took in a long, deep breath. They were still about twenty minutes outside London and they had company—another SUV weaving through the dribs and drabs of traffic, lights on full beam, heading straight toward them.

Ani had stripped Joe's phone of the battery and SIM back when she'd worked out the true purpose of Palgrave's call, but the guy must have gleaned enough information from it to have a pretty good idea of their route back, and had obviously sent someone to catch up with them before they made it back to YETI.

Joe doubted it was to offer them help.

"I'm an idiot," he said, hitting the steering wheel with the flat of his hand.

"You couldn't have known—" Ani said, but he cut her off.

No matter how many times he ran through the situation in his head, he couldn't make sense of it all. What was Palgrave up to? What were they missing? How was he connected to the events that were unfolding? This seemed way past an overprotective father fearing for the well-being of his X-Core-obsessed son; this seemed much deeper and darker, and had some kind of twisted logic that Joe just couldn't see.

Then he thought of what the two men had left behind at Pabody/Reich and saw the truth.

"That box in Klein's office. Palgrave was listening in. That's how we were followed. He's always been one step ahead of us."

Ani was checking alternate routes on the tablet, trying to

find an exit that would give them the opportunity to shake off their tail, but she was getting frustrated and Joe knew that the pressure was starting to take its toll on her. How could it not? In the past forty-eight hours her entire world had been upended. She'd been chased by mercenaries, had been subjected to that creepy .wav file three times, had been deputized as a member of a top secret teen spy ring, had seen Klein turn into something unspeakable, and now they were being chased by people sent by a politician for who knew what reason.

Joe was feeling the weight of it all pressing down on him, and he'd been trained for this kind of stuff.

"How're you holding up?" he asked.

"Okay. Sort of. Could you try Abernathy again?"

Joe did, but got no more than he'd been getting since Abernathy first went dark: absolutely nothing. That scared him more than anything. If YETI HQ was offline, that meant a whole lot of nasty possibilities. It could, of course, be nothing more than a technical hiccup. The Joe 2.0 communications system could have just bugged out, leaving them high and dry. But he doubted it. The timing was too convenient. Which meant that the signal was cut off, was being jammed, or that YETI headquarters itself had been compromised.

The last possibility made Joe feel lost, cut adrift, and utterly alone.

"Nothing," he said as the SUV fell into the space directly behind them. It sped up, tailgating, and started flashing its lights. The message was clear: pull over.

Joe stamped down on the accelerator even more and the turbo under the hood kicked in. They passed a traffic cam that flashed and Joe hoped that Abernathy was still in a position to kill the ticket when it turned up on his desk at YETI.

Joe thumped the steering wheel in frustration. "We need to get off this road."

"You've got an exit in a couple of miles, but they'll only follow us."

"We'll see," Joe said through gritted teeth. "What are they up to?"

Their pursuers were moving out into the next lane, and Joe guessed they were going to try to pass them before the turn off. Joe hoped that the cars were pretty evenly matched and gave the accelerator a little bit more pressure.

"This is where it gets a bit sketchy." He turned the wheel and began edging out into the outer lane, attempting to block the other car's hostile maneuver before they could draw level. The other SUV made it clear that it wasn't going to yield for Joe, but he knew a bluff when he saw one and carried on moving out. The other SUV braked to avoid the inevitable collision and Joe floored the accelerator, pulling the car onto the dividing line and keeping on it, straddling both lanes.

Their pursuers moved to undertake on the left, waiting for Joe to try to block them, but he figured it was only a feint and they were going to go outside as soon as he made a move, so he stayed where he was. Whichever way they came at him, he was ready to swerve and cut them off.

But it was a temporary measure at best.

He needed to gain an edge, get off this highway, and lose the other SUV as soon as possible. That meant taking the next exit. But without looking like he *meant* to take the next exit.

The mile marker came up and, due to the speed they were hurtling along at, the half-mile sign wasn't far behind it. The chevrons counted down and Joe snatched the steering wheel right and gave it the last jolt of speed the SUV had in her. He passed the two chevrons exit marker, then the one chevron, and the mouth of the exit ramp yawned wide. The other SUV was making to cut him off on the inside, just in case he was going to try for the exit. Joe shouted, and wrenched the wheel over to the left, almost rolling the car; he aimed for the space between the SUV and the guardrail, and just went for it.

He clipped the lip of the rail, jostled across some grass, fought with the steering, and then made the ramp. The driver of the other SUV realized what Joe was doing a second too late.

A second was all it took for them to overshoot, try to adapt, swing their vehicle across, and smash into the guard-rail. Joe watched them disappear behind him in the rear-view mirror, took his speed down to something approaching sane, and got Ani to plot him a route back to the city.

CHAPTER FIFTEEN:
GOING TO GROUND

Abernathy led his team down the tunnel and tried to figure out what had just happened. No matter how many times he played it through in his head, he came no nearer to an answer. Armed men had just stormed YETI HQ, and it was pretty clear that they weren't there to fix the coffee machine. A strike team, dispatched to a secret law enforcement unit in the heart of London. It was unthinkable!

The tunnel was long and mostly dark and the air was musty. What little light there was came from overhead fixtures that hadn't been serviced in a long time, so many of the bulbs were dead, the rest choked with dust. Smartphone flashlight apps would have made the task of negotiating a path a whole lot easier, but all devices had all been discarded as soon as the panic had faded from Abernathy's mind and he'd realized that it was a whole lot harder to escape pursuit when the phones in your pockets continued to broadcast your location. His was exempt from the mobile phone mass grave, only because it was *impossible* to track.

But just because it was the most secure phone in the YETI building didn't mean it worked underground.

He tried to think of things that they had going in their favor.

First up, the repeated evacuation drills had meant that the people who'd invaded YETI had found the place empty, and they would waste no small amount of time trying to figure out how that could be. They'd search every inch of the place, every room and closet, and they would find no one. Abernathy thought that it would be like those sailors who boarded that old ship, the *Mary Celeste*, and found the traces that people had left behind—breakfasts laid out, cups of tea still steaming—but no people. Then he remembered that those last details had been fictional embellishments from a story by Arthur Conan Doyle and decided that his analogy was severely flawed. The intruders wouldn't find the hidden door through which they'd escaped, of that he was one hundred percent certain. And pushing the button that opened it would do nothing, not without a reset of the system that could only be accomplished with the chip implanted in Abernathy's arm.

There was no way that the invaders could follow them.

But his team was in a state approaching hysteria. They were analysts—incredibly good at what they did, but essentially just desk jockeys—and they certainly weren't trained for fieldwork. So, of course, they were completely unprepared for a sudden flight from the safety of their office into the unknown.

Abernathy wanted to tell them everything was going to be all right, but even he wouldn't buy those words, so how could he expect his staff to?

That's not good enough, he chastised himself. *They're looking to me for guidance, and I need to find the words and the time to offer it.*

So even though time was ticking and he really needed to be aboveground sorting this mess out, he decided to show the leadership and solidarity his team needed, and he took precious minutes to stop and try to calm everyone down, to take a quick mental inventory of them, and to generally reassure everyone that things were going to be okay.

It worked.

To a point.

And then they continued on their way down the tunnels.

Still, he turned it all over and over in his mind.

Someone had sent an assault team into YETI, but who? And, perhaps more urgently, *why?*

There was no reason that he could see. Unless the men with guns had intended to slow down an investigation—of which Abernathy and his team had a half dozen running at the moment. But why would anyone want to shut his department down? Apart from the weird turn that Joe's inquiry had taken, everything else was standard fare, nothing different from any other cases they ran day in, day out.

It *had* to be the X-Core case; nothing else made any sense.

But how had the investigation led to this mass exodus?

He was missing something.

All right, he told himself, *think about it. Ignore that it's personal. Ignore that these cowboys came into my house with guns. Treat it like any other case.*

He didn't know who had organized the invasion, but he could think about the other details that every investigation needed to uncover. Three things:

Motive. Means. Opportunity.

The cornerstones of a case against any criminal.

First was motive. Simple. To shut down the investigation into X-Core. But there was a motive *behind* that motive—a darker purpose hiding behind that basic assertion. Why? Why would anyone want to shut down an investigation of national—no, global—significance?

Because they had something to gain from it.

But what?

Onto the second thing: means.

It was obvious to Abernathy that whoever sent an assault team into YETI HQ had all the means they needed at their disposal. Either that was an authorized team—which meant government forces lay behind the masks—or it was unauthorized, and that meant mercenaries, a private security firm, or terrorists.

The idea that it was terrorists seemed too paranoid. But all of the options were possible. Probable? That was another matter entirely. That the prime minister had authorized a raid into one of his own services seemed ridiculous.

Unnecessary. If he'd wanted to shut YETI down, then he could have done it with a phone call.

So that left soldiers for hire.

But sent by whom?

Opportunity, then.

The timing of the attack.

It tied in directly to the timing of Abernathy scrambling a team to Shrewsbury to secure what Joe maintained was an *alien creature* hidden inside Professor Klein. It was surely no coincidence that one had followed the other. But where did that leave him?

That someone had a vested interest in shutting down all mention of the events at Pabody/Reich? That someone already knew what was going on there but, for some unknown reason, was keeping it quiet, with armed troops?

They were nearing the first exit from the tunnel and Abernathy performed a quick calculation, weighing the fact that they were still close to YETI HQ against the need to get topside and start making some calls.

He wasn't going to get scared off of an investigation by a bunch of rent-a-killers.

YETI was coming out of the tunnel, sure, but they were going underground until he sorted this mess out.

And then heads would roll.

Joe drove two miles until they reached a small village, then he started looking carefully left and right.

"Gotta ditch these wheels," he explained, and Ani looked out the windows, too, until she spotted a car parked in a blacked-out driveway.

"That one will do," she said. "Screened on two sides, no lights on, can't see any motion sensors . . ."

Joe pulled over and they got out of the SUV.

They made their way toward the house cautiously, but there was no one around and the lights stayed dark.

"Don't suppose you know how to hot-wire a car, do you?" Ani asked.

Joe shook his head. "Not in my training schedule. You?"

Ani wrinkled her nose.

She approached the front door and, seeing a generous mail slot on the front door that was close enough to the door's lock, she put her hand through it, reached upward until she was sure that she was in approximately the right area, felt around until she bumped into a bunch of keys hanging there, maneuvered her hand around until she could grab them, pulled the front door key out of the lock, and extracted the whole bunch back through the slot.

Whatever dumb luck was working for her tonight, it had delivered in spades. Hanging from a fob was a miniature teddy bear, a few house keys, and the key to the car.

She tossed it over to Joe, who snatched it out of the air and nodded his approval.

"Pretty good," he said. "Want a lift?"

He unlocked the car and slid into the driver's seat, ratcheting it back so he fit. Ani got in beside him. He started it up and, to Ani's surprise, he headed back the way they had come. "They won't be looking for this car. And they're not going to think we're stupid enough to head back *toward* them."

"I hope you're right."

"So do I."

The SUV passed them halfway back to the main road. The front bumper was mangled and pretty much hanging off, and there was a long scrape down the side, but Joe only allowed himself a smile when it disappeared out of his rearview mirror.

The car they'd just commandeered was a strange little Korean number from one of those companies that keeps the costs down by paring back on the luxuries. The gearbox was a little unforgiving, but a few miles toward London he thought he was getting the hang of it. He checked the fuel tank and saw that there was more than enough to get to the city, checked that the SUV wasn't creeping up behind them, and managed to relax a bit.

He tried Abernathy again, but still no reply. It was worrying him more than he dared to admit to Ani.

Still, she had enough to be dealing with at the moment, and voicing his fears was no way to make her feel any easier about things. In all the craziness, car chases, and car stealing, he'd almost managed to forget about Klein and X-Core, concentrating instead on the enigma of Abernathy's radio silence. He thought about it, weighing the pros and cons, and made a decision.

"I need my phone," he said. "I know they'll just track us with it, but without a line to Abernathy we're useless here anyway."

Ani shrugged. "Not necessarily. I know you think that I'm playing *Crossy Road* or *Deadman's Cross* here, but I'm actually working on something. Give me a few minutes, though."

Joe drove until Ani said, "Okay."

"Okay, what?"

"We-e-e-e-ell, if I had some tools I'd just take your phone apart and disable the GPS. It's just a chip, easy to remove. But we haven't got any tools, so the problem stops being hardware and starts being software."

"And?"

"Hold your horses, Agent Dyson. This is the part where I get to tell you about the clever solution I've come up with. It's . . . it's the part where I get to show off, you tell me how brilliant I am, and I nod and agree with your wise words. Okay, we'll skip that. I'm going to boot up your phone into DFU mode, connect it to this tablet, and I'm going to flash your phone a firmware update that I just thrashed out. It isn't going to be tidy, your phone might turn into a brick if it all goes wrong, but if it works it'll teach your GPS a very important survival skill."

"Which is?"

"How to lie, my friend. I'm going to teach your phone to report a bogus route to our naughty little MP friend and get him chasing us all the way to Canary Wharf."

"You can do that?"

"We're about to find out. You have a USB cord for this thing?"

Joe looked embarrassed. "I didn't bring one with me."

"Then I am your dream come true." Ani reached in her jacket and pulled out a handful of cables, found the right one, connected his phone to the tablet's USB port, and said, "Here goes something."

She booted up the phone and Joe waited.

And waited.

Modern phones took so-o-o-o long to start up.

They were pretty close to London now, and then Ani let out a whoop, fist-pumped the air, and handed him back his cell.

"There you go, sir," she said. "That should confuse the enemy for a while."

"You're sure they can't track us?" Joe asked, and Ani thumped him on the bicep.

"Of course I'm sure. Now call Abernathy and find out why he's freezing us out."

The assembled workforce of YETI's technical and operational teams emerged from a hatch in a garden by a house on a deserted cul-de-sac that had surely seen better days. The few houses that remained were run-down and unloved. Which, Abernathy had to admit, made it a perfect place to lead his people out into the Promised Land.

Aboveground.

He helped people off the ladder and on to *terra firma*, lugged the Shuttleworth brothers' cases up onto the overgrown lawn, took another head count, and then gave himself a moment or two to catch his breath.

And, more importantly, to let his people catch theirs.

Abernathy had to admit that the air tasted pretty sweet after the staleness of the tunnels.

Still, the work was far from done. He had to get everyone to another location where they could set up a temporary headquarters using laptops and whatever the Shuttleworths had brought, and then they had to focus their attentions on the "why" behind the invasion of their HQ.

First, though, he had some pretty important protocols to take care of. Phone calls to key people. It was going to be hard to explain the situation, but he needed his HQ back, and was prepared to send in the entire British Army to make it happen, if that was what it took.

He was reaching for his phone when it started ringing.

Abernathy felt relief flooding through him when he saw the caller ID and pressed ACCEPT with a finger that hardly shook at all.

"Joe!" he said. "Are you and Ani safe?"

"Of course we are. Things got a little . . . hectic . . . for a while back there, but we're coming in."

"No, you're not. Nowhere to come. An armed tactical squad hit YETI HQ about twenty minutes ago and we only just managed to get out."

"Emergency drills finally paid off?" Joe's voice hardly wavered, and Abernathy realized that Joe was back on his game.

"They certainly did," he said ruefully.

"Who hit you?"

"We only just emerged into the night air after a lovely slog through the tunnels so, to be honest, we don't know. I was about to make some calls."

"You might want to hold up on those for a minute. I think I know who was behind the attack. And it may change your contacts list."

"You're telling me you have a name?"

"Thanks to Ani," Joe said, and Abernathy heard warmth and pride in Joe's voice and knew that he'd made the right choice pairing them up. "You're not going to like it or—most likely—believe it, but Ani and I have just escaped from gorillas sicced on us by Victor Palgrave, and the timing of our respective troubles seems too precise to be coincidental."

Abernathy took a few seconds to think before replying.

This was a whole other level of trouble.

Victor Palgrave? Sure, he was an ambitious politician—weren't they all?—but was he really capable of organizing the assault on YETI? And if he was, then what was his motive?

Put all those details aside for now, he told himself. *Forget things that need evidence to prove. Think about this, and only this: you've met him a few times—do you think he's capable of it?*

Abernathy thought about the kind of man Palgrave was—how he was charismatic but manipulative, charming but self-serving, outwardly modest and humble but inside confident and superior. He thought about the man's practiced focus-group persona, and the depths that shallow patina of PR covered. He thought about the way the man smiled with a studied warmth that never seemed to reach his eyes. He remembered the rumors he heard of just how right wing Palgrave was politically, and how meeting him had done nothing to dispel those rumors.

And Palgrave had been calling, demanding information about the investigation, but wrapping it up in concern for his son. A concern that had only started when Five started looking into Lennie's lifestyle choices and X-Core had thrown up a red flag that demanded that YETI take a closer look. Before that warning, Palgrave had sought no help, called in no favors, made no appeals, hadn't even mentioned it to an intelligence head over a drink in the bar.

It was like he only started caring about his son when his son was being investigated, and it would have looked pretty strange for him not to care.

Abernathy closed his eyes and thought about what he'd been told about this investigation when Ben Hoolihan from MI5 first came to brief him on the matter. In particular, he came up with a whole bunch of questions that he should have asked about the case, if it hadn't been for Hoolihan's charm and lightning-fast evasions.

"I am such an idiot," Abernathy said to himself.

The parameters of the investigation had been wrong. A "routine vetting" from Five? That's how it had been sold to him, and he'd been duped as surely as if Hoolihan had given him a handful of magic beans. The investigation was far from routine—it was part of a deeper and more comprehensive look into the life and behavior of Victor Palgrave.

Analysis?

Joe was right.

The enemy was a powerful man in the government.

And the million-dollar question became, how high up the ladder did the conspiracy extend?

Abernathy suddenly saw what Joe meant about his contacts list. Until he knew who he could trust, he was going to have to play a different kind of game. The enemy was hidden among the people that YETI was supposed to serve, and the stakes were higher than any he'd ever played for.

His control center was down.

His team had nothing but rudimentary equipment and the ingenuity of the Shuttleworth brothers.

He had two operatives in play, and they were both teenagers. One had only just returned to duty after the traumatic death of his partner. The other was an absolute beginner, with no field experience at all.

He didn't know who he could trust, and the case had taken so many strange turns that it covered both political intrigue and alien invasion.

For the first time in half an hour, Abernathy smiled.

Mess with us, will you? Well, here's where we start messing back.

While Joe conferred with Abernathy, Ani took stock of her mind and body.

Physically, she was exhausted—maybe even way past exhausted. Her body ached in every muscle and joint, and her eyes were dry and scratchy and in need of sleep. She felt like her body was bent into the shape of the car seat, and wondered what it would be like to stand up again. Adrenaline was the only thing keeping her going: the fear of staying still for too long.

Like a shark, she thought grimly. *I'll die if I stop.*

The horrible thing about that thought was, maybe it was true. The guys following them in the SUV hadn't seemed particularly cautious about forcing them into an accident back there, and she had a nasty feeling that the thing one saw written on wanted posters in the old westerns—"Wanted: Dead or Alive"—might be true for Joe and her, too.

So, physically, a wreck.

Mentally, she wasn't sure she was in much better shape. A trapdoor had opened up beneath the world she'd thought she knew, throwing away certainty, comfort, and her usual reference points, and she had been propelled into this shadowy other world full of terrifying threats. Corrupt government ministers, astronomers who were alien creatures, music that made monsters, car chases and men in black with weapons, sounds from outer space.

None of it made any sense when you tried to fit it all together.

Every new discovery threw the old ideas about what was going on out of the window.

A sound that only kids can hear? That had been a reasonable working hypothesis: adults seemed unaffected by it, so it seemed the only explanation. But Klein had heard it. And it had changed him. Changed him in a way that none of the kids at the Warhouse had been changed.

How did that make sense?

It didn't. It simply didn't.

Unless . . .

The thought hit her with the force of a physical blow, and she actually felt shaky as if reeling from the weight of the idea that had just struck her.

Unless, she thought, *it's not the same sound.*

She let the idea float around for a while, looking at it from different angles, gauging its size and importance. She felt a reassuring squeeze on her arm.

Joe was off the phone and there was confusion clouding his features.

"Okay," he said. "We are in big trouble."

He told her what the conversation with Abernathy had revealed, and Ani listened, feeling another trapdoor giving way underneath her. She'd been aware of the existence of YETI for a few hours, had been drafted in as a deputy for a little less time, and already the organization had been attacked, exiled from its home, and was trying to find a place to regroup so that they could continue the fight.

That Victor Palgrave was caught up in all of this seemed too likely to dismiss, but how? Was he trying to secure the sound file for himself, for his own use? Was he trying to shut down the investigation? And what did he have to gain from shutting down YETI? If his concern was *truly* for his son's safety, then YETI provided a way to meet that goal. Shutting it down meant that there was something else going on. Ani suspected that it was dark and dangerous and full of betrayal.

"What if he blames X-Core for the rift with his son, and this . . . private army he's put together is his personal revenge squad?" Ani said, knowing it sounded like she was stretching for an explanation. But that was because she was. "He wants YETI out of the way because . . . well, they're in the way."

Joe thought it over. "It's better than anything I've got. But there's something else here, something that we can't quite see. . . ."

"The sound from space—it's the start of everything. A message sent by an alien race, captured by the Pabody/Reich radio telescope, and converted into a sound file. It's the prime mover—the thing that everything else follows from. We need to concentrate on it."

Joe nodded. "A sound that was substituted before it was sent out to the world. Swapped out with another sound that ruined Imogen Bell's career. But then she goes and joins a rock band, which is incorporating the same sound from space into their music. What's that all about?"

"We're pretty certain that the sound received by Imogen Bell and the one sent out to the world's authorities were *different* sounds, right?"

"The sound that Klein played wasn't the one that revealed him as a monster from space, so I'd say yes."

Ani caught a flash of something in her mind: the worms inside the music, the worms crawling in and out of Klein.

A sound that makes monsters, she thought.

And then it hit her.

Hard.

"Are you okay there?" Joe asked.

"Think differently."

"Cryptic," Joe said. "Think differently, how?"

"Maybe we're looking at this thing the wrong way 'round." The idea firmed up in her mind more with every word. "Examine the chain of events. A message is sent into space. A radio telescope following that message's path hears something in space. What's the assumption? Something just heard the message and answered it. Sent a message back. So what are we saying *sent* that message?"

"An alien intelligence. A creature out there in the depths of space."

"Exactly. But what if it wasn't answering our message? What if it just happened to be passing through?"

"I'd think the odds of some alien intelligence passing through the same area of space we're monitoring would be millions to one."

"But things that have a likelihood of *billions* to one happen all the time. There are so many things happening in the universe. Bear with me on this. Let's just say that, however unlikely it may be, it's possible."

Joe nodded.

"What do you think aliens look like, Joe?"

"Like that thing we saw back at the observatory."

"But before you saw that? How did you picture alien life? Gray men? Green men? Daleks? Klingons? Those are just things we made up, that probably say more about us as a race than they do about what might be out there in the enormity of space. The one thing I'm sure about is that if we encounter an alien race it will be nothing like us. Nothing at all."

"But it was human-shaped at the observatory. . . ."

"Was it? Really? Think of the different types of life on just this planet. From humans, to sponges, to camels, to bacteria, to wasps that lay their eggs in spiders. So much variation from just one planet.

"Now think of a completely different kind of planet. Different gravity, different air composition, hydrochloric acid instead of water, knock yourself out on the details. Just imagine a truly alien environment. Now populate it. With a variety of creatures as diverse from each other as the ones in this world. Think of the changes such an environment would create."

"Okay. Aliens are *really* alien," he said, nodding. "Really, really alien. So?"

"Did you imagine arms? Legs? Eyes?"

"Yeah."

"But they're the things that this planet has; it doesn't mean that every form of life in the universe will follow the same rules."

"Tentacles?"

"Maybe. The fact is we just don't know. But I figure that alien life will be *completely* alien. Not just a different color skin, or bigger eyes, or even tentacles. Here's the mind-blowing bit. You ready?"

Joe nodded.

"What if the alien that strayed into the path of Pabody/Reich's transmission didn't send a message? What if it *was* the message?"

"You've lost me."

"Bear with me. The first thing we need to realize is that space is vast. Like, really, colossally vast. And who knows what's out there? I got to thinking that maybe an alien would be so alien as to be unrecognizable to us *as* life. What if the alien *was* the sound? What if there's a creature out there *made* of sound? What if Pabody/Reich heard it, the sound that is a creature, and only thought it was a message? Recorded it? Brought it down to Earth?"

"Hang on. What?"

Ani fished for another way to explain. "I know how crazy this sounds. But think about it. An alien that is made only of sound. A living creature composed of sonic vibrations. It could travel through space without a craft."

"And Imogen Bell caught it?" Joe said. "The sound doesn't create creatures, it *is* one. And it reproduces, just like any other creature. Oh, Ani . . ."

"Possible?"

"I haven't got a clue. But that's one truly terrifying explanation."

They sat in silence for a while and then Ani asked the question that was on both of their minds: "So where do we go from here?"

"We need to wait until Abernathy figures things out. And we have to ditch this car. We need somewhere safe to hide."

Ani took out her phone. "I might know a place. Give me a minute."

ooo

Joe looked around the library, awed at the number of books Ani's friend had in her house.

Gretchen had listened to the latest developments without comment, then she'd gone over to a table, retrieved the china teapot, and refilled their empty cups. She added sugar and milk and stirred, all without saying a word.

Then she sat down, looked at Ani, looked at Joe, and laughed.

The reaction was so unexpected, but somehow so perfect, that Ani and Joe joined in. It might have been borne out of hysteria, but it still felt great.

When they were done, Gretchen said, "Look, kids, you really need to make those drab lives of yours a bit more interesting."

"I'm thinking of taking up gardening," Joe said.

"Knitting," Ani responded, joining in.

"Both good choices," Gretchen said, a twinkle in her eyes. "Other high-scoring answers would have been painting fantasy miniatures, trainspotting, and Sudoku. Ready for the bonus round?"

"I'll take 'famous composers' for twenty points," Joe said.

"And I think I'll plump for 'MPs with a hidden agenda' for fifty," said Ani.

Joe had to admire the girl. Even when offered a few

moments' rest, she went straight back to the problem at hand.

Gretchen nodded and pulled out a handful of computer printouts and passed them around.

When Ani had suggested that they come here, Joe had been skeptical. By Ani's admission, she'd only met the woman the day before, and he hadn't expected Gretchen to be so welcoming, so sharp, and so ready to accept the story of their day with such easy charm.

Another tick in the "make Ani Lee an operative now" box, Joe thought. *Good people have a habit of picking up other good people along the way, and Gretchen is great.*

Joe looked at the papers he'd been handed and found a comprehensive description of the meteoric rise of one Victor Palgrave, from his humble beginnings right up to the present day, which saw him as a potential leader of the country.

Joe noted that some of the pages came from sources that required a high level of clearance, including one that suggested that Palgrave was losing traction and support within his party, and had "close ties to Aeolus," a private security firm engaged in "questionable operations" around the globe. There was also a suggestion that his "urbane, poor-boy public image" covered a "megalomaniacal hunger for power," and that his views took him "to a level of right-wing hysteria unmatched since the rise in Germany of one Hitler, Adolf."

"I'm not going to ask how you got this," Joe said, waving the sheet in the air. "I doubt that even Abernathy has seen it."

Gretchen just gave him a sweet, innocent look.

"Speaking of your boss . . . has Mr. Abernathy found a place to set up an alternate command center, or do you think he's still leading his team through the streets of our fair city, making them the best-trained homeless people in London?"

"All the usual safe houses could be compromised," Joe replied. "I figure he's still out there."

"Then why don't you invite them to our little party? We could use the company."

"Are you sure?" Joe asked, feeling almost impossibly grateful.

Gretchen nodded. "Call him. I've got soup."

They laughed and then Joe dialed the number.

Abernathy and the rest of YETI's exiles turned up twenty minutes later and, after some quick introductions, the team got to setting up their gear around Gretchen's house. She watched with a faint smile on her lips, and guided operations as best she could.

"My dear," Abernathy said, "I simply cannot thank you enough for allowing this intrusion."

"Thank Ani," Gretchen said. "I suspect you might have uncovered a rare treasure there. She needs . . . guidance, though, and I'm sure that you'll repay my hospitality by providing it for her."

She raised an eyebrow in a schoolmarm kind of way and Abernathy nodded agreement. "Already a priority, if we ever get YETI back up and running."

"Yeah, about that. It might be time to call in some favors," Gretchen observed. "There must be some emergency protocols that come into play when your HQ is attacked."

"To be honest, there isn't a procedure to cover what we've just suffered." Abernathy's voice betrayed the personal affront that he saw YETI's invasion as. "It was simply my own limitless paranoia that made me build an escape route, rather than a thought-out strategy. And before I make any calls, I need to figure out who I can trust."

"I'd take Victor Palgrave off speed dial, as well as anyone who might let any information slip his way. Anyway, I know a couple of YETI agents who need some beauty sleep. Can I send them off to bed, or do I need special authorization?"

Abernathy smiled. "You have it. I really can't thank you enough, you know."

"If I can help out a friend and *her* friends, then that's all the thanks I need."

"Are you looking for a job?"

Gretchen laughed. "I doubt you could afford me. But I'll help Ani out for free, whenever she needs me. Just make sure there's a good Christmas present in it for me. And yes, I love shoes. Size eight. The higher the heel, the better."

Abernathy smiled. "Here's the plan: we get the team up and running, we find out what's going on, and then . . ."

"And then?"

Abernathy's face clouded over, and his eyes were dark and unfathomable.

"And then, my dear, there's going to be hell to pay."

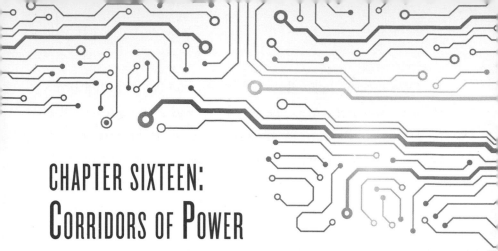

CHAPTER SIXTEEN:
CORRIDORS OF POWER

Victor Palgrave put the phone down and stared at the wall, his teeth clenched. The voice of the chief whip of the Conservative Party was still ringing in his head, and a hundred thoughts swirled there, too.

He felt on the very edge of panic.

His party was asking questions now.

Not just the bumbling muddlers at MI5.

Not just Abernathy and his army of sociopathic whelps.

His party.

The desperate efforts he'd made to derail Five's investigation had backfired. Instead of retreating into the background where he'd needed to remain until all aspects of his plans had fallen into place, he had found his head forced up above the parapet, and now the chief whip—the prime minister's human-shaped pit bull—was taking potshots at it.

He took a few deep breaths and, with a supreme effort of will, squashed down the panic.

"We need to talk," the chief whip had called to tell him. Palgrave was not naïve. The word *talk* was a euphemism: the party was putting him to the axe. His days in the corridors of power, on which his whole scheme depended, were numbered.

He knew in that moment that his careful planning had come to nothing.

He had run out of time.

Despair tried to fill the spaces recently vacated by panic. He had been so close! He could almost taste it! Power beyond imagining would have been in his hands, and with it he could have brought order and sanity to the country.

To the world.

The crazy thing was: he wasn't even doing this for himself. If only people could see that. Understand it.

Catastrophic societal problems of the kind that had infected the UK required unprecedented actions, and it seemed that he was one of the few who saw the path that the nation was heading down.

The tide of immigrants that was flooding into Britain—an island nation, with finite resources and a dwindling relevance on the world stage—was draining the country dry. It was basic mathematics. Every foreign mouth that was fed took food from the mouths of the people who really belonged here.

And were they grateful? These interlopers?

The lawlessness, permissiveness, secularization, and apathy of the country's citizens were providing the perfect growing medium for the radicalization of religious ideologies. When the flame was applied to that particular fuse, the outcome would be explosive. His country, the land that he loved, would be forever changed.

He simply could not allow that to happen.

His long-term plan might have failed, the extreme measures that would have seen the UK rise again as a leading world power, but there was still a chance that he could at least make a statement.

And it would be something that no one would be able to ignore.

Something that would never be forgotten.

But first he had a call to make.

He picked up the cell phone that even his wife didn't know he owned, and speed-dialed the only number it held.

It was answered immediately.

"Drummond." A clipped, military voice with the faintest hint of East London about it. Along with a not-so-faint hint of fear.

"Ah, Mr. Drummond. Just one quick question for you: how many times are you intending to fail me this week?"

"Sir, I understand that you're angry . . ."

"Angry, Mr. Drummond? Have you added *understatement* to your rhetorical repertoire, or do you truly not know the intensity of my feelings at this moment in time?"

"We tried . . ."

"Everything you have tried, you have failed at,

Mr. Drummond. You failed to catch either of the hackers who stole my file; your men bungled the interception of Joe Dyson, a seventeen-year-old *boy* who still managed to outsmart and outdrive a pair of supposedly combat-trained mercenaries; and you and your team secured YETI headquarters without finding a *single member of the organization*! These are not just failures, Mr. Drummond, these are total redefinitions of the word 'incompetence.' It's over, bar the inevitable shouting. But I still want you to concentrate your efforts on tying up a few loose ends. . . ."

When he had finished outlining Drummond's last set of instructions, Victor Palgrave sat in silence.

He had one last play open to him. Not what he'd planned, of course, but maybe it would be good enough.

Finding out about the existence of the .wav file had been the result of a shot in the dark.

Alien first-contact situations certainly weren't in his brief within cabinet circles, and the discovery of a suspected signal from space should have gone straight through to the Post-Detection Task Group for verification.

But Palgrave was nothing if not a forward thinker.

His business interests lay in the gray world of secret wars and weapon procurement. It made sense both financially and ideologically: there was never a shortage of people willing to pay for the latest weapon technologies, and by deploying those technologies strategically, a person could gather together a lot of power and influence.

His Research and Development had gone from strength to strength, and his R&D team made that of many nations look inadequate and outdated by comparison. And what he couldn't develop through innovation, Palgrave was able to gather by industrial espionage. He had lines into computer systems the world over, a digital spiderweb constructed to detect any new scientific or technological breakthroughs that could be turned toward the construction of new weapons.

After he'd heard about the Arecibo affair—the first time he had ever seriously considered that there might be other life out there in the depths of space—he had added SETI to his watch list, more in faint hope than in actual expectation. For Victor Palgrave, spaceships were the kind of thing his son Lennie read about in those stupid books of his. Still, he had seen no harm in monitoring SETI on the off chance.

That it had actually borne fruit was nothing short of a miracle, but the moment his software had recognized the event and patched it through to his desk, he had *known* that the rules of the war games he played had changed forever.

Space had come calling, and nothing was going to be the same again.

It had taken months to even begin to understand the importance of what the Pabody/Reich Observatory had discovered, and the better part of two years to convert it into something that he could actually use.

There had been many twists and turns, many sacrifices made and much money spent, people to be silenced and secrets to be hidden. Lennie finding a copy of the sound file while poking around on the Palgrave family server had at first been unfortunate, but later, having him as a guinea pig had turned out to be remarkably fortuitous. Imogen Bell, too, had been a great subject for experimentation; and all she had needed as an inducement to leave her old life behind was the promise of a chance to clear her name and work on the signal from space. She had gotten a chance to work on it, all right. Or, more accurately, Palgrave had given the signal the chance to work on *her*.

The idea of embedding his project in music had been suggested by his work as culture secretary, and seemed an efficient way to disseminate the signal to those he would need if his dream of a new British Empire were to reach fruition. It had been surprisingly easy to start a new musical genre from scratch. He had just funneled some lottery funding into the hands of some early adopters of the .wav file—the Brewster boy and some of his friends—and let them spread it through what they laughingly thought of as "songs." They hadn't even realized that what they thought of as "rebellion" was actually orchestrated conformity to Palgrave's plan. It had gained an impetus all on its own, and all he'd needed to do was wait in the background until a critical mass of youths were in the thrall of X-Core.

But then, with only days to go from the implementation of the first phase of his plan, the walls had started coming down around him.

Fools within the party had jumped the gun and started tipping him for prime minister. And although becoming PM had always been part of his overarching plan, the timing couldn't have been more inconvenient. Suddenly, people were looking at him with rather keener eyes than he could withstand.

When the MI5 vetting had uncovered Lennie's involvement in X-Core, Palgrave's life had become an exercise in damage control. He had been sure that he could deal with it, but then he'd learned of the hacked file—that the original, undoctored .wav file was out there in the world—and suddenly he was fighting a war on two fronts.

Abernathy and Joe Dyson entering the fray had been the writing on the wall, writ large.

Still, he wasn't going down without a fight.

It wasn't the endgame he'd planned, but maybe it would be good enough.

His party might be turning its back on him, but he would give them—and YETI—something to think about tomorrow.

He'd give the world something to think about.

Something it would never forget.

Perched on the brink of disaster, his political career in tatters behind him, and with years of planning coming to so much less than they should have, Victor Palgrave looked up from his desk and smiled.

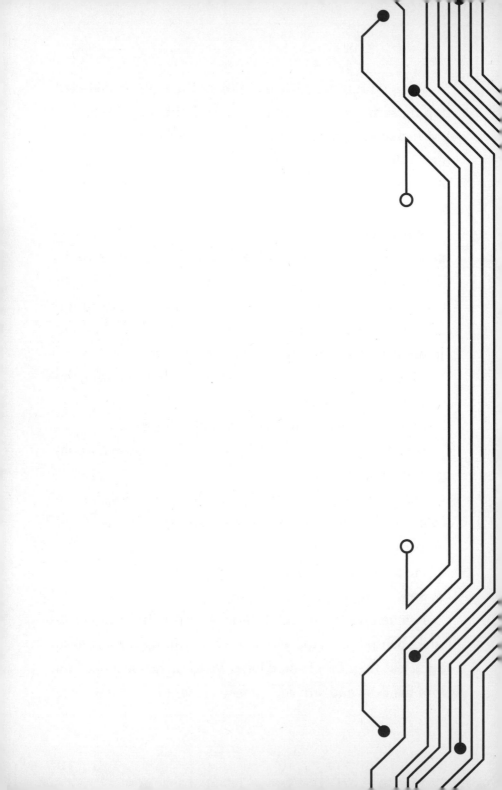

PART 03:
GOING VIRAL

The machine is not your friend
It sings on wires
Its melodies are cold
It wants to take your face.

And when you dream in 1080p
It is you.
It always was.

"Etude in Code"
Precision Image

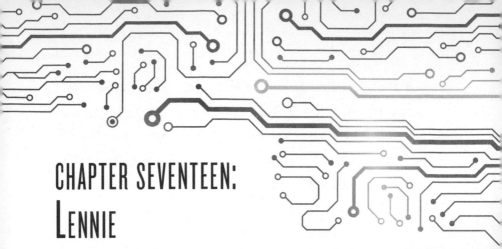

CHAPTER SEVENTEEN:
LENNIE

Ani found it hard to get to sleep—too many thoughts float-ing around in her head—but when she finally did crash, it was more like a coma than sleep. Her brain played back the day's events in garbled, exaggerated fashion in her dreams until she was awakened by Gretchen and a cup of tea.

"Your new employer seems to be getting things in order," Gretchen said. "He's quite the gentleman. If I were in his shoes, I think I might just start to let my good humor slip, but he's keeping a lid on it, playing things well."

"I'm so sorry about dragging you into this . . ." Ani began but Gretchen ssh-ed her.

"It's actually the most fun I've had in years. Now, why don't we go downstairs and grab some breakfast? I have a feeling that today is going to be a lo-o-ong one."

Ani grabbed her clothes and followed Gretchen.

Joe was sitting at the breakfast bar eating bagels. He nod-ded at Ani and then directed her attention over to where one of the Shuttleworth brothers, the taller one—she'd been introduced but she couldn't remember which one was which, and had a secret theory that they were two halves of the same person, anyway—was in a heated discussion with another member of Abernathy's team about whether *Battlestar Galactica* was better than *Star Wars*.

"That's Dr. Ghoti," Joe whispered as she slid in next to him at the breakfast bar. "Going head-to-head in a nerd war."

"There's really no debate here," the Shuttleworth brother said, exasperated. "*Star Wars* is fantasy, dressed up in science fiction clothes. *BSG*, on the other hand, is pure science fiction . . ."

"With roots in fantasy," Dr. Ghoti, a dark-haired woman with Southeast Asian skin tones, said dismissively. "Has happened, will happen, blah blah blah. Predestination. A series that takes the journey from pantheism to monotheism as one of its strengths? I mean, really? It's a heavy-handed Christian allegory at best. Gaius Baltar is Jesus, the twelve Cylon models are the twelve apostles; Starbuck even becomes an angel . . . hello?"

"That's only one way of looking at it," the Shuttleworth said defensively.

"I'm waiting for another, better one," Dr. Ghoti replied.

Joe gestured for Ani to move closer and when she leaned in he whispered, "I genuinely never thought I'd see it happen. Geoff Shuttleworth being out-nerded."

Geoff Shuttleworth suddenly decided that it was high time to go back to work, leaving Dr. Ghoti looking smug.

When he was gone, she turned to Gretchen and gave her a high five.

"Thank you," she said. "I've been wanting to do something like that for a long, long time."

"It was a pleasure. He'll think about it for a while, and then come back with something he thinks will confuse you."

"And that's when I come back at him with *Babylon 5* and *Firefly*, right?"

Gretchen nodded. "He doesn't stand a chance."

When Dr. Ghoti was gone, Gretchen asked, "So what are you kids up to today?"

Joe shrugged. "I guess we need to keep busy until we meet up with Ani's mysterious hacker friend later on. It would really help if we had some goal to head toward."

"Something will turn up," Gretchen said, and at that very moment Joe's phone started to ring.

He held up a finger as if to say "one minute" and then answered it. "Hello?"

His brow furrowed, and then his whole face brightened.

"Ellie. Ellie Butcher, of course I remember you. What's up?"

Gretchen gave him a look that said *See, I told you so*, and then Joe was grabbing a memo pad off the breakfast bar and scribbling down an address.

"That was some really good thinking," he said into the phone. "I can't thank you enough."

He listened for a few more seconds then said, "Yeah, that sounds good. I'll give you a call and we'll set something up. Brilliant. See you soon then."

When he hung up he said, "That was Ellie. She lives in the same house as Lennie Palgrave. Seems he turned up early this morning, and picked up some of his stuff. So Ellie, knowing that I was trying to locate him, followed him to an address in Camden and reported back to me."

"Got your own little network of operatives?" Ani said. "What's it costing you?"

"A meal," Joe said, then very quickly changed the subject. "I'll get the okay from Abernathy, and then we'll head out."

"I'll freshen up," Ani said.

Abernathy sprang for a taxi that took them to an address in Camden Town, and they stepped out onto a street that looked like it had been frozen in amber sometime about 1990. The place seemed to be stubbornly resisting the tide of boutique shops and restaurants that were hoisting property values, preferring instead to rot in peace.

Joe watched the cab pull away and then approached the door that matched the address Ellie Butcher had provided him. A three-story townhouse that looked more like a derelict building than somewhere you'd find the son of an MP. Crumbling brickwork, flaking woodwork, and a front door that looked like it would cave in under a decent knock. Luckily, a doorbell provided an alternative to punching a hole in wood, but its bare wires and lack of attachment to the door frame didn't exactly inspire confidence.

He had gleaned from Ellie's call that she'd tried to talk to Lennie when he came back to her place, but he'd been distant and evasive and she hadn't managed to get through to him at all. He'd left with a bag of his belongings and Ellie had felt both angry and frustrated and had decided to follow him. She'd stayed out of sight—which Ellie had admitted hadn't been *that* difficult, because Lennie seemed not to be seeing the world around him, paying little attention to anything except his destination—and she'd even gotten on a bus when Lennie did.

Abernathy had looked like Joe had just brought him the Holy Grail when Joe told him about the address they now had for Victor Palgrave's son.

"Do you need backup?" he'd asked urgently, as if there were a chance of securing any from the thin air that the invasion of YETI had created. Abernathy was still avoiding calling someone and Joe secretly wondered if it was less to do with fear about talking to the wrong person—although that surely played no small part in his decision—and more to do with Abernathy wanting to see if they could still operate the task force out of a couple of suitcases. If there was one thing Abernathy liked, it was mixing things up, keeping people on their toes, and getting their best work out of them through adversity.

Or maybe he really *was* scared that his contacts in all branches of law enforcement, and at every level of government, really could be in on some massive conspiracy. It seemed awfully unlikely, but then you *were* talking about a man with such paranoia that he'd hidden an escape hatch in the back of his office.

And there was always the chance that Abernathy was suddenly playing *his* cards close to his chest and already had something in mind.

Joe reached out his hand and pressed the doorbell.

Lennie Palgrave opened the door, and Joe was sure that he wouldn't have recognized his friend if he hadn't known there was a chance he'd be the one to answer. If Joe had seen Lennie in the street he would have walked straight past him without giving him a second look.

Sure, it had been over a year since they'd last seen each other, but even the passage of that amount of time seemed inadequate to explain the somewhat dramatic changes in Lennie's appearance and demeanor. Gone was the confident, eager to please, rakishly charming kid who had been Joe's first friend in his new life under Abernathy's direction. He had been replaced with this sallow, nervous young man.

Foppish brown hair was now a disorganized straggle of badly bleached straw, the boyish roundness of his face had been carved away and replaced with gaunt lines and sharp angles, his twinkling blue eyes now hid so deep in his sockets that they might as well have been a doll's eyes for all the life they conveyed.

Lennie frowned at Joe and Ani, didn't pick the person he knew out of the meager lineup, and sniffed.

"We've already got one," he said in a monotonous drawl. "That's if you're selling something. Either that or 'no, that's okay, we're renting the house and I don't think the landlord will let us' in case home improvements are what you're pitching. I also have 'while your beliefs are quaint and must bring you a lot of comfort, I myself find it difficult to subscribe to the notion of a benevolent sky-god who punishes the just and unjust alike' in case you're trying to convert me. That should just about cover all of the possible reasons you rang that bell, so if there's nothing else, good-bye."

Joe forced his face closer to Lennie's. "It's me, Lennie. Joe. Joe Dyson."

Lennie just gave him a blank stare as a reply and Joe could smell stale sweat and hair grease emanating from him in waves.

"You know, from Horace Walpole Secondary?" Joe persevered, trying to sound guileless, without an agenda, like this was just an ordinary visit to a long-lost friend. "I stopped by to see how you are."

"I'm fine, Joe Dyson from Horace Walpole Secondary," Lennie said. "Let's do this again sometime, huh?"

He made to close the door, but Joe got a shoulder in the gap and used it to pry the door open again.

Lennie just stood there, swaying slightly from side to side. He wasn't angry that Joe had barged the door back open, or offended, or . . . anything, really. It was like he hadn't even noticed.

"Lennie?" Joe asked, acting offended. "Don't you remember me?"

"Sorry," Lennie said, and it was clear that he just wanted to get rid of Joe and get back to doing whatever it was he'd been doing inside. "I've got a lot on my mind."

Then he seemed to notice Joe for the first time, and recognition dawned in those oddly sunken eyes of his. There was even the faintest hint of a smile threatening to spread across his lips. "Joe?" The monotone was gone, replaced with surprise. "Joe Dyson."

He even pointed at Joe with a finger as if Joe himself might not know his own name, even though he'd just reintroduced himself a few seconds before, and Lennie had repeated Joe's name then.

"The Yank. From school. What are you doing here?" Lennie almost sounded pleased to see him.

"I was walking down this road a while ago," Joe lied, effortlessly, "and saw you going into this house. I had some errands to do, but thought I'd stop by on my way back. And here I am. This is Ani, by the way. She's my . . . girlfriend."

Ani smiled at Lennie, not missing a beat, and placed a hand on Joe's shoulder. A small, but proprietary gesture that backed up the lie.

Lennie looked at her, and the blankness returned. The look turned to a stare and he held it for thirty seconds, utterly still, until it got *really* uncomfortable and Joe felt he needed to intervene.

"Are you okay, Lennie?" he asked. "I mean, you seem a little . . . *off* today."

Lennie snapped out of it, and looked back at Joe. "I'm just tired," he said. "Well, isn't this a trip? Joe Dyson."

Then Lennie pulled back, straightened up his loose-hanging frame, and a suspicious—almost wounded—look turned his face hard.

"Didn't you go off and join the police or something?"

Joe shook his head.

"I lasted a week." Joe was manufacturing trust pheromones in industrial quantities. "You know me, Lennie. Not particularly good at following rules. Hey, remember when that history teacher—what was his name? Mr. Norris? Mr. Morris?"

"Wallace."

"That's the one. Mr. Wallace. When he demanded that I read my essay to the class, the one on Lenin . . ."

"And you refused," Lennie said, nodding. "The essay was perfect, man, I mean absolutely perfect, but you didn't like him putting you on the spot like that and you told him that you wouldn't read it out loud. I remember you said 'It's an essay, not a presentation.'"

"And he threatened me with detentions, and letters home, and giving me an F . . ."

"And you compared him to Stalin, even came up with evidence from that book by Bullock on Stalin and Hitler to back up the claims. Man, that was legend."

"Yeah, well, imagine that kind of being put on the spot and multiply it by a hundred and you've got my reason for not making it into a second week."

"So what are you doing now?" The suspicion was still there, just lessened, but Joe knew that he was treading a very thin line here and needed to be very careful how he proceeded. He cranked up the pheromone factory and served up some *trust*.

"Joe's writing a novel," Ani piped up, and he felt his one opportunity to engage Lennie slipping away. Still, he hadn't come up with a quicker lie, so he couldn't blame her for filling a potentially awkward silence. Then she continued, "But it's really an indictment of modern values, the military industrial complex, religious hypocrisy, our suicidal push toward the end of the world. It's about teens fighting back against the whole corrupt system."

The more Joe thought about it, the more he realized he'd have been hard-pressed to come up with something better. An author was believable. He'd been pretty good at essay writing—good enough to ghostwrite for a few classmates when they were falling behind. And the stuff Ani had strung on to the end about fighting against a corrupt system seemed to agree with the philosophies of the three X-Core fans he'd met before the Warhouse gig.

"Wow, that's really cool," Lennie said, and it looked like his suspicions were calmed for now. But there was still something distant and guarded about him that made Joe angry. The Lennie that he knew was no longer here. Or, if he was, he had gone so far into hiding that Joe thought it made little difference.

Do you have one of those . . . things inside you, Lennie? he thought, and the idea made him break out in goose bumps. *Are you like Professor Klein, hiding something else beneath a human layer? Something impossible? Something alien?*

Instead, he tried the trivial.

"So what are *you* up to these days?" he asked brightly.

Lennie looked shocked that the conversation was still continuing, and kept turning his body toward the hallway to leave as soon as it was politely possible. "This and that."

It was frustrating, to say the least. If Lennie had been an arms dealer, or a thief, or a potential terrorist, then Joe had been trained to handle the conversations that would have resulted. He knew the switches and levers and buttons to push. He could work his way into all manner of tricky situations with some practiced patter and the ability to adjust that patter on the fly.

But if what he was dealing with was a cult, Joe was at a loss as to how to proceed. If Lennie was harboring an alien life-form that had infected him via a .wav file from outer space, then no amount of training in the world was going to prepare Joe for breaking through its defenses.

"Joe talks about you a lot," Ani said, interrupting an edgy silence that had sprung up. "He told me that you were a true friend when he really needed one, and it meant a whole lot to him."

Lennie looked at her, hollow eyed and . . . and *something else.*

Was that an actual emotion? Had Ani's words managed to break through to him, to the real Lennie, to the nice guy that Joe knew he had once been? Joe wasn't sure, but he thought he saw that Ani's words *had* penetrated the outer shell of Lennie's caution.

He thought maybe it was time to bring on some real empathy with a little hit of the pheromones *regret* and *remember.*

Neither of them was a precise weapon to use: *regret* was too broad and often caused introspection and *remember* was vague and rarely worked, and even when it did, it often caused the wrong kind of reminiscences. Still, beggars really couldn't be choosers in this situation. He needed to try, at least, to capitalize on any chink in Lennie's armor if he was going to keep him talking.

"Joe?" Abernathy said into the chipset. It sounded like he was turned up to 11, echoing inside Joe's head. "This link should be up and running, but I'm using a poor version of burst transmissions and it's crude, so I apologize if I haven't got the calibrations right. I probably either sound like I'm shouting or whispering. Anyway, I'm sending someone to collect young Mr. Palgrave. My personnel's limited right now, what with all the adventure of last night, but I think it's high time that I started working with the resources I have. And I've been meaning to test Dr. Ghoti in the field for a while. She assures me that she has a chemical spray with her that should make Lennie very compliant—if *compliant* is a synonym for *unconscious*—but I digress. Make sure Lennie doesn't leave the house. If he does, tail him. Don't let him out of your sight. And now, as you were."

Joe wished that it was a telepathic link rather than one that required him to speak, because they were at an important point in the conversation, and Joe couldn't think of something to say that would show he'd received Abernathy's message and also keep Lennie onboard.

So he just went in for the kill on Lennie:

"I don't know what I'd have done without you. I really don't." For once the words he used to manipulate his subject were entirely true.

Lennie looked torn, divided, like the gratitude Joe and Ani were offering him was both welcome and unwelcome. Like he was fighting a mental battle between his better nature and whatever it was that X-Core had filled him up with; and it was by no means certain which one was going to win.

Lennie started to sway, big arcs from left to right and back again, and his eyes rolled back in his head.

Joe remembered Klein's eyes doing the same thing and

looked desperately at Ani, but she was just looking at Lennie with a horrified expression.

Guess she's thinking what I'm thinking.

Lennie's body was shaking now, as if he was having a seizure. Or, more accurately, a whole bunch of mini-seizures. His arms started to flail, his head ticced and tossed, and then he fell over backward.

It happened so quickly, so unexpectedly, that it took a couple of seconds for either of them to react. Then Joe stepped over Lennie and into the house, dragging him into a hall that looked straight out of *Hoarders*. When Lennie's feet had crossed the threshold Ani came in, too, and closed the door behind them.

There was a nasty smell in the air like rotting food, and the carpet that Lennie was lying on was filthy and spongy. His head lolled to one side and foam had started drooling from his mouth and nose.

"Is he choking?" Ani asked, but Joe didn't know the answer.

Or if he did, he didn't want to accept it.

He feared that Lennie was about to become one of those . . . *things*, and he didn't know what he was going to do if it happened.

But Lennie resolutely refused to change into anything. He just lay there spilling foam from his open mouth. Joe could see it being sucked into the carpet. It made him feel queasy.

"What do we do?" Ani asked.

Joe didn't have a clue.

Ani saw that Joe had pretty much frozen, and she stepped forward, removed the tablet from her pocket, took off her jacket, balled it up, and put it behind Lennie's head.

"Get some water," she said sharply, putting the tablet on the floor next to Lennie. Joe seemed glad to have an actual goal to accomplish and set off into the house to find some. Lennie's brow was hot, and the beads of sweat seemed inadequate to deal with the heat that was raging inside him.

He's burning up, she thought grimly. *He's fighting something, and it's burning him up inside.*

She made soothing sounds and stroked his brow and, for an instant, it looked like Lennie was returning to normal. A look of pain danced across his face and then was gone, and Ani thought that maybe they had seen the worst of it.

Half full glasses are also half empty.

There was a sudden brightness like a thousand flashbulbs going off at once that seemed to emanate from all over Lennie's body, a sudden halo of intense, blinding, white light. She felt it buzz through her fingertips where they were touching Lennie's brow and she was thrown back by the sudden electrical discharge. Landing heavily on the base of her spine, the pain, paired with the fact that she'd just had all of her breath forced out of her by the sudden impact, meant she just stayed there, crunched up against the wall of the hall, staring at the blazing white halo surrounding Joe's friend.

She saw what looked like *soundforms* moving across the skin of the electrical field surrounding him, but these were far different from the ones she had seen at Pabody/Reich. Sodium white, cruelly jagged, less wormlike, like blasts of electrical shocks rendered into a form that almost seemed cartoonish, like one saw in a comic book to depict electricity. All that was missing was one of those awful sound cues, *bzzzzzztttt!*

There was something almost contrived about the way the nastiness of the *soundforms* she'd seen before had been made more comprehensible to the human eye. It seemed to her that she was no longer looking at something that her mind couldn't understand and just chose the closest it could come to it. Now it was something that was just as it appeared.

Electrical fields.

Discharging power.

Voltaic forces.

Joe was back with a dirty glass filled with water, and he stood motionless in the nearby doorway. The look on his face said that he thought water probably wasn't going to bring Lennie out of it.

Whatever *it* might be.

Ani heard Joe speaking, obviously to Abernathy: "How close is Dr. Ghoti?"

However close she is, it's not close enough.

Because the battle Lennie was fighting—and having felt *soundforms* invading her own mind, she had a pretty good idea what that battle felt like—was not going well. Lennie's mouth, which had been hanging open slackly as it foamed onto the carpet, was now stretching wide in what could only be an expression of terror and agony. His hands were steel-sprung traps snatched tight over his palms, and she could see his fingernails biting into the meat. And the jagged spikes of the aura that surrounded him were growing larger, stronger, sharper, and more jagged.

She spotted a colored flicker out of the corner of her eye and thought that it was another manifestation of this horrible phenomenon, but when she turned her head she saw the screen of the tablet flashing. She moved closer. The screen was filled with a graphical representation of the thing that was enveloping Lennie, a kind of digital reflection plucked out of the air. But the tablet image was turned ninety degrees, showing a portrait view. From a different angle, Ani recognized its shape.

Back in Cambridge, what seemed like an age ago, when this was all just starting, Uncle Alex had opened the .wav file in some software that had showed what the sound looked like—a series of peaks and troughs, jagged spikes along the timeline of the player software—and that was what she was seeing on the screen.

The spiky aura that surrounded Lennie Palgrave was a graphical representation of the sound itself.

She knew that it was an important piece of evidence—it might be useful to have a graphic representation of the sound for later reference. She had to fight through a flood of fear, helplessness, and self-doubt, but it was an opportunity too important to miss. She shoved her personal feelings aside, grabbed the tablet, and took a screenshot, then spent a few moments trying to clear the digital echo from the screen. It took a reboot, but the tablet was so fast that hardly mattered. She downloaded some sound editing software—again, lightning fast—displayed the graphical representation of the .wav file, took a screenshot, then opened both files and lined them up side by side.

Triumph and fear combined into a new, composite emotion as the stray pieces of the puzzle that had been floating around inside her head suddenly meshed together.

The more she thought about it, the more the thought gained weight and clarity.

She had a few things to check, a meeting to keep, and a favor to ask of Uncle Alex, but she thought she had a lot of this mess figured out now.

She only hoped she was wrong.

Joe saw Ani reach for the tablet, and the purposeful expression on her face told him she was onto something. He left her to it and bent over to attend to Lennie.

Joe knew better than to touch him. He'd learned that at an early age: you don't stick your hand into something containing electrical sparks. But he'd also learned that sometimes hard-and-fast rules weren't always without exceptions.

To even *begin* to understand this phenomenon, Joe knew that he was going to have to risk it.

He extended his hand, then stopped just short. He could already feel the immense power crackling through his hand, but he didn't feel pain, exactly. It was more like the odd tingle of static electricity.

He took a deep breath, reached out farther, and touched the jagged shell with his fingers splayed.

Joe heard the current rather than felt it, a collection of jumbled sounds in his head, different from the experience at the Warhouse. The sounds didn't seem to be trying to work their way into his brain. He was overhearing them, not being attacked. The phenomenon was focused on Lennie, and Joe was afforded a rare opportunity to listen in without it sensing him as something that needed to be attacked.

The jagged shell expanded—grew even spikier—and the sound got a whole lot louder. Its melodies rang and echoed through Joe's skull: high sounds that hurt; bass sounds that vibrated through his bones. But it was the mid-range sounds that gave him pause.

They didn't seem *quite* connected to the others. They

stuck out. And it took Joe a few seconds to work out why. It was like they were coming from a different set of instruments, which was sort of true, but not entirely the answer. He concentrated harder, and it came to him. Where the treble and bass sounds were otherworldly, alien, phrased and arranged in structures that seemed unique and strange, the mid-range notes seemed recognizable, or at least understandable. The treble/bass followed no musical patterns that Joe could recall, clicking and buzzing and falling away in chaotic patterns. The mid-parts seemed more organized, more . . . *human*.

Joe pressed his hand harder against the shell of sparks. The surface tension would not allow his hand to pass through to Lennie inside. The more forceful contact seemed to fight against him, the sounds growing louder inside Joe's head, and his entire body felt like it was resonating along with the sound, as if he had become a tuning fork through which the vibrations passed.

The incomprehensible madness of the alien sounds became unbearable. If he listened to them this loud for too long he thought they might just drive him out of his mind. The other sounds provided him an anchor—something to hold on to to keep him from going adrift in the voidsounds that surrounded them.

Alien sounds, he thought, *but they have a terrestrial middle.* Joe tried to focus on the mid-range sounds, and for a moment he thought that he was on the verge of something: understanding? Recognition?

Then the shell collapsed beneath his hand and he was touching Lennie's arm.

The sounds died down.

Lennie lay there unconscious.

There was a knock at the door.

Emari Ghoti was standing outside looking tense but supremely capable. In one hand she held a set of car keys, in the other a plain, unlabeled aerosol can.

Tall and slim, with dark butterscotch skin, Dr. Ghoti was a rising star medic who had tired of the National Health Service and the lack of funding for research that didn't have an immediate cash value application. She'd traded her old life for an unlimited research budget at YETI.

Once, she had joked to Joe that her name could be pronounced *fish*, if you used the "gh" as it was pronounced in the word *enough*, the "o" from *women*; and the "ti" from *nation*.

"You have a patient for me?" she said, stepping through the door, wrinkling her nose at the state of the hall, then frowning at Lennie's body spread out on the floor. "Started without me, huh?"

"We just left him where he fell," Joe said. "We need to get him back to Gretchen's and find out what's wrong with him."

"What are the symptoms?" Dr. Ghoti bent down and made a *give me space* gesture to Joe and Ani.

"He had a kind of seizure," Ani said. "Sudden fever. Oh yeah, and then he got swallowed up by alien electricity and started throwing out sparks. Sparks that mimicked the shape of the sound waveform that got him into this state in the first place."

Dr. Ghoti tilted her head at Ani, as if expecting a punch line, but when none came she turned to Joe. "I have a car outside; help me lift him."

Joe grabbed Lennie's shoulders, and Dr. Ghoti and Ani took the feet.

CHAPTER EIGHTEEN:
ZUGZWANG

Back at their makeshift hideout at Gretchen's house in Islington, and with Lennie sedated in an upstairs room, Joe sought out Abernathy. "I'm losing it. When Lennie went down, I just seized up. Ani had to get me back on track."

Abernathy surveyed him coolly and Joe felt uncomfortable under the scrutiny. Then Abernathy said, "*Pah!*"

"Pah?" It certainly wasn't what Joe had been expecting.

"Joe, a friend of yours went down and you froze for a few seconds. What happened to Andy raised its ugly head again and stopped you in your tracks. You're human. You make connections. Some of those connections are positive, some aren't. But you make them, that's what's important. Next time you'll be okay."

"I'm not sure I can deal with a next time."

"Of course you can. Look, I can't tell you that no one else is going to die on you in the field. I mean I *could*, but it would be completely dishonest of me. We play for high stakes. You know that. But the ends always justify the sacrifices we make. That's why YETI exists. What we do is important enough to lay our lives on the line."

"It's not me I'm worried about. It's the people I'm supposed to be looking out for. The people I'm supposed to be keeping safe."

"That doesn't cover the circumstances in Andy's case or, for that matter, Lennie's," Abernathy reminded him. "Andy could look after himself—insisted upon it, remember? The mission just turned bad. They do that sometimes. Think of all the missions that have turned out well, though. Think of all the people who are walking around on this planet because you stopped bad people from doing bad things to them.

"Lennie is different: a casualty of circumstances that are outside your control. That *were* outside your control. Because we're going to make sure that it ends with him. Stop second-guessing yourself, Joe. There is no one I want more on the front line for this."

"There's no one else to call," Joe said jokingly.

"Ah, there's that, too. Although I have just reached out to some . . . agencies that owe me some pretty colossal favors. I told them I'm cashing in. I think we'll be back in YETI HQ pretty soon."

"Why not just call the prime minister?" Joe asked. "I don't think he has any love for Victor Palgrave. And if Palgrave was behind the attack on YETI, then he's declared war on the justice system. He needs to be stopped."

"Our gracious host showed me the party's file on Victor Palgrave. Although there is plenty in it to provoke concern, we do not yet have the smoking gun that ties him to any of this. It's going to take evidence to implicate him directly, otherwise the party will stand beside him. Rumor and conjecture are not enough to bring him down, and he is both powerful and an ally of some very powerful people. Politics is full of some very complex beasts, and many of them serve more than one master."

"I thought politicians served the electorate. . . ."

"That's really funny. I must remember that one. Anyway, I myself am subject to political pressures and duties—party and otherwise. Committees oversee us, committees oversee those committees, reports crisscross Whitehall and weakness reflects poorly on all of them. I lost YETI to an invading force, Joe. I'm keeping as quiet about it as I can."

Suddenly, Joe realized that Abernathy was telling him the whole truth. That he was playing this exile through until he sorted it out himself, simply because he wanted the taking of YETI to remain secret from the people he should be turning to for help.

He wondered which agencies Abernathy had reached out to, and what Abernathy had on them to trust them to keep his own embarrassing secret.

The world was quite possibly in deadly peril, and Abernathy was holding out on calling in the big guns because of *pride*.

At least he's human, Joe thought. *It's nice to be reminded of that occasionally.*

Ani had a long talk with Gretchen, took a while to process the information she gathered from it, then called a meeting. A working class, fifteen-year-old kid from South Cambridge, calling a meeting of law enforcement personnel, analysts, a doctor, and Gretchen the human library—she felt both exhilarated and terrified.

They met up in the living room/library overflow: Ani, Gretchen, Joe, Abernathy, Dr. Ghoti, the Shuttleworths, and an analyst who introduced herself as Leeza Marsh.

No one seemed to think there was anything strange about taking time from their vital business to listen to Ani, and that encouraged her.

She'd fleshed out her suspicions with a lot of input from Gretchen, and had reached some pretty stark conclusions.

Conclusions that she was now ready to share.

"I've been baffled. There seem to be too many things going on here. We know they're all connected, but the connections are so vague I haven't been seeing them.

"Well, I'm starting to see a pattern now, and I need to say it out loud, just to hear your objections and take your input onboard.

"We begin with the science fiction part: an alien sound, brought down to Earth by a radio telescope. I'm absolutely certain that the message that Imogen Bell received that night *was* extraterrestrial in origin. But I'm pretty sure that what she recorded that night wasn't a message from an alien being. I think it *was* an alien being."

She saw how that idea struck the others from the surprised expressions on their faces: Abernathy's surprise appeared laced with skepticism; Joe's with amusement; Dr. Ghoti's with thoughtfulness; Leeza Marsh's with incomprehension; and the Shuttleworth brothers' with excitement. Gretchen merely smiled back encouragingly.

"Explain," Abernathy said.

Ani nodded, then continued. "We imagine alien creatures by combining elements of things we know. Whatever is out there in space must be, in some way, similar to us, or the other creatures on this planet. The alien from *Alien*, while terrifying in the context of the film, is humanoid; it has two legs and features that might be inspired by insects, but it's basically a product of a human imagination. Alien life will follow no such rules, I'm sure of it.

"I was talking to Joe yesterday, trying to find a way into this, and I suddenly realized that an alien creature wouldn't even necessarily be made up of the same stuff as us. It would depend on the start-up conditions of the planet it evolved on. Maybe it's made of rock. Or liquid. Or electricity. Or gas. Or magnetism."

She waited a few seconds. "Or sound."

Abernathy raised an eyebrow and nodded. "Ingenious. Please continue."

"Imagine it: a creature composed of sound, traveling through space, with no need for spaceships or warp drives. It could be its own vehicle."

One of the Shuttleworths—the taller one—put up his hand. Ani ignored the humor of it, a scientist asking her permission to speak, and pointed to him.

"Sound can't travel through space," he said apologetically. "Space is a vacuum. Sound needs matter to vibrate against so it can carry on its journey. I mean it sounds good but, sorry . . ."

Ani nodded. The simple fact that sound needed molecules to travel through, and there were no such molecules in space, was something it had taken her quite a lot of thought to find a way around. Or, rather, it had taken *Gretchen* a lot of thought.

"No need to apologize for stating the truth. That's why we're here. And, yes, it's true that sound *as we know it* cannot travel through a vacuum, but when I say that it's a sound from outer space, I'm kind of using shorthand. *Sound* is sort of a stand-in for something stranger and more complex than *just* a sound. I'm not saying it's like any sound we have here on Earth, or even that it has the same properties of sound as we understand it. Radio waves travel though space, carrying sounds wrapped up in electromagnetic radiation. And they travel at the speed of light. Maybe our creature is more like a radio signal . . ."

The smaller Shuttleworth put up his hand, but Gretchen had coached her for just this interruption.

". . . but unlike a radio signal it is free from the inverse-square law that says its power should degrade because it is *a living organism*. It maintains itself. It eats. It produces its own energy. It's actually its own transmitter, too, but from there it all gets a little hard to wrap my head around. The point is that it doesn't *have to* degrade."

The Shuttleworth hand went down again.

"It is a living, thinking creature. It holds itself together, and maintains its systems like any biological organism maintains its body.

"Maybe we'll find out its precise composition one day. But not from the creatures we brought down to Earth—Joe and I have only seen one of *them* with our own eyes. I don't think that X-Core teens are infected with the creature that the Pabody/Reich telescope detected."

There was the sound of multiple intakes of breath.

"Wait, what?" Joe asked. "I think even I might be getting lost here."

Ani smiled. "I was lost, too. But I started thinking about the limits of human recording. About how when we record an orchestra, it's not the orchestra itself—just the sounds it makes. We might capture those sounds in amazing detail, with a clarity that allows us to hear everything from the deepest roll on a kettledrum to the faintest trill of a piccolo, but what we don't record are the actual people or their instruments—their physical forms.

"What if Imogen Bell recorded the *sound* of the creature she found out there in space? She captured some of its essence, if you like, but not really the creature itself. The creature is energy, radiation, information. To us it's a sound, because it's close to being a sound, and the human mind loves its analogies. So our flawed human recorders captured some of the creature: its sound. But that's *enough* of the creature for the recording to copy some of its sentience, too. Its intelligence. Its thoughts. Imogen Bell basically made a terrestrial copy of the creature that *lives* in the medium of the recording, but it isn't the creature. Just a reduced *version* of it."

"The recording is *alive?*" Abernathy said. "Is that what X-Core is? A second-generation copy of a creature from space? Finding a home inside our children?"

Ani shook her head. "Sort of. Kind of. No. Look, it's important to think about what happened next. The creature that Joe and I saw at Pabody/Reich was very different from the one we saw Lennie becoming. The thing Professor Klein was harboring . . . It *was* a copy of the alien. But Lennie? I think he was something different. Connected, but different."

She took the tablet from her pocket and displayed the two waveforms side by side. "Compare and contrast. You can see, quite plainly, that they *are* different. The first one is the creature, as recorded by Imogen Bell. The second one has been altered."

"You make it sound intentional," Abernathy said.

"I know." Ani pointed to the Lennie waveform. "But I'm convinced this is *not* a recording error. It could not have happened by accident. It's as if terrestrial sounds have been incorporated into the creature's *shell*, so it has properties like the original, but with a more specific purpose. I believe there is a human hand at work behind this."

There was a long silence, and then Abernathy said: "Check everything Ani just said. I want proof one way or the other. What are you all still doing here? I want it yesterday."

Then he came up to Ani, and slapped her on the shoulder. "Very nicely reasoned."

Ani thought, *I could really get used to this.*

Baker Street was crowded with people, many of whom seemed determined to get in between Joe and his view of Ani. The street was uncharacteristically busy, and it made Joe nervous. Ani was waiting outside the Sherlock Holmes Museum, trying to blend in. Tourists took photos of the museum, and of the man who stood in the doorway of 221B dressed as a Victorian policeman. Ani always turned away or drifted out of shot by the time the shutter was pressed.

Joe nodded every time she did. It was good spycraft, made all the better by being natural, instinctual, untaught.

A reflex to stay out of people's photographs might be borne out of a hacker's paranoia, but was a skill that perfectly transferred to being a YETI operative.

Joe was playing lookout: scanning the crowd and addresses nearby, watching for something out of place that could pose a threat. Buses and cars passed, people walked by either looking around or focused on their own thoughts—the perfect way to tell a tourist from a local—but there was nothing to get his investigative hackles up.

Except, of course, the time.

It was 2:10. Ani's hacker friend was supposed to have shown up ten minutes ago. Maybe he was doing the same as Joe, scouting the area for signs of danger, his caution preventing him from approaching Ani until he was one hundred percent certain that she was alone.

Which, of course, she wasn't. She had Joe. Maybe Jack had spotted him, but Joe doubted it. He was shifting position every few minutes, pretending to consult a map, and he was doing his best to look lost. He'd occasionally pick out passersby who looked like tourists and would have no idea of the area's geography, and ask them for directions. If they didn't know, the deception was intact. If they did, then he pretended they didn't and carried on. Joe was actively drawing attention to himself, which was one of the very best ways to hide in a crowd.

It was a necessary precaution. Joe had nagging doubts about Jack's motives for this meeting, based on the undeniable fact that he should have experienced some kind of reaction to the .wav file. Jack not warning Ani about the file's danger made Joe suspicious. Maybe Jack was one of *them*.

Joe was about to approach some more tourists when he caught movement from the door of the museum. He studied his map, looking over the top of it to watch the person exiting the building. A bulky youth in a *Halo* T-shirt was looking around surreptitiously, and if he was trying to look inconspicuous he was failing, miserably. Joe could see the tension in his face and movements. Jack—it had to be him—spotted Ani, pretended he hadn't, and made such an act of not looking at her that Joe felt a little embarrassed for him. Jack approached Ani, keeping her quite obviously in his peripheral vision, and Joe crossed the street on Jack's blind side, taking up a position between Ani and the museum's entrance.

Jack drew level with Ani and made awkward contact with her—he seemed to pretend to cough, maybe hiding her name in the noise. It was such a rookie move that Joe felt like squirming.

Ani nodded. Jack moved away and Ani followed him a few paces behind. Joe fell into step behind her.

They passed a realtor's, and some other stores, before Jack crossed the road, led her another hundred or so feet, and then ducked left into an alleyway. Ani shook her head, and followed him. Joe got to the opening of the alley, but hung back and waited around the corner.

He hoped this was worth the time it was taking out of their day.

Ani thought she would have recognized Jack even without the half-baked attempt at saying her name while pretending to cough. It was a dumb thing that kids stopped doing around the age of eleven, but Jack seemed to think it entirely appropriate for a clandestine meeting.

Still, it was better than one of those contrived passwords you heard in spy movies like, *The winters in Moscow make my grandmother grow irises.*

But only just.

They rolled into an alley and Ani checked that Joe was just behind them before turning. Then she had her first face-to-face with the legendary hacker who she'd never thought she'd hook up with in meatspace.

"Were you followed?" Jack asked urgently, and the slight nasal tones, coupled with the subtle pink device in his ear, cleared up the mystery of why Jack had remained unaffected by the .wav file.

He was partially deaf.

"Were you?" Ani asked, dodging the inevitable lie until it was necessary.

"I don't know. I don't know anything anymore."

In the flesh, Jack "Black Hat" McVitie was either exactly as she expected, or not even close. He perfectly fit the stereotype of a kid who spent too long at his computer and not enough time exercising, but Ani had anticipated something different. He was such a legend, she kind of expected a Hollywood-style hacker, dashing good looks and a lightning-fast mind.

Instead he just seemed awkward and sweaty.

"I've been on the run since you sent me that file," Ani said. "Men with guns. Chasing me. Where did you get it?"

Jack's pudgy face made him look like he was about to cry. "Government server. Very hush-hush. I was looking for dirt, I found that."

"It's okay. I just need you to confirm something for me. Was there an account tied to the file? An identification code? Some way we can track it back to its owner?"

"I knew whose stuff I was poking around in. I mean, I wasn't fishing an uncharted river. I'd heard some negative chatter about an up-and-coming politician and I wanted to confirm it before I launched a massive DDoS campaign against him."

"His name?"

"Palgrave." Jack wiped his nose with his sleeve. "You know, the one they're tipping for PM someday."

"Were tipping," Ani corrected. "I think he blew that shot a while back. And you think it was him who sent men after you?"

"Who else? They were private goons—the kind his data says he's been financing in Africa and South America—fighting his private wars for money and influence. I even traced a few of his shell accounts rerouting funds to groups who look like terrorists, to be honest, but then I found that stupid file and got distracted. I had to see what was in there. It was the highest-protected data on his system. I thought it had to be a record of his sketchiest deals, but it was a sound file that called home. The rest you know."

"Do you have proof that it came from Palgrave?"

"Proof?" Jack's features took on traces of suspicion and distrust. "Why would I need proof?"

"So he doesn't get away with it."

"Get away with what? Hunting us down? Man, if we tell anyone about the hack, we're toast. After some of the stuff we've done together, we'll be the bad guys. Don't even think about telling anyone about all this, Ani."

Something about Ani's expression must have given him an inkling that that particular ship had already sailed because his face turned red.

"You've already told someone, haven't you? Of all the stupid . . ."

He moved toward her, and Joe picked that moment to come around the corner.

Joe saw Jack make a move toward Ani, and stepped in to make sure it didn't turn violent. It seemed unlikely—the guy was about forty pounds overweight and looked like the closest he came to fighting was playing *World of Warcraft* online—but Joe felt protective toward Ani and didn't want to take a chance.

Jack saw him immediately and ran.

Down the alley, away from Joe, not particularly fast but pretty determined.

Joe didn't think he looked scary enough for that kind of overreaction, but then he saw that Ani was still looking past him, and he turned to see two guys coming into the alley, reaching into their jackets. Joe recognized them from the security footage that Klein had shown him back at Pabody/Reich just before he went all extraterrestrial on them, and the thought of the guns they were drawing sent him right back to the moment that Glenn Tavernier pulled out his own weapon. This was a moment that would pretty much define the rest of his life.

He guessed he'd felt it raising its ugly head back when he'd first seen the bulge in the first guy's jacket on-screen in Klein's security room, but he'd squashed it down and kept it away from the forefront of his mind, put it back in the darker parts of his memory where he hid his failures, like the red chamber where Andy died again and again and he was unable to prevent it every time.

Freezing was out of the question.

Doing nothing was not an option.

He had a new partner now, and he wasn't going to let her suffer the fate of his last one.

The two guys already had their weapons half drawn, and if they drew them fully, Joe and Ani were at their mercy. He couldn't say for certain that they had murder in mind, but Joe believed that a man didn't pull a gun unless he was prepared to use it, and he didn't use it unless he was prepared to kill with it.

Joe readied himself, closed his eyes, accessed his chip—the way he wished he'd accessed it on the night Andy died—and turned on its *eidetic reflexes* function.

The basics of every type of physical combat, from bare knuckle brawling through to jujitsu, were stored there, ready for activation.

He thought about Andy, and Ani, and did something he had always avoided.

He turned off the safety switch, just by imagining it as a physical switch and mentally flipping it.

Now he welcomed the anger he'd always tried to suppress, feeling it flooding through him like a red tide.

He opened his eyes.

Ani realized that they were in big trouble and looked at Joe for guidance, a strategy, reassurance, *anything*.

She was shocked to see him close his eyes and just stand there, immobile.

Great time to freeze, she thought and turned to the first of the incoming goons. His gun was in his hand and he was bringing it around to point at her. She felt sick and alone and afraid.

She steeled herself, made her body into a shape that seemed similar to a fighting stance she'd seen on TV, and thought, *Well, this is stupid.*

She looked over at Joe again, fear and sickness growing within her, and saw his eyes flick open, his face get gravely serious, then determined, then slightly insane.

He took a few paces forward and the first guy stopped the arc that would bring his gun to rest upon her and swung it around until it was pointing at Joe.

He settled into his aim.

Ani saw Joe grin.

And then things went kind of crazy.

The guy was pointing the SIG at Joe's body, playing the averages. The torso was a better bet than a limb, or even the head, simply because of its greater area. And there was plenty inside the torso that would be messed up enough by a bullet to end any resistance.

It was the easy play.

It was also flawed.

Because the guy had his stance locked down, and it would take time to readjust. Oh, it would only take milliseconds, sure, but they were milliseconds that Joe simply wasn't going to give him.

He knew that the longer he drew this out, the less likely it was that he could emerge victorious. Two adult targets with about equal strength, stamina, training, intelligence, and guns, against Joe and Ani who were unarmed, had teenage strength, moderate stamina, Ani with no training, they both had unpolished intelligence, and no guns.

Speed and surprise were the only weapons in their favor.

That, and a catalogue of digital files full of violence, and the righteous rage that was already filling Joe with increased adrenaline.

With the chip engaged, time passed in a very different way for Joe. The Shuttleworths called it *the edge*, while Abernathy preferred *the quick* because of something he'd read in a thriller once. But whatever you called it, it was like Joe was moving at full speed, while the people he fought looked like they were at half.

Joe swerved out of the guy's line of sight, then ducked and wheeled around as he cut down the distance between them. The guy tried to track him, but Joe's path was random, and it brought him within striking distance of the guy in less than two seconds.

Up that close, a gun didn't need to be accurately aimed to do fatal damage, but it did need to be pointing in Joe's direction. He bobbed underneath its firing line and came up fast and hard, pushing off the ground, straightening bent legs and concentrating the force of all that energy into the flat of his right hand. The hand hit the guy's gun arm midway between his wrist and his elbow and it pushed the arm upward. Joe stood up to his full height while the arm was still traveling and windmilled his left hand—curled into a fist—so that it came from high up and hit the topside of the guy's arm at the junction of his hand and his wrist.

Joe's right hand remained flat beneath, and the guy's arm hit it as Joe's left fist drove the arm down with devastating force.

The gun flew out of the guy's hand, and the bones inside his arm made a horrible noise—somewhere between a pop and a crack. Joe moved fluidly aside, spinning around the guy until he was behind him, and delivered a flat-foot kick to the back of the guy's left calf. A stamping kick that focused all of Joe's power, rage, and digitally enhanced skill into a single spot, all delivered at lightning speed.

Joe checked the position of the other guy—three yards out and gun aimed, but the barrel wavering because things were happening too fast for him to be able to risk letting off a shot without hitting his associate—before watching the first guy take a heavy, headfirst fall onto the pavement.

Joe gauged his resting place, turned to face the second guy, and set off for him, kicking off hard and making sure that his spring forward used the back of the first guy's head as a starting place.

Joe figured that was one down, one to go.

The second guy tracked Joe with his gun and his finger was tightening on the trigger, so Joe feinted right, feinted left, and then dived to the ground, hitting a forward roll and coming to a stop at the guy's left, seated on the ground, legs drawn back, hands splayed.

The guy tried to adjust, but it was far too late.

Joe braced himself with his hands and he kicked out with both feet, hitting the guy's knees, knocking him backward. Then Joe was up and flashing two quick punches into the man's solar plexus. Joe took a quick count: two knees screaming in pain, and the blows to the abdomen would have thrown the guy's diaphragm into spasm, causing a momentary, but total, loss of air.

Keeping the gun in his sight line, and keeping his body away from it, he reached up with two stiff arms and clapped them together—hard—on both of the guy's ears.

The fight went out of him. *The rule of three.* Deliver three agonizing strikes and let overload do the rest. Joe stuck his leg behind the guy's legs, pushed him backward, and he tripped and fell. Joe stamped on his chest and kicked the gun from his hand. Then he ran to Ani, grabbed her by the arm, and together they raced out of the alley and back onto Baker Street.

Not a shot had been fired.

Not a blow landed on him.

Joe shut his eyes, checked the combat log, and saw that the fight had lasted thirteen seconds, then switched the safety mechanism back to "on," powered down the *eidetic reflexes* part of his chip, and he and Ani made their escape.

"That was, like, that was . . . I mean . . . *wow!*" Ani said when they were clear. "You took them both out . . . I mean . . . *how*? What was that you were using? Ninja skills?"

"A few things I picked up. But, truthfully, I'm a little disappointed."

"Disappointed?" Ani asked, bewildered.

"It took thirteen seconds to take them both down."

"Yeah, to take down two armed mercenaries. With guns. What's there to be disappointed about?"

"I was aiming for under twelve."

Ani noticed that he was only half joking.

He knew that he'd probably come across as arrogant, or unnecessarily glib, but it was a strange feeling, all that fighting skill and expertise just fading away back into his chipset. Turning off the anger control made it even more difficult to adjust, because all the rage that came out—and that was responsible for at least two of the blows that he landed—wasn't augmented at all. It was his natural state without the chip. And it scared him. It always had.

Then he'd joined YETI and the same neurological disorder that made his anger uncontrollable turned out to be the precise thing that made the Shuttleworths' chipset work in his head, and the anger had disappeared.

But taking off the suppressor, or switching off the chip, always reminded him that it was only YETI technology that kept him from losing his temper. He saw his propensity for violence as a weakness, and—even though it had just helped him dispatch two armed men in thirteen seconds—it was also a source of shame.

Shame that hid its vulnerability beneath defensive statements like *I was aiming for under twelve.*

Better Ani thought that he was cocky than ashamed.

He contacted Abernathy and told him what they had confirmed about Palgrave's position at the head of the conspiracy they were steadily unraveling.

"It would help if Mr. McVitie could provide indisputable proof of Palgrave's involvement."

"Yeah, well, he took off. Paranoia multiplied by the arrival of two guys with guns."

"Thirteen seconds? You disarmed them and took them down in *thirteen seconds?*"

"Had to. So what are we doing now?"

"Well, Dr. Ghoti is hard at work on your friend Lennie, but it's difficult to know exactly what we're dealing with. And we've got a lot more questions than answers. I mean this must all be leading up to *something,* but I can't figure out Palgrave's strategy. The taking of YETI HQ must mean that we're very close to his endgame. You can't take out a government task force without some kind of blowback. He must have something in play. We must be missing something."

"What?"

"Ah, that is the question, isn't it?" Abernathy sounded

frustrated. "All I know is that you don't make a play like Palgrave did last night unless you think that no one is going to notice in time. That means there must be something happening now that is going to make an armed takeover irrelevant."

"Have you checked Palgrave's calendar for the day? I mean there should be some public record of an MP's movements, shouldn't there?"

"There's nothing there," Abernathy said. "We checked."

Ani was listening to Joe's side of the conversation. She'd started looking up something on her tablet, then raised her eyes from the screen and said, "Uh-oh."

Joe asked Abernathy to wait and turned to Ani.

"What's 'uh-oh'?"

"Twitter. Palgrave's setting off for a gig in Hyde Park. Some free entertainment he's organized . . ."

"Did you hear that, Abernathy?" There was no answer. A few seconds later he got a reply.

"How did we miss this? A sophisticated intelligence gathering network at my fingertips, and I find out through Twitter and Google? There's a free concert in Hyde Park for the city's youth, and it's starting in about thirty minutes. It's being webcast. Around the world."

"Don't tell me. Precision Image is playing?" Joe said.

"Could be. 'Up-and-coming London bands' is all the information I can find. Joe, we have to stop this. We're under-resourced, understaffed, and way behind the curve on this one, but if that sound is anywhere near as dangerous as it seems, then we can't let it go global."

"We'll stop it. We have to."

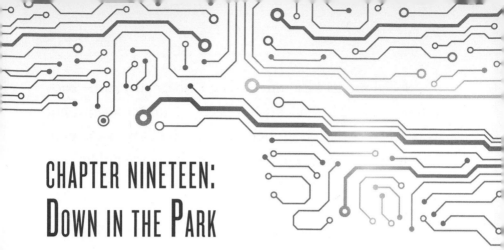

CHAPTER NINETEEN:
DOWN IN THE PARK

Joe and Ani grabbed a cab and it crawled through London traffic toward Hyde Park. They had no plan, no strategy, no ideas, and Joe had a terrifying feeling that they were too late and Victor Palgrave's scheme was about to reach a terrible fruition.

Ani took out her phone and made a call: a cryptic conversation during which she muttered about sound waves and antinoise—whatever the heck that was—and she refused to speak about it, other than to say it might not come to anything, and if it did it was their "very last fallback plan."

Joe was too wired to argue.

He willed the traffic to break, to allow their cab through, but it seemed resistant to his mental commands and they made slow progress. They took a right at Selfridges, then a left onto Park Lane, and then traffic stalled. Joe paid the driver and they took off on foot.

The area was in chaos with throngs of teens heading for the park.

"Social media has gone insane," Abernathy came back to tell them. "The concert has been set up for weeks, but its organizers have been holding back the bulk of the publicity until now. Suddenly it's a secret gig made public, and everyone wants to go. I can't tell you how many people are heading there. . ."

"I can. Freaking thousands. Lambs to the slaughter. Can't you call in the army?"

"I've called in *everyone* I can think of. This is as short a notice as I've ever had to organize anything meaningful for a situation so grave. Get in there, Joe. Shut it down. And most of all: make sure that .wav file doesn't play!"

Hyde Park was one of the places where London's urban and commercial sprawl tried on countryside clothes, and the city was better for it. Ani had been here before, for a gig with a band that she now could not believe she had *ever* thought was cool, and she had marveled then at the park's size, the beauty of its landscaping, and its sheer capacity for human audiences.

Now, though, she felt sick.

The crowds of young people filling up the park were completely unprepared for the sound from space, or the modified version of it. She had no doubts now who had modified the .wav file: Victor Palgrave. And when it played, everyone in the park would be subjected to its devastating effects.

Thousands of kids would become just like Lennie

Palgrave—normal on the surface, but inside, hosts for those electric impulses that would make them no longer completely human.

Had Lennie been used as a lab rat for the experiments his father would have needed to run in harnessing the .wav for his own dark purposes? Ani wondered what kind of father it was who could be *that* cold and manipulative. Still, maybe it was lucky that he *had* gotten Lennie involved. If he hadn't, MI5 wouldn't have set YETI on Lennie's trail. That was Palgrave's big mistake.

She was starting to see the sequence of events that had brought them all here: Palgrave obviously hadn't been expecting MI5 to start investigating his son, and when YETI was asked to infiltrate the weird world of X-Core just days before this "free concert" that would provided Palgrave with an army, he must have gotten spooked and thought he'd take YETI out of the equation.

Jack's discovery of the .wav file must have thrown Palgrave into a panic, too, so he'd sent mercenaries to shut Jack up. And anyone he'd been in contact with.

Ani supposed she shouldn't be surprised, but she was.

First contact had been made with an alien life-form—of which Professor Klein was probably the purest terrestrial manifestation—and Palgrave had quickly seen a way to turn it to his advantage. That was the way humanity seemed to operate.

Humans couldn't help but exploit *everything*.

There were still a few things that Ani couldn't figure, though.

First, what was Imogen Bell's role in all of this? It seemed certain that she had heard the sound from space, recorded it, played it to Professor Klein, and then she or Klein had substituted it for another sound. Did that mean that Imogen Bell was, like Klein, a recipient of the real creature's essence? How, then, had Victor Palgrave gotten his hands on it? How had he figured out the route to power that was to be gained by adding his own messages to the creature's code?

Still, there was no time to waste on endless questions and speculative answers.

They were entering the park.

They had to stop Palgrave taking over the minds of everyone gathered here, and then they could hunt him down and just ask him.

The crowd was converging on an area that had rapidly been turned over to a stage and a huge public address system. Joe didn't know how powerful the speakers were, but he was sure they would be more than sufficient to convey Victor Palgrave's terrifying sound with devastating efficiency.

The area around the stage was already thick with spectators, and there was a tangible buzz in the air. As far as the crowd was concerned, they were here for free entertainment. They had no idea about the terrible things hidden beneath the music.

Technicians were busying themselves on the stage, connecting instruments and checking microphones. Joe felt futility wash through him, a tidal wave of doubts and fears. But he had to concentrate on making sure that his fears stopped before the band took the stage.

"Abernathy," he growled. "Where's my backup?"

"On the way," Abernathy snapped. "But you need to buy us time. Get to the mixing desk and make sure that sound doesn't play."

"I'm on it."

"I've got a helicopter on its way, an RAF Puma. Kill the music, Joe. *Now!*"

Ani tapped him on the arm and pointed up to the stage.

The technicians were gone.

The crowd roared.

The kid that used to be Harry Brewster was emerging from the side of the stage. Imogen Bell followed. Then the rest of the band.

Precision Image was onstage.

Time had just run out.

The first note of the song reverberated around the park, and the crowd screamed in fevered appreciation. It was a low, industrial sound that Joe could feel vibrating through his skeleton, and it made him feel anxious and more than a little scared.

Onstage, Null-A had his eyes turned up toward the sky as he struck a defiant, messianic pose, looking too much like the image of Jesus dying on the cross for it to be accidental. Flashes of light from a rig above the stage made a flip book of Harry's posing.

Joe scanned the park quickly, noticing that Ani was doing the same, desperately searching for the location of the mixing desk. "There are thousands of people here," he muttered. "Tens of thousands. This is bad."

"Ignore them," Abernathy told him. "Just concentrate on the job."

"Easy for you to say. How about telling me where the sound engineer is hiding?"

"*Find him!* We're trying to pull the plug from here, but I have nowhere near the options available to me that I would at HQ. We're seconds away from killing the webcast, but that isn't going to help the kids in the park. I've got multiple teams moving in on your location, but right now you're our only hope of preventing a disaster."

Joe felt a tug on his arm. It was Ani. She was pointing to a figure raised above the heads in the middle of the crowd. A man in a baseball cap, with a ponytail sticking out of the hole in the back, was working at a vast mixing desk about fifty yards from where Joe and Ani were standing.

They started pushing their way through the crowd, but it was like moving through molasses. People stubbornly stood their ground, not giving an inch as Joe and Ani tried to pass, their eyes fixed upon the stage. Joe tried shouting for people to get out of his way, but he was completely ignored. He realized that being polite wasn't going to work. They'd have to force their way through. He aimed forward with his shoulder and kept moving at a brisk pace.

He bounced his way through a few rows of people and then the crowd seemed to draw in around him and he completely lost sight of Ani.

Joe experienced a moment of pure panic, which had more to do with the crowd pressing in on him than it did with what would happen if he didn't stop the alien signal being transmitted. A primal, potent fear of the crowd just swallowing him up. But fear was useless unless he could channel it. So that's what he decided to do: he'd convert the panic into fuel, diverting it into a force he could use.

Ani appeared out of a wall of people, pushing them aside with a determined look on her face, and Joe felt relief replace his fear. She was tough, that much was certain, and she seemed to have an ability to reformulate plans and procedures on the fly, adapting and evolving strategies as they were needed. If this was Abernathy's idea of a field examination for Ani, and if they got out of this alive, intact, and sane, then Joe was going to give her a passing grade.

With honors.

But right now they had other things to concern themselves with.

Joe and Ani continued to barge their way through the static crowd, but when they were about ten yards from their target, the music suddenly changed.

Joe saw Ani stop and throw her hands up to cover her ears.

He knew then that time had *really* just run out.

Ani was following Joe through the crowd when it hit her.

Hard.

The .wav.

Amplified a millionfold.

Earsplitting.

Brain-crunching.

.wav.

She put her hands up to her ears to block it out, but it was like trying to block a tsunami with a cotton ball. The sound was just too loud, too powerful, too raw. She felt it move into her brain, full of its insidious information.

First, the deep bass sound, descending until it was like a physical pain. Then the mid-range sounds spreading through her body. Then the second type of *soundforms* trying to insinuate their way into her brain and body, all electric heat and crackling power.

She tried to fight it, tried to push the *soundforms* away

before they could spread and multiply throughout her. Again, it was in vain. They were too loud, all-consuming, fierce and hungry, and there were far too many. At this volume the command for her to *"OBEY! OBEY!"* was impossible to resist.

She reached for something—anything—inside her brain with which to arm herself, and suddenly remembered the way she had banished the sound at the Warhouse gig. Just as she had been on the very edge of the musical precipice, when all the kids around her had been giving into it, she had broken free. It had taken the most horrible remembrance—her mother, arms sleeved with blood, hands gloved with it, that awful look in her eyes as she stared at Ani, pleading and lost.

The memory wasn't strong enough this time.

Not against something this loud, this concentrated. Not when it was all around her, ten times louder than it had been at the Warhouse. A hundred times . . .

She felt the *soundforms* battering against her resolve, felt her defenses breaking under the onslaught.

With one last supreme effort she managed to let another memory out of her store.

A memory she never revisited.

A dark thing that she had always kept hidden away, caged and locked and hidden from view.

One she never brought to mind.

One she never dared let loose.

Still, in extreme circumstances, extreme measures were needed.

She took the lid off the box and let the demon loose.

She is thirteen years old and she and Dad are visiting her mother in the HOSPITAL. Dad capitalizes the whole thing every time he speaks its name, HOSPITAL, and the stress he puts into that single word shows all of the fear and horror and shame he feels about the place.

It's a small but well-lit room with a bed and a couple of chairs and not much else. There's a hospital smell that always makes Ani feel queasy.

Mom is distant, and that usually means she's heavily medicated, so they just sit there for what seems like a long, long time and, at some point, her dad leaves for some fresh air and Ani says she'll stay, even though it's the last thing in the world she feels like doing. The full, blunt, brutal truth is that she never wants to come here, and as soon as she does she always wants to run away.

But that's selfish thinking. That's putting her wishes ahead of her mother's needs.

A mother needs to see her child, Ani's father usually says in the car over to the HOSPITAL, it's the only thing she has left.

Sadly, it is true.

Ani's mother has little remaining.

Her illness has subtracted so much from her that it's like it's only her shadow sitting there on the bed; or an impression that has been left behind in the air that her mom once inhabited. She is physically frailer—that's undeniable—but it's not just the measure of her physical mass that isn't adding up for Ani: it is something else.

Something vital, but hard to describe.

Part of her mom's essence—the brave, loyal, devoted Sandy Lee, who'd crossed Vietnam in search of a better life—has been siphoned off, taken away, replaced with blankness, void, coldness, distance, and inscrutability. It all leads to the overwhelming thing, the thing that she cannot tell Dad, that she cannot tell anyone.

Her mom scares her.

More than anything else in the world.

More than any of the monsters and murderers from horror films put together. More than the crazy people she hears about on the news who kill and torture and eat their victims. More than the unspecific dread of the things that hide in darkness. More than she fears her own mortality.

Her.

Mom.

Terrifies.

Her.

She can hear her dad moving down the corridor, his rubber soles squeaking on the floor as he walks away, sounding like a manifestation of the screams and wails that he always manages to stop from escaping. Ani may only be thirteen years old but she could see the tears welling up in Dad's eyes just before he left; and she could empathize with the pain that had put them there. She feels that same pain now, sitting in the visitor's chair, looking over at the shadow sitting on the bed.

Seeing, but not being seen.

Her mom stares right through her.

Haunted, sunken eyes with a cold sparkle beneath, as if a chip of ice is buried under the surface of each.

Her mother never sees her when she visits; her eyes seem incapable of latching on to anything close, and faces don't seem to hold the same fascination for her as they do for the rest of humanity. When Ani talks to people, they look at her face. They watch her mouth. They study her eyes.

Not her mother, though.

When Ani talks to her mom, her mom never sees her. She doesn't know if her mom can even hear her voice.

This is how visits with Mom always go.

Sitting and trying to reconcile the person in front of her with the person who only exists now in Ani's memory; trying to spot the overlaps between the two women. Searching for a sign, a trace, even a hint of the lively, lovely woman who had brought Ani into the world, and had brought her up.

Ani is suddenly aware that something in the room has changed, and it snaps her out of her thoughts.

Her mom is watching her now. Not looking through her, because her eyes seem focused on the near distance instead of the thousand yards removed she usually views the world at.

Ani feels that those eyes are actually seeing her.

"Mom?" she says, her voice barely more than a whisper.

Her mother does not answer, but there is a flicker of something—recognition?—in her eyes. The ice chips that smolder with cold fire seem to have melted.

Suddenly, the woman in front of Ani looks like her mother.

Not like a shell of her mother, not an imprint, nor a shadow.

"Mom," Ani says again, and leans in toward her. And that's when the mother-facade breaks. That's when the woman in front of her screams at the top of her lungs and launches herself toward Ani. Suddenly, her mom's face is feral, enraged, insane. Her lips are pulled back from yellow teeth and bloodied gums. Her eyes are wide and staring and demented. And her hands—usually so thin and delicate-looking—are like claws. The fingers seem twisted, knotted, the nails look long and sharp. And they are aimed, Ani is sure, for her throat.

The sheer, unexpected shock of it has frozen Ani to the spot for just a little bit too long, and she only manages to get her neck out of the way as those clawed hands come past her face, and one of the nails trails across her cheek, drawing blood. The quick movement unbalances Ani, and she falls from the chair. She hits the floor and then her mom's body falls on to hers and that mad, twisted, feral face is just inches from Ani's own.

Ani's mind is reeling. It seems impossible that things can go so horribly wrong, so frighteningly quickly. In clock time, from Ani thinking that her mom was herself again to her ending up beneath the clawing rage of the same woman, it's all taken less than ten seconds.

Less than ten seconds for her entire world to be turned on its head.

Her mom's hands in her hair, pulling, twisting.

"Is she safe?" her mom asks in a maddening falsetto. "Is she safe? Is she safe? Keep away from her. Keep. Safe?"

Whatever memory path she's locked on, it's overwritten the present. Ani has no idea who her mom thinks she is, what character from her past Ani has been cast into, and the terror grows.

Her mom's mouth moves silently next to Ani's chin, and for a horrible minute she thinks that her mother is about to bite her neck. One of those twisted claws moves in front of Ani's eye line. One of the fingernails moves toward her left eye. Ani tries to turn her head away, but finds she is trapped beneath her mom's weight, with her face pressed against the side of the chair.

The fingernail moves closer.

The memory was sharp and jagged and profound enough to distract her from the *soundform* invasion. The image of her mom clambering over her—just before she was pulled away from Ani by Dad and an orderly—pushed the invaders away.

She thought about the way that music worked on the human brain, and that maybe the euphoria and joy that a person feels when listening to it must produce something in the brain—probably endorphins, the opiate-like chemicals the brain manufactures to create pleasure. Maybe they were the *soundforms'* way into human consciousness.

If music made people feel *good*, then perhaps that was the state the invaders needed to make their takeover possible. That would explain why music had become the perfect medium for their transmission.

By thinking of bad things, Ani had suppressed any good feelings. She had poisoned the ground that they had been trying to seed themselves into.

She looked around her. Joe was way ahead.

He'd left her, but then what choice had he had? When it looked like she was succumbing to the sound, he must have thought that he was on his own.

But he wasn't.

She pulled out her phone and speed dialed a number.

Uncle Alex answered immediately.

"You got something for me?" Ani shouted to be heard over the noise in Hyde Park.

"You gave me an impossible mission and next to no time to complete it, so it's rough as heck. And it will need to be exactly the same volume as the sound you're trying to cancel out. It's not exact, but then I wasn't working with a sound, I was working from an image."

"But it *will* work?" Ani asked urgently.

"It *might*. That's the best I can offer."

"Have you sent it yet?"

"I sent it."

"Then wish us luck."

She'd sent the screen grab of the Lennie sound over to

Uncle Alex while she was in the cab, and then called and told him what she wanted him to do to it. He'd been skeptical at first—at the idea of scanning the image and then re-creating the .wav file from its visual representation, and by comparing it to the original, unmodified .wav file—but then he'd taken it onboard as a challenge. She'd also managed to impress upon him the urgency of the situation, and now—checking her tablet—she saw that the file had arrived.

She bounced and jostled through the crowd until she'd made it to the foot of the scaffolding that raised the mixing desk above the heads of the crowd. Joe was already there, and he was fighting with the technician. Ani climbed quickly, almost gracefully, and soon she was standing on the platform overlooking the crowd and stage.

"*Unplug everything!*" Joe shouted. *"Stop it! Now!"*

His fist hit the technician on the chin and the man went down hard.

Ani looked over the platform and saw the sea of people beneath her. She knew that this was her one shot at saving them all. And about time, because the shells of energy that encased every member of the crowd were the same as the one she had seen Lennie Palgrave encased in: the impossible sound spikes of the terrible alien notes, harnessed by Victor Palgrave in his greed for power.

She froze for a moment as the energy began to connect each member of the crowd into a shining web of force, and she saw the people trapped within it start to distort, to

396

change, their bodies stretching like warm toffee, their limbs elongating, their heads swelling.

They are becoming something else, she thought, *something neither alien nor human. Soldiers. For Palgrave's new order. Slaves.*

It pulled her out of her inactivity.

"Time for Plan B." Ani screamed to be heard above the noise, then she located the cables that fed into the mixing desk, wired her tablet in through its *sound out* port, opened up the file Uncle Alex had sent, closed her eyes, and shouted, *"COME ON!"*

Joe watched, openmouthed, as Ani plugged her tablet into the mixing desk. Rather than pulling out power cords and sound cables, she was doing something else entirely.

This had better work, he thought and then:

Suddenly there was quiet.

Complete quiet.

Only the dull thrum of an incoming helicopter disturbed the unnatural silence that had instantly descended on Hyde Park.

"What did you do?" he asked, and Ani turned and smiled.

"Antinoise. I called the best sound technician on the planet and he came up with the idea. He made me the exact opposite of the second version of the .wav file. My uncle Alex saves the day."

Joe didn't know what she was talking about.

"Antinoise," Ani explained. "My uncle says it's a sound with exactly the same amplitude, but its precise inverse phase." She must have seen Joe's blank look because she tried again. "Like heat can cancel out cold. I just played the opposite sound, and the two sound waves together made a single interference pattern. They canceled each other out."

Joe looked around at the crowd and was just in time to see them fall, as one organism, to the ground.

"Are they going to be okay?" he asked.

Ani shrugged.

"I sure hope so."

They unplugged the mixing desk from the power source, and shut it all down.

In all honesty, it was a bit anticlimactic.

Even the band onstage was unconscious. There was no movement anywhere in the park. In the sky but still distant, an RAF helicopter was coming in. Soon, it would need to find a clear space to land. Ani wondered who it was carrying.

That mystery would have to wait, though.

The park wasn't *quite* still.

Someone was moving through the crowd, flanked by bodyguards, aiming for the exit, and Ani thought she knew who it was.

"Palgrave!" she said to Joe, who followed her gaze, nodded, and then started climbing down the scaffolding toward the escaping man.

Ani wasn't just going to stand by and wait, so she followed Joe, and they both hit the ground at about the same time and took off in the direction that Palgrave was heading. He had a two-hundred-yard head start, maybe more, but he wasn't running. He was just steadily walking and didn't look worried at all.

Joe and Ani broke into sprints, leaping over unconscious teens and running as fast as their legs would take them. Ani took small pleasure in the fact that she was matching Joe stride for stride.

They caught up with Palgrave on the outer edge of the concert area, and Joe screamed his name.

Victor Palgrave turned around, a smile on his face. His minders stood behind him, hands inside their jackets. Their gun hands, Ani was certain.

"Give it up!" Joe yelled. "There's no escape."

Palgrave's smile widened.

"Joe," he said with a fake warmth that had presumably been spliced into his personality when he decided to take the political route through life. It was the warmth that allowed him to shake hands with people when he despised everything about them except their ability to vote, and helped him kiss babies that he longed to deprive of state benefits. "How lovely to see you again."

"It's over."

Palgrave feigned surprise, which was the only thing less sincere than his smile. "Oh, I'm sorry, you seem to have misunderstood my actions. You truly believe that I was making a getaway, right? Running away from the scene, hoping to jump on a plane to Ecuador? Or Argentina? But I wasn't trying to escape. I was just getting far enough away so that I could do this."

He reached into his jacket and pulled out a small silver device, about the size of an iPhone. He held it up theatrically and made a big show of pressing some buttons and then he laughed, a sound that was cold and hateful and terrifying.

"I'd think about running, if I were you. You and your little friend there. Is that the American in you showing through, Joe? Does it make you feel enlightened, politically correct, to run around with someone so obviously your inferior? Run, and take her with you. You won't get far, to be perfectly honest, but it'll make your ends so much more . . . dramatic, don't you think?"

"What are you talking about? We stopped you. Shut off your signal from space. We won."

"You put them in standby mode. Impressive work, though. Completely unexpected. What was that, by the way? Antinoise? Anyway, it doesn't matter. Here's the thing: I just woke them all up. But wait, there's more. You see, I put the programming parameters for this new form of the space sound in place."

"To turn them into your slaves!" Ani spat.

"Oh, my dear, how tiny your imagination is. What a view there must be from your head, so boring and bland and unable to see true greatness. But people like me have vision. Vision enough to see how an army of privileged kids at my disposal—"

"Soldiers?" Joe said dismissively. "All this for a bunch of remote-controlled soldiers?"

Again, Palgrave seemed amused. "The first phase was supposed to be quiet, with the slow, steady, covert infiltration of all the levels of society that matter. Young scientists, and lawyers and politicians and . . . well, you get the picture: the elite.

"You and Abernathy lucked your way into that one, making me . . . evolve my plans. The second phase was to be consolidation, with my secret helpers chipping away at all structures of power, authority, and control. The third phase would have been glorious: the takeover of all political power in this country. The moment when I would finally assume the power that I was born to inherit.

"Not just with an army, Joe. That's just so last year. No, I made it so that my puppets could become my greatest *weapon*. I have to confess that I have simply been *dying* to try it. I had hoped for more time to make this a bit more . . . global. Still, it would be a shame to waste the opportunity to go out—as they say—with a bang."

He pressed another couple of buttons on the handset

and nodded over Ani's shoulder. "Now why don't you take a look at what you've won. I think it will redefine, for all time, the whole concept of *a prize*."

It started with random sparks, leaping between the unconscious individuals spread out across the park, rekindling those strange electrical shells that seemed the only outward sign of their true nature.

Joe had really thought that Ani's plan had worked. That it had been ingenious, immediate, and that no one had gotten hurt. Canceling out the sound had, he thought, canceled out the menace.

No such luck.

The sparks were already turning into bolts of white light that arced through the air, leaping from person to person, lacing the fallen crowd together in a complex network of unearthly power: forming a crisscrossing pattern that missed no one in its hunger to spread, to connect, to grow.

Static electricity filled the air, making it taste metallic. Burnt ozone filled Joe's nose and lungs.

"What have you done?" he shouted.

"I have *created*," Palgrave replied, his voice full of pride. "It looks like I won't have my new British Empire, but at least I have this."

He gestured over Hyde Park.

The lines of power continued to glow, throwing out more and more strands, pulling the fallen people closer together, binding them with the alien fire.

On the stage, the members of Precision Image were being drawn into the mass that was forming in Hyde Park. Joe saw Harry Brewster—Null-A, one of the high priests of this new religion of electricity and power—being flipped and bumped across the stage, pulled with tentacles of incandescent brightness.

The electric lattice was not just connecting people: it was pulling them together, squashing them against each other, and wrapping electric bindings around them to hold them there.

Joe had no idea what he was seeing. His shocked senses could see no pattern, no logic to it at all. The electrical lightning was just gathering the crowd together into different-sized piles in front of the stage, then working at the piles with its bands of force until they were bound together in formless masses.

"You're killing them," Ani screamed. "Stop it! Stop it now!"

"Oh, is that what I'm doing?" Palgrave said. "Then stop it yourself, little girl."

Palgrave had made a comment about her "inferiority," and now he was calling her out on her size and sex. Oh yes, he was quite the charmer.

She wondered what a country under this man's rule would have been like, and shuddered. It would have become a country for people who Palgrave thought deserved it:

white and full of xenophobia, no doubt; straight and full of homophobia. The UK would have become strong, probably, but it would have been a country that drew its strength from being scared and insular and full of hate.

Power was wasted in the hands of those who desired it.

There were piles of people stacking up on the grass, piles of kids, all fizzing and crackling with energy. An energy that seemed sentient, that appeared to have a purpose, although she could think of no purpose for piles of kids.

Whatever it was, she decided, it was *very* bad.

Worse than her worst-ever nightmares, and she'd had some doozies.

"*ARISE!*" Palgrave screamed, for theatrical embellishment again, because it was surely that infernal device in his hand that was doing this, rather than his sub-Frankenstein demand.

Ani wished that Joe had thought to take the stupid thing out of his hands before all this could come this far. She guessed that he had been as surprised as she had to find that not only hadn't they stopped the sound from taking over thousands of kids, but that Palgrave had some kind of fallback plan.

Suddenly that backup plan started to make some sense.

Insane sense, sure, but it was finally possible to see what was happening out there on the grass in front of the stage.

"I guess we're in *real* trouble now."

The piles of humans that the electricity had gathered together—one big mass in the center, two smaller ones below it, one still smaller to the left and another to the right, and the smallest of all at the top—were being pulled together with remarkable speed and precision.

Once the final drawing together began, it became clear that the shape was both intended and familiar.

First the two small masses—each containing over a thousand people, Joe figured—started building upward, with the electrical force nudging them carefully into place and maintaining their positions. Two large, flattish bases with columns stretching out of them ever higher, until their shape became so obviously recognizable that Joe could only look at them in terror.

A huge part of him wanted to take the device out of Palgrave's hands and smash it into a million pieces. With his reflexes, it would be easy. But would he be solving the problem, or just taking away the last chance they had of stopping this madness from happening?

"Abernathy," he said. "Are you seeing this?"

"That giant pair of legs standing in Hyde Park? Yeah, they're kind of hard to miss."

"I hope you've got a plan."

"Half a plan. And a couple of prayers to alien gods. We'll be with you as soon as we can."

The legs complete, the force moved onto the central

mass, reeling in skeins of people and weaving them into a body. If it hadn't been so utterly horrible, Joe was sure that he would have been impressed. Unfortunately, the human aesthetic sense seemed to wither and die when confronted by the truly unthinkable.

The feet and legs themselves—composed of two thousand or more people packed in tight rows and held in some kind of electrical suspension that shored them up and made sure that the lower bodies weren't immediately crushed by the tremendous weight bearing down on them—had to be fifty feet high at least, and the ribbons of force were adding a body that was that high again.

A vast colossus constructed out of people and electricity.

The arms were being assembled and pulled into place, and the final mass of people became a vast sphere that rolled up the right leg, and then the body, before taking up position at the top of the human structure as its head.

Blinding white electrical light blasted outward from the human outline, and Joe couldn't begin to guess where all of that power was coming from. Enough to hold thousands of people in place . . . enough to power . . .

Thum-thump

The creature took its first, tentative step forward, and the ground beneath Joe trembled with the vibrations.

Behind him, Palgrave laughed again.

"How *do* you stop a war machine made out of children? Because when you attack it, only innocents die."

"You're insane, you know that?" Joe said. "Completely and utterly insane."

"Oh, like a crazy person could build that," Palgrave said, pointing at the creature as it took another unsteady step forward.

Thum-thump

"*Only* a crazy person could build that," Ani said. "It makes no sense. It makes no sense at all. *Why?*"

"The alien sound," Palgrave said. "Our first-ever contact with an alien race. When Imogen Bell recorded it, she had no idea what it was that she had brought down to Earth. Her and that stargazing buffoon, Klein, just put the carefully laid *first contact* protocols into operation and, guess what? Bell's first call? Came to me. *Me.* If that's not destiny calling, then I don't know what is."

Thum-thump

"But, here's the thing: the sound may have only been a pathetically poor copy of a larger organism from out there in the dark depths of space, but it was still *alive*. It was still *life*. Not quite life as we tend to think of it, but a whole new category of being.

"Of course at the start, it was so weak, so primitive, it didn't have the strength to do anything but sit in a file on Pabody/Reich's computer."

Thum-thump

"I instructed Imogen Bell to substitute the sound file for another one; some instinct told me that if we had made contact with an alien race, then I wanted it to be *me* who defined the terms of that contact. She sent me the file and I just forwarded it to some . . . acquaintances I keep on my payroll. Weapons developers of the *hush-hush* kind—always looking to build the next bomb, the next gun, the next nerve gas agent, the next biological weapon. They analyzed the file, and discovered something odd. This . . . *sound* . . . it was alive. It thought, it fed, and eventually it grew. It did what all life does: it reached out and tried to make more copies of itself.

"And we found ourselves in a rare and incredible position. We had a new form of life. That life had been digitally encoded into a file. Sound files can be edited. That meant that this life-form could be *edited*. It took a lot of time, and no small amount of trial and error, but in the end it was easier than you'd think. We had a sound that was capable of tremendous things. We just wrote some new instructions to be inserted into the file, and my team edited them in. Rewriting its code to change its purpose.

"An alien creature loose on planet Earth, living in sound? That's not good for anyone. But an alien creature, tamed, reprogrammed, loose on planet Earth to do my bidding?

"*That* is just too good an opportunity to pass up."

Thum-thump

The creature was still making awkward, slow progress forward, but it seemed to be getting better at moving with every step. Joe figured that they needed to stop this now before that thing *really* learned how to move.

He moved toward Palgrave, thinking he was going to snatch the device from his hand, but the man knew what he was intending and shook his head.

"Turn it off and they *all* die," Palgrave said. "That thing falls apart and suddenly it's raining men. They're bound together using some kind of electric bands that even my scientists don't fully understand. The way they see it, this creature that Pabody/Reich discovered was a space traveler, a creature of energy: some of it sound, some of it radiation, probably a whole bunch of stuff we'll never truly understand."

Thum-thump

"But perhaps a creature that is just waves of energy, moving through space, needs a physical form every now and then. You know, to interact with things, maybe to feel, or touch, or break, or eat, or destroy . . . It's hard to know what space monsters really think about, isn't it? But the electric field that's holding our giant friend together over there is the way it makes things—tools, arms, a mouth—out of the junk it finds in space, or plunders from the planets it passes."

"So why did you think that making a monster out of living beings would a good idea?" Joe said.

"It's an engine of destruction," Palgrave said. "And it's

made out of innocent kids. You've got to agree that is *some* human shield."

Thum-thum—

Whap-whap-whap-whap-whap-whap

The steady advance of the human colossus was drowned out by the sound above them, and Palgrave looked up. The barrels of three rifles were trained on him from the open door of a RAF helicopter. His minders went for their guns, but Palgrave shook his head and they stopped.

"Stay still and don't move," Abernathy's voice came through a loudspeaker. "Or move, and give me an excuse to put a bullet between your eyes."

Palgrave lifted his hands in the air, and the helicopter landed, throwing dirt and dust up in clouds around Joe and Ani.

"Abernathy and the cavalry?" Ani yelled over the roar of the helicopter rotors.

Joe shrugged. "I sure hope they have a plan," he said, "because as of five minutes ago I'm all out of ideas."

Abernathy got the pilot to swoop down low next to the vast creature that was stalking across Hyde Park. If he weren't seeing it with his own eyes, there was no way he'd ever have believed it. Put this up on YouTube and every comment would be the same: FAKE!

But it wasn't a fake.

This was as real as things got.

An animated creature made of rows of unconscious human bodies, neatly stacked in columns, held together with pulsing lines of electrical force. This close up, Abernathy could see the faces of the people on the outside of the creature, the ones that made up its skin and musculature, and he felt a terrible sadness.

If you put the terror, horror, and wonderment aside, sorrow was the remaining feeling: these were human beings, robbed of their very individuality, now serving as the makeshift body of a poorly copied creature in service of a fascist megalomaniac.

Abernathy knew that it wasn't a CGI special effect, or a digitally manipulated image.

He now knew *precisely* what this thing was, how it was formed and—although he hadn't been expecting Palgrave's madness to spill over into such an obscene construction—he had the ultimate ace up his sleeve to deal with it.

An ace that he'd spent the afternoon organizing, that he'd had helicopters crossing the sky to secure, that he'd managed to put together with video conferencing and an impassioned plea to someone he'd never even met in the flesh.

As they came in for a landing next to Joe, Ani, and Palgrave, he ordered the troops onboard to point their weapons at Palgrave. Palgrave looked smug, and Abernathy hoped that his ace wasn't beaten by a better hand.

ooo

Ani saw Abernathy climb down from the helicopter, flanked by armed soldiers, and she saw something in his face that puzzled her.

He looked calm. Confident. In control.

She felt far from calm. If the striding monstrosity that Palgrave had built out of the audience made it out of Hyde Park, then who knew what damage it could cause? It was already creating a wake of destruction and panic, making slow but deliberate progress toward where they were standing, on the edge of the park nearest speaker's corner. Past that it was city. Past *that* it was destruction on a mammoth scale.

She'd grown up watching *kaijū eiga*, those weird and wacky Japanese movies where giant monsters tore up cities with their claws and a veritable arsenal of special powers, and she'd always felt them to be a bit of a guilty pleasure. Seeing Godzilla and his ilk—Ghidorah, Rodan, Destroyah, Baragon, Hedorah—laying waste to skyscrapers, stepping on people, fighting each other with no regard for collateral damage was fun, sure, but if you put that kind of destructive power into the real world, then the effects would be tragic.

Palgrave had made that crazy dream of *kaijū*—which literally translated as *giant beast*—come true. What he had made out of his arrogance and lust for power was nothing less than a nightmare, with the potential for 9/11 times a thousand.

Palgrave was kneeling down, his hands behind his head, and he still held the device that had made this . . . horror . . . possible.

Abernathy walked up to him, nodded to Ani and Joe, and then told Palgrave, "Stop this. End it now."

"I have thousands of hostages," Palgrave said. "And they are all tied together into the most devastating weapon this planet has ever seen. I hardly think you're in a position to issue orders."

As if to underline the point, Palgrave stroked the device behind his head and the air was instantly full of the crackle of electricity, closely followed by a truly horrible sound—thousands of voices screaming in pain.

"I want safe passage," Palgrave said. "For me. My wife. Or I will just let . . . that . . . run free. It will feast, I'm sure. It will destroy, I'm certain. And it will . . ."

". . . not make it another step farther!" Abernathy said, and his voice was full of steel. "I gave you a chance to end this, to redeem yourself if only slightly. Ani?"

"Yes, sir."

"I just sent you a file. Use it."

Ani took out her tablet and there, sure enough, sat a new file on the home screen called *Earthlink*.

"I thought I'd let you do the honors," Abernathy said. "Call it a reward for your excellent work so far. A present for joining YETI."

She clicked on the file and it opened with a map of the world, places highlighted by red dots.

Text scrolled at one corner

```
>connecting to observatories

>>

>>>

>>>>

>connected Jodrell Bank

>connected Mullard

>connected Pabody/Reich

>connected Pushchino

>connected Arecibo

>connected Guadalajara

>connected Hat Creek

>connected Green Bank

>connected Magdalena Ridge
```

Ani recognized a couple of the names as observatories, and as the names scrolled down the screen, she realized that the program was linking together every radio telescope across the planet.

```
>connected Mauna Kea

>connected Miyun

>connected Nobeyama

>connected Murchison

>connected Hartebeesthoek

>connected Amundsen-Scott
```

"Professor Klein has been a *massive* help," Abernathy said. "I mean, once we explained that we meant him—and the creature he was carrying—no harm at all, he explained the reason behind Pabody/Reich's rocketing electricity bill."

Palgrave looked entirely confused and Abernathy laughed.

"You didn't know." There was a mocking tone in Abernathy's voice. "You thought that Imogen Bell was the only one who'd heard the *real* sound, and that was why you kidnapped her, and used her as your first test subject? She became your first guinea pig. For two years you threw so many variations of the sound at her until, finally, one stuck.

Then you could include your own instructions into the mix and *voilà!* Instant zombie slaves. But just to make sure, you played it to your own son. You started your music movement and selected new converts for your mind control judged on their intellectual and socioeconomic merits.

"But what you didn't know was that Klein was sitting there at Pabody/Reich, desperately trying to phone home. He didn't have the power to reach the creature that he was a part of, but guess what?"

Palgrave looked baffled. His arrogant air was already fading away, leaving him looking out of his league.

"Do the honors, please, Ani," Abernathy said, and she looked at the screen and saw a deep red button that read TRANSMIT.

"Oh, you beautiful man," Ani said, and Abernathy might even have blushed as she pressed the button.

"Every observatory across the globe just called out," Abernathy told Palgrave. "Loud. Clear. The message, if you're interested, was *HELP!*

"We've been transmitting a message for . . . well, long enough, actually . . . because as of ten minutes ago something entered our solar system, something that was traveling at enormous speed, and I mean really *really* fast. Astronomers and physicists are going to be writing papers about this for years.

"Oh, did I say that the message *HELP* was on the precise frequency of the original message, and also a few variations on your modified version. It's heading here because you put all of your eggs in one basket. Ani here just sent it our exact location. Hyde Park, London W2."

The sky went dark above them.

"Mommy's home," Abernathy said. "She's probably pretty angry."

Joe knew that Abernathy had timed that speech to the second, knew that he was being fed the location of the creature from the stars, all so that he could achieve the dramatic effect of mentioning their location and the sky going dark.

Although *dark* didn't quite fit. But Joe wasn't sure there was a word that could do any better. Human language described things that human beings were capable of describing. If you passed beyond the sum of human experience, language would, inevitably, start coming up short.

No one was trying to talk anyway.

It made a nice change.

Everyone was looking up into the sky.

It *was* the only show in town worth looking at.

Above Hyde Park there was an area of sky that surely wasn't quite the same as any sky that had ever appeared over it before. It just took a while to figure out why that was. Joe found that he needed to actually *force* his eye to translate the shape that was threaded through—or rather *between*—

the sky. The eye kept trying to flee away, to pretend that it could not see the vast pattern that boiled and churned and twisted in the spaces *between sky*.

He kept thinking that: *between sky*, because whatever it was that hung there above them was not actually *in* the sky, it was not *across* the sky, or even *on* the sky; but, rather, it seemed to fit in the spaces between, as if it existed slightly out of phase with earthly things and tried to slip, unnoticed, through them.

When Joe realized that he needed to force his eye to connect with its form, and needed to look in a slightly different, almost sidelong way, he found it became easier to pull a shape out from what had seemed at first formless. Now he could understand how it fit together—maybe only intersecting with human reality, rather than existing within it. He could begin to say what it might be, what it might look like.

Areas of the sky had become stretched tight around spherical bulges—many dozens of them, like transparent blisters—and the spheres were linked with a complex network of ragged cables and distended tubes; spheres, cables, and tubes that were only made visible because of the way their presence forced the sky to bend around them. Tubes connected the spheres in a kind of ever-shifting lattice, while the cables seemed more random in their distribution, carrying sparks from section to section as if moving power to where it was needed.

There was no sense of the head/body/limbs structure

favored by Earth creatures and Joe wondered if this . . . space traveler . . . was more like a cosmic box jellyfish . . . or coral . . . or bacterium . . . or . . .

It was no good.

Analogies fell down as soon as they were made, and comparing it to terrestrial things seemed nothing more than a distraction from the true wonder of the thing.

Joe saw the shape in the sky flex, and dozens of neon-bright electrical bolts rained down from it, all angled in toward the striding sculpture of human kids that Palgrave had thought was going to buy him out of the trouble he was in.

The electrical bolts didn't *hit* the colossus, not exactly, anyway. What actually seemed to happen was that they stopped just short of its surface, then changed state from bolt to liquid, a liquid that poured across the colossus, coating every inch of every surface in seconds, before exploding into incandescent light.

Joe shielded his eyes from the light's intensity, then watched as that brightness traveled back upward into the sky creature. The creature was draining power from the colossus, and Joe could see the bonds that held the whole thing together breaking apart, being pulled upward into the creature.

It was like skinning the creature with lasers.

They'll fall, he thought bleakly. *Take away those bonds and they'll all die!*

Already Joe could see hundreds of kids starting to spill from the wound where a huge swath of electrical force had been peeled away from the surface of the composite creature and fed back into the parent above.

Joe couldn't watch. He turned his head away.

When the kids started leaking from wounds on the *kaijū* creature's body, Ani found herself wondering what had been the point of it all. They'd stopped Palgrave, okay, but if those kids out there died, then it hadn't been worth the price. Not even to see Palgrave's look of abject terror as the creature from the sky set about dismantling the only thing he'd actually "achieved" with almost casual ease.

Ani wondered if all Abernathy had really done was shift the blame. If the army had thrown bombs at that thing and succeeded in stopping it, then there would have been the blood of thousands of kids staining their hands. If an alien creature stopped it with the same result, then something else was to blame.

As the first few hundred bodies started pouring from the loosening bonds, as they started plummeting toward the ground, Ani wondered if Abernathy would *ever* be able to truly live with the consequences.

Awake now, the kids could see the ground rushing up to meet them, and their screams were sounds of terror ripped from their throats. A cascade of human bodies . . .

. . . suddenly stopped in midair.

Ani thought that she was imagining things—that she was wanting *something* to happen so badly that she had invented an ending for this where nobody died—but one of the soldiers was risking Abernathy's anger by gasping and pointing, and she knew that it was true.

The people freed from the body of the composite creature were hovering in the air, attached to the alien mass in the sky by beams of light that were either fields of energy, or tentacles, or hands, or wires.

The remaining mass of people suddenly burst, but those beams of light were there to prevent their fall. They were close enough that Ani could see the strands that tied them together, holding them in the air above the park, and she felt her fear evaporate, giving way to wonder as she saw the people descend slowly toward the park, handled gently by the alien network. It flexed again and the people were suddenly organized back into a crowd, albeit a crowd that seemed for all the world to be standing on nothing more than air. A tremendous pulse of sound tore through the park, a deep sound that Ani felt reverberate through her body, making her feel like a tiny part of some vast, cosmic orchestra, and she felt light spread through her, filling her with a sense of limitless space and dimension, and then before her eyes, the crowd began to descend slowly toward Earth, bathed in an unnatural glow, before they were deposited—with absolute care and precision—onto the ground.

The creature in the sky thickened—became completely

visible for the first time, and Ani was reminded of neurons in the human brain, of jellyfish, of hoses, of bacteria, of electric cables, of neurotransmitters, of planets in orbit, of the darkness of space and the brightness of stars, of atoms and electrons and seaweed and cells and circuits and wires and octopi and nebulae—and the people that had been part of that terrible mass of Palgrave's design were all looking upward into the heavens, staring in blissful awe at the *thing* as it contracted into one huge comet-shaped mass.

The air felt like it was charged with impossible forces and Ani felt tears streaming down her cheeks as the comet-creature flexed again and then the *soundforms* were pouring upward from every person in the park who had absorbed them, not wormlike at all, but more like infant versions of the thing that hovered above them.

The *soundforms* were drawn into the parent mass, fusing with it, making the shape grow and shift shape one last time until it was like one of those single-celled creatures they'd looked at in science one time—protozoa—although she knew that the comparison, once again, fell short of describing the phenomenon and was just her human mind's attempt to draw meaning from something it was not ready to truly comprehend.

Soon all of the *soundforms* were swallowed up by the creature, and it flowed through the sky, trailing behind it reverberations that seemed forged on the soundboard of infinity and made all music she'd ever experienced seem dull and cold and lifeless. It pulsed, throwing cilia in all directions, before it turned itself upward and disappeared into the sky.

She was left there feeling lost and empty and sad, like she had touched something profound, had been on the verge of understanding things beyond her mind's capacity, and then it had been snatched away from her.

A voice behind her snapped her out of it and she turned, but not before she watched the crowd in the park suddenly awaken, looking as puzzled and lost and empty as she herself felt.

It was Abernathy who broke the silence.

"Joe," he said, his voice strained, but still commanding. "Take him down."

Joe realized that this was Abernathy's idea of a reward for him, much like Ani's had been to trigger the final call to that . . . that . . . whatever that had been.

Joe turned to where Victor Palgrave stood, a pistol in his hand. When all else failed, he'd turned to a concealed weapon. As if it were going to help him. Three AK rifles were trained on him, but Abernathy waved them aside and Joe took three giant steps forward and stood facing Palgrave.

"Put the gun down," Joe ordered, and his voice was hard and made fear dance across Palgrave's eyes.

He held the gun with a trembling hand, looking for a way out that simply refused to arrive, and then he let go of it and it fell to the grass in front of him.

Joe hit him hard in the gut, and when Palgrave bent over from the blow, Joe grabbed his arm, twisted it until it was behind his back, caught a cable tie that Abernathy tossed him, and bound Palgrave's hands behind his back.

"You have the right to remain silent," Joe said. "So please, remain silent."

Then he handed Palgrave over to the soldiers, picked up the gun, emptied it of its magazine, and jettisoned the round from the chamber. Then he walked over to Ani, put his arm around her, and led her out of the park.

CHAPTER TWENTY: ENDS ARE ALSO BEGINNINGS

Gretchen poured tea and put cups down in front of Abernathy, Ani, and Joe.

"So you got your headquarters back, then," she said with a faint smile on her lips. "Did it take a lot of explaining?"

Abernathy sipped his tea, made an appreciative noise, and then shook his head.

"Several law enforcement agencies got caught with their pants down. Since YETI was the one that managed to sort things out for them, losing our HQ to invaders has been overlooked. We're back and—without meaning to boast—we're actually bigger and better than ever."

"And how are my favorite spies holding up?" Gretchen asked, looking over at Joe and Ani.

"Good," Ani said. "I'm looking forward to the training program, but I know I have a long way to go. It's good to find something to fight for, something tangible. Somewhere that I can actually make a difference."

"We couldn't have done it without you," Abernathy said, and Joe nodded agreement. "Or without you, Gretchen."

"I just looked some things up," Gretchen said modestly. "Information is power, not the person who provides it."

"You made the connections," Joe insisted. "You found out that Klein was trying to contact that space thing. . . . What ever happened to him, anyway?"

"The thing inside him went home with mommy," Abernathy said, "along with the things in Lennie Palgrave and Imogen Bell and the other kids we picked up from the Warhouse and the kids from the park. And the .wav file is gone, too, pulled from every system that held it. Space reached down and plucked up every trace of the sound, and took it back out there with it."

"So it's over?" Ani asked. "Once and for all?"

Abernathy started to nod, then stopped himself. "I don't know," he said. "We just called that thing down from space. It knows where we are now. Maybe it doesn't care. Maybe we're nothing more than ants to it. Or maybe it will start to get curious about us. Could be we haven't seen the last of it."

Gretchen wrinkled her nose. "Thank you, Mr. Gloomy. If it took all trace of itself back into space with it, I think it's gone for good."

"I hope you're right," Abernathy said. "Anyway, I just wanted to say thanks. You put a lot of the pieces together for us. Made me feel quite inadequate."

"I wouldn't have *had* any pieces to put together if it wasn't for Ani and Joe. I take it this is the beginning of a new partnership for our intrepid heroes?"

Abernathy stood up, buttoned his jacket, and winked at her. "We'll have to see about that."

The bar was empty and quiet and also just what they needed. They found a table by the big windows at the back, sat down opposite each other, and looked out over the River Cam. The water was still and calm, with hardly a breath of wind to disturb its surface, and then the blade-like body of a rowing eight cut through it, sending indignant ducks scattering, turning the area of river into an interference pattern of tiny waves and ripples.

Ani took the drink from her dad's hand and gave him a rueful smile.

"It's weird, you know? When those men showed up at our place with guns, the last thing I thought would come out of it was a job offer. A new beginning . . . moving away . . ."

Ani looked at her dad. He was studying her over the top of his cider, his blue eyes twinkling in the light. This was the hardest part of the whole process. The part that made it all real. Made it final.

"It's not weird," he said, squeezing her arm. "I've always known that you were meant for better things. More than I could ever offer you."

"But you've given me everything I've ever wanted. And don't think for a moment that I don't appreciate all of the sacrifices you've made for me."

"That may be so, but I haven't been able to give you what you *needed*. And this Abernathy guy sounds like he'll be able to give you that. I'm just glad that you're rebelling against your old dad by picking a path of law and order."

Ani sipped her Coke and stared at the table.

"Could have gone either way," she said.

Her dad nodded. "But it didn't."

They sat in silence.

"I'm going to miss you," he said after a while, and Ani thought she'd misheard until she looked up and saw that there were tears in his eyes.

They had never been very good at expressing emotions, settling instead on *showing* rather than *telling*. If Dad was choosing to break that tacit agreement, then she thought she'd been given license to.

"Oh dad, I'm going to miss you, too. You've always done right by me, always looked after me. You've been there when I needed you and butted out when I didn't. You made me the person I am today."

"You've done that *despite* me, my dear girl," he said and stared out the windows at the ripples spreading across the river.

"You do know that you're never going to be able to cope on your own."

"It's certainly going to be quiet. . . ."

"To new beginnings," Ani said, raising her glass.

"To new beginnings," her dad said, and smiled.

They sat there in silence for a few moments, letting the whole thing sink in.

"You were right. It *is* weird," her dad said.

Joe arrived at the building and experienced a mild feeling of déjà vu because it was another place you needed to be looking for to find. But, unlike the Pyramus Club where he'd met up with Victor Palgrave, this place didn't even have a little brass plate to confirm its identity.

Some places are built for secrets.

Not ordinary secrets like a lie told, an object hidden, or a lover betrayed; but deep, dark secrets that could—Abernathy assured him—topple governments.

It was a tall piece of nineties architecture hidden away among the loft apartments, restaurants, pubs, and clubs of Clerkenwell, and if you didn't *know* what was inside, you probably wouldn't *believe* what was inside.

Joe rang the buzzer and was greeted by a young man in a white coat. He looked like a nurse or a doctor if you ignored the concealed earpiece, the weapon bulge on his belt, and the cold, dead eyes through which he surveyed the world.

"Joe, right?" the man asked pleasantly.

Joe nodded.

"Can I see some ID?"

Joe handed over his card and the man studied it carefully before handing it back.

"Excellent. Follow me."

He led Joe to the elevator that was the sole way out of the building's foyer. There were two levels of security just to work the elevator. It took an ID card and a twelve-digit code to open it. The man ushered Joe inside and pressed the button for floor six. There was a flash as he did so and Joe nodded, impressed.

Three levels of security.

A fingerprint scanner was built into the elevator buttons.

"You have temporary clearance for floor six," the man said. "It expires in an hour, and it's non-extendable."

"Meaning I have to be back down here in an hour."

The man nodded.

The doors closed between Joe and the man and the elevator started climbing.

On the sixth floor the doors opened and Joe stepped out. A row of blue lights lit up in the floor and Joe followed them down a white corridor to a door at the end.

Its illumination led to two doors that clicked open as he arrived outside them.

"I'll try door number one," he said, and pushed it open.

Inside was a bed, a dressing table, a shelf with books, a wide-screen TV and, on a chair in the middle of the room, Imogen Bell. She was reading a big fat book with no identifying marks and looked up when Joe entered. She closed the book, but not before Joe saw a mind-boggling collection of equations.

Light reading, then.

"Hi. It's good to meet you at last," he said. "My name's Joe Dyson. I thought we should have a little talk."

"The secret agent kid?" Imogen said, surprising him by grinning. "It's good to finally meet you. I . . . I hear I owe you . . ."

"Nah. It was all in a day's work. It's worth it to see that you're okay. I've got some news for you, though. My boss said I could be the one to tell you. . . ."

Imogen Bell looked at him expectantly and Joe saw that there was something fragile and broken about her, as if being the repository for the alien energy had depleted her, eaten some of her natural self-confidence, some of her own life energy.

Joe could see why.

She had endured almost three years of having the alien sound living inside her; of Palgrave's relentless experiments to weaponize the sound; then of being a slave to the dictates of the sound. Joe couldn't imagine how that would feel. To be locked away inside your own mind while an alien intelligence called the shots. It must have been like being a prisoner inside your own body.

"I came to tell you that you've been exonerated. Completely absolved of all the bad press you received. I have a list of places offering you professorships of your own—Cambridge, MIT, Japan, Cornell, Princeton—and as soon as you're cleared here, you'll be walking into any job you want."

He paused.

"What was it like?"

Imogen looked down at the floor. "It was like a nightmare that I couldn't wake up from."

"Well, the bad dream is over now," Joe said. "And the future looks bright."

"Why?" Imogen asked, looking up again with tears in her eyes. "Why did he do this to us? To me?"

"Victor Palgrave? Because he was insane. But you're going to be okay. You can start again. He's going to be in prison for a long, long time."

They talked for a little longer, then Joe wished her well and left her to her book.

Door number two opened onto Lennie Palgrave's room.

Lennie was sitting on his bed, gazing into empty space with a fixation that looked part terror, part despair. He didn't seem to notice Joe coming in.

"Hey," Joe said.

Lennie turned, his face warming. "Joe. Joe Dyson. I understand that you saved me. Is that true?"

"Not really. Maybe a little. I didn't come here for that, though. I just came to see that you're okay, to tell you that you'll be out of here soon, and to say thank you."

"Thank you?" Lennie sounded genuinely shocked. "It's me who should be thanking you, surely? I mean that . . . noise . . . those things . . . they were in my head, Joe. And my dad . . . my own dad . . . put them there. If it hadn't been for you . . ."

"If it hadn't been for you, then I don't think I'd have been able to save anyone, Lennie."

"What are you talking about?"

"I lost a friend. A case went bad, my partner took a bullet, died, and that was it for me. I was out, Lennie. Finished. Done. Through. I couldn't find a reason to go on. Just a whole load of excuses not to bother trying. Then another friend—you—was in trouble, and that . . . that brought me back from the edge of a pretty steep precipice I was learning to fall down. If it hadn't been for you—I'd probably still be falling now. You saved me just as surely as my people saved you."

Lennie stayed silent and they sat there while he collected his thoughts together.

Finally Lennie said, "You know the serial killer's neighbors?"

"Huh?"

"On the news. After they catch some bad guy, usually a serial killer, and his neighbors all go on about how he was quiet, a bit of a loner, but he seemed like a nice guy."

Joe nodded.

"My dad was never a nice guy. But you are, Joe. A good guy. A good friend. If helping me helped you out, then I'm happy."

"Let's call it even. I'll come see you when you get out of here, okay?"

"I'd like that," Lennie said. "I'd like that a lot."

"See you, then," Joe said, got up, and started toward the door.

"They *are* going to let me out, aren't they?" Lennie asked.

"Of course they are," Joe said and left.

"Was that the truth?" Joe asked when he was out in the corridor. "That he'll be getting out of here?"

Abernathy sucked in a breath and then said, "I think so."

"They're better. The creature has gone. Why are we still holding them?"

"It's out of my hands, Joe. Certain people just want to be sure that they're not a threat. . . . But I'm pushing for their release. It might take some time. . . ."

"This place. It's full of people who *aren't* getting out, though, isn't it? People involved in other cases who have become . . . inconvenient."

"National security, Joe."

"I know. Doesn't make it sting any less, does it?"

"No, it doesn't."

"Ani settling in at Gretchen's?"

"Seems like it.'"

"Good. I'm taking the afternoon off."

"You've certainly earned it. See you tomorrow, Joe."

He rode the elevator down, nodded at the guard in the white coat, and then walked out onto the street.

He checked his phone and saw he'd gotten a text message while he was inside the building.

Joe. I'm so proud of you. Mom. X

He stood there for a full minute, reflecting upon how that was the nicest thing she'd ever said to him, and being unable to decide if that was a happy thought, or a tragic one.

He sent her an *x* back and then made his way down the street.

He'd gotten about twenty paces when his phone started ringing, and smiled when he saw the caller ID.

"Ellie. We still on for a late lunch?"

He listened for a few seconds, put his phone back in his pocket, and stepped out into the fresh air.

The sun was high, burning off any clouds, and Joe loosened his collar, looked up to the sky, and smiled again.

It was, he thought, going to be a beautiful day.

He made his way to the car he'd been issued—Abernathy's treat, a racing green TVR—opened it up with the fob, got behind the wheel, started it up, and drove away.

ACKNOWLEDGMENTS

All of my books have been a team effort, even though it's only my name that ended up on the covers. This book truly would not have been possible without the invaluable efforts of some pretty amazing people.

First up is my long-suffering wife, Fran, without whom none of this would have been possible. Or even worth doing. When I falter, she picks me up. When I'm lost, she sets me back on track. She is, quite simply, the best.

Then there's Jon who, in a friendship spanning over three decades, has always been there for me; and is still always on hand to beta test the latest project. Words are not enough to convey the value of his friendship, which for a writer is a pretty hard thing to own up to.

Then there's Becky Bagnell, my jewel of an agent, whose comments, suggestions and support were crucial at every stage of this book's genesis. She helped get the book's balance right, and never doubted, not for a second. Even the book's title was her suggestion.

Next up is my wonderful editor, Alison Weiss, who has not only believed in this book enough to acquire it twice, but without whose polish, attention to detail and joyous enthusiasm the final product would have been a whole lot less than it is now.

I also want to take a moment to offer my heartfelt thanks to some amazing advocates for my previous books: the bloggers who have taken my works to heart and helped spread the word. It humbles me to know that you're out there and you care enough to take the time to tell other people. I just want you to know that I truly appreciate it.